"This book is easily within the top 10% of the novels that I have read since my grade school days. It captured my attention and keen interest immediately and it was sustained right to the last page. The Holy Spirit also ministered to me in and through this book."

John Lewis Walton, B.A., M.Div., OSP (Clinical Member)

Voices in the Wilderness

written by

Judith Utman

This story is purely fictional. Any resemblance to persons, names or locations is completely co-incidental.

WestBow Press books may be ordered through booksellers or by contacting:

WestBow Press
A Division of Thomas Nelson
1663 Liberty Drive
Bloomington, IN 47403
www.westbowpress.com
1-(866) 928-1240

Quotations from Bible from The Message

ISBN: 978-1-4497-6754-9 (e)
ISBN: 978-1-4497-6755-6 (sc)
ISBN: 978-1-4497-6756-3 (hc)

Library of Congress Control Number: 2012917047

Printed in the United States of America

WestBow Press rev. date: 10/29/2012

To all those who have yet to find their calling in God

Acknowledgments

Above all else, I profoundly give God credit for anything that is good in this book. He planted the seed that Inspired the reason to write this novel and the ideas that rolled forth into an actual story. I give Him the Glory!

To my husband, Tom, I thank you for your ever present support to read and re-read my drafts. It is your encouragement that propelled me forward through all the phases to this finished product.

Thank you to Pat McAinsh who not only read my first draft and saw the glimmer of talent within the pages, but also designed the fabulous cover photo for the finished product. You provided the impetus to keep working on the book when my frustration was greater than my energy.

I also want to give my gratitude to my friends, Sandy White and John Walton, who had the courage to read very raw first and second drafts and yet urged me to continue to edit and make positive changes in this manuscript. The time and care you took in finding even the smallest mistakes is so appreciated. I am forever indebted to you.

I want also to express my appreciation to Debra Wade, my close friend, who challenges me to grow and be the person God has designed me to be in Him. Thank you for catching those last proof reading changes.

Thank you so much to Chris and Carol Palko who patiently answered all my questions regarding their passion for off-roading with their Jeeps. It was fascinating and so informative.

To all the people I interviewed in St. Martin and Jamaica about the signs of the coming hurricanes and how the people were affected, I owe you a lot. You provided insights into the storm that could only come from someone who had experienced the real thing.

And lastly I want to express my joy of having friends who have constantly asked how the book was coming along. It is so nice to know you actually care about a fledgling author. Without your interest, I may have given up the idea of putting this novel into print.

Introduction

Before one enters this tale, some facets must be explained to the reader. First, the drama is set in a nonspecific location somewhere in the U. S. northeast. It could be anywhere; perhaps Maine, New Hampshire, Vermont, Massachusetts, or New York. The city mentioned could be Augusta, Manchester, Montpelier, Boston, or New York City. After much prayer, I am satisfied that giving these details would only detract from essential ingredients of the story itself. It is vastly more important that the reader understand that this adventure is a plausible scenario that might occur soon and could involve anyone of us. Events often sweep us into unforeseen circumstances and before we know it, we are there, 'in the midst of' a crisis. How would we respond? That is the essence of this parable.

The reader will also notice that, as the writer, I have chosen a curious style. You will find that words are sometimes capitalized in the middle of a sentence. It is done to distinguish between things of the everyday physical world and those that are of a deeper Spiritual, Divinely Inspired and Empowered nature. It has done for emphasis and clarity. I realize that it is unconventional, but I strongly believe it will give an additional dimension to aid the reader's understanding of the underlying message.

I invite you now to enter this journey with the characters. As darkness descends on Seeley's Mountain, walk with these men and women as they face an unseen evil the likes they have never faced.

Prelude: The Storm Conceived

The scorching afternoon sun shimmered off the desert sands of the Sahara, radiating waves of searing heat that silently ascended toward the heavens. Air currents, buffeted by mountain ranges to the east, dipped and twirled in a westward dance across this changing landscape of the African continent. Seeking to quench its arid core, the wind greedily sucked in the warm moist air rising above the waters of the Atlantic Ocean. Freed from earth's constraints, the moisture soared into the cool upper atmosphere, instantly appearing as clouds that twisted and skipped high above the Cape Verde Islands.

No human eye noticed as an evil seed silently slipped into this air mass, churning the winds in the innocuous cloud formation. Encouraged by the earth's rotation, the swirling air mass crept over the warm waters, incubating, breathing, sucking in moist air from the sea. More wind, more rotation and now friction. Electric impulses jumped from cloud to cloud. Thunderstorms jolted one into another, uniting until one giant evil army advanced in rotational formation ever westward.

The evil force deep in this plodding mass grew and stretched its tentacles outward; its malevolence was now visible in the darkening clouds. The storm marched, progressing relentlessly, driven by the growing cancer deep in its core. Fear was its fuel, destruction its aim, death its desire, a thief by nature. Mankind chose its name and Hurricane Igor was born.

Chapter 1

Jack Davidson sat on the porch steps of the small cabin he used as the base camp for his business and his life. Another group of students was set to arrive, and he needed to start his preparations. No doubt that he was making a good living. He was pursuing his greatest passion in life, survival training, in an idyllic setting, yet he could not understand his impatience with the impending arrival of a new gaggle of trainees.

It was approaching the end of August now and the season of summer vacationers would soon be ending, providing more serious clients, those who came out despite the seasonal changes. This may be what had spurred his restlessness. Like so many others this season, this current group would be here merely for entertainment, with no commitment to the training. Corporate clients and the serious wilderness enthusiasts better suited his life philosophy. The discipline of the training made sense to him. These summer trainees were just looking for a diversion from their mundane lives, an experience to share over a beer or coffee, allowing them to show a few frivolous photographs to shallow friends.

Jack had seen all kinds come and go over the last eight years since he started offering wilderness training. He had used his military training to good advantage, and he was now making a good living from his expertise. Survival techniques made sense to him. He had to rely on his skills set, the materials at hand and the talents with which he was born. It was an uncomplicated existence. Everything made sense in his world. The environment itself made the rules, not erratic, confused people. The landscape had basic elements and his tools were simple; the rules of the game were predictable. He just had to pull all the components together to his advantage so he would win, hence survival.

People themselves were all too often the problem. They came with far too much baggage, literally and figuratively. It seemed impossible for some of them to detach themselves from the trappings of the city–cell phones, designer hiking boots and jackets. Why could they not just bring stuff that was practical to the environment? That was the basic problem, they just had no idea what to expect outside the cocoon of the city.

Out here, although technology was available, using what nature put in front of him is what made his heart sing. To him, that was luxury. Sure, there was a place for a nice hot shower and dry soft bed, but at the end of the trail, not in the middle of the bush. What were they expecting when they signed up for these courses? Jack mused on the need for a Wilderness 101 course for the bored sophisticates to whom he had been catering lately; something that caused less discomfort for them and less whining for him.

Jack sighed and rubbed the dark stubble along his jaw line as he looked over the papers on his clipboard. What would this bunch be like this weekend? Two males and two females were scheduled on this run. It was just an introductory orienteering lesson. Compass navigation was a routine course. It would be an easy weekend for him, especially in this warm weather. He hoped that the bugs would be the biggest problem for him. He would do some simple lessons on reading a compass, following a bearing, measuring distances and finally build up to following directions in an open field. Once they had mastered those techniques, he would take them into the bush for the final challenge of following the charted course over unpredictable terrain. This course was child's play to him but all too often it brought these urbanites to their knees.

Paul Montgomery glanced up at the sky above him as he drove through the countryside. Above him there was nothing but blue sky with a few scattered clouds. He knew that there was nothing to be concerned about, yet there was something nagging at him. He had neglected to look at the long-range forecast before he left and Evangeline, or Gel as most people called her, would be upset if there was rotten weather this weekend. Although she now sat beside him quietly watching the changing scenery, she had been reluctant about accompanying him on this trip. She was anything but a country girl. Her carefully coifed shoulder length blond hair and designer clothes reflected her love of city life. She had agreed to go because this trip was given to him as a gift from his friends at work when he turned thirty-five the previous month.

His workplace seemed so distant from this road. What a change in atmosphere a few miles made; with the dark green hues of late summer foliage, the blue sky, brown earth and the occasional brightly painted house. His office was housed in a concrete gray building, bordered by concrete sidewalks. A few neon sale signs along the street broke the monotony. Everything was man-made, manufactured for the convenience of urban dwellers. The pace of city life was dictated by urgency–to reach the next deadline, to beat the other person to the next promotion, the next client, the next bonus. The business executives on Fulton Street wore stress lines etched on their faces as deep as the pain in their stomachs. Paul had always thought it was exhilarating; after all, who would not want the adrenaline high that comes with beating the other person to the deadlines and the corner office?

He had begun in sales at the newspaper. He could always sell advertising space. He had a smooth demeanor with clients, appealed to their egos, highlighting the client's strengths and how a little publicity about their company would promote their growth in the community with an edge over their competition. He could usually produce an advertising line that was "catchy" and his graphics were always "bang on."

He had taken his journalism degree at night while working full-time, and soon wrote a human interest story with edge that caught the eye of his friend, Mike, who was a reporter with the newspaper. Mike had brought it to his editor and it impressed him enough to give him a shot. Imagine his work in print, not just advertising space!

It was a good story, although not spectacular by his current standards. He had discovered a young man in his old neighborhood who had extraordinary talent in mathematics and science. He had no hope of going to university, much less a big name school. His single mother hardly made the rent each month. His ticket to success lay in his other ability. He was a gifted runner. He would get out on the track and it was like his legs took wings. He would fly over that track propelled by impulses that no one could explain. His stride and pace were exceptional. He had been running since elementary school, the ribbons he had won filled the walls of his bedroom. Combine his academic prowess with track abilities and he suddenly became a coach's dream. The next thing he knew he had two university scouts on his doorstep vying for his attention, offering full ride scholarships at prestigious universities. The decision was all his. That would have been wonderful, except he had misgivings about leaving his mother. She had been his support through all the rough times and he had been hers too. Could he make the break? It made for a captivating story and the readers of the paper loved it too.

The next thing he knew, Mike asked if he had any other articles up his sleeve. He had a few already floating around in his head. He chose two and whipped up the pieces with equal success. He had a knack of finding the human angle that people could understand without sounding soppy or too saccharine. Before long, he had the readers writing in, asking for more of his articles. That, of course, caught the eye of the editors, always wanting anything that could boost sales of the paper. They soon found that they liked his style too. He became more adventurous and tried a few investigative pieces that went over well with the brass as well as readers. Anything that sold more papers had the approval of the publishers. His work fit with the journalistic slant that pervaded that daily newspaper and sales were good, so everyone was happy. He knew enough not to rock that boat so the checks kept rolling in. Before long, he resigned from the advertising department to write full-time for the paper.

Paul had never looked back, or, had he? It had been ten years now, but lately, the grind of producing novel pieces was starting to nag at him. He had to maintain his edge or risk losing the notoriety he enjoyed. There could be another writer with a little more talent and innovation, some young college graduate hungry to make his name as he had. The upper brass was always pushing for articles that would drive up circulation. He had many sources, so producing the articles never was a concern. What itched at him was his desire. He knew he wanted to write and it never was a problem for him. He just sensed deep inside his gut that he was approaching a crossroad in his life.

He had been travelling too often lately in search of the next story. The time away from his wife was beginning to cause friction. Evangeline had been hinting not so subtly about the possibility of starting a family. This could not happen at a worse time, with the mounting pressures of producing more at work was driving him further a field for stories. The mounting conflict he felt was becoming more than a minor distraction in his life, far more than he liked and now he would have to soon tackle the problem, before it affected his work and his marriage.

As Paul looked at these new surroundings, he felt satisfied that this holiday was the right break for him. Evangeline should understand his need to get away and after all, his friends had paid for the trip.

Solomon Penfield, or "Sol" to his friends, pulled his red van into the laneway beside the cabin. Well, it was not a cabin in the regular sense. It was large by the standards of the lake. Lacey McCrae owned the house. It was a hub of activity for a select gathering of people in this area with meetings on Tuesday evening, but people dropped in for coffee most afternoons. They wanted to keep up with the pulse of what the group was "hearing." The atmosphere was shifting and everyone could feel it now. The weather had been hot all month and with each degree the thermometer had risen, the tension had climbed with it. Something was moving in and they knew it had to break soon. The only question was where and when. The sense of urgency for the group was now palpable.

MacKenzie "Mac" Donnelly was behind the wheel of his beloved Mustang convertible. Sarah was beside him, as she had been now for twelve years. Life was good, especially now that he had vacation time in front of him. Tall, dark and slender, Sarah was the love of his life. They were devoted to each other. They had been sweethearts since high school. Always athletic, Mac had played any sport that came his way. He excelled at hockey, although baseball, football and lacrosse had been also part of his repertoire. He had gone to the same university as Sarah, both obtaining athletic scholarships. It had not begun that way though. Sarah had accepted a rowing scholarship down in Tennessee but found that the coaching was not what was originally promised. Through his connections at his university, she obtained a scholarship at the same school in her sophomore year, so they finished out their education side by side again.

They had not taken the same courses in school. Sarah loved mathematics and science and children. The logical choice for her was education. Sarah taught high school mathematics and science and, of course, was coaching the rowing team. They had spectacular results this summer and it had been a scheduling nightmare to get away this week, having just completed regional championships for the girl's junior team.

Mac's mind was business oriented. His father owned a small manufacturing firm producing gloves. It was not a glamorous industry by any means, but it provided a good living for his family and had given Mac a venue for gaining experience in the business world. Mac had graduated with a master's degree in business administration and had started a consulting firm.

Recently, competition had forced his father to sell his company to a larger multinational organization. Such was the way of business these days; the big corporations consuming the local family owned firms. But his parents were ready to move into retirement with a tidy sum, well invested. It was a good legacy for their sons and grandchildren. Now his mother was hinting that it was time to produce some little Mac's soon, but the time had to be right and up to now it had not been. There had been too many obligations and loose ends in their lives to commit to a family yet.

Mac's career had intensified especially lately. He had been away from home more than he cared for. He had thousands of air miles accumulated but no time to use them for pleasure. He had been providing consulting expertise, coming in as the ax man, trying to find ways for corporations to trim their expenses. Tight budgets were the concern these days. He had become effective at advising firms how to eliminate excess in their organizations, but was becoming increasingly uncomfortable with some results of his recommendations lately. Several firms had used his expertise to justify significant staff layoffs. This caused him consideralbe stress, his conscience nagging at him after his father was forced to sell his factory last year. Maybe he was too good at what he did.

This weekend was just the ticket away from it all. Sarah was a close friend of Evangeline Montgomery. The two couples had 'buddied' up together several times on holidays, when time permitted. Gelly was Sarah's nickname for Evangeline. They were coworkers at the first school Sarah had taught at following graduation. Although Gelly had switched careers twice since then, the friendship had grown over time.

Gelly had put her major in literature to good use and worked for the publicity division of a publishing firm on the West Coast for a year after she left teaching. She had met Paul during her stint in the publishing world, though they did not get together as a couple for a few years. Gelly was based in California and Paul, though he travelled for work, was centered on the East Coast. Logistically, it made for an impossible relationship. Sarah had thought it strange though when Gelly had suddenly quit her high paying job in California to return home. She had said her affection for children had called her back to teaching but Sarah often wondered what had triggered the abrupt departure from the corporate world.

Once Gelly was back East, the common connection of writing had lured her into a deeper relationship with Paul and soon a bond of love developed. It was not long after that she and Paul jumped from serious dating into marriage.

Gelly and Sarah had never lost touch over the time Gelly was away in California. They had kept in contact, sometimes by phone, but more often by Internet. Gelly had not given many details of her life on the West Coast, but Sarah sensed that it was not the happiest time for her. She merely said that it would help her to appreciate the good things she now had. Gelly was back working at the same school with Sarah now. Gelly and Sarah had something in common beyond teaching though. Their husbands both had consuming professions and were travelling for work more than they liked. It had forged an indelible friendship.

Sarah was excited about the weekend away; three days with Mac and her best friend, Gelly, and her husband, Paul. The clear mountain air invigorated her senses. No smog, no traffic, no obnoxiously rude people. Imagine trees, sunshine and blue skies! It was Paul's treat for them. He had been given the gift of the orienteering course at work. It would be a good weekend away. It was a change from coaching rowing and she was up for a challenge.

She was not so sure that Gelly was as enthusiastic though. She was a city girl at heart and the thought of snakes and bugs made her cringe. Sarah knew she could have her laughing about it all by next week though and Gelly would make the best of it for Paul's sake. It was his birthday after all and you only turn thirty-five once in your life. She told Sarah that she sensed it was a turning point for him. She seemed uneasy when she had said it, as though she were hiding something. *It might be a mystery now but I'll have it out of her by Monday!*

Chapter 2

The bright-yellow sun rose early over the Caribbean island. By all appearances it was just heralding another hot, humid late summer day. The locals, however, knew differently. The animals were restless in the fields, looking for shelter from an unseen menace. Trees even bore their fruit, ripening before their time, as if they knew their season would soon be cut short.

Long rolling waves crashed on the shoreline, yet no winds brushed the beach to explain their appearance. Local fishermen, muscles straining as they pulled long nets into shore, catching whatever fish ensnared in it, glanced skyward, knowing these large waves were not the norm. No clouds betrayed the storm's arrival yet, just waves pushed by an unseen hand.

By the time the fishermen had finished their toil, drawing their nets to shore, sorting their catch and cleaning their nets, the winds had shifted. The flags had picked up in salute of the day. Curiously, one set of flags at one end of the beach flew west, the other set pointed east, an omen of the coming confusion; a swirling breeze had begun.

Out on the horizon, dark clouds were barely visible, far out to sea. Locals prepared for the onslaught they knew would soon overtake them. Anxious animals were corralled and brought into shelters, houses protected by storm shutters, food and water stored.

Constant radio warnings echoed throughout the towns and villages. Apprehension was rising with each repeated message. Most residents had seen this tyrant before. They knew his heartless fury, marching forward, ever closer to their shores. The animals were not the only ones with fear in their hearts.

Reg Langley opened the squeaky screen door and entered John's Market Square in the village of Lofton. It was an inflated name for such a small grocery/gas station, but it often was a heart of activity on this country highway. Residents of the area, both permanent and summer transients, relied on its stock of food, gas and drinks.

John Brompton had been the proud owner of the store for more than twenty years now. When he moved into the area from Stockbridge at age forty-two, it seemed remote. It was just as he liked it; far from the intense crowds of the city. He had had enough of the stress back there: Lofton was far enough out of the city and even beyond the local towns. It was country living; surrounded by trees, trees and more trees, rocks and lakes. Life progressed at the pace of the person living it. John preferred to take life slowly.

Some of the summer residents persisted in the city pace, but he was stubbornly on country time. If you wanted to get service at the city tempo, then he figured you could go there to get your stuff. It made no difference to him anyway. He opened this store as something to do with his time. He had a sizable inheritance from his grandfather and did not need the income from the store. Rumor had it that he had millions invested somewhere, but you know how rumors go. Anything could be true or a complete fabrication around here. Stories cropped up weekly about one person or another. It did not matter to Reg, though; he just wanted the newspaper, a frozen pizza and a little information.

Reg walked into the market with a loping stride and asked John, "So what's the latest weather report? I heard that hurricane is on the move. What're they saying?"

John glanced at the television set behind the counter. It was perpetually on the weather network, a small consideration John gave to his customers who wanted the forecast for their weekend activities. He stroked his full, gray beard thoughtfully and spoke in his slow manner, "Well, they said it was headed straight for Jamaica then veered north. Looks like Haiti's in trouble with the thing. It's building strength too. May be a Category 4 soon. It could get nasty."

Reg raised his eyebrow in response, "That doesn't sound good. It's a wonder how they predict these things. I guess they know what they're doing. Looks like they're going to have to evacuate folks with a hurricane of that magnitude."

John nodded, "Said they're watching it. Ah, you know after that mess with Katrina and Rita back a few years ago. Nobody wants to be responsible for warning people too late. They're sending out notices now for the Carolina's, but that's a big area. You can't evacuate two states."

Reg frowned and shrugged, "Yeah, but they'll have to institute some sort of plan. You know the kind of mess a storm like that can cause."

John shook his head slowly, "Well, they'll have to be more specific where it might hit landfall before people will move on out. After all, they've had a lot of false alarms over the years. My sister, Sadie, lives in Charleston and is tired of it. She told me last year that she would rather take her chances than to board things up again for nothing. She said she'll wait longer this time then head inland to her niece's home."

"I don't know, John. It seems foolish to wait, especially with the way storms have gone these last few years. Look at the damage down in New Orleans. People are still recovering even now this long afterward! If I were her, I'd just board things up and head to her niece's anyway. You have only one life, no sense taking a chance at losing it over a storm."

John had heard it all over the years and did not like to rush into anything. He did not have patience with these worry-warts like Reg. "I'll call her, like I do every time there's a storm. But I don't have much influence over her. If you think I can be stubborn by times, you haven't met Sadie. If I say much to her, she'll probably just stay there out of spite to me."

Reg grabbed a deluxe topping pizza out of the freezer case then picked up *The Journal* from the newsstand. Plopping them down on the counter, he asked John how much he owed him. John replied, "That'll be $9.53 to be exact." Reg pulled a $10 bill from his wallet and waited for the change. "So I guess you'll be fishing on Saturday. Is Jason coming in to handle the store?"

"Yeah, he should be here. But I'll have to wait here to see if he shows up on time. Sometimes, he doesn't get here until almost 9:30. If I wasn't here to open the store, I'd have customers angry with me all week. He says that his parents have been giving him a hard time lately, wanting him to do more chores before leaving to come here. I'm not so sure it is that so much as he can't get out of bed after partying the night before. You know, he's at that age. Anyway, I'll see you when I get there."

Reg picked up his bag and walked out to his jeep. It sure was muggy again today. Maybe if would make the fish bite better, he thought as he took off down the road.

Jack stopped by Lacey's house to drop off his rent money. The cabins he used for the courses were owned by Lacey. He had one comfortable cottage for himself; a rustic wooden structure clad in stained cedar. It had an adequate kitchen with a table and chairs to eat at, two bedrooms, and a bathroom. A large central room served well for relaxing in as well as teaching any theory for his courses. The large wrap-around veranda overlooked the hillside where the other cabins were dotted on the slope toward the lake. The main house had electric services but the cabins were basic, providing a little more protection than tents in case of inclement weather. A shower and washroom building for the campers were at the top of the hill to the side of Jack`s house.

It worked out well for his business. Before Lacey bought the property, Mason Grimly had run the place for fishing and hunting groups. The day Mason turned sixty-five though, he packed up and left; saying he had had enough traipsing around the countryside in the cold and mud and he moved to Florida. The property was up for sale for only three months before Lacey came along and bought it.

Some people wondered why a middle-aged widow would move this far up the mountain to live by herself. She said she wanted solitude to do some writing. Jack knew she was an author of some sort, but he never asked what sort of books she wrote; he was not that interested anyway. She must have had some success because she had quit her city job and she lived comfortably. She traveled often in the winter; sometimes she toured to promote her books and other times to take vacations and do research. But she did use the place to run writer's retreats several times a year and she stayed put up here for the rest of the year. It didn't matter much to Jack because she made for a good landlady and was a pleasant woman. She did not ask much of him and that suited him fine. If anything needed to be fixed, he could usually make the necessary repairs himself and she paid for them quickly. He could not ask for a better arrangement.

Jack pulled his old blue Chev truck into Lacey's yard. It was more than a driveway. You could park at least half a dozen vehicles by the side of her house. The house itself was a story and a half wood frame house with dormers front and back. The wood was stained cedar, with a matching wraparound balcony like his house, but much larger. Her house had at least four bedrooms, and she used one extra room on the first level for a study and a library. She had a passion for reading books as well as for writing them.

Jack knocked on the screen door. The inside door was open to catch what little breeze was available this afternoon. The aroma of chicken simmering in the slow cooker wafted out to the porch. Lacey knew how to cook. He had been invited to dinner a few times with her friends from the village. Calvin and Jan Talbot were their names, a congenial couple, no-nonsense people who had a cottage up here for twenty-five years and recently become full-time residents since retirement the previous spring.

"Well, hello there, Jack. How're you doing? The weather hasn't gotten any cooler with all that rain we had this week, has it? What brings you by this Thursday afternoon?" Lacey was drying her hands from doing dishes as she answered the door. The screen door squeaked as she opened it. She was tall, slender and athletic, and did not look her fifty years with her short curly auburn hair. She was wearing blue shorts and tank top. She did the physical work of the garden and simple house maintenance. In addition, she kept active with a daily swim in the lake and liked to hike year round.

Jack dug into his jeans pocket producing the cash. "I just wanted to bring the rest of the rent. I appreciate your letting me split the rent into two payments this month. I had some unexpected expenses on the truck. I probably should start looking into getting a new one soon. When things slow down in winter, I'll take the time." Jack was thankful that Lacey was easygoing about the rent arrangement. It was not a problem for her because Jack always produced the money eventually.

"So you have people coming up this weekend?" Lacey was always curious about his clients. She liked people and they were always drawn to her and her compassionate demeanor.

"Yeah, two couples. I think one is a writer. Perhaps you know him. I think he writes for *The Journal* in the city. Paul Montgomery is his name. Maybe you have something in common, writing and all."

"Well, I think his kind of writing is differs from mine and we don`t exactly run in the same circles. He's a journalist. He deals primarily in facts and events. I tell stories. It's not the same thing," Lacey commented with a smile. Jack wondered what she was getting at with that comment but did not say anything.

"From what I have read of his pieces, he doesn't just report the news. He tells the story behind the news items. He does some digging and tries to help the reader understand the people involved. I kind of like his articles." Jack always made a point of reading the newspaper and following the news on the television when he had a break between clients.

"I suppose then we do have something in common. I tell stories about people and how they deal with life. The difference is that I probably have a little more creative freedom in what I do." Jack had to admit that he had never read any of Lacey's books, so he had no idea of what type of stories she told. He thought that they were probably some romance novels anyway.

"I imagine that the topics aren't the same. Maybe you'll have a chance to meet him over the weekend. Would you like that?" Jack offered.

"You never know, we'll probably bump into one another over the three days. I have a hunch that it might be a busy weekend here."

"You got something planned for the weekend, Lacey, or just the usual drop-ins?" Lacey seemed to have an open door for all the locals, especially with the people attending the Tuesday night meetings. It had been busier around her place than last summer.

"No, nothing out of the ordinary. I just sense it could be busy. Maybe it is the unsettled weather. Have you been watching the hurricane? It looks like it could hit the coast soon. Didn't you say that your sister is staying down that way?"

Jack ran his hand through his hair and sighed. He hadn't focused on the weather as much as usual with all the trouble he had been having with the truck. Laurie was in Wilmington, North Carolina caring for their aunt who was in hospital there. Aunt Liz was seventy-eight with bad arthritis and emphysema. She was already finding the humidity brutal and had come down with pneumonia. Laurie was a registered nurse who could not say no to anyone. She had taken a leave of absence from her job to help take care of her aunt's personal affairs while she was critically ill in the hospital. If the storm was soon to hit the mainland, perhaps he ought to check in with her.

"Thanks for reminding me. I hate to admit it, but I have been spending so much time on the transmission in the truck, I haven't called Laurie this week. Do you have any idea where the storm is headed?"

"Well, the current path is looking like the Carolinas but which area, I'm not sure. Come on in and we'll check the weather network." Jack stepped into the house. The chicken smelled even more inviting than out on the porch. Jack sniffed and smiled. Lacey caught his expression and replied, "If you have time, come on back at 6:00 and dinner will be ready. I used the slow cooker today so it wouldn't heat the house."

"You do make the best chicken around here. I suppose you have some secret recipe." Jack was warming to the idea of a dinner out of someone else's kitchen.

"Well, I just use fresh herbs out of the garden, Jack, and a pinch of love. Every meal needs a pinch of love," she replied. Lacey was always making obscure comments like that. It befuddled Jack at times but he put it down to the writer in her.

Jack and Lacey walked into the great room. Two tan leather couches with a matching chair were set in a u-shape in front of the large fireplace. A dining area with a rustic carved wooden table and chairs were conveniently placed between the kitchen and living area. They switched on the television to the weather station. Satellite photographs revealed the typical vortex cloud formation over the Caribbean moving on a track toward the Carolinas. The announcer was talking about the current damage in Haiti and what was expected in the Bahamas. Concern for Savannah, Georgia was mounting but warnings were being sounded in case the track should head further north toward Charleston, South Carolina or as far north as Wilmington, North Carolina. FEMA and state officials wanted to issue evacuation orders, but had to be sure of the course it would take before sounding the alarm. Everyone still had Katrina and Rita on their minds, so no one wanted to be in error.

Jack had an uneasy feeling in his stomach when he heard the announcer say Wilmington. He would try to call Laurie when he got back to the house. He did not want to worry her but he also wanted her to do what she should to be safe. It was predicted to be a bad storm and had already taken fourteen lives in the Caribbean. Aunt Liz's house was close to the beach and would take the brunt of any storm surge and that was where Laurie was staying while in Wilmington.

Lacey could sense the tension in Jack. The muscles in his neck tightened and that jaw was set and ready. "Do you want to call her from here, Jack?"

"No, Lacey, I'll get back to the house and call her there. Don't worry, Laurie is levelheaded. She comes from Davidson stock. We're a tough breed. Remember she was an army brat and did her stint in the military too. If anyone can prepare for a storm, she can." Jack did not want to alarm Lacey nor let on to her his concern for Laurie. Jack was not the type to let anyone into his private thoughts. He would address it on his terms.

Lacey knew Jack did not want to hear what she was about to say but she also realized she had to say it, "Jack, I will be Praying for Laurie and Liz for their Protection"

Jack tensed further and said, "Aw, Lacey, you know how I feel about that stuff, but I appreciate the sentiment anyway." Jack had always made it clear that the topic was off-limits in their friendship.

Jack glanced at his watch. Lacey caught on and said, "You go do what you have to get done. Come on back tonight at six and dinner will be ready and waiting for you."

"Sure, that sounds good Lacey. Is anyone else coming by for dinner?" Jack asked as he headed toward the door.

Lacey shrugged, "You know how it is around here, Jack. If anyone happens to drop by, the table is always big enough to hold one or two more. You never know who might stop in. It's always an adventure and keeps life interesting."

Jack let go of the screen door and walked down the stairs headed for his truck. "I'll be by later, Lacey, and thanks for the invitation." He was thinking as he walked across the parking area how all her friends who stopped by for coffee and dinner would probably end up as characters in her books. Maybe she had someone fashioned after him too. It made him chuckle to think of how she might describe him and his life. Maybe he should ask to borrow one of her books to read after all.

Mac steered the silver Mustang into the service station. The roads had been good until now. They had been travelling for more than two hours now. They had their favorite CD's playing on the stereo and with the sunshine and wind in their hair, it was as if they were teenagers again, no pressures, just out for a weekend getaway. It brought back warm memories of when they were first married. However, there was no Mustang in those days, but the enjoyment of being together was the same.

They had reached the turnoff for Route 15 north up to Seeley's

Mountain. It was a good spot to pull in for gas and a pit stop. Sarah needed to use the ladies room and a coffee break seemed reasonable to Mac.

Mac steered the car by the gas pumps shut off the engine. He unfolded his six foot two-inch frame from the sports car and stretched to work out the kinks that two hours on the road had caused. Sarah grabbed her purse and went into the store as Mac filled the tank with gas. The bell rang as she opened the door. Racks of snack foods were placed near the entrance; with rows of shelving containing various food staples and canned goods behind them. The television was on at the end of the counter where the cash register was sitting. As Sarah passed the checkout, she could hear a news report on the television giving the final scores of various sporting events. She spotted the sign for the washrooms and headed that way. The store was just large enough to handle all the necessities of living so the locals did not have to travel back to the highway to the chain stores. It probably was convenient but more expensive than in town.

By the time Sarah came back from the washroom, the newscast was reviewing the current weather predictions. The announcer gave a rundown on the damaging storm in the Caribbean and its imminent attack on the Carolina coast of the U. S. The tension in the news delivery caught Sarah's attention. Well, yes, she was concerned for the people living in those areas, but she had been so consumed in grabbing time with Mac for the weekend that she had become self-absorbed. She felt a twinge of guilt. Memories of her mother's admonishments about looking out for others flooded her mind. She promised herself to say a Prayer for them when she got back into the car.

Sarah wandered toward the snack display and picked out a bag of cashews for herself and some liquorice for Mac, then headed to the coffee counter. She thought that she might switch to decaf, having had enough high-test coffee in her system already to keep her awake all night. Thinking better of it, she spied the drink cooler and pulled out a strawberry-kiwi fruit drink that appealed to her and a bottle of water for Mac. As she turned back toward the counter, she saw that Mac was already paying for the gas. Mac headed to the washrooms himself as she paid for the snacks.

Sarah chatted with the clerk as the short plump lady made change for her $20 bill. She wore a name tag that read 'Shelley'. "So where are you headed?" the woman inquired pleasantly.

"We're going to up by Seeley's Mountain to Big Rock Lake for a wilderness survival course. Well, it isn't the survival part of the course, just compass reading, the basics, you know. But it should be fun, a little different from the usual grind."

Shelley asked, "Is that one of Jack Davidson's courses? He's made a fair business in the last few years. You should have a good time, if the weather holds."

Sarah answered, "I think that's the fellow's name. We're looking forward to it. What about the weather? Is it supposed to get bad?"

"Well, you know the mountain has its own weather systems sometimes, getting more rain than down here, like last week. We sure got a lot of runoff from it. The creek is higher than usual. But there's a low-pressure system in the Midwest that they're talking about bringing some rain by Sunday maybe. You never know what that hurricane will do to the overall weather picture. I don't think those weather trackers know half of what they try to let on that they do. Likely, as not, we'll be in sunshine here while the rest of the area will be in rain. Who knows?"

"Well, I hope you're right about the sunshine. It would be a drag to do the course in the rain. Maybe we could just stay in the cabins and play cards if it gets bad."

Mac was coming back from the rest rooms as she finished paying for the snacks. "Ready to go?" he asked. "Sure, I got you a bottle of water and a licorice. Do you want a coffee too?" Sarah replied.

"Yeah, I'll go grab one and I'll meet you out in the car."

Chapter 3

Flashback:

Her mind spun for a moment, taking her by surprise. That old haunting memory had returned for an instant, causing a familiar anguished sensation deep inside her:

That insidious feeling of uneasiness that crept up her spine had come over her again and for no apparent reason.

Of all times, this made no sense. She never understood the source of this fear; why it found its way into her soul. But it now tantalized her, playing with her in the periphery of her emotions. Why now, with everything going so well and the new job offer she had been dreaming of for so many months? The adventures it offered were captivating. The money they promised was irresistible. So why did she feel so uneasy?

"Oh, well, no sense dwelling on it, I have to get going anyway." She grabbed her keys and ran out the door, slamming the door in defiance.

The ogre flashed his teeth with blinding lightning. It bore down heartlessly on the small mass of land in the Caribbean Ocean. An angry roar discharged from its belly as winds escalated. It lashed out, tearing at anything in its way, no obstruction too large for its vengeance. Rage spilled from its gut; whining, moaning, screaming emanated from the demons of hell it unleashed. The sounds mounted, ever increasing in intensity, until it sounded like a thousand freight trains rolling overhead.

Walls shuddered, roofs loosened and vibrated to the tune of a crazy drummer. Windows buckled and shattered as the hideous monster plodded along the shore. Palms bent low to the ground, bowing to an unseen prince of darkness as he demanded penance in his path. Trees were stripped of leaves, houses sandblasted clean of visible paint, scoured bare.

The ocean waters rose ever higher, whipped in equal fury as the monster marched on. Tempest tossed, wave after wave battered an already beaten shoreline. Higher and higher the ocean rose; arms of water stretched toward the heavens, vicious tongues thrashing for stray victims. Walls of water pushed forward, ripping all moorings close to shore, moving inland, not satisfied by shoreline alone. Rising higher; higher still; the waters consumed the land, ripping everything in its path.

Eli Belkert arrived at Lacey's house in his new silver Chev four by four truck about an hour after Jack left. Lacey commented on the improvement over his rickety old 1990, half ton truck. "Well, Lacey, I was thinking that you were right about having reliable equipment. There's no sense living up on the mountain and not having a vehicle that can do the job, especially when winter comes along. Having the four-wheel drive will be a good addition, you know."

"Congratulations, Eli. I know you'll enjoy having it and I'm sure there'll be a few people who will be happy to pay you to transport them around in the winter and during the spring rains."

"Now, Lacey, I wasn't banking on having a new job as well as a new truck! So did you hear anything more since Tuesday night? I thought I'd give you a few days to gather more information."

"Eli, I'm not sure of all the details, but I do know that the hurricane brewing in the South has something to do with it. There's money involved but I'm not certain who it concerns yet. However, it is even bigger than that. I'm sure it also will focus on the West Coast soon. It confirms what Sol said at last Tuesday's meeting. I'm sure we'll get more information soon. It usually comes on a "need to know" basis, as you are already aware."

As eager as Eli was to pump Lacey for information, he knew better than that from experience. Only when she was ready and had spent time in consultation did she ever venture an opinion on how to proceed. It would be a group effort anyway. Though Bert Lawson was their senior member; each of them had an opportunity to offer their opinions to this close-knit group.

Lacey patted Eli on the shoulder and said, "Whatever we decide, it won't be just us handling the work as usual; you do know that, right?"

Eli perked up and said, "You are always so good at reminding me of that Lacey. We're merely one part of the situation. I realize that. I just get anxious sometimes to get going on it. It's hard to develop patience. I understand that I am the youngest one in the group. At least what I lack in restraint is made up for in eagerness!"

"Eli, I cannot fault you in that respect and you are learning to pace yourself better and better. Sometimes, perhaps, the rest of us can be a little too reserved and need the momentum you provide. I am always grateful for your presence."

"Well, thank you, Lacey. I need to hear that occasionally. Is there anything I can pick up for you when I go into town this evening? I have this new truck that's just waiting to be put to use, you know?"

"Sure, Eli, here's my list of things I was going to get tomorrow anyway. This money should cover it amply. I want to make sure we have enough supplies in case we have a bunch of visitors on the weekend. With the hot weather, there are sure to be extra people who are here from the city. I'll talk to you later. Thanks for helping."

Hour after hour the monster battered the island in the sea until all thought they could take it no more. All sanity was lost, all hope eroded like the shoreline. Then like an angry child tiring of its toys, it tossed them aside and muscled on, away from their island, on to new amusements.

People peeked out of shuttered windows, almost afraid to see the demon staring back at them. No, it was not the eye of the storm; that part of the storm had missed them. The ogre had merely given them a glancing blow, but God help those hit directly by this fiend.

Residents ventured out of their shelters to survey the damage. Devastation met their eyes wherever they looked. They gathered, hugging one another knowing they were safe, alive.

One by one, they started to pick up the pieces of their shattered lives, banding together to help each other retrieve broken belongings, cleaning debris out of trees, repairing houses, sharing their few remaining possessions. The sense of togetherness and mutual survival was pervasive as life moved on; restoration, starting over now became their goal.

They looked toward the horizon as the menacing clouds moved toward other victims, knowing they had narrowly escaped the monster's full wrath. Grimly they watched the storm power onward and knew that others surely would not be as fortunate as they had been.

The Montgomerys and the Donnellys had driven up in separate vehicles because Paul had to take care of some details at work in the city core before leaving. Mac and Sarah wanted to get away early so they could take their time and stop along the way if the mood dictated them to do so. The two couples were going to meet at a little motel about ten miles from Friday's destination. It was supposed to be a nice location with a restaurant frequented by many locals. The food was also reported to be good as a chef from the city had moved his restaurant there.

"What is the name of that motel? Oh, I think I wrote it on the bottom of the map I downloaded from the Internet. Yes, here it is. Umm, let's see Eagle's Rest Inn. We should be about twenty minutes away now." Evangeline remarked, breaking the silence.

She had been worrying about the weekend's events, trying not to be intimidated by it all. She had managed to accompany Paul many excursions in the past and had enjoyed herself once she got there. She always seemed to over analyze events and think of negative possibilities, the "what ifs" in life. It frustrated her enormously that she could not be as free and spontaneous as Paul. It was something she had talked about with Sarah several times, but she never could identify the root of her underlying fear. She hoped she could just deal with it this weekend. If nothing else, she would come away with another life skill and a packet of memories.

Paul roused from his thoughts when Evangeline spoke up. He had been trying to shut off all his musings on his next article, so he could just enjoy the experience. The guys at the office ragged on him before he left about not taking his work with him. That was difficult to do when the expectations were as high as they were on him. With the big salary, came bigger responsibilities. He did not begrudge the wages, just the stress he sometimes felt. But he did like the challenges it posed, so he would just have to get over it and move on. He had just made that decision when Evangeline had broken his thoughts.

"Yeah, about twenty minutes should do it. The scenery sure is getting nice, isn't it?" He decided to dump any outside pressures and enjoy this getaway; he owed everyone that. It had taken a lot to organize four busy people, so he wanted to have a blast while away. "That motel should be nice. The menu in the restaurant sounds like it should be high quality. We can relax and not have to go anywhere afterward, just back to our rooms."

"It'll be nice to catch up with Sarah. She's been away with her rowing team for the last while and with all the practicing before the competition, I haven't had a chance to talk to her for ages. A relaxing dinner sounds great. We can get to bed at an early hour and be up and ready to go up to the mountain first thing in the morning."

"Between my schedule and Mac's, we haven't had a chance to get together to play squash lately. It'll be a good evening. How far till the turnoff for route 15?"

"It shouldn't be more than six miles more. Oh, look, a moose crossing sign. I wonder how often people encounter them?" Evangeline was excited at the prospect of seeing wild animals, although a little nervous too. It wouldn't be so bad with Paul with her and it was not supposed to be an outdoor camping trip so it should be fine.

"I don't think it's something that happens every day, just a warning for motorists. I wouldn't want to tangle with one along these roads at night though. I'm sure they don't want any contact with humans."

"Oh, look, there's the sign for the junction. It's just coming up. Well, here we are! We're almost there. I can't wait to get there and walk around. With all these winding roads, I guess I'm a little tense. I'll be glad to get out of the car."

Jack went to Lacey's for dinner that evening as arranged; the food was as good as he had anticipated and the conversation was interesting too. Calvin and Jan Talbot stopped by for coffee after the meal. They played cards for a while. The conversation had traversed a broad arc from Calvin's fish stories to Lacey and Jan's woes with deer eating their gardens to where they would like to travel if the money was no object.

Jan had them all laughing with her description of a predicament with a stray cat that had made itself at home on their veranda the previous week. It happened the same evening the neighborhood skunk also paid them a visit. Unfortunately, Jan had been feeding the cat outdoors and the food dish was still out on the lawn by the edge of the porch when the skunk had arrived. While the skunk was having a feast on those tasty morsels, the cat decided that the skunk's tail made for a marvelous toy. Ripples of laughter met her description of how the cat hung over the edge of the veranda, reaching down to bat at the skunk's tail. Jan somehow managed to get the cat's attention through the dining-room window and scooped it into the house before the skunk had gotten angry and sprayed.

"I can't tell you how relieved I was to get that cat in the house. I had sworn I wouldn't take the cat inside. The last thing I need is a pet, but when I saw that cat playing with that skunk's tail, I changed my mind immediately. All I wanted was to get her inside at that point! Can you imagine the smell all over the deck furniture? Ugh," Jan exclaimed.

"I don't suppose the cat is still around is it? Or did it finally make friends with the skunk?" Lacey asked.

"Oh, we managed to find its owner the next day, and we're smarter about leaving food out as a lure for the skunk. It hasn't shown up since then, thankfully," Calvin replied.

The conversation had then drifted to more serious topics and when they started to talk about their Faith, Jack managed to make his excuses that he had to get back to prepare for his group arriving the next day. That was a topic he would rather avoid.

Paul and Evangeline arrived at Eagle's Rest Inn about an hour after Mac and Sarah. Evangeline opened the door to their Pontiac Grand Prix. She gave a quick glance in the visor mirror to see if she was pleased with the appearance of her shoulder length blond hair and makeup. She then unfastened her seatbelt, and smoothed out her designer tank top and shorts before she got out of the car. At five foot two inches tall she was petite but stylish. She stood for a moment as she surveyed the motel. It was quaint but seemed well appointed and cared for on the exterior. She hesitated before following Paul up the path to the office, taking in her surroundings. This truly was the country. All vestiges of city life were left there. She hoped that the rooms were comfortable and the food would be good. The best part of the weekend was that she and Paul would be having an exciting weekend with Sarah and Mac. She wanted to focus on that and not her mounting anxiety about her environment. She felt beyond her comfort. No matter what, though, she was determined to have an enjoyable time.

They quickly checked in to their rooms and had time to freshen up before dinner. The motel had a charming atmosphere but the rooms were surprisingly spacious and included all the required amenities. The restaurant exceeded their expectations. Although the menu was limited, the taste and presentation of the dishes rivaled any they had experienced in the city. The chef, Sebastien Lauzon, came out from the kitchen and greeted them when they raved about their meals to their server. He chatted with them for some time, even hinting at the ingredients that were distinctive in each dish. He obviously enjoyed all the attention, but also loved to share his expertise with people who appreciated his efforts.

"Too often, when I had the old restaurant in the city, people were too sophisticated. They rarely appreciated what they had and seldom did I hear anything positive. It was only when, on occasion, there was an error made in the kitchen did I hear anything. It was discouraging. People come in here and they don't expect much and get a lot. It makes for a different result. I feel as if I am achieving so much more, though the menu is scaled down here."

Mac thanked him again for the group and Sabastien disappeared into the kitchen. "Well that was nice. That's a good start to the weekend. What do you think guys?"

Evangeline quietly commented, "I can only hope the rest of the weekend goes as well."

No one but Sarah noticed Evangeline's hesitancy. She promised herself to talk to her the next morning before they set off up the mountain. It would have to wait until they had a quiet moment together, however, Sarah did not want to break the festive mood of the evening.

Jack managed to connect with Laurie at Liz's house before he went to bed. He thought it would be the best time to call as she would be back from the hospital after visiting hours were over.

"I realize that they are predicting the storm path to hit in this area,

Jack, but there's only so much I can do. I have a responsibility to Aunt Liz. I've asked her neighbor to help board up her house for me. He already has been helping Aunt Liz for some time because she couldn't manage any heavy work. After Uncle Stan died, she needed a handyman around to do odd jobs, so they made a financial arrangement for him to take care of things. I'll try to take my stuff to the hospital if it looks like the storm will be hitting us directly. That way I'll be prepared for whatever might happen. I figure that staying with Aunt Liz at the hospital will be one of the safest places to be, given that they'll at least have emergency power. So don't worry about us. I have it all under control."

That's the Laurie that Jack knew. She was gutsy and realistic. Her army training helped her during a crisis. She had been taught well and she used it in her civilian life, just as he had. "That sounds like a good plan, Laurie. I just wanted to find out how things were going. So how is Aunt Liz doing?"

Laurie paused, "Well, Jack, I'm not sure. She seems better one day and the next a new complication seems to crop up. Her blood pressure has been erratic lately. One day she seems to breathe better; the next it's labored again. They've been trying various meds to get it under control. At least she's alert most of the time. They've been getting her out of bed daily to help her strength and circulation. Realistically, I just wonder how much energy reserves she has left."

Jack realized he was talking with a professional. It was Laurie's expertise. Aunt Liz had the right person with her. "Well, you tell Aunt Liz that I was asking after her. Is there any point to me calling her directly? Can she talk on the phone?"

"Jack, she can't talk long enough to make a full sentence with the way her breathing is now. She would want to talk to you and that would just tire her out completely. I'll tell her you called and wished her the best."

"Okay. Keep me informed how things are going. Call me if there anything I can do from here."

"I doubt there's anything you can do from there. I'll stay at the hospital. I'm sure they'll need an extra set of hands around here if the storm hits the area. Thanks for calling. I love you."

"Yeah, I do too. Don't do anything foolish now, will you?" Jack was uncomfortable with all the mushy sentiment but he did love his sister. She was his sole remaining sibling since their brother had been killed in a car crash three years ago. Jack did not want to admit that he had been completely absorbed in his situation over the last few days and if Lacey had not reminded him, he probably would not have even made the call.

"Don't worry, Jack. I'm sensible. I'll just do what has to be done. I'll leave the heroics to others. By the way, have you talked to Mum and Dad lately?"

"No, but maybe you should call them and let them know what you told me. You know how Mum rags on us about not keeping them informed, especially because she can't keep tabs on us as easily since they moved out to the West Coast."

"Don't worry, I'll be sure to call them and let them know where I'll be. So, I'll talk to you later, then, okay?"

"I'll try to call you tomorrow. I have the number for the hospital and your cell in case you don't go back to Aunt Liz's. Bye for now."

Chapter 4

Jack rose early Friday morning and left the house to make sure Bob Fisher would be available on Saturday to help with the field training on the mountain. Bob called up the hill from his house as Jack approached, "Old man Horace has been at it again! "

"You don't mean what I think you are saying, do you?" Jack replied.

"Oh yeah, worse than ever this time though. Hammerford spied him streaking about midnight between Hooty's and Grissom's. Now that was something I am glad I didn't see!"

"Nan will have his hide for that one! Literally, I guess"

"I didn't even ask her for her thoughts on the matter this morning. I thought it best to put it to bed with the old man."

Bob walked with Jack into the house, shaking his head, perhaps a little more vigorously than necessary. The mental picture of old man Horace, butt naked, cutting across the yard was not an image he wanted permanently burned into his memory. Old Horace was a man who could be described as having wrinkles on his wrinkles. Naked, these would not be picturesque!

The old man was stinking drunk again, no doubt. Coupled with escalating Alzheimer's, it was a dangerous combination. Nan had her hands full. No matter how many times she confiscated his bottles, he somehow managed to replace them. Someone must be helping him get it. It was a wonder the old guy had made it to eighty-three, considering how much he'd been drinking lately. No one understood the grief Nan held inside her. It was decision time, for his safety and for the protection of those who had to go out at night to try to find him and bring him home.

"I hope Nan is now ready to talk to Dr. Jenkins about either some help or a visit to Sunnyview. It can't be good for her either." Jack replied. "So you ready to go Saturday afternoon? There're four in this group so I could use two helpers; one for the bottom of the hillside, the other partway down. It's the same place as usual, the same setup for the course. It shouldn't be a problem. It's straightforward, no complications that I can foresee. If anything comes up, I'll call you."

Bob nodded his agreement. "Just let me know if anything changes, otherwise we'll be there as usual, about 1:30. With only four of them, it shouldn't take that long. You'll send them down in pairs as usual?"

"Sure, these guys are from the city and I'm not taking any chances with this bunch. I'll arm them with radios, just to be on the safe side. One is Paul Montgomery, the reporter. The last thing I need is to lose some famous dude and have it splashed all over the newspaper the next day!" Jack countered.

"Sounds good. You've got it all covered then. I'll see you tomorrow afternoon. You headed to Worley's party Saturday night then?"

Jack made a face. "I'm not sure yet. It depends on this group and when they want to leave. I might have to hang around to babysit if they want to stay until Sunday morning. Depending on what time we finish they might not want to drive that late in the day. I'll let you know tomorrow when we're done, okay?"

"Sure. Whatever. Talk to ya later," Bob said to Jack as he left the house.

Paul and Evangeline went down to breakfast early. They were soon joined by Mac and Sarah in the dining room. Breakfast was as sumptuous as dinner the night before, with fresh fruit, eggs, pancakes, bacon and sausage. They packed all their belongings and were ready to drive up to the lake by 8:00 a.m. Jack was expecting them by 8:30 so they headed directly up Seeley's Mountain Road toward Big Rock Lake.

It was a continuous climb up the mountain taking them past rustic cottages and an outfitter supply store. They could see signs for campgrounds and bait shops on either side of the road. They passed a creek that seemed to crisscross the road several times. As the clerk at the gas station had said, the runoff from the rain earlier in the week had increased the flow in the creek. Soon they passed John's Market Square, which set off chuckles in both vehicles as they looked at the size of the store compared to the relative grandness of its name. Before long, they hit the turnoff for Big Rock Lake and they could tell that they had started down the other side of the mountain toward the lake below. The view was breathtaking. The vivid blue water of the lake was in sharp contrast to the vivid green hues of the evergreens, birches, aspens and ashes on the mountain slopes washing down toward the lake.

"Mac, you have to stop here. Let me take a photo of this!" Sarah cried. Mac slowed the car and putting on his blinker to warn Paul behind him. Sarah sprang from the car, camera in hand. Her excitement was clearly visible, like a child. Mac had to smile. This spontaneity is what he loved about Sarah. He could see why she did so well as a teacher. She could see possibilities in everything and wanted to capture those moments of wonder forever. She quickly returned to the car, not wanting to hold everyone up. That was Sarah. She would dart out to do what she needed but never to monopolize the moment. They were on their way again moments later, hardly adding two minutes to their trip.

Behind them, Paul and Evangeline laughed at Sarah and her darting photography session. "I'll have to get a copy of that photo. I don't know how she manages it, but she seems to capture these spectacular photographs without even trying. If I tried all day, I couldn't produce anything like that."

Paul remarked, "It'd be great if the guys at the paper could produce as quickly and as well as she does. Maybe she should moonlight for us."

"We must be almost there. There's the sign post Jack told us about. The names on it are McCrae, Davidson and Peltry. That's the side road to his camp. It looks like it's right on the lake. Maybe we can all go swimming while we are here! That'd be so good."

"I'm sure there'll be time for breaks and swims. That's half the fun of coming to the country. So you ready for this? We've arrived!"

"I think I am. What about you?"

"I couldn't be more ready. It'll be such a change from work. Uh, let's see, I guess I can park it in here."

They parked and got out of the vehicles. Although it was still humid, it was fresh mountain air that filled their lungs; no smog here.

They surveyed Jack's house and the cabins below. They had been warned to bring sleeping bags, pillows and flashlights. It was not going to be a luxury stay. They were here to learn new skills and understand the countryside better. Evangeline eyed the cabins, realizing that any vestige of glamor she expected had just evaporated. *Well, he sure didn't lie about the accommodations, did he?* She would not verbalize this comment, not wanting to let her reservations about the trip be obvious to the others. She was determined to have a good time for everyone's sakes, especially Paul's. She took a deep breath, ignoring the nagging fear she had been fighting the last few days and stepped toward the others.

Jack Davidson opened door of the house. He was a tanned, slim and muscular six feet tall. With blue eyes and dark-brown hair, he had chiselled good looks that led many to mistake him for an actor. He smiled and immediately put them all at ease. Looking at Jack, Evangeline and Sarah smirked at each other, thinking, how bad could this be? It could be a good weekend after all. It seemed they were in capable hands!

The news was on the television in Eli's living room. The big story was Hurricane Igor. It had taken a turn to the northwest now and was picking up speed and intensity. The announcer was comparing its track with the 1954 Hurricane Hazel. "That hurricane pounded ashore with winds of 106 miles per hour and reported gusts between 130 and 150 miles per hour in the area between Myrtle Beach in South Carolina and Cape Fear along the southern coast of North Carolina. Evacuation orders, starting with areas most vulnerable to storm surge, have been in place for the last twelve hours. As expected, traffic out of the region is back logged as many people are in the area for the last of the summer holiday season before the children go back to school. . . ."

Eli turned off his television set. The details were not especially important to him. He knew that it was the beginning of a set of events that could turn everyone's lives upside down. The only thing left to do was to Pray. Many people were going to get hurt. He did know that and they were running out of time to do anything about it.

Jack welcomed his new clients to Big Rock Lake and showed them to their cabins. He apologized that there was only one building for bathrooms and showers, explaining that at least the men's facility was separate from that of the women although housed in the same structure. He thought that the beds were at least comfortable and they were welcome to stay at the house until they wished to retire for the night.

Each couple brought their knapsacks and gear down to their bunkhouses and settled as best they could. Considering the circumstances, even the women had to admit that they were cozy for cabins with no utilities. When they had enough time to use the facilities, they regrouped up the hillside in the house where Jack was awaiting their arrival.

He offered them coffee, juice and water. Mac and Paul each accepted a cup of java and both women asked for juice. Once they were seated around the living-room table, Jack began his introduction to orienteering. He handed each of them a compass. "So are any of you experienced with using a compass?"

Mac and Sarah both nodded that they did. They were scuba divers and had taken navigation as part of their advanced certification. Paul had used a compass when he was young in the boy scouts and Evangeline had been given some basic instruction by her father who used to hunt when she was young.

"Okay, that makes it a little easier then. If you pick up your compass, I'll review the basics." Jack went on to describe the basic parts of the compass as a piece of survival equipment. He expanded to review the points of the compass, the 360 degrees of division on its face. North corresponded to 0 or 360 degrees; 90 was east, 180 was south and 270 matched with west. The points between could be further broken down to northeast, southeast, southwest, and northwest. The individual degrees allowed for more precise directions than the general categories would allow. Soon, because of their experience, each person was comfortable with these basic concepts.

"Okay, then, what conditions will screw up the use of a compass?" Jack then asked.

"Well, I suppose dropping it wouldn't be good for it" offered Evangeline.

"No, it sure wouldn't be, but that is not exactly what I was getting at," Jack answered patiently.

"I don't think you can use them in the extreme North, can you?" Mac said.

"That's right. You're too close to the magnetic north for them to be operational. Do any of you plan a trip up there in the next while?" They laughed and agreed that it wasn't on their agenda.

"So what might be another situation that might cause trouble with the compass?" Silence met his question, so Jack offered a hint, "You mentioned the difficulty in the North because of magnetic north. Is there anything else which may also mess up the use of a compass?"

Paul offered this comment, "Well, I imagine that if you're near a large mass of a metallic substance it causes problems."

"That's exactly what I was getting at."

"Oh, yeah, that's right. When we were taking the scuba navigation, the pier had large metal girders. When we got into the water, we had to take a bearing on the shore and match it up with objects on the shoreline so we could find our way back to our exit point in case we got lost. The girders played havoc with the compass, so we had to get far enough away from them to be able to read the compass."

"That's a great example. Usually you won't encounter a metal of that size in the bush, but you never know and you always have to keep it in mind. Even a metal belt buckle can cause problems."

Jack got them to do several exercises getting comfortable holding the compass level so the needle was free to move, then finding particular compass bearings and turning the bezel or housing.

Once they had completed that, it was time for a break. The room was filled with upbeat chatter and Jack knew he had achieved what he wanted in the first session. They were ready to build on their knowledge and start work outdoors.

Bert Lawson was on the phone with Lacey. "It looks like the lion is loose. Things are heating up to the South, don't you think?"

"Yes, Bert. It probably means that we have to step up our activities for a while. Jack has a sister in Wilmington and John Brompton's sister, Sadie, lives somewhere in the Carolinas. No matter how you cut it, someone around here has a relative or friend or acquaintance down there. It affects most people. We all have to do our part until we can get together again. First we should all make a few phone calls and get our contacts involved. The time is getting closer and it's more urgent than the last time."

"I agree, Lacey. It all falls in line with what we were warned about last year and last month. It's consistent with what we've been preparing for this past year. Everything's in place and ready to go. It's time to start now. There's no time to waste. What about our contacts out West?"

"They're preparing too. I'll call Danny after I finish talking with you. Bert, you do know that we're ready for this, don't you?

"Yeah, I think we are. As ready as you can be for something like this. I'm glad that we've been preparing this long. It should make things easier."

"Okay then. I'll get things started with our western contacts. I'll talk to you later."

Bert hung up the phone. He took a long heaving sigh. He had hoped that it would not have to come to this. Nevertheless, he knew they were as ready as they could be under the circumstances. However, he also realized that you are never prepared for it until it happens.

On the North Carolina coastline, where it butts up against the South Carolina border, the prevailing breeze began to pick up as the first evidence of the wall of cloud was visible on the horizon. It was dark and menacing against the brilliant blue sky and sparkling waters. Soon, as the barometer fell, clouds overwhelmed the sky. Rain, coupled with the wind, moved in together like an overdue express train. It began to howl and moan, building in pitch and intensity, screeching into every corner of buildings. No place could escape this demon.

Battered and molested, all boards loosely adhered on buildings broke from their moorings. Large pieces of debris flew as if no longer tethered by gravity. Roofs flexed, buckled and peeled off, becoming enormous flying missiles, seeming as light as a piece of paper on a summer breeze. It was no breeze; it was an uninvited, hideous monster that had invaded their territory. It seemed to have a life of its own; no, this thing was not life and it brought the stench of hell with it. No life or light was in this fiend. It was death itself.

The rain came incessantly, blown in horizontal sheets across the streets. This ogre did not weaken; instead, ever-increasing gusts threatened to explode everything in its path. Street signs were ripped from their posts and became violent projectiles against anything they encountered. It was far too dangerous to be outside.

They were helpless against this onslaught. No physical effort could stop the storm. People just had to stay put and hope that their building held together, outlasting the storm. No, it was beyond a storm; it was a beast that breathed and screamed at them. It was angry, dark and boiling like a cauldron. It slammed into the coastline with a viciousness no one around there had ever remembered. It was a monster unleashed from the pit of hell.

Jack took his crew outside in the grassy field leading down toward the lake. It was time for practice what they had learned. He reviewed their instructions from the earlier session. This time he got them to follow some basic coordinates on their compasses, starting with easy ninety degree turns, then building up to forty-five degrees followed by 135 degree turns. They fumbled a little, and got confused at times, but it then worked out well. Soon they would be able to follow a bearing, take sightings of landmarks that lined up with their coordinates, and manage to periodically check their compasses to make sure they had not veered off course. They now understood the fundamentals of navigation on a flat terrain.

"Okay, guys, you've earned your lunch break. Does anyone want to take a swim before we eat?" Jack asked.

Mac answered enthusiastically, "Thought you'd never ask! When do we have to be back?"

"We can break for about an hour, then we'd better be ready to start again. Go ahead and enjoy your swim. By the time you get back up here, I'll have lunch ready for you."

Jack had prepared sandwiches and drinks the night before. It was warm and muggy and everyone was happy to have an opportunity to cool down with a swim in the lake. The mood was festive and the group was enjoying themselves. Jack began to relax and think that this group was going to be less hassle than he had originally anticipated.

When the class had reassembled following lunch, Jack started to explain their next hurdle in the session. He brought out topographic maps. Jack explained the symbols and how to read the contour lines. He built on these concepts to introduce how to use a compass in relation to those maps; how to find your way from point A to point B, considering the dips and inclines that the land throws at you.

He brought them back outside to illustrate his point about changing terrain. A massive outcropping of bedrock lay between the top of the slope by Jack's house and the dock by the lake. He had them take a bearing on the dock and follow that course to the dock itself. The problem was that the granite boulder lay in their intended path. He asked them to imagine it as much larger than it was. "You have a choice here. You can climb over it, perhaps at risk to your safety and adding considerable time and energy expenditure to your trip. What is your alternative?"

Evangeline offered a choice, "You could go around it, then your compass bearing would be messed up, wouldn't it?"

"Yes and yes. Sometimes you have to go around obstacles, especially when it involves a cliff or steep ravine."

Mac piped up, "That's something we never had to worry about in our scuba navigation. If there was an obstacle it was easy to just rise in the water column over top or descend if necessary, remembering the scuba rules for not ascending too fast to off-gas nitrogen. I hadn't thought about that problem before."

"That's true. Scuba has other technical issues that we don't have to work around here."

Jack then explained how to make a detour around an obstacle. "You have to make a series of ninety degree turns around the rock formation, being careful to precisely measure the number of paces required to walk around the obstacle. If we began on a path due south, we need to turn twenty paces east to get around the obstacle, then another thirty paces south to get to the other side of the rock. To compensate for our detour, we would then need to go twenty paces west to bring us back to the original sighting that we started on. You must take a sighting on a landmark on the other side of the rock before we start making the course corrections. When we land up on the other side of the obstruction, we can then check if our landmark and our compass bearing line up."

"Okay, I'm confused. You'd better go over that one again." Evangeline said, looking perplexed.

"No problem. Just watch me as I illustrate it for you." Jack paced out a rectangular path around the boulder outcropping in the field. Their faces brightened as they caught on to the pattern. "Now, it's your opportunity to practice the same thing. Go ahead now."

On they went down the slope making course adjustments as necessary until they made their way down to the dock. Once there, Jack said, "Now you've earned your swim! Go ahead and get cool."

The winds had started to abate gradually until there was an eerie silence. Surrounding them was devastation. The sea had risen with the storm surge, and with it, the ocean had picked up boats and houses with its massive arms and thrown them hundreds of feet inland. Waves which crashed on the shoreline had pulverized piers and underpinnings of beach houses. The ocean had mercilessly climbed above the doorsteps of shops and businesses along the seaside highway, waves now licking at second-story windows. But it was quiet, no more howling from this ogre.

Above them was a hint of blue sky, the sun pulled back the drapes of darkness and dazzled all below with radiance. Was it a call to hope amid the bleakest moments of a lifetime or was it the monster teasing an offering of peace that he had no intention of giving?

Those, like Laurie, who had not been exposed to this type onslaught before, mistakenly presumed the worst was over. No, no, that was not to be. It was the eye of the devil, the center of its deception, a ruse to lull them into a false sense of security. Take a breath as you may, the tail of the demon was more monstrous than its head. Battered and bruised, weakened and ready to quit, he had you where he wanted you-fearful and without hope. No place was safe to hide; the tail would lash at you in your shelter, your refuge, from the other direction. No; there was nowhere to escape now.

It was more than Laurie had ever envisioned a hurricane to be. It was worse than the photographs and news reports could ever convey. The fear, once seeded inside her, grew and overtook her despite her training. Nothing could prepare her for this evil force. They called it a category 5 hurricane now, but it was not merely a storm, it was an out of control demon. Any relief, however momentary, was welcomed by all. It was a long instant to sit and breathe once more before bracing for winds from the other side of hell.

Sol stopped into John's Market Square intending to buy a tub of ice cream for dinner that night. Hildy, Sol's wife of thirty-two years, was planning to barbecue chicken on the patio, anything to keep the heat out of the house. He could just taste it now, as it turned lazily on the spit. Ooh, those juices, the spices. So what better way than to finish with an icy dish of chocolate peanut butter swirl? Oh, so delicious.

John spied the ice cream and commented, "I thought the wife said no more of that this month, Sol. She said your cholesterol was up."

"Aw, John, you know how to spoil a good daydream. It's low fat, so I'm allowed a little. Anyway, Hildy will have most of it and any visitors who drop by. You can't take away everything good in life."

"I suppose you're right, Sol. Just don't tell Hildy I said so. Did you see the television? That storm slammed into the coast as at least a category 4, maybe even a 5. Now, of all things, they are predicting with the force of it and its track, it's supposed to continue north. Then they're not sure what it might do. I can't imagine it being much by the time it gets in this direction. They usually dissipate over land, don't they? We're not hurricane material here."

"Well, if you recall, Hurricane Hazel did a lot of damage through here back in, what was it now, ah, '56?"

"No, it was '54. I was three then. My aunt and uncle lost their house in the flooding. That date has been talked about in my family all these years. They almost lost their lives, as well as their house. It was a near disaster. Something like that you remember. I just thought it was a fluke, not to be repeated."

"Well, anyway, it could be worse than we think. Better make sure you have flashlights and candles ready for us to buy. It could be here in a day or so they said. In fact, better give me a pack of those D batteries and a bundle of emergency candles. I might as well get them now or Hildy will have me back here when you open in the morning!"

Jack let them have their break with a swim in the lake. Only one more exercise remained for them to do today anyway.

Once everyone was dry and ready to go, he brought them to the hillside above the house. It was lightly treed and would be easy to walk through. Jack handed around the bug spray and told them it might be stinky but they would appreciate having it on once they got into the bush.

They had backpacks with water, snacks, compasses and the map Jack had handed out. He pointed out the land features compared to the contours on the map. They noted the elevation changes in relation to the starting point that Jack had marked on the map and their destination. He then asked them, as a group, to agree on a feasible path to plot to descend the hillside. They soon realized that the most direct route took them down a steep rock face and that they should make a detour around it toward a gentler slope. It would take a little longer but would be safer.

Then Jack helped them in plotting their course and compass bearings necessary to achieve it. "So I'll go up with you and walk you through the course changes, landmark taking, measuring out your paces for course correction. Once you get up there and walk it out, it'll make practical sense. Does anyone have any questions before we start?"

No one seemed to have any problems with what was covered thus far, so they climbed the hillside. This time they realized that rock faces and boulders were not the only obstacles that might pose a problem. Fallen trees lay in their path and a stream that flowed down toward the lake. The rains earlier in the week had made the ground muddy around the streambed so the footing was slippery at some points, especially where there were exposed rocks. If it were a larger creek or river, plotting a course around them would pose a much bigger challenge.

"There's a lot to learn about this, isn't there?" Evangeline commented as she swatted some pesky mosquitoes. She was beginning to realize why they had put on the bug spray.

"Yeah, it's a beginner's course. There are a lot more skills that could be covered in a longer course."

They fell silent for a moment contemplating this. A couple of blue jays could be heard overhead in the trees, squawking out at the disturbance the group had created in scuffling through the leaves and pine needles as they made their up the steep grade. Suddenly, they could all hear the rustle of leaves on the hill above them. Evangeline startled and shrieked.

"Oh, Gelly, it's just a couple of red squirrels fighting over territory. It's nothing!" Sarah said as she put her arm around her friend.

"I'm ok-kay. It just startled me. It's darker in the trees, isn't it?"

"Don't worry; we'll all stay together on this trek down the slope. And tomorrow you'll always be with a buddy for safety. Is everyone ready to get started?" Jack responded.

They agreed to begin and with Jack's expertise, he made it all seem easy. Slowly they descended the slope, making the necessary course adjustments as they encountered a large fallen spruce, then an outcropping of granite that was too steep to traverse. It all seemed so sensible when Jack led them around these detours. They were becoming one with the terrain. Sweaty, but satisfied, they descended foot by foot until they had made it back to the road below.

"Lacey, I just received word from my people on the West Coast. They've put their people in place now, so they should be in sync with our efforts. They understand what's at stake here, and for that matter there, too."

"We should have another meeting tonight, once things settle down for the evening. It shouldn't take long, just to solidify things and see if we've missed anything. You never know, there could be some last-minute instructions we haven't expected. I realize we're not infallible. What do you think, Bert?"

"It sounds like a plan. I'll call the others. What do you say, 9:00 okay?"

"Perfect. We can meet here. Just tell everyone to come prepared to listen."

The winds lashed out again with supernatural vengeance, as though anything that withstood the first beating deserved to be crushed beyond recognition. Now the winds rose from the opposite direction as the other side of the monster smashed the shoreline. The waves grew larger and mightier, lashed by forces pushing out of the deep. The waters expanded, pushed ever upward by an unfathomable power. Battered shoreline was consumed by the angry waters, rising higher and higher. Recognizable landmarks were obliterated. Street signs strained to stay above the surge and were soon consumed. Buildings crumbled under the constant mauling waves. This demon showed no mercy. It was as though indescribable forces had gathered behind a reservoir of evil and the dam had broken on to their coastline. Nothing remained to do but Pray. No human effort could save them now.

The group trudged back to Jack's camp house. Hot, sweaty but satisfied with their achievements, they were ready for a break. They had learned a lot in a short period of time.

Jack directed them back to their humble quarters and suggested they clean up with a swim and come on back to his house for barbecued hamburgers when they were done. It did not take any convincing and they were off to suit up for the swim.

Laughter filtered toward Jack's open windows from the lake. They sounded like a group of teenagers down there. They were jumping off the dock, racing one another to the raft anchored fifty feet out. Once on the raft, they took turns pushing one another back into the water as he used to do with his brother and sister. It brought back fond memories of their uncle's cottage they had visited while growing up.

That was where Jack had developed his love of the wilderness. Those roots were there long before he entered the military. Whenever possible, depending on where his father was stationed, his mother and siblings would travel to Uncle Stan's hideaway. That was what Aunt Liz called the cabin. It had been his dream to have a cottage by the lake. That was long before they retired in Wilmington.

Uncle Stan had spent considerable time with Jack and his brother, Matt, while their father was away working. He taught them so much of what Jack knew and understood about survival in inhospitable terrain. They had gone on backpacking treks, tenting it sometimes and other times making shelters from what was around them. They had so much fun in those days.

Jackie, as he was fondly called in those days, was never intimidated by the bush or the creatures that inhabited it. He had a deep respect for nature and what it could unleash on the unprepared, but he was not afraid of it. It had a rhythm and a flow. You could use it to your advantage if you understand what it had to offer you. Be prepared was what Uncle Stan would always drum into him. Know the elements, the possible problems and plan for them. That is the way Jack lived his life now.

Laurie loved the cottage too. She, Aunt Liz and their mother did activities with other families around the lake more than he did. Times had surely changed since then. Life had become more complicated and complex. It was eons ago; before Matt moved away to work in Oregon and the car accident that took his life so suddenly.

Jack shook his head at the memories. Thinking of Laurie and Aunt Liz brought him back to reality. He would have to try to contact her once dinner was over and he had the place to himself again. He wondered how bad the conditions had gotten since he last checked the news. He knew that it could not be good given the category 5 status.

Eli sat watching the evening news report. One of the big items was the devastation that had been hitting the Carolina coastline from Hurricane Igor. It was much worse from the sound of it. He sat just shaking his head slowly. You could hardly comprehend the damage. It was a solemn moment.

Eli closed his eyes for a moment, as if doing so would make it disappear, but there it was again when he opened them. It did not matter anyway, when his eyes were shut, the image was burned on his retina. There was no getting away from it. It was going to devastate many people. It was obvious.

FEMA representatives were already talking about assistance that was ready for the area. Assurances were being given that the problems following Katrina and Rita have been worked out. "I hope so," Eli replied to the television, "because many will need it, that's for sure. Some will believe that they have no other hope than government aid in their lives, unfortunately. They feel they have nothing else to hang on to."

Jack chatted with the two couples while he stood in front of the grill. The burgers were on and, for a special treat, Jack had added ribs. The aroma from the barbecue was enticing. Everyone was hungry. Clear mountain air combined with honest exercise will increase your hunger any day.

Laughter and joking drifted in the air all evening. The food was simple, but oh so appetizing. Everyone was trying to get Jack to give up his sauce recipe. They claimed that it was the best they had ever had.

"I got the recipe from a buddy in the army and I promised I would never divulge the mixture because they use it in his father's restaurant in Louisiana. He would shoot me if he ever thought I told you. I kid you not!" was Jack's defense.

"But, Jack, we would never tell!"

"Ah, yes, but Bubba has his ways to get it out of me. I want to save your lives. He couldn't let you live if he thought you knew!" It was followed by peals of laughter.

Lacey strolled by on her evening walk and Jack gestured to her to come on over. He introduced her to everyone as his lovely landlord. "Why, Jack, that sounds so grand! We have a good arrangement around here and you fine people benefit from it. How's your course been going?"

"It's been good, so far. We've gone over a fair amount of information in a short time," Mac answered. "It is surprising how different the material seems when you put it into action on the terrain. Tomorrow is supposed to be our big challenge though. We'll head up the big mountain for our final test. I suppose Jack has put you through one of his courses before?"

"No, I can't say that I've had the pleasure yet. But I've had similar training in the past and camped and hiked a fair amount when I was younger. I imagine that Jack could teach an old dog some new tricks though!" Lacey's melodic laugh was contagious. Lacey then excused herself to finish her walk before darkness overtook the hillside.

It was a pleasant evening. Daylight soon waned and gave way to darkness. The days were starting to get shorter now and it was noticeable. When the women started to get chilly, it was decided that it was time to call it a night. They had another adventure planned for the next day so they had to be rested for an early start in the morning.

Each couple had a separate cabin. They had large portable battery operated lamps in each room so they were not completely roughing it. This pleased Evangeline because camping was not her favorite pastime. She and Paul snuggled into their bed together. "Just listen to those bullfrogs down there. Who would think that such a small creature could make such a loud noise?"

"Yeah, it sorts of sounds like the belching contests my cousin Ralph and I had as kids!" Paul remarked.

"Aw, you can be so crude when you want to be!" Evangeline chuckled.

"I only said it because I knew I'd get a rise out of you!"

"I thought you did. I guess I'm a sucker. I fall for it every time, don't I?"

"You sure do. It works every time. 519 times and counting!"

"It probably is, you know. I suppose that is why you love me, right. You can use the same stuff every time, you don't have to be original and I still take the bait. It must be why I'm still hooked on you."

"Now that was just plain corny."

"Yeah, but that's okay."

Jack dialed the number his sister gave him for the hospital. He received a recorded message from the operator saying that there were technical difficulties at the desired number and to please try the number again later. Jack immediately understood that the telephone lines must be down where Laurie was. He realized that there was nothing he could do at this point. He felt helpless. He wanted to go in to save the day, but here he was with his hands tied and nothing to do to change the circumstances for her.

He turned his attention to cleaning up the dishes in the kitchen. The television was giving bulletins about the conditions where Laurie was. It started to grate on Jack's nerves. "Why did they have to repeat it so often" he thought. "Enough! Give me something positive to go on!"

He flipped channels. One newscast followed another. He flipped to another station. "Ah, there's a 'who-done-it'; that should take my mind off things."

He watched about fifteen minutes of the show, realizing he'd already watched earlier in the season. He flipped the channels again, but found another news program. This time it was covering another story, but it was equally grave about some people who were shot outside of a dance studio that evening. He flipped channels again. Nothing appealed to him. "Why does television swarm to tragedy like bugs to roadkill?" he thought. "Enough!" He switched off the television. He had too much of it already. "Jack, it's not your fault that Laurie's down there. You told her to be careful. She's a capable woman!" he said loud enough to be heard. "Oh, great, now I'm talking to myself."

Jack finished cleaning and turned out the lights and headed for bed himself. He might as well get some sleep because there was nothing else he could do.

Mac and Sarah settled in for the night quickly. They kidded each other about being on a sleepover as though they were kids again at summer camp.

"I remember the silly campfire stories we used to tell around the fire." Sarah whispered.

"I bet you the ones we told at the boy's camp were worse than yours. We used to try to out-scare each other. We would make funny rustling noises behind us for effect or get one of our friends to creep through the bushes when we reached the climax of the story. It was a riot!" Mac said with relish.

"I'm glad that I wasn't there. That's the difference between girl's camp and the boy's. I think some things are meant to be separate at that age for a reason," Sarah replied.

"You're probably right. You okay with how everything is going so far this weekend?" Mac asked.

"I'm having fun. Gelly is doing better than I expected. She seems to have been a good sport about it all. She's even enjoying it," Sarah said thoughtfully.

"I imagine the big test for her and all of us will be tomorrow when we have to head down the harder terrain without Jack at our sides. I know he'll be there behind us to keep an eye out, and we'll have radios, but we'll have to figure things out ourselves," Mac mused.

"Yeah, it'll be a bit more challenging, but at least we have our scuba navigation experience to back us up. I just hope Gelly holds herself together in the bush with all the bugs and stuff. She sure has been a trooper so far though," Sarah said hopefully.

"I'll admit she has been so far. So are you ready to sleep yet?" Mac responded.

"Yes, just hold me a few more minutes, and I will be. I love you; you know that, don't you?" Sarah asked.

"You know I do. Sleep well."

Five automobiles pulled into Lacey's parking area, arriving minutes apart so they were ready to meet about 9:00. It did not have to be a long meeting, but it was necessary. In all, there were twelve people. They had been huddled on the leather sofas for about twenty minutes already.

"So this is it, then? You're sure of it?"

"Lacey and I discussed it earlier and we think everything points to it. I couldn't be surer of it if he were standing here before me now saying it." Bert said solemnly.

Nods and knowing glances were exchanged. They understood the significance of what they were saying. A growing resolve with an intangible shift in the atmosphere spread throughout the room.

"So we're one on this?"

"Yes"

"Yes"

"Yes"

Each of the twelve continued to say their agreement.

"Okay, then." Bert paused and drew in air as though with this breath came a force that was unbreakable. "You know that we have to be together, as one, in this? If not, it all could crumble around us. It can fall like one domino against another. You realize the full implication of what we have ahead?"

"Yes, of course. It's what we have been preparing for all these months!" Lacey asserted.

"It's the Truth and it's solid. We can stand together on it when things don't make sense. There's no doubt in it."

"Yes," each said, one by one.

"It might get messy from here on. It will. It's no secret to them what we've been up to, so expect trouble. We have information behind us that they don't, so we can stand together. Unified we can achieve the desired goal. No wavering from now on. Together."

"Agreed"

"Agreed"

"Agreed"

Again each of the twelve was resolved to stay united.

"See you tomorrow. We'll see what it all brings down. No matter what, we'll stay resolved."

Chapter 5

Paul and Evangeline had drifted off to sleep. Evenings were already perceptively cooler than earlier in the season and the mountain elevation gave more relief from the heat than the city would have felt.

Evangeline awoke with a start. She dared not move. She sensed a noise, but had not heard it. *What was that?* It was dark, intensely dark. She put her hand in front of her face and saw nothing, which increased her uneasiness. It must have clouded over, obscuring the Moon. In the city, however cloudy it was, there was always some light from somewhere. Here, when it was dark, it was inky black. This realization confirmed the notion that was uncomfortable on this mountain.

There it was again; the noise, or was it a noise? It sounded like breathing or something. Then there was a rustling. *Oh no-o-o, there's something outside!* Her heart skipped a beat. "What kind of animals are there up here?" She had made the last comment aloud, obviously loud enough to awaken Paul.

"Uh-h?" Paul grunted, thick with sleep as though drugged. He was about to glide back into his dream when Evangeline spoke up again, this time in a whisper, not wanting to disturb "the thing" outside their door. "There's something out there!" she hissed.

"What do mean?" Paul said groggily.

"There's something out there" she repeated.

"Yeah, so-o?"

"We're not alone!"

"Gelly, we're in the country here. What did you expect?"

It was not the response Evangeline wanted from her husband. Irritation sprang up inside her. She could manage a good front in the daylight and among her friends and instructor. But this situation was different. Everything familiar was gone and it was dark, so dark. She could feel fear mixed with the annoyance. She made no effort to control either one. "Well, can it get in here?"

"The door is closed; the windows have screens on them. I doubt it."

"I need you to check it out."

"What do you want me to do, go outside?"

"Just look out the window. Can you see it? Can you see anything?"

Paul sighed. This performance was Evangeline at her best. He had married her for better or worse; it was the worse side of things. He rolled over and slid out of bed. He then plodded to the window nearest his side of the bed. He chuckled when he saw what was making the noise.

"What's so funny?" Evangeline said thinking he was teasing her.

"Well, you come over and see."

"It's nothing dangerous, is it?" Evangeline said tentatively.

"I wouldn't say so. You'll probably like it."

Evangeline left the security of the bed and tiptoed beside Paul. Her eyes had adjusted to the darkness and she could just make out the objects around her. Outside the window, perhaps fifteen feet over was a raccoon scrounging about in the brush for tidbits of food. "Oh, look at that!"

"I thought you'd like it."

"It is so cute! I guess being in the country, you get all the scenery and the wildlife too." Evangeline remarked.

"Yeah, so can we go back to bed now? It might be a long day tomorrow if we're tired."

"That's fine with me. I'm just not used to these surroundings. I didn't know what to expect."

"Good night then."

"Good night." Evangeline rested there for a few more minutes. She soon could hear Paul's regular breathing. He was asleep. She knew it might take her a little while longer for her to do the same.

The screaming of the wind ebbed like the tide. Decibel by decibel the storm abated. The pressure against the buildings subsided. The demon was relenting. It had exacted enough satisfaction, sufficient devastation on this sector of territory. It would move onward, elsewhere. Those whose lives had been lambasted for the last twelve hours did not care where it went if left them alone. It was more than any human could endure. It was time to sit still and bask in the silence. Few ventured out yet, realizing what would greet their eyes. Those who survived huddled in a group, thankful that the beast had departed. Others lay battered, beaten, crushed by debris or washed away by massive wave after wave. Finding who was alive, who had been taken, would take days to determine in this broken chaos.

Evangeline awoke with a start. Her heart was pounding out of her chest. *Was that real or is this?* "Oh, it must have been a dream. Oh, thank goodness it was a dream" she panted to herself. It was so vivid; that figure lurking behind the trees out behind the house. She had been walking to the washroom and there was this voice out of nowhere it seemed. "You don't belong here. The rest of them do but, you don't fit. Give it up. Go on home or you won't make it." Was it a dream or an apparition?

Where did that come from? It was as though she had been visited by the henchman of fear himself. It was like one of those horror movies Paul sometimes liked to watch.

Evangeline tried to calm down, chiding herself for giving in to such silly childlike fears. Now she knew why she didn't like to watch those movies.

Chapter 6

Dawn's glimmer on the horizon came early and with it the birds broke their nighttime silence. One robin awoke and called to announce the morning. Silence resumed. A pause, a breath, then the robin sang out again, waiting for a response. Minutes passed and a chickadee then a nuthatch could be heard further down the slope nearer the lake's edge. The sun rose over the horizon and with it lazy rays of light crept through the trees to illuminate the wilderness again.

Flashback dream:

The travel schedule was hectic, impossible. One meeting flowed into another. They were in one city one day; another next. It was impossible to keep any context of normal life at this pace. What plane, what highway were they on now? What time zone was it?

Last night's reception went on far too late and there was way too much food and liquor flowing to keep anyone's head straight. She couldn't remember the conversations she had or with whom. It was crazy. Who had said what to her anyway? She had business cards in her pocket this morning and she had no recollection of faces to match them. Who were these people anyway? Everyone wanting in on the action, wanting to make connections with important people, or were they merely people they thought were important? She knew better, though. She had had enough contact with the inner circle to know what was behind the façade of grandeur. Sure they had control over careers, but at what cost? Oh, the cost. So many who 'sold out' to make it. And what was left of them now? What part of their soul was left in that reception room or another along the road or some hotel room afterward? Was she one too?

She looked at the suit she had worn last night. It smelled of liquor. Was it hers or someone else's? Judging by the way she felt this morning it was probably hers. "Why can't I remember what happened last night?" she moaned. The meeting itself had gone well, she knew that. The negotiations had progressed the way they wanted them. They had a product that everyone was clamoring. Yeah, timing was everything in this business. You either had to be flowing with a trend someone else had inspired or devise a new one which no one could live without. She was so good at what she did and her supervisors knew it too. She commanded a large salary for her talents. The stress was enormous but the payoff was terrific. Staying on top was critical and now she was staking everything she was for the pinnacle of her career. It wouldn't be long now and the promotion would be hers, upper level wages and all. Had she stepped on a few people to get there, sure, but the prize was worth it in this business. The cost to her inner self was temporary, wasn't it?

She awoke with a start. Was it a dream or memory? It had been a memory, wasn't it? After all, she had lived it. She had been there. Why would she dreaming about it all again? That was another part of her life, past, gone, done with. She had moved on. Why would it be back again?

Jack awoke early Saturday morning and could not go back to sleep. He had an odd feeling that he had something to do. What was it? He could not focus his mind yet to understand what it was. He showered, shaved and dressed. He sensed it might his last bit of luxury for a few days. It was a nasty impression that would not let go of him. He shook it off.

He flipped on the television to see the early news. Video footage of the overwhelming aftermath of Hurricane Igor met his eyes. "Oh, Laurie" he said under his breath. Jack punched her number into the phone. No response again. What else did he expect this early after the storm had marched through?

Mac and Sarah had slept well. Fresh mountain air, no smog or phones, no pressures or deadlines–what more could you want? Sarah had ventured to the washroom in the night but had not encountered any critters along her way.

By the time everyone assembled at the main house, Jack had a large urn of coffee ready and breakfast was half made. The aroma of coffee and pancakes wafted to their noses as they knocked on his door. "Come on in. Breakfast is almost ready. Any later and I would have eaten it and what was leftover would have gone to the raccoons. Get yourselves in here and eat. We'll want to get started early today and finish before the weather moves in. They are predicting that the hurricane might shift the weather fronts around a little, so we had better get a move on."

"An early start is good. Then we have more of the day together to play" Mac said mischievously.

"Mac Donelly, what are you up to?" Sarah responded.

"Nothing more than I ever did at summer camp when I was a kid! What did you think I might do?" Mac answered with a chuckle.

"Oh, nothing but visions of a frog in my sleeping bag!" Sarah said giving him a warning look.

"Enough, boys and girls! Eat before it gets cold" Jack said like a camp counselor.

Hurricane Igor, the name coined for this fiend, raced on through Virginia and Washington, DC overnight. It moved quickly, although its winds diminished to a down-graded "category 2" hurricane overnight. Residents of these states quickly realized that this monster was not done with its destructive habits. Its winds clawed open roofs, uprooted trees and dumped inches of rain on their lands, causing rivers and creeks to quickly overflow their banks. Many were taken off guard, ill prepared for a hurricane traveling so far to the north and inland. The evil that propelled it onward knew that people had short memories for its unleashed misery and even less defense for its destruction. Yet onward it sped, eager to rendezvous with a cold air mass to the north and more fuel for its devastation. Few were ready to receive this onslaught and it gave Igor far more pleasure.

Jack phoned Bob Fisher early in the morning to see if he could move their rendezvous up to the morning. "We covered a lot more than I expected yesterday and they seem fairly good at it all. Two have taken scuba navigation before so they caught on quickly. The other two are intelligent people and seemed comfortable with the skills by the evening. Paul's wife might be a little hesitant but if we keep them 'buddied' up it should proceed well."

Bob inquired, "Did you get the radios ready?"

"Yeah, they're all set. I charged them last night," Jack replied quickly.

"So you should be ready about 10:30 then?" Bob checked the timing to be sure.

"Yeah. Can you call Eddie and see if he can help earlier? I just want to get this done before it has a chance to rain. These guys are from the city and I don't think the women would appreciate a miserable trek down the mountain in a downpour. That reminds me, I'll have to get the rain slickers out of the back room to pack in their knapsacks," Jack commented.

"Well, I'll let you get to it then. We'll come over just before 10:30," Bob concluded.

Jack was a detail-oriented person. He wanted to take care of everything on his checklist before any distractions came along. He had enough on his mind with Laurie amid a hurricane and not being able to be there. He didn't need any other disturbances to mess things up. This should be a textbook instruction today then he could think about other things later. One event at a time and it would all get done.

The sky was brooding and gloomy, like Evangeline's mood. She slept fitfully after her dream. She did not want to let on to Paul how she felt, especially after the episode with the raccoon; he might tease her, and she was feeling vulnerable enough as it was. Something was wrong and she could not put her finger on it. Maybe it was just the threat of rain in the air that had dampened the atmosphere. She was not sure about the exact source, but she knew she felt unsettled and uneasy.

Lacey dropped into John's Market Square to pick up a few things that she had forgotten to mention to Eli to get for her. John's store was more expensive than the supermarket in Moulton but the cost and time involved with the trip into town far outweigh a few extra dollars.

"The hurricane blew through the coast already. It looks like it caused considerable damage," John commented.

Lacey picked up a bag each of potatoes and carrots and put several cans of soup in her basket. "Yes and the worst of the storm isn't over yet. They expected it to dissipate over land but somehow it has maintained most of its strength. They say it is because it is moving so fast. They've dubbed it Hurricane Hazel II. You know where that went the last time?"

"It seems we might be in for some nasty weather in the next while," John replied.

"It could be wet for a bit. I hope you got your roof fixed or you'll be bailing out the dining room again!" Lacey observed.

"Oh, don't you worry about that. It's all taken care of now. You don't think Melissa would allow me to let that slide do you?" John chortled. What he did not add was his concern for the roof over the store.

"And well she should keep after you about that. She lives there too. But you know me; I don't use the word worry. I manage those problems as they come along and don't carry the care with me," Lacey added.

"I know, Lacey, you seem good at it too," John said as he punched the prices of Lacey's goods into the register.

"Oh, John, it isn't always that easy and it has taken many years of practice!" Lacey retorted.

"Lacey, then you must have started early, because you're not that old yet!" John continued as he tore off the register tape and handed it to Lacey.

"John, you know what to say to a lady. You must use the same lines with everyone you want as a return customer!" Lacey said with a smile.

"No, Lacey, this time I meant it. I sometimes wonder where you get your poise and wisdom. My grandmother didn't seem to have it as together in all her ninety years as you do."

"John, your grandmother was a fine lady. Don't be putting her down," Lacey responded.

"Aw come on, Lacey, you know what I mean," John grumbled.

"John, it's by the Grace of God. Some days are harder than others, you know," Lacey said as she handed him the cash for the groceries.

"I do know," John murmured as he counted out her change.

"And John, I wasn't always like this." She looked down and was quiet. John realized that there was more to her story than anyone knew. Some things were private.

John took Lacey's cloth bags and helped her load her purchases into them as Lacey asked, "Do you still have your generator at the house?"

"What, do you know something I don't about the storm?" John looked up from his work and looked at her over his glasses.

"Not for sure, maybe; I just have a sense it could be nasty, that's all. Just make sure you have enough fuel for it is all I'm saying," was Lacey's quiet response.

John knew that when Lacey made a comment like that, he had better act on it. She had been right more times than not.

With that, Lacey scooped up her parcels and was out the door.

Back in their cabin after breakfast Paul was packing his knapsack getting ready for their final lesson, he sensed something was wrong with Evangeline. It wasn't so much what she said or did, as much as what she didn't say or do. She was quiet and ate little. Something was on her mind and he wasn't sure what it was. The reporter in him had spent enough time observing people to realize that something was afoot. The problem was that he was often better at sizing situations in other people's lives than in his relationships.

"Gel, you okay? You seem quiet."

"Yeah, sure. I just didn't sleep well last night. It must have been the different bed or something." Evangeline did not want to admit it to Paul how a dream had shaken her up so much. It was just a dream after all. "Did you pack the rain slickers? I can't seem to find them."

"No, the forecast wasn't for rain before we left. I just assumed that you had. You usually do that stuff," Paul retorted.

"Paul, I especially asked you to take care of that before we left. We'll just have to hope it doesn't start to rain before we finish on the mountain!" She had said a little more sharply than she had intended.

Paul lowered his head. *Okay, there is something going on here,* he *thought. Maybe Sarah will be able to figure it out.*

"So did you get everything else? We'd better get going. We don't want to hold everyone else up," Evangeline said in short staccato bursts.

What happened to that cheerful attitude she had yesterday? It was a question both Paul and Evangeline asked themselves. Only one had a clue to the answer and Evangeline was not planning to tell anyone about her fears.

By the time that the four students arrived back at Jack's cabin with their gear, Eddie and Bob had arrived in Bob's weathered van. Jack introduced them to everyone and explained, "We'll go back up the mountain in Bob's van. It has more seating and Bob and Eddie will take my truck down to the bottom of the hillside to our rendezvous point. They can position themselves for our exercise from there."

Jack had an array of provisions out on the picnic table outside the house. "I just wanted to give you some general supplies that you should always have before going out on a hike of any kind. Too many people get themselves into severe problems each year thinking that the little hike they planned will take a short while and they don't need to take any provisions with them. I also have a rain suit for each of you. I hope we won't need them, but given the change in the forecast, you never know."

Paul nudged Evangeline lightly. She managed a small smile for him. That's more like it, he thought.

"Here are some bottles of water as well. Never go on any trail without a supply of water. I also have some protein bars. They're light to pack but will sustain you in an emergency. You also have a basic emergency first aid kit here, as well as matches and multiuse knife. I realize that these items are not part of the course you have taken yet, but I don't let any of my students into the bush without a basic kit."

Mac and Sarah picked up their items and handed the others to Paul and Evangeline. They busied themselves with packing their gear. Each student had their compass and map to put away as well.

Jack then gave a quick review of all the procedures they learned yesterday. "Does anyone have any questions?"

"How far up the mountain will we be going?" Mac asked.

"Oh, not that far, but it may seem so. It is just far enough to get the hang of the techniques in real life situations. I won't kid you, though. The bush is denser than yesterday. Take the bug spray again. You'll probably need it."

"Yeah, the bug spray. It'll be one of my most pleasant memories of this trip!" Sarah quipped.

Jack continued, "I have radios for each of you. You'll always be in communication with me or Bob Fisher on the downward slope. If you have questions, problems or get stuck or think you've gotten turned around, use the radio to contact us."

"Well, we shouldn't have any trouble figuring out the direction we came from. It will be up the hill, won't it?" Mac asked.

"Yes, the general direction will be. You have no idea how some people without training panic and get turned around. Remember your training. If in doubt use the teaching you had in scuba-stop, rest and think. Don't move on until you get your bearings and your landmarks. Remember, there'll always be someone a short distance in front or behind you who can steer you straight if you get stuck. I have confidence in you guys that it will be an easy exercise for you and we'll be back here for lunch," Jack responded looking each trainee in the eye in turn. He then nodded at Bob and Eddie, who moved out to load the gear.

The phone chirped in Lacey's great room. She walked toward the table, checked the call display and picked up the receiver. "Hello, Sol, what's up?"

Sol was always warmed by her cheery voice. No matter the circumstances, she managed to sound happy to be alive. "I suppose you've seen the status of the storm?"

"Yes, if it stays on its current path, we could see considerable rain soon. The winds haven't diminished much either surprisingly. It could get ugly for a while. I hope not for a long time though."

"It confirms the information that we've been thinking lately. It's hard when you're only given bits of information to work with. You've always said that it's a need to know basis."

"Well, Sol, human nature often fills in the gaps with too many unnecessary details. It eliminates extra time and energy if you wait and act only when you're sure that you're right. I never thought that this might be a situation I would have to encounter up here. I'm sure that I would have made wrong assumptions and been moving in the wrong direction if I'd acted earlier."

"I'm glad we met last night. Bert's let the others in the group know what we think we might expect from this. They're preparing now. It's essential to have all twelve of us involved at this point" Sol commented.

"There's no doubt about it. This may be merely the beginning of it though. I don't think this one event is what this is all about, by any means. Neither does Bert. If anything, it could be a diversion for something more serious" Lacey added gravely.

"I hope you're wrong, but sense you may be right. So far your instincts have held," Sol responded.

"We just have to remain true to what we do know. Don't get sidetracked off the primary concerns," Lacey added.

"Agreed. I'll talk to you later," Sol finished.

"No doubt you will." With that Lacey hung up the phone, walked into the study and closed the door.

The group took Bob Fisher's van and drove back up the mountain toward the village of Lofton. Jack pulled into a clearing beside the road and put the van in park. He turned in his seat. "We've reached our point of embarkation. It is a straightforward run down the mountain below to where Bob is waiting for you. I'm not saying that you won't encounter obstacles, but they're easy to manage if you follow the rules. Keep your heads on straight and you should have no problems.

"I'll send you down in pairs. Stay together and work together. Once one couple has had enough of a head start, I'll the send second pair down. This isn't a competition of who can get to the target first. It is about teamwork and using the skills you've been learning.

"I also have Eddie Warren stationed halfway down the hillside, but off your planned path, to make sure that you do not get too far offtrack. If it looks like any one of you is in trouble, he'll guide you in the right direction."

They got out of the van. The gray skies had turned three shades darker. The lowered ceiling gave the impression that they had climbed several thousand feet overnight. A fine mist was in the air already.

"You might as well don your rain gear now. It looks like it might start to rain in earnest by the time we hit the bottom of the hill" Jack instructed.

They all pulled out their rain pants and jackets and started to put them on. "I suppose the rain makes it a more realistic wilderness experience," commented Sarah.

"It wouldn't be a survival course without some discomfort," Jack laughed. "It shouldn't change anything that you have learned. Just be careful of your footing if it starts to rain harder. The moss on the rocks can be slippery. Fallen logs can be treacherous, so be careful where you step. I think the worst of the rain will hold off until we get down to the bottom."

Evangeline eyed Jack with doubt in her heart as he gave these final words of encouragement. It was the part of being out in the country she disliked. At home, if it rained, she just preferred to stay inside. Paul would go biking in any weather, but she was not fond of the rain. As far as she was concerned, the sooner they finished the better. The thought of a nice lunch back at the cabin was inviting.

In Wilmington, debris lay everywhere, but much of it was unrecognizable. Twisted, mangled metal lay strewn carelessly by a madman. Many buildings stood like ghostly sentinels, bared of their roofs and awnings. Shops had windows smashed out by flying projectiles. Power poles hung at precarious angles over the street above. A 2x4 was wedged in at an awkward angle in the side of a wooden building.

Rescue workers continued to pick their way carefully through debris laden streets. Incomprehensible sights met their eyes; a child's doll floated by in the flood waters. They did not want to contemplate where the child was now or how this cherished doll was separated from its owner.

They continued wading through the waters in stunned silence. As they neared the beach area, the full magnitude of the power of the storm was emphasized. Full-sized yachts were lying on their sides two blocks from the water's edge. Houses had been lifted from their moorings and deposited hundreds of feet from their original locations. Other buildings no longer resembled structures of any sort, beaten by the pounding waves and winds of the tyrant. Automobiles lay cast aside on their sides, piled one against another like discarded children's toys.

Rescue personnel could hardly breathe at the sights. It was too much to take in, much less comprehend. They stood still, just looking around them. They slowly did a 360 as they committed the images to memory. They were on sensory overload now. The last twenty-four hours, its horrific sounds still vibrating in their heads, had left them unable to feel. They were numbed by terror. They had held it all in, never letting others see the fear. They could not hold it in any longer but they could not process all they had seen and gone through either.

It was decided, mostly at Evangeline's urging, that Mac and Sarah would go first, map and compass in hand. She wanted to know that someone had made it down before she entered into the dense bush below her.

They had carefully plotted their course on the map, taking note of the terrain and possible barriers. Mac entered the bush first, followed by Sarah. It took no time before they were lost to Evangeline's view, engulfed by the thick forest.

Mac and Sarah had turned their radios on, but Jack instructed Paul and Evangeline to keep theirs off until they started down the mountain. They were also to use a different channel than Mac and Sarah. "I don't want you guys getting any hints from each other. It's not a test, just a learning exercise that works most effectively if you do it in separate groups. But don't worry. You'll all do fine, judging how you did yesterday."

To Evangeline, it felt like it was taking them forever to make progress. After what seemed to her like a lifetime, she heard Mac's voice on Jack's radio, although Jack was not letting them hear the conversation. He did not want them to get clues to their chosen trail from their discussion. Jack seemed happy with their radio transmission so Paul and Evangeline assumed that they were making good progress. They could also see Jack picking up a second radio, set to another frequency, to talk to Eddie on the hillside. He talked for a short time then walked toward them.

The clouds had seemed to have thickened and lowered even more, bringing with it a more pronounced rain. "It's not the best weather to be doing this, but we should be finished before the worst of it moves in, " Jack commented as he looked up toward the sky. He then walked back over by the van again, listening for more radio calls.

Paul kicked a stone on the ground in front of him. It was a little habit he had when he was anxious about something. Evangeline spotted his stance and walked over to him. "This should be easy, shouldn't it?"

"Sure thing" Paul responded looking down at the ground.

"You're not feeling competitive with Mac, are you? I've seen that look on your face before you go play squash with him. This isn't a competition, you know."

"I know. It's just a course. We get down the mountain and go have lunch. That's the plan. It's not a big deal."

"I just want to do this right, Paul. No heroics or anything. Let's just follow the rules he taught us, please?" Evangeline let the tone of her voice speak her concern. She knew he did not want to take longer or have more problems with it than Mac and Sarah. She also realized that she could hinder his efforts. Mountain climbing had never been her forte. The last thing she wanted him to do was rush her in this rain.

Paul shot her a glance. She knew better than to respond to it. The last thing she wanted to do was start a fight before entering a strange dark forest.

Jack occasionally checked in with the Mac and Sarah if he had not heard from them for a while to track their status. Eddie was on another channel and piped in when they passed his position. They had moved past the halfway mark. That was good, thought Jack. It was going smoothly. Mac reported in when they reached the rock face. They had chosen to detour around it then work their way back to the desired course below it. Mac said to Jack, "You neglected to tell us that there were two possible routes to bypass this cliff. We now have a decision to make!"

Jack responded, "Use your best judgment there. Pick the easiest route down. Remember your footing is important."

"Roger that" was Mac's response.

It took a few minutes before the next comment came through, this time from Sarah. "I hope that was the trickiest part, because if it is, we're home free!"

Bob Fisher radioed in when, through his binoculars, he sighted of the couple partway up the hillside.

"Okay, you two, are you ready? Mac and Sarah have negotiated themselves into range of our catcher at the bottom of the hillside" Jack announced.

"We're as ready as we will ever be. Our radios are on. We have everything prepared" Paul responded for both of them.

Evangeline hoped she was as set to go as Paul was. Together, they should be able to manage things with no trouble. Working together, it should be easy to check their compass heading with their chosen landmark. She set her eyes on the opening in the trees, took a deep breath, picked up her backpack and followed Paul into the bush.

Paul called back to Jack, "See you at the bottom!"

Jack sat on a boulder by the side of the road. "Have fun, you guys," he called after them.

The weather report came from the radio station. "Severe storm warnings have been issued. You can expect high winds and torrential rains for the rest of this afternoon and this evening. Hurricane Igor has come to town!"

"Well, isn't that a cheerful statement!" Jan Talbot remarked. "I suppose because we're in for a mess of weather for the next bit, we might as well get some work done in this place. Calvin, can you bring out the vacuum for me?"

"Why don't I vacuum while you get something ready for dinner? If the power should go out, then we won't have to be cooking on the barbecue outside in the rain."

"Good idea. If Bert and Lacey are right in their hunches, things might get busy later anyway, so we had better get to it now."

Paul and Evangeline found the bush much denser than during yesterday's exercises. It also was considerably darker given the dense canopy of trees and the clouds above them. The only thing that Evangeline liked about it was that the trees gave some cover from the rain.

A thicker growth of mature trees covered this mountainside and many fallen branches and tree trunks made it difficult to negotiate. Paul's long legs stepped over limbs that Evangeline had to physically climb to get past. She was panting to keep up and finally, with a sharp edge of exasperation, she said, "Paul, if you don't slow your pace, you're just going to lose me altogether!"

He stopped short. He sighed and said, "Sorry."

"Can we just look at the map again? I think we've gone far enough. We had better make sure we are still on our heading."

"Okay, we should be about here. I've been counting my paces and it should be about right."

"That looks good. Could you just go at little slower so I can walk and check my compass? I just don't want to break any bones doing this. It won't help if you get there fast and I am left up here with a broken leg!"

"I'm sorry, Gel, I'll try. I have long legs. It's the way I walk. So the next landmark could be that pile of fallen branches. What do you think?"

"Yeah, it seems to line up well. Okay, let's keep going," Evangeline agreed.

They walked down the slope until the grade started getting steeper. Evangeline slowed a little more to be sure of her footing. Paul was not having the same difficulty she was encountering. He looked back, saw that she was lagging and stopped long enough for her to catch up again.

"It is untouched countryside, isn't it?" he commented. "Some of these trees must be a hundred years old or more." The moment she was beside him, off he marched again.

The rain was coming down heavier now, making its way through the trees above. Paul thought that it would be good to finish this soon. Unconsciously, his pace quickened again. Evangeline was panting as she slid to a painful stop on her butt.

"Paul, help me!" She was plainly annoyed at him now.

Paul took a quick look at this landmark, turned and helped her up. "Are you alright? Nothing hurt?"

"No, but you have to go slower for me. Jack called it the buddy system for a reason, you know that?"

The radio chirped. "Jack, here. I haven't heard from you two for a while. What's up?"

"Paul, here. Nothing much. We're just arguing over whose legs are longer, that's all." Paul said this with a mixture of irritation and mischief.

"Paul! You didn't need to tell him that!" Evangeline was clearly embarrassed.

"We're making slow progress here because the ground is getting wet and a little slippery. It looks as if we're on track though."

"Okay, I won't hold you up then. Keep going. Jack, out."

"Talk to you shortly. Paul, out."

Evangeline was glaring at him as he looked up. *Oops, I said the wrong thing again.* "Sorry, Gel, I didn't realize it would bother you. It was the truth though."

"Sometimes you don't have to be that honest! Okay, where were we?"

"That pile of branches, remember?" Paul answered, happy to change the subject.

"Oh, yeah. So let's go, but slower," Evangeline pleaded.

They walked another hundred feet and checked their bearings and landmarks again. "That rock outcropping looks good. Kinda looks like a bear, don't you think?"

"Paul, you are not helping the situation, you know? I don't want to be reminded about the wildlife out here under these circumstances. A raccoon is one thing, a bear is another!"

"Gel, I was just commenting. You don't have to be so touchy."

They walked in silence for a while. She played the last few minutes over in her mind. Why was she so cross? She did not have to think for long, but she would not tell Paul. The dream had stirred up old fears. She had often wondered what Paul had seen in her. She was not the brave adventurous type that she expected he would be drawn to. She realized that she had always been a little insecure in their relationship, half expecting him to announce one day that he had found some strong heroine type who fit with his image better than she did. This course had raised a raw nerve. Well, she would just have to get over it, do her best at this and prove to him and to herself that she was capable after all!

Mac and Sarah were excited as they finally made it out of the trees. They had thought that they had done an excellent job, but found that they had missed the target by nearly fifty feet.

"How could we be that far off the mark?" Mac was disgusted with himself.

"Wow, I thought we had done a better job that that too!" exclaimed Sarah.

Bob Fisher strode to their position. "Well, you did a good job compared to most people who come through here. Don't beat yourself up. A small variance in your compass bearing isn't much over the first hundred feet or so, but you came a lot farther than that down that mountain. By the time you come this far, it makes a big difference to where you finish. It's like shooting a rifle with a bad sight. You won't hit a thing even if you think your aim is good."

"I guess you've got a point there" answered Mac. "I hadn't thought of it that way before."

"I think that's one of the points that Jack wanted to drive home to you with this exercise," Bob responded nodding his head.

"And he did a good job. I probably wouldn't have believed him so much had he just said it in the classroom" Sarah remarked.

"Over a longer distance, it might be the difference between arriving in Boston instead of Myrtle Beach! I guess that is why they have GPS on jets these days" Mac said excitedly. "Well, I sure learned something from this course."

Eddie's voice came over Jack radio. They just passed my position. They're over halfway down now. Over"

"Gotcha. That's good, we should be out of here before you know it. It's starting to rain on my parade and I don't like it much. I can't imagine they will either. I'll bring the van down now. Bob, you monitor their channel in case I get out of range. See you soon."

"I'll follow them down at a distance just to make sure nothing goes wrong. Talk to you shortly. Eddie, out."

"Bob, here. I'll listen and watch for them. Bob out."

Lacey looked outside at the rain. *Those clouds couldn't get much lower without lying on the ground. What a miserable day. I think I'll forgo my swim today. The winds have started to pick up too. Hmm, they had forecast this and for once they were right.*

She felt an internal nudge. Oh, this wasn't good, she thought. Something must be going on. She could not put her finger on it, just a sense that something was amok. Lacey turned and headed back in to her study and closed the door.

Chapter 7

Flashback:

She parked the car in her usual spot in the underground parking lot. Thirty steps separated her from the elevator taking her up to her apartment. Thirty, long steps. Too many steps. Unfamiliar sounds in the garage echoed in the darkness beyond her row of automobiles. She sat there frozen. Her mind would not focus. What could she do here, alone in her car? She could just drive back to the street and hope that when she got back the noises would be gone. But what if they weren't, like those other nights? She'd still have to face getting out of the car and walking those thirty steps to the elevator alone, in the dim parking lot lighting. How long would the elevator take to come? She wished there were a remote control for the elevator call button. She would summon it and have the door open already as she reached the elevator doorway. Thirty steps. It might as well be a trip to the Moon; it seemed such a long walk.

Her heart raced as she picked up her purse and briefcase. Putting her hand on the door release, she took a deep breath as though it might be her last. Images of the aftermath of the vicious attack on Natalie in her office building ran through her head. Her chest constricted as she stepped out of the car. I have to do this. I can't keep living like this. She locked the car and paced out the thirty steps, unconsciously counting them out in her head. Her heart was beating so loudly in her ears, it blocked all external noise. She pushed the 'up' button, glancing over the end of the row of vehicles. Were those shadows over there? Control yourself! Where is that elevator? It was taking forever to arrive. She drew a breath as the elevator door opened. Finally! She launched herself forward the moment the doors opened and ran smack into a short burly man, then fainted from terror.

As quickly as the image had appeared, it vanished, leaving her momentarily breathless. Annoyed, she shook her head trying to dispel the vision lingering in her brain. She did not need this, especially not now. Of all times, she needed a clear head.

Paul and Evangeline progressed well until they hit the rocky cliff. "Whoa, that's a sharp drop-off. Jack obviously chose this heading for a reason!"

Evangeline pulled up short behind Paul. "Well, he surely did, didn't he?"

"I guess we have to decide which way to go now. This ridge runs a fair distance. We could go that way but the cliff seems to continue for a long way. If we go this way, it looks as though we might be able to climb down the rocks themselves partway down." Paul scouted out the ridge to see if it would be possible to descend safely.

Evangeline was rooted to the spot. It was the last thing she wanted to do. She did not want to be climbing down a slippery rock face. Paul returned saying, "Gel, it looks feasible. There appear to be footholds in the rock. I think we could do it."

"Uh-uh. I don't want to be taking chances on this mountain, Paul. It's raining. Maybe if the conditions were good, I'd be willing to try it then. But it's raining; it's slippery. I have already fallen once. No way!" was her emphatic retort.

"Aw, come on, Gel. Do you realize how much time it will take if we go all the way down to the end of the ridge? Be reasonable!" Paul spit the words out, eager to get moving.

"Who's being unreasonable here? You want me to take a risk like that? My legs aren't as long as yours are. Why do you have to make things so hard?" Evangeline responded yelling over the sound of the rain on her hood.

Paul stood glaring at Evangeline. Evangeline would not look at him, knowing that if she did she would give in then who knows what consequences would ensue.

"Come on down with me, Gel. I'll help you." Now he was trying to be conciliatory. "I know you can do it."

Maybe, but this time she would not. This time she could feel fear rising in her gut. She could not face trying to climb down there in these conditions. It just was not going to happen.

"No, Paul, I can't. That's final."

Paul was fuming now. "Okay, I'm going to start down. Follow me or not. It's your choice."

She watched him walk down the ridge away from her. He was counting his paces so he could line himself up appropriately when he made it to the bottom. She hesitated for a moment, almost following him. Something stopped her. She felt physically restrained. *This can't be happening. He left me alone! How could he do that?*

Anger rose out of the fear in her gut. Two could play that game! She started down the ridge in the opposite direction, counting out her paces. He was not going to force to do something so ridiculously dangerous. Not this time.

"Gel, don't do that!" she heard Paul call after her. "Okay, have it your way. Just make sure your radio is on. You know the landmark tree, the pine with the gash in the trunk."

She hardly heard him as she plodded down the ridge. *I'll follow the techniques I was taught to a tee and I will show him I can do this!*

Paul carefully made his way down the ledges in the rock. At one point, he thought he might be stuck. *Maybe, Gel was right. Oh, no, there's another foothold. There, the rest should be easier.* Inch by inch he made his way down until he was about three feet from the bottom. He jumped the rest of the way.

Evangeline finally made it to the end of the ridge. Paul was right. It was a long way. The terrain was sloping now, still rocky, but manageable to climb down. She had counted 105 paces in all. She would climb down this incline and make her way back another 105 paces. It might take a few extra minutes but she would have all her limbs intact when she rejoined Paul. *Why does is he so stubborn? He's probably thinking the same thing about me. Probably thinks I am a sissy or something. Well, I've blown my chances of showing him what I can do to keep up with him!*

Jack arrived at the rendezvous with Sarah, Mac and Bob. "So you managed to get down in one piece, I see! How did you do on the target?"

"We were off at least fifty feet. Imagine that!" Mac said ruefully.

"Don't be so disappointed, you've had one of the better results we've had lately. It's not hard to miss the mark by a lot more than that."

"That rock ridge was a pain to get around, but we paced it out and got back to our landmark on the bottom," Mac added. "Now we just have to wait for the others to arrive."

Evangeline was relieved that she had made it down the ridge with no problems. She just hoped that Paul was equally intact. Her anger was beginning to simmer down now that she had made it past this hurdle.

She retraced her steps a few yards because the footing seemed a little better on the rocks than the slippery moss and peaty dirt. A cluster of scrub brush lay in her path at the bottom of the rocks. She stepped to the side a bit to get by, not realizing that there was more rock under the leaves. Her footing started to slip. Suddenly, she felt the ground fall way under her feet and she began to slide downward. *How could this be happening? It was the bottom of the ridge and the ground seemed so firm?* The next instant, she was sliding past ground level, down further and further. She let out a scream. That was the last thing she remembered when everything went black.

Lacey walked out to the wrap-around porch and surveyed the brooding clouds overhead and frowned. It was not going to be good. She had weathered enough storms here over the years to read skies, the signs of the seasons. This instance was different. The wind had picked up too. She was glad that she had taken the time to move the patio chairs and umbrella to the shed behind the house. This looked like it could get nasty before it finished.

Lacey glanced over at Jack's house and noted that his truck and Bob's van were already gone. He would be on the mountain today, no doubt. He had better finish soon though or they would have a miserable time of it. She shook her head; then paused. Something felt wrong, but she could not put her finger on what it might be. Lacey looked up the mountain, trying to see any signs of trouble, but all that met her eyes were low gray clouds obscuring the top of the mountain and, of course, the rain, ever heavier by the minute. The sound of the wind in the trees was noticeable now, creating a gusty moan. Lacey sensed that would soon become constant and get much worse before it got better. Many old trees in this area were likely to sustain significant damage if the forecast was right.

A lingering sense nagged at her that something was not right. She was starting to get wet from the windblown rain so she stepped back inside the house and shut the door behind her. She took note of the preparations she had made. Lanterns and flashlights were within easy reach. She had checked the generator last night and knew it worked well. She had plenty of water and canned foodstuff in storage. They had plenty of fuel for the barbecue for cooking and, if necessary, they could haul water from the lake if there was a prolonged power outage. Once she was satisfied that she had done all she could do at present, she went into her study and closed the door behind her. In the relative quiet of this room she knew she had some pressing work to do.

Bert Lawson hung up the telephone. Lacey had given him a quick call to let him know about her feeling that something was amok on the mountain. Lacey was usually right with those 'hunches' of hers, so he did not lightly dismiss it. He had no idea what it was though and neither did she yet. No doubt he would know soon enough. The atmosphere was charged today and not just because of the lightning that had started streaking the darkened sky. It was going to be a nasty day and probably night too. The hair on the back of his head bristled. Now he sensed it too, something was wrong and he had the impression it was serious as well.

Paul stood by the pine with the gash on it for several minutes, with no sign of Evangeline. He calculated in his mind how long it might take for her to negotiate the end of the ridge, then climb down and come back an equal distance in this direction. *It shouldn't be more than about ten minutes at the most. I know she has shorter legs than mine, but that should be enough time to execute the descent. Where the heck is she?* He was starting to get impatient with her now. He glanced at his watch and looked down the ridge to see if he could spot her jacket or any movement in the distance. He could see nothing, nor hear any rustling of the underbrush as she walked. The only sound was the rain pelting on the overhead canopy of trees and his hood. The wind had picked up, evidently, because the branches above were swaying in rhythm with the gusts. A rumble of thunder could be heard in the distance as well, but no signs of Gel anywhere.

The wetter Paul got, the more agitated he felt. He picked up his radio, "Gel, are you there? What's the holdup?" No answer was given.

"Gel, can you hear me? It's Paul. Look, I'm sorry if I made you angry. Come on over and I promise I'll make it up to you later." There still was no response from Evangeline. "Gel, this is no time to be playing games; it's wet and miserable here. Did you head down the mountain without me?" Again there was no response.

An uneasy feeling crept into Paul's gut. What was going on here? It was not like Evangeline to play games like this especially in an environment that made her so uncomfortable and with the rain to boot. *No, something must be very wrong. What could have happened? I had better find her.* He shook his head and closed his eyes for a moment before starting out. *If this turns out badly, I just know I'll be paying for this one for a long while!*

Paul followed along the lower part of the ridge looking above him for any sign of Evangeline or her backpack. She had been wearing a blue rain jacket with black trim and it should show up in the underbrush. Her backpack was black with red trim and should be visible as well. He walked slowly at first, scanning above him as well as along his path, but there was no sign of her anywhere. He finally made it to where the ridge sloped to his level and he stopped. *What could have happened to her? I know she was upset with me but, I don't think she would go down the mountain by herself, it isn't like her. Well, I'll go up top of the ridge and look around.* Paul climbed back up the slope of the rocky outcropping. He could find no sign of her there either.

"Paul, Jack here. I haven't heard from you for a while. Are you guys having trouble up there? Your last transmission sounded odd. Did you split up or something? Jack over."

Paul froze when realized that they had overheard his last appeal to Evangeline to quit playing games and his blood pressure raised a couple more notches. It was bad enough to be in this circumstance, much less having everyone else overhearing it all. He took a deep breath and responded, "Well, Gel didn't want to climb down the rocks on the ridge so she went the long way round, but she didn't come back to the rendezvous point. I just went looking for her down the ridge and there's no sign of her here. I was hoping that she decided to head down the mountain to you on her own. Is she down there yet? Paul over."

"No, she hasn't shown up here. You stay put where you are and I'll send Eddie over your way. Do you understand? Don't move. Jack over."

Paul stood still, not because he wanted to obey so much as because he was not sure exactly what he could do at the moment. He wanted to do something, anything would be better than standing here feeling like a fool. *What could have happened here? One moment we were making our way nicely down the mountain and the next Gel had traipsed off doing her own thing; then, of all things, disappears! She's starting to get me angry now. If it's some sort of game she's playing on me to intentionally hold us up, I'm going to be angry. I don't think she's that vindictive though.* Paul let out a long, exasperated sigh. *What does she think she's doing anyway?* "Gel, are you there? Why don't you answer? Quit playing games here!"

Paul looked up when he could hear Eddie's footsteps in the distance. He started down toward him, Paul atop the ridge, Eddie on the bottom. They looked at each and Paul just shrugged. There wasn't much he could say. He continued walking until he could climb down to the rendezvous point so they could talk. Paul explained what had happened.

"So you expected to meet at this tree. The ridge isn't that long. Let's retrace her steps and see what we can see."

"I already did that and there's no sign of her," was Paul's brusque reply.

"Yeah, I know Paul, but you might not know what details to look for. Let's just walk back along there and see if she left any tracks," Eddie said patiently.

"Okay, I guess you guys know what you're doing." They climbed back up the rock face and walked along the ridge line. Eddie pointed out some broken branches and impressions in the peat forest floor that if Paul squinted with his eyes just so, he could imagine them to be footprints. "The trouble is that you've already been walking along here after her so it had mucked about with the footprints. The rain makes it all the harder to get good visible tracks."

Eddie stopped at this point and radioed Jack down the mountain. "Eddie here."

"So Eddie, what's the story up there? Jack over."

"There's no clear sign of where she went that I can see. You might want to come up here yourself. You're the expert. Maybe you can see something I haven't. Paul walked along the ridge too, so there are conflicting signs along her probable path. Eddie over."

"Okay, you stay put. I'll leave the others down here to wait and see if she comes out down the bottom and I'll go up and meet you at the ridge. Jack out." Jack was a little annoyed. How could a basic exercise as easy as this go so wrong so fast? And now given the conditions, it could turn so completely out of control so quickly. He was running out of time to beat the weather as it was. It would have been just fine if they had not had their little tiff. He shook his head in disgust. His mind began to rapidly play out possible scenarios. *If she heads downhill, she'll intersect with the road. She would have to go uphill or parallel to the ridge to get lost. It's common sense to just go downhill.*

Jack drew Bob aside from the others and set his jaw, deep in thought for a moment, then said, "Bob, she'll probably just head down the mountain if she got messed up with their rendezvous point. We obviously need someone down here to catch her if she emerges from the bush down here. I don't want to leave these two alone and take the risk of having them wander off looking for her."

"Don't worry. I'll make sure that Mac and Sarah stay where they are. We don't need anyone else lost in this weather."

"We sure don't. Make sure they don't move an inch," Jack called back as he took off up the mountainside.

Eli drove to Lacey's house. The television weather report was grim. The storm was supposed to get progressively worse as the day wore on. The winds were expected to rise steadily, gusting up to ninety miles per hour by evening with driving rains. Hurricane Igor was being dubbed a Hurricane Hazel clone. Emergency agencies were being mobilized in anticipation of the damage. The power companies were calling all off-duty personnel as they expected countless downed power lines owing to the high winds. Police were warning people to evacuate low-lying residential areas near flooding rivers. Officials also asked people to stay off the roads during the storm. It was going to be a significant gale with substantial damage along its path, as it showed little signs of slowing yet. The concern was a cold air mass over the Great Lakes that could refuel the hurricane as happened with Hurricane Hazel back in 1954. The meteorologist signed off by saying, "Hold on to your hats and buckle in for the ride of your lives."

Eli looked at Lacey as they switched off the television. She looked grim. He did not expect anything else because it was how he felt too.

"Have you prepared everything on your end of things?" Lacey asked as she went into the kitchen to check the food she had been cooking all day.

"If you mean, have I tied down everything; yes. I also got all the supplies in we might need. I did call everyone else to be on standby to help should we run into trouble in this area. I expect the biggest problems might be down the mountain, though, by the river. The highway is vulnerable to flooding, especially because the water levels are already high with the rains last week. The local officials will take care of that. But we have to help around the lake here and down toward Lofton. It will take the pressure off the emergency crews if we do our part up here."

"You're right about that. I'm a little concerned about Jack and his bunch though. They've been on the mountain all day and I haven't seen any sign of him coming down. I don't think he wants to be there with a bunch of novices in this weather, do you? It just doesn't sit right with me that they aren't back yet. You didn't see anything when you drove up here did you?"

Eli though about it for a minute and relied, "Well, I did see Jack's truck at the bottom of the mountain, you know, where the clearing is. But I didn't see anything unusual, if that is what you mean."

"Eli, I just don't have a good feeling about this. Maybe we should go over and check and see if everything's alright. If it's nothing, then we've been over cautious. But if it turns out that they need some help, it is better done sooner than later," Lacey said as she was already grabbing a few emergency items from the storage room beyond the kitchen. She turned off the stove and put the pot in the refrigerator.

Eli headed toward the door and was putting his boots on by the time she got back. "We can take my truck. It has four-wheel drive, in case there are any problems. Grab your rain gear and let's go look anyway. You never know. I trust your gut feelings on things."

The monster raced along a familiar track, one it had taken before. A groove was already worn in its memory of where to go and what to do. It had been successful along this destructive path once before. It did not matter that it had been years since the marauder had come this way; after all, it made people complacent and unprepared for the attack and the victory so much more satisfying. A surprise assault caused so much more fear which fuelled the storm and its rage. The energy it needed was fear, it always had been; for it was not merely a natural phenomenon as many people suggested. It had a life of its own, born out of hatred and a lust to steal and to kill and to destroy. Fear was the necessary component to keep it moving, although people did not realize it. And fear they would experience before the day would end.

Jack had raced double time up the now slimy slope to where Paul and Eddie were positioned on the mountainside. "Tell me again what happened here. I need to understand the events so I can retrace her steps and get this thing sorted out quickly."

Paul retold his story, realizing how stupid the exchange of words he had with Evangeline seemed when repeated to another person. Paul tried to raise a response from her on the radio again, but heard no reply.

The group went to the crest of the ridge to retrace her probable steps, Jack in the lead. He instructed the others to stay well behind him as he did not want them to obliterate any visible tracks. He paused several times, bending to examine undergrowth for signs of broken branches, plants, moved leaves or stones or other disturbances on forest floor caused by a footfall. He muttered several times about how there were several sets of footprints confusing the track.

When they reached the end of the rocky outcropping and Jack looked perplexed. "Well, I seem to have lost her trail here. I don't know what to make of it. Either the rain has obliterated her tracks already or she double backed along the rocks themselves and didn't leave any signs. It doesn't make sense," he grumbled. "She couldn't have just lifted off the mountain, so there must be some logical explanation."

Paul was getting over his embarrassment and was moving into anger now. "What do you mean, you don't know? You know this mountain, don't you? What's the most likely thing that would have happened? How does a person just disappear?"

"Look, Paul. I wasn't the one up here with her. You tell me what you saw and heard; anything unusual? Sounds maybe, birds, animals? Anything?"

"I don't know; maybe there was a sound. Ah . . . I don't know, a blue jay or a crow or something. What, you think a crow picked her up and brought her back to camp?" Paul muttered sarcastically.

Jack shook his head, trying to keep his composure. "Sometimes, sounds play tricks on you on the mountain. Over a distance, a woman's voice can sound like a bird's call. Think about it Paul. What did you hear?"

"Well, I don't know. Yeah, it could have been a voice, not a bird. But it was short, sort of like a squawk, just once, not repeated, come to think of it."

"Just one noise. That's it?" Jack was in interrogation mode, his mind calculating all the possible outcomes at once.

"Yeah, just once. You know it could have been Gel; it just didn't occur to me that it was her. Do you think she cried out in trouble or something?" Paul asked in response. His mind was starting to race now, too.

"Paul, anything's possible. I don't have much to go on; unless you want to agree with the theory that she disappeared into thin air!" Jack turned to him as he answered. The conversation was on the edge of being confrontational at this point.

"Of course not! So where does that lead us? Did she encounter someone else or did she get hurt?" Paul mused. His mind was reeling and it took all his control not to lash out at Jack.

"If she got hurt, I would expect to find her laying somewhere over here, but I haven't found her, have you? So either she wandered off and we've somehow lost the trail or someone helped her, hurt or otherwise," Jack bit back.

"What are you suggesting? Someone grabbed her? This isn't the city here. Do you often get a whacko on the mountain grabbing people? "

"No, Paul, I am just brainstorming scenarios," Jack countered. *I'll have to be careful what I say around him. I don't want to cause any panic. Panic! Well, isn't that what I'm feeling here? The weather, the circumstances, why wouldn't I want to panic? Okay, calm down, Jack. Let your training talk you through this. You can do this!*

The rain pelted through the thick overhead canopy, while thunder rumbled frequently now. The wind was causing the trees to groan and strain. The forest sounded like it wanted to speak, to give up its secrets if only someone could listen.

Paul shuddered as he looked up into the trees above. What sky he could see was dark and ominous. The mountain, that seemed harmless two hours ago, now had a life of its own, strange and foreboding. New sounds brought life to inanimate trees, rocks and underbrush. It was no longer a game; it was life and death with death moving in ever closer. With it, fear rose like a presence in this forest, stalking in the periphery of their vision, watching silently for their responses, their thoughts and words. Paul trembled slightly, physically shaking the presence. But it did not leave. Its claws had wrapped themselves firmly into the back of his neck.

"Jack, look this isn't my expertise here, but I have covered enough stories with similar themes that did not turn out well. Forgive me if my imagination is running wild. What's our next step?" Paul said, avoiding his gaze.

Jack stared at Paul. His mind was going through mental checklists and finding no explanations. *Yeah, Jack. What is our next step? You're supposed to be in control here. Or is this beyond your training? What do you plan to do about this one?*

Chapter 8

Lacey and Eli pulled out of her parking area and on to the access road along the lake until they hit the highway. The windshield wipers were on full speed, hardly keeping up with the wind driven rain now. It was a nasty day and it looked like it would only get worse. Branches strained against the wind, bowing low to its pressure. It would not be long before they would snap, becoming projectiles and roadblocks. Lacey glanced at Eli as he concentrated on the road before him. It was another quarter mile to where they expected to see Jack and his crew. Eli felt her look and replied to it, "I'm glad I'm not doing their training today, Lacey. They should be finished by now though."

"Jack knows what he's doing, Eli. It isn't his first course on this mountain, even under lousy conditions. He's always managed fine. He has training and experience under worse conditions than these, you know." It was as though she were trying to convince herself.

"Yeah, I know. I just don't have a good feeling about this though. I know you don't either. You said so yourself."

"I'm going to speak positively from now on though, Eli. We already have enough possible problems. I don't want to add to them. Fear will get us nowhere."

"You're right. Enough said," was Eli immediate response.

They drove without a further word; only the rhythmic slapping of the wipers broke the silence. They rounded the corner and saw Mac and Sarah in the parking area at the bottom of the mountain. Eli pulled the truck into the clearing and rolled down his window. Rain immediately splattered his face and arm. "You guys finished for the day?" Lacey queried.

Sarah walked to the truck and replied, "Well, sort of. There's a problem with Paul and Gelly up the mountain though. We're waiting for Gelly to come down here," Sarah replied.

"Sarah, Mac, this is Eli, a friend." Lacey introduced her companion.

"Pleased to meet you," Eli said, nodding at Bob. "Are Jack and Paul still up there? Why would Gelly come down separately?" Lacey asked.

"We don't know. That's all we know. We were given strict instructions not to move and to watch for her if she comes out. I'm not sure what happened up there. It was such a simple exercise. I can't imagine what went wrong." Sarah did not want to admit that she suspected that Paul and Gelly probably were arguing and got separated. It did not seem to make much logical sense to her why any of it would happen.

Eli rolled up the window as he put the truck in park. He looked over at Lacey and they got out of the truck. Immediately they were thankful for the full rain suits they had put on before leaving, as the rain lashed their faces. Lacey ambled toward Bob and asked, "You have radios, right? Have you heard anything from them?"

"Not lately. It's been a while now. I'll call up and try to get an update." Bob offered. "Jack, it's Bob here. What's going on? Bob over."

"Jack here. Ahh, well, we're not sure yet. Evangeline seems to . . . ahh, she's not here now."

Mac piped in at this point, "So you know where she was headed, right? Mac over."

Along pause was followed by this response from Jack, "Not exactly."

Sarah exchanged glances with Mac. The expression on her face showed immediate concern and urged him to get more information. "You mean, you don't know where she is?"

"Not at the moment," was Jack's short response.

Sarah's eyes implored Mac to ask more questions. He looked at her and shrugged. "What do you want us to do down here? Lacey and Eli have just arrived, is there anything we can get them to do. Mac over."

"Could Eli check if she got turned around and headed down by Pointer Road. It's the only logical explanation at the moment. We're going to make another run along the ridge. Jack over."

Lacey and Eli nodded their agreement and Mac replied, "Yeah, that's no problem. Is there anything Sarah and I can do here?"

"You stay put in case she surprises us all and comes out where you are. You never know what might happen and I want all my bases covered, especially with this weather. Jack over."

"Jack, Sarah can stay with Lacey and Bob and I can come on up to assist you. It never hurt to have an extra set of eyes," Mac answered. He could not believe he was just standing there in the rain doing nothing if there was an emergency. He was a fellow who usually had things under control, in business or leisure time. It made no sense to him that they could not use his help.

"Believe me, Mac, I appreciate the offer but we'll probably be down the mountain before you make it up here. Just stay put for the moment and we'll be there before you know it. Just stay put. You hear me?" The strain in Jack's voice was evident to everyone, so Mac did not push him any further. "Bob, could you head to the west side of the cut and check to make sure there are no signs of her coming through there? Just make sure that Mac and Sarah stay with Lacey."

Bob glanced over at Mac to make sure he agreed and replied, "Sure, Jack, we've got it all under control down here. You just finish what you have to do there." It was Bob's responsibility to keep this couple in one piece and he did not want more problems than there were already.

"Mac, are you okay to stay with Lacey and watch for Evangeline? Jack over."

"Sure, Jack, whatever you say. We'll stay here and wait for Gel to make it down. Mac out."

Eli shook his head and said, "Lacey, you alright staying here?" Eli asked as he headed back to the truck.

"Eli, you just do what Jack requested and we'll be fine here," was Lacey's reply. The rain was dripping off her yellow rain slicker on to her nose. It was getting miserable and as she looked up toward the thick forest above, she thought that it would probably get much nastier before it got any better. This could be a long day and an even longer night ahead. Good thing they were as prepared as they could be under the circumstances. *What does this dark day have in store for us?*

Bob locked eyes with Lacey as he prepared to leave. He wanted to be sure she would not let Mac and Sarah out of her sight. She nodded at him, knowing what he meant and said, "You do your jobs and we'll wait at the 'base camp'. If it gets too miserable, we can all climb into the van. You did leave it unlocked, Bob?"

"No problem, Lacey, help yourselves," Bob replied as he walked back toward the bush.

As Eli drove out of sight, Lacey felt the gloom of the mountain descend on her; a presence she had not felt before. *I'm sure there's more to this than I can see now.* Lacey thought it, but said nothing to Mac and Sarah. *I hope that they are prepared for what lies ahead. There could be more to this adventure package than these folks thought they were buying.* The grim reality of the situation was starting to settle in as all of them huddled waiting for more news from the mountain above them. None of them seemed prepared to retreat into the comfort of the van, while so much uncertainty remained.

Hurricane Igor moved determinedly toward the northwest, fuelled by a cold air mass over Ontario. It had no thought of stopping until it had spilled all its remaining fury. Why stop over land when the terror could continue onward, northward? With plenty of fear to draw from, it need not cease its movement and there would be even more panic before it was through. Oh, the fear! How it strengthened the storm's resolve to continue onward. How unprepared were these people for its intended rage. What devastation could it pour out below? Memories of Hazel were dim in this thoughtless generation and it only excited the storm even more.

Jan Talbot watched the branches outside the window as they swayed in the erratic dance dictated by the gusting winds. Rain lashed against the windowpane across the room, then, with seeming unpredictability, it pelted the window beside her. It could not decide from which direction it would approach. It was probably the collision of storm fronts that dictated this fickleness.

Is it my imagination or is it cooler now? They did say the temperature might drop with the cold front. Jan busied herself with making dinner, while the power was still intact. Who knew how much longer they would have it, given the strength of the winds that exploded from the storm. A draft through the door made her shiver. What made her pause though was not the temperature change, but a chilling sense inside her. It was not something she recognized, but it did catch her interest. It was not natural or welcome. It was unmistakable though and she also realized that it needed her attention now before it took root and grew.

"Calvin!"

"What's up? You need help with something? I was just checking the …" He stopped short when he saw the look on her face. He had seen it before and he knew to take it seriously.

"I don't know what it is, but something's wrong. I just got this strange feeling. It's sort of as if we aren't alone here. Uh, I'm not sure what it is. Could you check the doors and windows?"

"Aw, Jan, I already did and you know it. The storm can play tricks on you. The change in air pressure has my knees hurting, that's for sure."

"Calvin, it's different than that. Just hush for a moment, will you? Don't you feel it?" Jan said as she held up her hand to silence him.

Calvin stood still, just listening to the wind in the trees around their house. It was intense, but what was Jan getting at? Then it crept in like an escaped draft under the door, but it was not a breeze, at least not what he had felt before. It was unusual; however, he could not grasp what it was about the sensation that caught his attention. This felt like something was there, watching them, waiting for his response.

"Yes, you're right. It's odd. Lacey talked about this at the last meeting. I didn't take it seriously at the time, but that sure is strange!" Calvin replied slowly. His eyes carefully scanned the room and saw nothing unusual. However, he could not deny what he sensed.

Calvin added, "Well, I'll phone Bert and ask him to start the calls to the others. I guess it has begun after all. We've been preparing for this. Now's the time to put what we studied into action." Jan and Calvin exchanged knowing looks.

"Just be careful what you say. It could make all the difference at this point," was Jan's response.

Jack felt his blood pressure rising with the winds. He ran all the possibilities over in his head again. *It's just plain stupid. She must have walked along the rocks for a distance to have made no tracks. Was she trying to cover her trail? This couldn't be some practical joke they had pulled?*

No, not with this weather. She just didn't seem the type to participate in something like that under these conditions. I'm sure she just wanted to get down that mountain as fast as she could. Wilderness conditions were not her thing; that was obvious. But where did she go?

Jack retraced his steps along the ridge, looking on the forest floor for clues, glancing down the ridge for signs he might have missed when he was down there. Something just did not sit right with him. He knew he had to be missing something, but for the life of him, he just could not think of it at the moment. *Okay, buddy, use your instructions: stop, rest and think. What's logical here? If she isn't playing games with them, what else could have happened? Are there any signs of another set of footprints? It's difficult to tell with all the traipsing around they did before I arrived. But I'd better look again; maybe further along the slope I can pick up signs. If there was another person there who lured her off course, I'll surely see some signs of it. If not, then there's no logical explanation.*

The rain was persistent now. It also seemed cooler, which only made him more conscious of the chill from the sweat trickling down his back. It could be from all the exertion of racing up the mountainside and tracing their trails, but it might be from the increasing uneasiness in his gut. This just could not be happening. It made no sense to him. Again he ran down the list of possibilities in his mind, only to come to the same empty conclusions.

The trees above creaked with the wind. The swirling gusts matched his thoughts and his apprehension grew. It was one nasty afternoon and he sensed it would get worse. He shook off the unfamiliar feeling. His training would not fail him. It never had in the past. He would run the drill of probabilities once more and it would soon all make sense as it always had before.

John Brompton's store had seen a lot of business this afternoon, to the point that he was getting low on some stock. People had been listening to the weather reports. Given the history of electric blackouts in the area in previous storms, many had thought it prudent to come in and make sure they had all the necessary supplies to take them through for a few days. It often took that long for the electricity to be restored.

The atmosphere was as gray as the skies. Vacationers were grumpy about losing their weekend of sunshine. It was even too miserable for the anglers to be enthusiastic about their sport. Although the locals were just ready to hunker down for the duration, the city folks left their mountain retreats early, not wanting to be without their usual conveniences should the power go out.

John smiled as he reflected on those city dwellers. Cottage country was pleasant when it was hot in the city and they wanted to be cooler, but give them a little discomfort and they were out of here. Better that they go though, because if the river should flood, they did not need more people to tend to. He knew some would do stupid things, like driving through flooded roads just because they had some SUV. It always amazed him that these people did not seem to have a lick of sense. If the water was too deep to walk through, what made them think it was safe to drive through? There would be fewer people for the emergency personnel to rescue, and maybe, one fewer casualty reported in the papers the next day.

Lacey surveyed the hillside above her. The bush was reasonably dense but not impenetrable; otherwise Jack would not be using it for his exercise. This adventure was deteriorating quickly for these couples. No one wants rain for a weekend away, but this could prove to be more than any of them had bargained for. A gust of wind forced her to grab Mac for support.

She glanced down at her watch. How long had it been since Eli left? Mac saw her gesture and asked her, "How long do you think it will take Eli to check down the road?"

Lacey shrugged and replied, "I imagine he'll be back shortly, unless he ran into someone or something."

Confirming her thoughts, Eli's truck could be heard as he rounded to corner and came into view. He put the truck in park and climbed out.

"Any signs of her?" Sarah asked with a hopeful expression.

"None that I could see. Maybe she flagged down another vehicle. Did any come by while I was gone?" Eli answered. They shook their heads almost in unison. He looked up the mountain. "You hear anything from up there?"

"Not since you left," was Mac's reply.

"Why didn't you climb into the van and get out of the rain?" Eli looked at them, rain dripping off them like waterfalls.

Mac shrugged and Lacey laughed, "I don't know. That probably would have been too logical."

Sarah countered, "I think we were just watching for Gelly. It would be hard to see her if we were in the van. I don't know, somehow it just doesn't seem right for us to be comfortable in the van, when everyone else is out here in the rain."

"I guess . . . whatever," Eli said as he looked up toward the trees.

Following Eli's gaze, Mac offered to call up to Jack again. "Jack, Mac here. What's the story up there?"

"We haven't found anything yet. I think we'll come down there and regroup. Any sign of her down there? Over."

"We haven't heard back from Bob but Eli didn't see her on the road. I don't suppose you have an explanation for all this. What did Paul have to say about it? Over."

"Wait till we get down and we'll talk about it then. Jack out."

Having heard the last exchange over the radios, Paul met Jack as he returned along the ridge. He was fuming by this point. He was not sure how much of it was anger or how much was worry, but the result was the same. He was ready to draw blood to get some answers at this point.

Eddie had done little to calm his nerves. Eddie was a quiet man, doing what he was asked to do on the mountain, but he was not much for conversation. That only fuelled Paul's anxiety as he waited at the rendezvous point. Jack had made it clear that he did not want any 'help' scouting out the terrain. Paul would likely have done just that, just to be doing something. However, his help was not welcome at the moment and it left him feeling useless.

Then there were the questions floating through his mind. *Why would she just go off like that? What was I supposed to do, anyway? She was being so unreasonable and whiny. It wasn't such a big deal to climb down those rocks. I could have helped her down and it wouldn't have been such a big deal. Why did she have to go and wander off? What was I supposed to do to stop her anyway? I couldn't just tackle her down in the bush. If she wanted to wander off, then she would. I know there was nothing I could do about it.* She was still missing. Paul could justify his actions all he wanted but he did not know whether she was safe. It was not like her to just disappear and he did love her, even with her quirky ways. *What was going on here?*

Just as Paul could not stand there another moment with nothing to do, he heard the sound of Jack's footsteps in the underbrush coming his way. He had heard the exchange on the radio and it did not make him happy. As Jack approached, Paul said, "You can't be serious about leaving the mountain. You haven't found her or explained what happened!"

"Look, Paul, standing around here isn't going to help her any. We might as well get together and discuss our options. Once we have a plan, we can proceed more effectively."

"You don't think I'm willing to leave her do you?" Paul said, ready for a fight.

"That's not what I said, Paul. I meant that we would just go down the mountain for the moment and strategize. We can enlist some help, just in case she did somehow go down the hillside without us knowing it."

"Well, I am not going to leave this mountain until we know what's going on. I'll go down with you, but I want to search more before I go back to the camp. It just doesn't make any sense to me; how could she just disappear?"

Jack spoke calmly now, distinctly, trying to get Paul's cooperation, "She didn't. There has to be a logical explanation to it and that is what I want to discuss. If we put all our heads together, we might have a better shot at figuring it out. You know her better than I do so I want to talk to you and get your ideas of what she's like and what she might do in an unusual circumstance."

"Why don't you just ask me, after all, I'm her husband? I think I know her better than anyone else," Paul countered.

Jack sighed slightly, trying to keep his composure with Paul. "Yes, you are her husband, but you're a man and maybe Sarah, as a woman, might know something that she wouldn't confide to you," Jack continued.

"Jack, what are you implying?" Paul retorted.

"Nothing. Just that sometimes women talk to each other in ways that they don't with men, even their husbands. I just want to proceed with this logically, sensibly and not wasting time. Let me do what I am trained for," Jack responded. He was starting to get exasperated with Paul at this point. They were wasting precious minutes arguing over moot points.

Paul shrugged and took a deep breath. Trusting Jack under these circumstances was all he could do, but it did not make him happy.

"Well, I'm going to try calling her again. Maybe she was just angry with me before and wouldn't answer." Again, Paul radioed Evangeline. "Gel, we need to hear from you. Let us know if you're okay. Just answer us. Can you hear me? I'm sorry, okay, just answer us." He stood there and waited for a reply that did not come. All he could hear was the wind in the trees above and the rain on the hood of his jacket. The peaty aroma of the sodden forest floor wafted up assailing his senses, emphasizing the lack of response from Evangeline.

Paul looked around him searching for some sign that she might respond but the radio was deadly silent. Paul closed his eyes for a moment as the full impact of the predicament settled in. "Maybe her radio isn't working," Paul remarked in exasperation. "Gel, can you hear us?" he yelled. "Gel, answer us!" Still there was no response, just the creaking of the branches above him.

Reluctantly, Paul followed Jack and they proceeded down the mountain. The rain had not let up and it made for even more slippery footing. The moss covered rocks were especially treacherous under these circumstances.

Branches creaked above them with each gust of wind as they made their way down the mountainside. Paul's mood dropped with each foot they descended. It was not the way the weekend was supposed to go and he did not like what was happening. Life suddenly had taken a turn out of control. Confused thoughts swirled about his head with no logical answers to bring any sense to the matter. No story he had covered with similar circumstances ever turned out well. He did not like the sense of dread that was planting itself in him.

Jack, Paul and Eddie made their way over the parked vehicles at the bottom of the mountain. From the grim look on Jack's face, Lacey realized the circumstances were serious. She had a little more difficulty reading Paul's expression, although he was obviously upset.

Lacey was not sure if Paul was angry with Jack or the circumstances. He was out of his normal surroundings here, she could see that. He may be used to camping and into outdoor activities, but it was not his usual beat. He did not like being on the other side of a 'story'. A disappearing wife was not something he had experienced before and he obviously was uncomfortable about it all. The weather was just making it all the worse.

Lacey closed her eyes for a moment and said a quiet Prayer for Wisdom. They would all need as much as the Lord could provide.

The first casualty of the storm on Seeley's Mountain occurred as a departing weekend resident rounded a corner on the road leading out of their lakefront property of the other side of Big Rock Lake and ran smack into a fallen pine that spanned the road. The driver was knocked unconscious and two passengers had abrasions and bruises from the sudden impact. Emergency vehicles were dispatched from Moulton down on Route 15 below Lofton. The driver was taken immediately to hospital by ambulance. The passengers were attended to at the scene and taken to hospital shortly afterward.

Crews busied themselves with cleaning away the debris and cutting up the fallen tree so no further incidents would occur at the site.

"It's one big old tree. The roots must have been loosened by the rain earlier in the week. It didn't take much to send it down," said Larry Walters.

"Yeah, it's too bad. We might see more come down if the storm is what they're predicting. I just hope that no more get hurt like that. It looks as if they might have avoided the tree if they had gone a little slower though. They were in a hurry to clear the area before the weather got worse and look at what happened to them! I hope the rest of this bunch has more sense than that. Nothing is worth doing that fast if it costs your life," replied Parker Johnson. His tall lanky frame towered over his fellow worker as he cut away branches and tree trunk.

It was not long before the roadway was clear to traffic again. Small twigs littered the scene, the only visible remnants of the accident as they packed their truck and headed back toward Lofton. They did not realize how much work they had ahead this day.

Jack heard the sirens in the distance as he walked out of the bush with Paul and Eddie. He was uneasy at the sound. He walked toward Eddie and quietly said to him, "Could you get on the phone and see if you can find out what those sirens are about? I want to be sure it has nothing to do with our client, so go back to the van to make the call, okay?"

Eddie shrugged then agreed to be quiet about it. He walked to the van and climbed in to make the call to a friend on the other side of the lake and he was given details of the accident. They did not get much activity this far up the road, so it made the local "wire" report rapidly. Most residents nearby were involved in directing traffic around the accident and helping the rescue crew as was necessary.

Eddie sauntered to Jack who was deep in conversation with the group at this point. He leaned toward Jack's left ear and whispered, "The problem down the lake doesn't involve us. It's just a quarrel between an SUV and a pine that had fallen across the road. The SUV lost."

Jack responded with a nod, but his blood pressure lowered a notch. It did not improve things, nor did it make it suddenly worse either, which he could easily live with.

Paul had just finished explaining what had occurred up the mountainside from his point of view. "I don't understand how she could just disappear like that. It defies explanation. I know she didn't just disappear, but at this point I'd believe in alien abduction or some story in the tabloid news rags. It is not like Gel to just wander off. She's not comfortable in this kind of situation and would want to get back to everyone quickly. She might have been ticked off with me initially, but I know that she would've cooled down once she found her way around the ridge. It just doesn't make sense."

"We went along the ridge; it was a fair distance, but not unreasonable. We cut down the bedrock about halfway down. We figured that we could negotiate the rocks at that point because it wasn't as steep. We sort of cheated too. We didn't go right to the end and see what was over there. So what was there at the other end?" Sarah inquired.

"Nothing much that I could see. Just more of the same, but not as steep," Paul answered. "Jack, what did you see that I missed?"

"I wish there was something. I was checking for tracks and evidence of where she walked. She must have doubled back down the rocks a bit, because I lost her trail when she hit the end of the ridge. It was frustrating because she should have made some sort of track. I look for broken branches, crushed stems of small plants, disturbed leaves on the ground. But there was nothing to see. It makes no sense. Your wife is either good at dodging a tracker or there is some logical explanation that eludes me at the moment," was Jack's response. From the expression on his face, it was evident his mind was still up the hillside checking possibilities. He had not given up on the search yet, that was obvious and it gave Paul something to hang on to at the moment.

Rustling could be heard from the bush not far from where they stood. Jack was the first to hear it and looked toward the source of the sound. As they followed his gaze, they saw Bob emerge from the trees; looking as if he had taken a swim fully clothed. He had a grim look on his face, which made Sarah spirits fall even further than they already were.

Jack walked to Bob and fell into stride with him. The others were rooted to the spot, not wanting to hear any bad news sooner than they had to. Jack's look was enough of a question for Bob and he answered grimly, "I saw no sign of Evangeline, however, I did run into Carmen Loughrey as I came out above his property. He said that there was a bear sighting last evening. You know the one that has been creating havoc over by the campground. It's been doing considerable damage among the campers, especially in the tents in the last week. They scared it away from the campground. They got animal control involved and their presence seems to have spooked the bear to this side of the lake. That would not be good news for our missing client."

Jack drew a long breath. He did not want the others to see his response to Bob's new information. It was bad enough that he had a client who was unaccounted for, but having a bear nearby made it far worse. He realized that this woman was not the type to deal well with that type of situation at the best of times, let alone under these conditions. "We'd better be careful how we share this information. We need to keep it in mind, but let's not drive everyone into a panic about it. Let me handle it, okay?"

"Sure thing. Well, as you know, it's better if the bear hears you before you come across it. You don't want to be startling it. We might want to be sure we've got some whistles and other stuff to use. Shouting will work to a degree. You got anything with you?"

"Not with me. I have some whistles and bear screamers and bangers back at the camp, if we need them. I didn't bring much stuff with me because it was supposed to be an easy exercise. Man, I sure didn't need this on top of everything else! Well, we haven't found her yet so we might be here for a while. Umm, well, could you go back to the camp and get that stuff and my rifle? I'm not about to take any chances here," Jack said in disgust.

They walked to the group who were expectantly waiting for any news. Jack was the first to speak, "Bob didn't find any trace of her on the other side of the hillside. I'm going to send Bob back to the camp to check things there, to make sure she didn't somehow make her way back there without us knowing it."

Mac replied, "Sounds good, but what do you want us to do?"

"Well, I might just have to give you a little more training than your lesson plan included. We're going to have to do a modified grid search to see if there are any clues we might have missed."

Paul piped in, "What about getting more help?"

Jack nodded and said, "Yeah. I'll have Bob recruit some assistance for us while he's at the camp. With the weather closing in on us as it is, we need to finish this quickly, before . . . "

Sarah looked startled and said, "Before what? Things get worse? It's about as bad as it gets, isn't it? We've lost one person already!"

Jack held up his hand to stop her and added, "No, I was going to say before other emergencies crop up in the area because of the storm itself. There was an accident already on the other side of the lake when an SUV ran into a fallen tree. Before all the personnel get tied up, it would be wise to notify the authorities to look for her and to recruit some assistance in our search."

"I'm sorry I jumped to conclusions," Sarah replied.

"Jack, Eli and I can go back and bring some of our group. We know the lay of the land as well as you do, so we could be of some help," Lacey offered.

"Okay, Lacey, that sounds good. I've got something in the truck for you to take back with you for me. Come on over and I'll get it for you," Jack answered. As they walked to the truck, Jack added, "Lacey, there's something you guys might as well know before you go. A bear was spotted on this side of the lake last night. It's an added complication that we just didn't need but we must prepare for it. Anyone coming should know what they are getting into and if they have clackers or bear spray it would be helpful to bring it along. I don't want a lot of people traipsing around with loaded rifles, but anyone who is well trained to use one might bring it with them, just in case. I don't need a bear mauling to happen on top of everything else."

Lacey faced him and looked into his eyes. Jack averted her gaze quickly. He was not comfortable with the kind of penetrating look that Lacey could deliver. "We can do that with no problem. What's your best guess of what happened here?"

"Lacey, I only wish I knew. People don't just disappear, they either walk out by themselves, they are helped out or they're injured and can't go anywhere. If she were injured, we would have found her, I'm sure of it. She either walked out on her own accord or she was helped."

"By helped, you mean what?" Lacey asked.

Jack sighed. He did not want to voice his concerns. "Well, a person might have redirected her but there was no sign of a struggle anywhere that I could see. If it were a bear, we would have heard a lot more noise. It makes no sense for there to be no signs of anything. I've been doing this for enough years to know that this doesn't follow a rational pattern. You know that I've worked in search-and-rescue operations in the area for years now. We've located enough lost anglers and hunters to know what we're doing."

"Jack, I don't doubt your abilities for a moment. When things seem out of control there is one thing I resort to, you know what I mean?" Lacey added.

"Sure, Lacey, you do your thing and I'll do mine. Just make sure your group comes prepared for the weather and the possible conditions. You've have been helpful in other searches, so I know I can rely on you for the kind of help I need," Jack responded quickly, changing the track of the conversation.

"So do you have something in the truck to take back or was that just a diversion to talk to me?" Lacey asked.

"Oh, yeah, it was a diversion but I'd better give you something or I'll have them on my case before I even get back to them. I'll give you a couple extra maps of the mountain terrain to take with you for your people. You probably know the mountain better than most around here, but it might be helpful for you anyway."

"Okay, Eli and I'll take off now." Lacey motioned to Eli to meet her at his truck. "Where do you want us to meet you when we come back?"

"Here, take one of the radios and call me if you don't see me when you arrive. I can let you know our location. Bob will notify search and rescue. I just hope there are enough available. Given the weather, a bunch of them might have been called in to work. There may be a few still on standby though."

"Jack, I'm sure that there will be enough and with our experience, we should be able to help where you need us," Lacey countered. She sounded surer of it than Jack felt at the moment. His mind was working overtime, trying to find an easy explanation of the scene before him.

Unfortunately, he realized, life usually liked to throw the unexpected in to the worst of situations. This was one of them.

"And Lacey," Jack added as Lacey turned to go. Lacey stopped and faced him so he wouldn't have to raise his voice for the others to hear. "Make sure you bring just your experienced friends. I don't need well meaning rookies on this expedition. It's serious, given the conditions. I don't want another casualty or two among the helpers."

"Jack, trust me, I don't either. I don't want anyone getting injured. I wouldn't ask anyone to venture in beyond their training or abilities. Trust me to do what I am good at and I'll do the same for you"

Jack realized he had been scolded by Lacey, but he did not care. He was doing all he could to hold a situation together was rapidly falling apart despite his planning.

Chapter 9

Evangeline began to awaken, slowly becoming aware of her new surroundings. It was dark, cold and wet. Her mind tried to grasp her new reality. Where was she? What was this place? Her head hurt; oh, did it hurt. And her leg was twisted under her at an odd angle. What was this place anyway? She tried to move and pain shot up her leg and back. She felt drowsy and drifted off again, to a place where it did not hurt so much.

Hurricane Igor was what they called it, but it did not matter what name they gave it. It was merely a tag to identify what they could not control. It was beyond their abilities, and the storm knew it, even if people did not yet understand it. They were its victims, its prey. The evil contained within it delighted in their ignorance of the devastation it planned.

It was entertaining; watching them scramble to take cover, to escape the inescapable; to prepare for what they thought was coming. But always, the storm took command. It had them at its mercy and mercy was not in the plan. It was a sport with no rules, except to do what was necessary to see these creatures squirm in terror.

Yes, terror, that was a game it could understand. Terror was the aim, whatever destruction happened was just the means. Fear fuelled the storm as much as colliding low-pressure systems could achieve and these foolish people were quick to oblige. Now, watching the show below, it excited the storm into increased agitation and a wicked frenzy. This would be the storm these mortals remembered for years to come.

Calvin picked up the phone on the second ring. It had startled him at first, but pulled him back into the reality of the day. He had been reading his Bible and deep in contemplation. It was the thing to do when you knew that circumstances were about to whirl out of control before you. He was sure of it. So was Jan. They knew they had been training for such an occasion, but the details were hazy. They would just have to take it a step at a time. They would just let it play out. It was beyond explanation, but that was where Trust came in. Yes, it was big. They knew it.

"Hi Lacey. Yeah, we feel it. It sure has settled in, hasn't it? What a strange atmosphere though. It's not we expected. It's nasty, this one is. What's up?" Calvin replied.

"Calvin, we have a situation on Seeley's Mountain with Jack's training group. It seems one of the students is missing. She didn't make it down the mountain with her group and Jack is mystified what happened to her. He would appreciate some help with the search."

"Sure, Lacey. That won't be any problem. We've helped before in other searches. Jan and I can help coordinate things. Anything we should know about?"

"Well, there is another complication. That bear that was causing all the raucous over at Chaney's campground has been spotted on this side of the lake near their training exercises. We'll have to come prepared for the animal. I doubt that we'll see it in this weather, but you never know, if it's hungry enough without the food from the campers."

"So who's missing; male or female?" Calvin asked.

Lacey answered, "It's a female, wife of one of the fellows taking the course. She's not an outdoor enthusiast from the sounds of it, so she may not know how to take care of herself in the wilderness. It probably wouldn't take much to get her turned around in the bush. She separated from her husband coming down the mountain on a navigation run and just disappeared, with no trail to follow and no logical explanation how she went missing. You and I both know there is probably an explanation no one wants to confront though."

"I don't imagine you suggested anything to them either, Lacey," Calvin commented.

Lacey paused before she responded, "Calvin, this bunch is not ready to hear about it much less act on it. We'll just have to respond as it unfolds. We don't rely on conventional wisdom and we'll show them by our actions. We model our Teacher and that will say more in a situation like this."

"So what do you want us to do then, Lacey?" Calvin questioned.

"You know the routine, Calvin. Could you start the calls and ask everyone to meet over by the base of the mountain that Jack uses for his training runs? Just remember to get everyone prepared for a long day with appropriate supplies and rifles with ammunition for the trained hunters. Jack doesn't want anyone armed who doesn't already know how to use a rifle though. So let's not have any stupid stuff going on. If we make a lot of noise, it will probably scare off any animal anyway. With the number of people we'll have, it'll be easy to make that much noise, I'm sure," Lacey said.

Calvin then inquired, "Has anyone connected with the rescue team?"

Lacey nodded her head on her end of the conversation, "Yes, Jack was getting Bob to go back to the camp, to get supplies and make the necessary contacts. I hope he was going to let the sheriff's office know in case she shows up on the road instead of staying in the bush. You never know what might be involved with this. You put city folks into the country setting and people do strange things. I assume that it was merely a situation with two couples away for a pleasant weekend retreat, but you never know what their motivations and plans were."

Calvin paused before asking, "Are you trying to say that it was all staged?"

Lacey was quick to respond, "No, Calvin, I'm just saying that people do strange things sometimes. You watch the television as much as I do and you've seen the news reports. People can be bizarre at times. We'll just have to be prepared for anything. You don't need to start any rumors either. Just give the group the facts we already know. We have training that'll prepare us for the other stuff. Come with your 'radar' on, is all I am saying!"

"Well, Lacey, I suppose that explains the odd atmosphere. It isn't a nice one and we should be ready for anything this time. This may be what we've been getting ready for all along," Calvin said solemnly.

"Calvin, it may be, but I sense it's just the beginning. I'll talk to you later when we get together on the mountain. Remember, rain gear and good footwear, because it's slippery," Lacey reminded him.

"I sense it could be slippery in other ways too. See you there. Godspeed," Calvin concluded and disconnected the phone.

The winds gusted in a steady rhythm now. The trees above strained and groaned with each damaging blast. The rain lashed out against every crevice on the mountainside. No place was dry, even in the densest bush. The treetops no longer gave protection from this storm.

The wet penetrated the forest floor, already moist from previous rains earlier in the week. Streams and rivulets formed along paths of least resistance. Dips and furrows in the rocks and dirt gave way to runoff, gathering speed with the dropping elevation. Soon new waterways were shaping, carving new pathways in the dirt. Water descended the slope toward the lake below. The lake emptied its new deluge into the creeks, which now flowed more like large streams and small rivers. How long these avenues could contain the current was debatable. It soon became evident that new landscapes were about to appear; ones that were unpredictable and violent in nature.

The storm was moving along the face of the Earth now, no longer content to hover overhead and ravage from above. This terrain required hands on pressure and movement, so far from the fuel of the ocean. The hurricane mutated across the mountains and valleys creating terrors as it descended on the earth's surface. With proximity, came the intimate pressure of the evil in its core. Its center throbbed, ebbed and flowed with evil desire, pouring it down on these complacent creatures. Not one knew what to expect and that gave the hurricane fuel for the terror it was about to unleash.

Sam Fowler recognized the name on the call display and picked up the phone on the first ring. "Jack, what's up?"

"Hold on, Sam, it's not Jack. It's Bob Fisher. Jack asked me to call you. We have a situation over on the mountain here and we could use help if you've got some available hands."

Sam responded immediately, "Sure thing, Bob. Anything for Jack. I've mobilized all our people to be ready to come in today given the possible conditions with the storm but so far haven't had to do all that much. What's the problem there?"

"Well, we've got a party missing from the navigation course. It doesn't make much sense where she went, but she never made it down the mountain on the compass reading exercise. A woman separated from her husband partway down the hillside and seems to have disappeared," Bob explained.

"Bob, people don't just disappear. There must be some logical explanation for it," was Sam's response.

"Yeah, Sam, I know, people don't just disappear, but this one seems to have done a good job somehow," Bob reluctantly responded.

"Are there more details we need about this; more dynamics to the events?" Sam asked.

"Darned if I know. They're a close bunch; four of them, two couples that get along well. One, a newspaper writer, was given the course as a gift, and the other couple decided to tag along for an adventure. Some adventure it's turned out to be! Now one's missing. That will be some story for them to tell their friends later. We'd rather clean this up quickly though with the weather moving in on us like it is. We don't want to give this guy something to write about for the newspaper. That wouldn't be good for business, would it? Do you think you can help?" Bob explained.

"No problem. Are you at the usual place?" was Sam's immediate answer.

Bob confirmed, "Yeah, Sam, the same place Jack uses. Lacey McCrae is mobilizing bodies too so we should have a number of people soon. Jack just wanted some trained personnel to keep this a tight operation, especially given the conditions."

"I can have our people over within a half hour," Sam reiterated.

"Oh, and Sam, you should know that we have a bear sighting on the mountain last night. Just some extra possible complications, you know. Everyone should come prepared," Bob added.

"Well, doesn't that make things interesting? Okay, we know the drill. I'll get everyone mobilized and meet you over there ASAP."

"Thanks Sam, we owe you one."

Sam said firmly, "No, I owe Jack more than I can count already, so this isn't a big deal. I'll see you soon."

Chapter 10

Flashback:

She took one drug to go to sleep, another to wake and still another to get through the day; some prescription, some over the counter, some from other sources. Who cared where they came from if she could perform at work? Then there were the men. How many 'relationships' had she had this year already? It was just a diversion and the comfort of knowing someone was there, someone who could take care of intruders if necessary. It was just so she wouldn't be alone at night. Oh, those nights; the dreams that came suddenly, so vividly, and so ominously. Did the men mean anything to her; no, anyone would do. Just so she wouldn't be alone.

Never be alone. Never be alone with the fear she had named her 'companion'. It was her constant 'companion' now; no longer a creeping sensation occasionally when making a big decision. Now any decision could trigger its entrance. Second guessing was a game with the 'companion'. No decision was easy. She constantly looked over her shoulder, wondering who was after her job, her status, her name. The 'companion' reminded her constantly that she was easily yesterday's news and would be replaced without hesitation.

The last deadline was almost missed and she took a lot of heat for it. After all, it was her job to keep things tight. A missed deadline meant lost contracts and money. It would be her fault and her name was on the line. Was it worth it anymore? She was beginning to doubt it. She wasn't sleeping well or eating well anymore. She looked ten years older than her age when she looked at her image in the mirror. It took more makeup to create the illusion of beauty that the heads upstairs seemed to desire.

Minutes ticked away on the clock; precious minutes. Each minute took her closer to the new deadline, then another. But would there be another if this one wasn't successful? No, she realized, it was the determining one. This one had to be good, successful and dramatic or she would be out the door. The writing was on the wall. Jackson was young, energetic, enthusiastic and able to make himself 'the name'. And she was nearly out of ideas to outsmart him now. The minutes ticked away, one by one. She knew she had to make her move now, not later. Her 'companion' stepped into the room, made its entrance and dread did its dance in her heart once more.

Evangeline slowly became aware of the wet dirt between her fingers. Jumbled thoughts drifted across her mind. Images of dark figures melded with ominous shadows and dissolved into cold darkness. Her eyes were closed and her lids felt too heavy to open. She shivered in the dampness as she listened to the trickle of water somewhere beside her. She struggled to comprehend these sensations. As she moved her hand, she realized there was more rock than dirt. What was this place? She managed to open her eyes, but saw an eerie darkness, just dim shadows. How did she get here?

As she regained consciousness, she also began to feel the pain. Her head throbbed intensely. She lifted her hand to the side of her head and felt wet, sticky blood matted in her hair. It had trickled down her forehead into her eye, making it difficult to focus. Her leg was twisted under her at an awkward angle, but when she tried to move it sent searing pain up her leg into her back. She groaned in agony, waiting for the pain to subside, afraid to move lest it start again. She panted with the pain, trying to regain her composure, while a wave of fear washed over her.

What had happened? She could not focus her thoughts long enough to remember. Where was she and how did she get here? Could this merely be another nightmare? No, this pain was real enough. She reached out again, groping in the gloom to feel her surroundings. Dirt, rock and water met her fingers. She realized she was partly on her side, with something strung over her shoulder. She felt a band or something was pulling against her chest making it hard to breathe. As she felt around, she soon realized it was the strap of a backpack that was at her side. She was tangled in it somehow. Her thoughts would not focus enough to allow her to figure out how to remove it. Every movement was excruciating. Why was she here? She felt a wave of panic rising inside her. What is this place?

She heard a sound on her left. What was that? With so little light, she could not make out shapes. "Who's there?" she called out weakly. Her voice sounded like a whisper but seemed to echo, mocking her. No answer came; just the sound of trickling water. She closed her eyes again, something she did in childhood when she was feared the dark. If she could not see out, then the hidden monsters could not see her either. It was silly and foolish, but somehow gave her some comfort now. Anything seemed better than the sheer terror that was rising in her now. Was she alone here in this miserable place?

Sol hung up the phone. Standing in deep contemplation, he was startled back into reality as Hildy entered the room. "Who was that on the phone?" she asked.

Sol had his back to her as he stood in front of the picture window. The view before him had gone from gloomy to nasty over the last hour. The normally placid lake was whipped by whitecaps and as gray as the sky above it. He was glad that he moved the boat into the boathouse this morning. He would not want to be out in the storm now, fighting to reposition the boat without scraping the sides on the dock. "It was Calvin. You think you might like to go for a drive?"

"Are you nuts? In this weather? Sol, you had better have a good explanation for this one. I was just thinking that it was crazy when I saw the last car drive by the house. Who'd like to go out on a day like today, especially with the forecast the way it is, predicting such winds and driving rain?" Hildy looked at him in disbelief.

Sol turned to face her now. The solemn look on his face let her know the call was serious. "Now, don't get too upset, Hildy. This isn't for a joy ride. Calvin says there's a situation brewing up the mountain. They've got a missing person and they need people to help find her quickly before the weather gets even worse, especially before dark."

"Well, why didn't you say so from the beginning? A scenic drive is out of the question, but I am always willing to help the neighbors. Who is missing? Anyone we know?" was Hildy's response.

"No, no one we know. It's one of Jack's clients. They were doing an orienteering course, and she disappeared on the way down the mountain on the training exercise. I guess she'll fail the course then, won't she?" was Sol's attempt to lighten the atmosphere.

"Solomon Penfield! How can you joke about such a serious thing?" Hildy responded.

"Well, Hildy, if you can't keep things humorous, there's no fun in life. There's enough misery to go around and you know it. You've been with me enough years to know I take things seriously though I joke," Sol answered indignantly.

"Thirty-two years, to be exact! You're right. You take me by surprise sometimes though. I suppose that's why I've stayed attached to you for so many years. You keep things unpredictable; like taking me out on such a miserable day. Who else would I go out with in this weather?" Hildy said shaking her head at the idea.

"No one else I hope, Hon. We'd better pack some supplies to take with us. We should take some food to feed the crowd. It's likely that the rescue squad will need to be fed, as well as any others that Calvin has gathered to go there," was Sol's reply.

"I'm glad that I made those extra sandwiches in case the power went out. Now they'll be put to good use. I'll make some lemonade and put it in the large drink cooler. We'd better put a case of bottled water in the van too." Hildy was halfway into the kitchen before Sol could reply. "Could you grab the rain suits from the garage? And pull our boots from the closet, too."

Hildy was always efficient and a good organizer. She probably would have made a good drill sergeant, Sol thought, as he went to do what she asked. She had always kept Dr. Kemp's office running smoothly and miraculously on time. No wonder, the doctor was probably afraid to run overtime with his patients with Hildy setting out his schedule. He could no longer hear her orders as he went into the garage to get the rain suits, nonetheless, she continued to talk.

As Sol returned to the kitchen with the yellow rain gear in hand, he found that Hildy had already partly filled the food cooler with a feast. How she could work so quickly always amazed him. She stopped as she heard him return. "You know, I sense this could get ugly before we're through. I think we'd better do some serious Praying before we leave. Have you got the flashlights?"

Sol chuckled to himself. Was that what she was telling him to get when he went into the garage? He never did hear it, but would redeem himself quickly by coming in with them anyway. He nipped back into the garage and emerged with flashlights in hand. Hildy smiled as she saw him with them, knowing why he had to go back for them, but saying nothing about it. "Can you think of anything else we're missing?"

Sol paused before he divulged the next bit of information. He was not sure how Hildy would take it; nevertheless she needed to know about it. "Calvin also mentioned that the bear that has been messing with the campground has been sighted near the mountain. The presence of the animal control officer seems to have spooked it and it has moved back into the woods for the moment. Unfortunately, it might mean that it will be in our backyards or on the mountain itself. Either way, it's not great. I'd better bring the rifle, just in case. No sense coming unprepared."

Hildy thought for a moment before she spoke. "That will give us one more thing to Pray about, won't it? We'll have to add Psalm 91 to our covering Prayer of protection for all the searchers, as well as our missing lady. We'll need those angels to blanket the area for us under the circumstances."

"It never hurts to have all the help we can muster. Are we ready to leave then?" Sol replied as he grabbed an ammunition box from the locked cabinet in the den.

"Almost. I just have to grab my Bible and I'll be set on my end. We can Pray when we get into the van before we leave. I didn't expect this type of excitement when I got up today; then again, I suppose that is what we have been gearing up for, isn't it?"

"This and maybe a lot more, you never know," was Sol's observation as he grabbed the cooler to load into the van. "How much did you pile in this thing? It weighs a ton!"

"Just enough to feed the army I expect we'll encounter today. Tomorrow, I'll make more. Just be glad I didn't pack for two days!" was Hildy's cheery reply as she picked up the thermos and her Bible. "Now I'm ready to leave. We're Armed and Dangerous."

As Evangeline lay in the utter darkness, terror climbed from the pit of her stomach into her chest. She was not sure if her difficulty breathing was owing to her rising panic or the awkward position in which she found herself. *Close your eyes. You'll be safe then. Concentrate. What is*

the last thing you remember happening? The course. The mountain. The ridge. Oh, yeah, the ridge. She could not remember what was important about the ridge or what happened after she reached it. Her thoughts were muddled. She sensed her emotions more than the details about what occurred on the mountain. She felt anger and frustration, exasperation, perhaps desperation. But why, she did not know.

What had happened to bring her into this dank, dark cavernous place? *What was that? It sounds like a rumble. The earth isn't shaking so it can't be an earthquake. Maybe a heavy truck or something. Was it a motor? No, no it's fading.* Her mind would not focus long enough to be logical. *What could cause a noise like that? There's water trickling close by. Is it a stream?* The sounds did not make sense. What did they have to do with this predicament? She squeezed her eyes as if the action would force her brain to comprehend the events.

Then another noise caught her attention. This one sounded like scratching followed by pebbles trickling down the rocks. She held her breath. *What was that? I'm not alone. Is it someone to help or hurt me? It is a person or an animal or what?* Now she faced a decision, to open her eyes and try to look for the source of the sound or continue to close out any possible image of danger. Panic was rising like her heart rate. Her breath constricted in short painful gasps. *Paul, where are you when I need you?*

Paul was in Jack's face now. He wanted answers, concrete ones, no more evasiveness. "What do you mean; we should wait for the rescue team to arrive? We're able-bodied people and can get started now."

Jack held up his hands for emphasis as he said, "Paul, slow down. We need to go over a few things before we go up the mountain again. We need to do things systematically. I don't want to waste time here anymore than you do. With the weather closing in like it is, I want to do this quickly too. Trust me, I've done this many times before and there's a good way to do it and, well, a not so good way to attack the problem. Let's do it right, okay?"

Jack was trying to slow the pace of things to avoid panic from anyone. He had enough experience to know that circumstances like this could boil over for the most reasonable, placid person. A rescue scenario followed a logical sequence and he was not going to be goaded into by-passing what he knew best. It was his area of proficiency and his training was kicking in now. In any rescue there was one-part training, one of preparation and another measure of pure instinct involved. If Paul pushed him too hard, he knew that the latter might slip past him. He knew this mountain like the back of his hand, or so he thought. Nothing usually got by him here and he was going to use all his gut feelings to perfect a plan.

"Hey, you're the man here, Jack. We're at your disposal to work this out, right Paul?" Mac intervened. The rain was pelting now, driven by stiff gusts of wind. "Why don't we climb in the van and discuss what you need us to know?"

Paul glanced over at Mac, about to reply, then thought better of it. He just looked down at the ground and shrugged. He clenched his jaw, fighting off his urge to charge the mountain without them. Flashbacks of stories he had covered whipped through his mind, reminding him that impulsive moves usually ended tragically. It took all his logic to overcome his fear. He reluctantly followed the group as they climbed into the van.

A flash of lightning illuminated the blackened sky. Immediately, an earsplitting crash of thunder cascaded around them. It sounded like the mountain would descend with the sound. Sarah shuddered, suddenly drawing in her breath as though it might be her last for a while. She looked over at Mac without saying a word, but her message was clear. She never liked storms, especially not thunderstorms with gale force winds, and this experience was quickly stirring up her fears. Mac knew this but did not betray her confidence. He grabbed her hand and squeezed it and looked into her eyes. It was the reassurance she needed and she slowly exhaled.

Jack turned in his seat to face everyone. Eddie sat beside him in the front seat, Paul, Mac and Sarah in the second row of seating. It was a snug fit, but no one seemed to care under the circumstances. "That's better; out of the rain, we can discuss this better. I'll put the heater on so we can get dry. It may still be warm weather, but it doesn't take much to chill you when you're wet and the wind is blowing like it is. There's no sense causing more casualties by not protecting yourselves. The first rule of rescue is staying away from situations that put you at risk of needing rescue yourself. We don't want to be either looking for a second individual or having to extricate someone else. Does everyone understand this?"

Each person nodded and murmured agreement. Jack looked at Paul a little longer than Paul found comfortable. He wanted to gauge his mood. He realized that Paul was ready to go off like a firecracker at the least provocation, so he measured his words carefully as he continued. "When we go back up the mountain, we'll go in groups. It would be better to wait for assistance to be more effective. I know you want to go immediately, but given the conditions, I would prefer to have backup with people I've worked with previously. No offense to you guys, because I know you'll do the best you know how. It is just that I need you to know more than you do now to be effective without more supervision. I can't be concentrating on watching over you and doing my job in a rescue capacity the way I should. I'll go over the techniques we'll be using and assign you to Eddie's care while I work with the rescue personnel when they arrive. You'll still be working with us. We just need to structure your help to prevent accidents. Is that all clear?"

Paul was about to speak when he thought better of it. He realized that there was no use continuing to batter his point home the need for urgency. It was not his mountain or his territory. His opinions were just that, opinions. His comments would be based on emotion and partial knowledge and he should shut his mouth until he gathered more facts. That was what a good reporter would do and that was what he was trained for, not mountain rescue. Paul reluctantly agreed with Jack, as did the others. For the moment, he would allow Jack to lead the rescue, at least if they were still making progress, doing something that made sense and would get Gel off that mountain in one piece.

"The fundamental method we'll use is to break out into groups to search patterned areas. That way we don't miss anything and don't have to cover ground more than once. We will be looking for clues of any sort. It could be bits of cloth or clothing, footprints, broken stems that convey a trail, the direction that the person has walked. Nothing should be overlooked; even the most trivial can be significant. If you find anything that might be relevant, stop where you are immediately and let your team leader know. In this case it will likely be Eddie."

"We want to begin our efforts where Paul and Evangeline separated. The variables are how far apart each searcher will be from one another and how far we expand the search area. That will be partly determined by how many people show up to aid us and if we find anything relevant to pinpoint the search."

Jack paused before he went any further. He did not want to proceed with the instructions, if he had lost them at this point. He realized that the emotional investment they had could have deafened their ears to hear what he was saying. He could not tell where their minds had wandered since he began to speak. "I just want to make sure that we're in agreement. What do you understand from what I just told you?"

Mac glanced at Sarah and Paul and replied on their behalf, "Well, I guess, uhh, that we'll start at the ridge where Gel started to walk westward. Paul, Sarah and I will join with Eddie to walk out a grid of sorts, looking for any signs that she went in a particular direction. We'll space out, how far would you say, Jack?"

"Oh, to begin with, probably a few feet at most, so you don't miss anything. After that, it will depend on how many people we have to help us. But I'd prefer that you stay close to one another. That way Eddie can be sure where you are. If we don't get much help, you'll have to keep Eddie in the middle of the pattern so he has contact with you. Let's leave the wider search to the pros who are joining us, shall we?" answered Jack, looking each in the eye but Paul, who was looking out the window.

"We can live with that, right Mac, Paul? We just want to help. I have no interest in making this harder for you and I am sure no one else does either," Sarah was quick to answer. She did not want to give Paul a chance to push the issue. As far as she was concerned, she wanted to rely on Jack's expertise. She had no interest in acting like a superhero and wanted to prevent Mac from doing it either. Paul, no doubt had separate motives, but she thought it was in their best interests to keep him contained at the moment.

"Good, then we can cover some things to look for in more detail," Jack continued. He wanted to give the rescue team a little more time to reach the embarkation point before he let this group loose on the mountain. The longer he spent on teaching, the better his chances were of getting an experienced crew here to back him up. He had enough understanding of these circumstances to realize skill was better than mere willingness to help. He needed people who he could trust in a bad situation. He had always had himself, his training and his buddies to rely on. That was where he was comfortable, and it was not about to change now in a miserable storm. But how long could he stall these folks?

Chapter 11

The wind picked up intensity as it swooped from the ever lowering clouds. It was as though the sky had fallen thousands of feet, preventing the clouds from rising. They now seemed hemmed in by an unseen force from above. This hand pushed the air into increasingly tumultuous gusts overhead and now from the sides, buffeting anything and anyone in its way.

Driven by the velocity of the wind, the rain pushed downward, gathering speed as it descended. Waters inched upward in reservoirs, lakes and streams, contained by banks that had not seen so much volume so quickly in many a year. The excess liquid searched for outlets into which to escape, overflowing wherever it was trapped. Where the rains had fallen in the previous week, the ground could not absorb any additional moisture. That meant overflow water was breaking out as it was pushed on by the law of gravity.

Gradually this onslaught of water searched for places to flow ever downward. It descended the mountain to the valley beyond the mountain where dry gullies longed for moisture. These ravines were unprepared for such a deluge of water; there was no time to absorb it as it tumbled down so vigorously. Mountain top to lake to valley in minutes, gathering momentum, the urgency of its descent multiplied as the seconds ticked by. An unseen hand massaged the path, pushed the water forward, downward, onward toward the unsuspecting people below.

Lacey toured the property taking inventory in her mind as she surveyed the scene. Everything seemed in order at the moment. It was all as she had left it a while ago, but something was nagging at the edges of her senses. It felt like someone or something was lurking in the periphery of her vision. It was not tangible; just a feeling that all was not 'right'. She had encountered the same feeling the day Warren had the accident. It was not something she liked to remember, much less replay. It nagged at her. The last time she had thought it was a silly notion to be brushed off. This time it skirted the fringes of her consciousness enough to tease her, tempting her into the fear she would rather avoid.

She was no longer the same woman that faced that situation. Time had passed; she knew more about her enemy this time. She recognized the calling card. She could smell its presence; the sense twisted a knot in her stomach. It was decision time now. Would she face it or run like before? Nausea tried to distract her focus.

"I'm coming for you again. I'll finish what I started the first time."

Lacey responded in righteous anger, "No, you don't! Not this time, you fool. In the Name of Jesus, you take your hands off what is mine! You don't know what you are up against this time. This time I am Prepared and I am not alone. This time you're going down; not me, not my family, not my friends! It's your turn. So now you'd better fear me. This time I am 'Armed and Dangerous' and I won't let up and I won't let go. I put you on warning; listen up and stand back. I will use my full Arsenal and I won't hold back."

The winds shifted in the trees, groaning and straining as they passed. A branch cracked off the pine to Lacey's left. It sailed through the air and landed with a mighty crash inches from striking her. Lacey looked up at the angry skies above her and nodded, realizing a duel had just begun. It was the first blow, but ineffective in its efforts. She was Armed as no mere mortal could understand. She knew her enemy more than it knew her this time. Her Preparation would reap benefits.

Eli headed back to Lacey's house, driving over the crest of the hill overlooking her property as the branch came down beside her. He put the truck in park and ran down to meet her. The look on her face startled him. He had never seen her appearance so stern and disapproving. He immediately thought she had been hit by the branch.

Lacey jumped as he reached her, not hearing him approach. "Lacey, are you alright? That was close. It didn't hit you, did it?" Eli exclaimed.

Lacey turned to look at him, half expecting to see someone else. When she realized it was Eli, she smiled. Chuckling, she answered, "It takes more than that to take me out Eli." She paused and took a breath. "I think we might need to change our tactics a little though. This storm is turning in to a monster and needs to be treated as such. I think we need to do some quick research to prepare us better. Come into the house. I think I know what we need to do now. I don't know why I didn't think of it earlier."

Eli was taken aback at her sudden change of expression and eagerness to get going. His curiosity was piqued. Knowing Lacey as he did, he was about to learn something he had never encountered. It was always an adventure when she got excited like this. It was obvious she was onto something and he was determined that she would share it with him. The problem was he also realized that they were in a rush. He did not want her to get sidetracked and waste time that they could not spare. What could they possibly research in such a short period?

They entered the house, quickly taking off their rain gear and boots, dropping them by the door. The house was quiet except the ticking of the grandfather clock in the hallway. Lacey flicked on the light switch in the hall leading to her study. *At least we still have our electricity. I wonder when the next strike will occur and with what force? That is his way, hit without warning; take you by surprise. Well, this time I will keep tabs on him better than the last. Now I have better resources!*

Lacey opened the door to the study revealing walls lined with books. This room always excited Eli. Lacey had books on every topic imaginable. When she did not have a suitable book, she knew where to look on the Internet. Her resources seemed endless. He was interested now.

"Hey, uhh, Lacey, you know that we have to get back soon, right? You know what you're looking for in all this? There has to be hundreds of books here. We don't have much time."

Lacey turned toward Eli. The look on her face surprised him. She had always seemed like a kind teacher in the past. He had not seen such fierceness from her before. It was not anger exactly, but a resolute appearance that gave him pause. Something had changed in the time since he dropped her off and he did not understand why.

Lacey immediately pulled out an index box, flipping through several cards until she hit the right one, she then pulled it out. She scanned down the list on the card and turned immediately, heading to the bookshelves to her right. She stood there for a minute or two, searching the titles until she found the one she wanted. She then pulled out a blue volume with no dust jacket, looking like it must be at least fifty years old. She then moved to the left side of the room, climbed a stepladder and reached to the top shelf to find another book with a leather cover of a similar vintage. Climbing down the ladder again she walked to her desk by the window. Beside her computer was a thick file folder. Lacey pulled out half the papers and put them into a manila envelope.

"Okay, I'm ready now," Lacey said as she turned to leave the room. She gave Eli no explanations as she headed out of the room. Reaching for the light switch, she gave Eli a look as if to say 'are you coming?' and as he started to follow her, she turned out the lights. Lacey was all business now and it was apparent she was on a mission. She grabbed her Bible from the coffee table in the great room, putting it and her other books and papers in a knapsack she pulled from the closet by the door. Before Eli could react, she turned to go back in to the kitchen bumping into him as he had followed close on her heels.

"Oh, sorry. I didn't realize you were there. We ought to bring a few more things with us for supplies. I was so intent on the research materials that I almost forgot the water and food. Could you pull the cooler from the back porch?" Lacey had an agenda and there seemed no stopping her.

"Whoa, Lacey. Hold on a second. I know I said we only had a short time, but now you're going too fast. We're likely to forget something at this rate. Maybe we should make a list so we don't leave something out."

"Good idea, Eli. My mind is a little preoccupied at the moment. So what should we bring then? There's a case of water on the counter over there, a cooler in the back porch to put it in, and bags of ice in the freezer. I know others will bring some, but you can never have too much. I'll pull some granola bars from the pantry and a few energy snacks. I put together a box of emergency supplies in the screened in porch as well; stuff like flashlights and ropes, rain gear, extra socks and T-shirts, a couple of sweaters. It's in the green storage bin. Oh, and there are extra batteries in the blue box beside it. You'd better pick that up too."

"Okay, sounds good. You said those boxes were out on the porch?" Eli responded as he headed toward the door.

"Yeah, but have you got room in your truck for all this stuff?" Lacey asked as she came back into the kitchen with an arm filled with loot from the pantry. Before she finished the sentence, she had dropped them into a plastic storage bin she had pulled from the shelves in the pantry.

"No problem, Lacey, I have room in the truck bed. I cleaned the storage unit out yesterday to make room for those boxes I took to Horace and Nan's. I still have the tool box in there for emergencies, but there is plenty of room for everything and we still have the back seat available for anything you need to keep dry."

"Oh, yes, I did forget that this truck is bigger than your last one. It has a back seat. That'll work well, won't it now?" Lacey mused. She was about to head out the door to begin loading up when she stopped. "I do suppose we had better come armed though, considering the bear sighting. This weather will probably have it looking for cover. But you never know, I guess, depending on how hungry it is we might encounter it. I'd prefer to be prepared, you know."

"Have you got a rifle, Lacey? I didn't take you for a hunter," Eli questioned.

Lacey shook her head and responded, "Warren was the hunter in the family. He taught me how to use it and care for it. I've continued to keep up with it a little now that he's gone, mostly for security, you know. We're in wilderness country. It can be isolated at times and as we know there are bears around the area. So, yes, I do have a rifle, but, because you're more experienced with it as a hunter, I'll gladly give it to you to use today. I'd prefer to concentrate my efforts in the areas that I am more comfortable with, like my books, research materials and listening for Answers. We all should stick with what we're good at in a situation like this."

Eli paused in his packing and turned to Lacey saying, "You'll have to tell me more about Warren someday. He sounds like the kind of guy I might have liked."

"When this storm is over and things are quieter, I'll be glad to, Eli. But now we'd better get going so we don't hold anyone up. I'll go get the rifle and ammunition and meet you out at the truck. I think I'll just say an extra Prayer for the place as I leave though, just for good measure. I want everything to be here in good condition when we get off the mountain. I think all of us might be back later and need to use the facilities. I want to be sure nothing happens while we're away, what with this storm and all."

"Good idea. I'll load up the truck while you do that." As he headed for the door, a flash of lightning illuminated the house, followed by an immediate crash of thunder. The storm was overhead. As he turned the handle to open the door, the wind caught it and blew it open with a slam. The lights flickered but stayed on. Lacey glanced back at Eli and they nodded, knowing what they might face later in the day when they returned.

"Don't worry. The generator is ready," Lacey said as she disappeared into the back bedroom to get the rifle. With that Eli continued out the door, boxes stacked in his arms as he headed toward the truck. He hoped they had everything they might need. The skies seemed to have darkened even more if that was possible. *We'll need the headlights on now. It's like dusk already and it's only mid afternoon. What kind of storm is this anyway?*

Evangeline lie there listening in the darkness. The sounds had stopped, except the running water; that had increased if anything. She heard the occasional rumbling noise though and it was loud at times. But the scratching noises had stopped and that was what concerned her the most. She feared the unknown sounds, the ones that made her sense that someone or something was there, but staying hidden. The thought that someone or something was hiding in this darkness just petrified her. Somehow, she reasoned, it was far easier to fight off the fear of an identified object than an unknown entity. She knew of too many things that her imagination could concoct to explain the noises and they were far too terrifying to contemplate at the moment. How could she be in such a predicament and why was she alone?

Okay, now what can I do to help myself? I can't rely on anyone else to help me. Take a breath. Slow your breathing, girl. I have to move this strap. It's digging in so tightly I can hardly breathe. I know it hurt to move before, but I just have to do it. Evangeline shifted slightly, inch by inch, whimpering with the pain, until finally the knapsack could be moved out of the way. *Oh, that's better. Maybe I can think now that it is off me. Now what about my leg? What can I do to make that better?*

Evangeline took a deep satisfying breath and just stayed there for a minute trying to make a plan. She knew she had to move. No matter what, she could not function while lying in such an awkward position. But how was she to disentangle herself without causing intense pain? She told herself she would have to go ahead and just do it. These words gave her pause. Had she not long ago said the same thing to a friend who was recovering from an injury and attempting to get back into a workout program? She regretted those words now. What was she thinking?

Just try to move your foot first. See what happens. You've got nothing to lose, maybe a little pain for a bit. She closed her eyes tighter as if that effort would transfer energy to her legs. Slowly she moved her right ankle. That was alright. Now was the test, the left leg was bent off to the side. *Just start with your toes. You can do that much. Okay, so they move. Now what about the ankle? Just try to move your foot a little at a time. Hold your breath if you have to, just do it.*

Evangeline winced in pain as she forced herself to move her foot. It did work, so clearly her foot was not injured. So now she had to consider the knee. This she knew would be a problem. She had already felt the pain and could hardly face it again. But what was worse? Staying here in the dark, alone, with whatever had made that noise before, or trying to do something to get out of there? She had to be able to assess her surroundings better and lying here in such an awkward position was not going to do it. Gingerly, as she grabbed her leg with both hands to steady it, she started to unhook her knee. She cried in agony as her foot seemed caught on a rock or something. Panting from the pain, she tried to regain focus. *Why won't this work? I can't move it.* Reclaiming her composure took all her energy. Panic seemed to surge inside her.

Lying here will get you nowhere. You have to do this for yourself, girl. Face it; you have no one to help you. You just have to do this however how much it hurts! She now felt fear of the unknown and the pain, but it was slowly being mixed with anger. She was not sure what she was angry with: maybe the pain, maybe the circumstances, maybe the lack of help. Nevertheless, it was giving her a surge of adrenaline that she needed now. With a sudden howl, she rolled to her left to free her leg from its impediment. She had never felt such agony in her life before, but she had liberated her leg. Next came the hard part, rolling right again to lie on her back. Surely it could not hurt as much this time, could it?

If you could do the last movement, getting back should be easy. You just do it now before you lose your nerve. She let out another wail, but this time it was not as loud. She slumped, exhausted from the effort, panting and half whimpering. The extreme exertion had left her drenched in sweat despite the cool, dank atmosphere.

Lying there, she calmed her breathing for several minutes. She could not move a muscle, except those used to breathe. Her exhaustion was profound. Her mind was numb. How long she remained there she was not sure, nor did she care at the moment. She might have dozed off for all she knew. Nothing mattered now. She just needed to rest.

Then she heard it again. It started at the recesses of her brain. It began as awareness, a sensation, growing in intensity until she knew she was awake and there was a sound and a presence a distance away. It was that scratching sound again. Her heart almost stopped when she realized that the noise was in this wretched hole with her. Apprehension rose in her chest as she caught her breath. *What was that? Is my mind playing tricks on me?* This time she heard it again, fully conscious of the noise echoing in her rocky prison; this time louder, distinct. Her mind raced through possible images. Fear mounted. She could sense something beyond her reach, not far beyond her position. A sound, a presence. Then it stopped, leaving her alone with her horrible thoughts.

Chapter 12

Sol and Hildy had gone about a half mile when they encountered a silver sedan by the side of the road. Sol pulled behind it and put the van in park. "What's up now, I wonder?" Hildy said to herself and to Sol.

"I don't know, but we'd better check things to make sure they don't need our help," was Sol response.

Hildy followed Sol out of their red Montana van. It did not take them long to realize the problem as they approached the car. The runoff from the side of the mountain had gouged a rivulet across the road, up to a foot deep in spots and almost two feet across. It was too deep for the car to cross and borderline for their van as well. The other driver was standing in front of the car weighing his choice as Sol approached from behind him. "That looks bad there, doesn't it?" Sol said as he got nearer to the stranger.

The man looked back at Sol, obviously surprised to hear his voice. "I didn't hear you coming with rain coming down so hard and the wind. Yeah, it's too deep to cross here. I was just wondering if I could fill it in with some dirt or branches or rocks. I was visiting the Coulter's up the road and thought I had better get back to town to make sure my wife was okay at home, but I didn't think the road would be damaged so soon. It's turning out to be some storm. You don't usually get them this bad up here, do you?"

Sol chuckled. "No, it's mighty unusual for us here. We might get strange weather patterns at times, where it rains up here and it's dry down in the valley, but this storm is way beyond the norm. It looks as if we've got some work to do before we can go any further. I'll go back to our house and get some shovels and whatever else I figure we can use. I hope you don't mind a little manual labor."

"Don't worry about me. I'm used to hard work," the man responded.

"Well, stranger, welcome to Seeley's Mountain and Big Rock Lake. My name is Solomon Penfield and this is my wife Hildy."

"My name's John Wilson. Pleased to meet you. I guess you've saved me some grief. I'll help you out with whatever you need to do to get us across this ditch. I suppose you have to help your neighbors at times."

"We work together to be a neighborhood watch. It's especially helpful for the residents who live here in the winter. We kind of watch each other's backs. It's the way of life up here, you know," Sol answered as he headed toward his van. "Why don't you stay here and flag down any drivers who might be coming along, so they don't get stuck in that trench. I won't be long; we're just down the road from here."

Hildy followed Sol back to the van and climbed in and called to John as they turned around, "Don't worry; we won't leave you here long. We'll be right back with the tools we need to repair this, however temporary as it may be. We'll get you going soon!"

With that, they drove off into the driving rain. The clouds had descended even further making it seem like early evening already. Sol and Hildy looked at each other without saying a word. They read each other's thoughts, which happened often after thirty-two years together. What they realized was it was just the beginning of what they had to expect over the next few hours.

Lacey and Eli came from the opposite direction around the lake. The creek that ran through a culvert under the access road was full to overflowing, tumbling over the rocks, splashing over its usual banks, finding new paths to flow on its way down the mountain.

"It won't be long before that messes up the road there, Lacey. I hope we don't have a difficult time getting back to the house later," commented Eli. "It's a good thing this truck has four-wheel drive."

"We'll just have to work with it when the time comes, Eli. I imagine this day's going to be exciting, so we'll just take it one problem at a time."

"I have shovels in the back of the truck still from helping Nan with her new garden. If we need 'em, we'll be prepared at least. It's a good thing I didn't take them out," Eli observed.

"Maybe you got a little extra Direction that you didn't realize at the time, Eli. You've been getting better at Listening lately, so maybe it was Planned for you," Lacey countered. "I've concluded that little happens by chance, you know."

"Yeah, I guess you're right," Eli responded. "Just look at that creek. Whoa, it won't take much more before it overflows over there. Wow!"

"Just as I suspected, Eli, we're in for a difficult day and night too, if this keeps up. Let's get back to Jack and get this search under way! There's obviously no time to spare."

Jack was relieved when he saw Sam Fowler's truck pull into the clearing. He could not hold this group off any longer. He was glad Bob had come through and convinced his friend of the urgent nature of his request. It had only been thirty or forty minutes, but felt much longer while handling an anxious husband and his friends. The tension was thick in the van and he could not fill the time with more instructions.

Sam's arrival shifted the atmosphere. He felt right in his element again. It was what he was trained for and now he had back up. Sam and his crew were better at talking with the worried family members. His expertise was in the actual search and rescue. Sure he was personable enough and everyone liked him. He treated people decently when he was around the victim's friends and family, but it was a strain on him. Once he got into a groove during a search and rescue, he preferred to stay in that mode. So far, today, there was already too much emotional baggage to distract him from the task at hand. He would prefer to give that job to those with expert training in that area. As far as he was concerned, he was better off sticking to what he did best and that was finding people.

Jack had always found his target alive; well, if you did not count the elderly hunter who had died of a heart attack before the search began. The fellow had collapsed with his buddy while hunting and his friend had gone for help, but could not remember where they had been before he left him. The outcome was a body recovery unfortunately, but the coroner had determined that he probably had died before his friend had left to get help. That situation had stuck with him for a while and he was determined not to repeat it.

That might be why he just wanted to concentrate on the search. He did not want to get too emotionally charged or attached in a rescue scenario. It divided his attention and was not productive use of time. He just wanted to leave it to the psychologist types. They could do their thing, he was better to do his. Unfortunately, this time he already was linked to the friends and family of the victim. He could not get around it. He just wanted to hand that part of the job over to someone else soon. He would explain that he could serve them better if he worked directly with Sam and they stayed with Eddie. They could still participate but in a much more controlled manner that way. *Man, I hate it when these things get complicated. Well, I never lost a client before; that might explain it. It makes no sense how this happened. Now how do I explain this one to Sam?*

Jack opened the van and nodded at Eddie to take care of the group in the back row. "Just stay put here with Eddie while I fill Sam in on what's happened," Jack said as he slid out of his seat. With that he slammed the door shut and ran toward Sam's truck, shielding his face from the driving rain. Sam met him halfway across the lot.

"Hey, Sam! How you doing? Thanks for coming," Jack said as he clasped hands with Sam. Sam was a mountain of a man, at least three inches taller than Jack with broad shoulders. He grabbed Jack's arm as he shook his hand. Despite his athletic build, he dwarfed Jack as he walked beside him back toward Sam's truck.

"No problem Jack. You know I'd do anything for you, buddy. You've saved my skin so many times, I'll owe you till I retire!" was Sam's quick reply. "So what's the story here? One of your clients took off on a course?"

"Yeah. I can't understand it. Maybe you can help figure it out. It was one of the easiest exercises I do with clients. I mean, really. How can you get lost if you just go down the hill? Something has to have happened that I can't explain yet. It makes no sense otherwise." Jack was talking with his back to the van in which Eddie was babysitting his clients. He did not want them to realize that he was so frustrated with them. He had enough trouble already and did not want to add to it.

"Look, Jack, you and I both know that everything has a logical explanation and end. We just have to backtrack sometimes to find it. Maybe you've just been following false leads so far. You fill me in what you know so far then I'll talk to your clients. Between the two we'll probably settle this thing quickly. I have a few other crew members on their way and they should be here soon. They just had to mobilize their gear. The roads are getting a little treacherous so it may take a little longer to get here, but they should arrive by the time we finish questioning your people."

Jack filled Sam in on all that had occurred on the mountain. He let Sam know the tension between Paul and Evangeline before she disappeared. This added dynamic was important to the event and could factor in to the actions of the missing person. "I don't know the status of the marriage. They seemed to all get along well yesterday. Evangeline seemed a little cautious about the wilderness environment. She's more a city girl, but was giving it her best effort from the looks of it. Maybe something spooked her or something. I just don't know." Jack shook his head in disgust.

Sam frowned a little. "There's something we're missing, I think. It just doesn't make sense the way you're telling it. Let's talk to the husband and see if he fills in more details."

They started to walk to the van. Eddie was keeping them occupied by talking to them about more clues to look for in the terrain. He was giving them examples of things he had found in past searches. He also pointed out that they had always had successful searches. This distracted Paul for a while, but Eddie could tell that he was beginning to get impatient again. Jack came back just in time. He did not think he could hold him down much longer.

When Paul saw Jack walking with Sam, he got out of the van immediately. He had had enough waiting. He was not going to tolerate more stalling from Jack or Eddie. Mac and Sarah were close on his heels. They too wanted some progress, but they also wanted to make sure Paul did not start to get into it with Jack again.

Jack and Sam could see the tension building as the threesome approached. It was not the first time they had counseled the agitated companions of a lost individual, but it was the first time it was one of Jack's clients. Jack deferred to Sam's expertise in this instance partly because Sam was good at what he did, and partly because Jack wanted to ease out of that role. It was good to let Sam seem to be in control of the rescue. Anyway, he was too close to this one to be objective.

"Folks, this is Sam Fowler. He's the director of the Search-and-Rescue squad in this district." He and I have worked together many times. Sam and his team are aces in their field. We need to let Sam execute what he's good at doing. I'd appreciate it if you would cooperate with him, even if some of it seems a little redundant. He's going to begin with asking you a few questions, just to make sure that we haven't missed anything. I realize we need to move quickly, but it will go a long way to narrowing our search and saving us time."

Jack introduced everyone; meanwhile, Sam was watching body language. Every little clue was essential in dissecting a disappearance. He did not want to miss anything.

Jack turned as he heard Bob pull into the clearing with his truck. Jack was relieved that he now had an excuse to leave. He glanced back to Sam and, said, "Sam, why don't you take it from here? Eddie and I'll meet the others in the squadron when they arrive and start filling them in with what we know so far. Then we can gear up and be ready when you finish here."

"Okay, Jack, sounds good to me. Is that alright with you?" Sam responded, looking at Paul, Sarah and Mac. He wanted to maintain a positive rapport with them, considering the high degree of tension in the air.

The threesome shrugged and nodded. They did not have much choice at this point and they knew they were at the mercy of the circumstance. What else could they do?

Jack breathed an inaudible sigh, relieved that Sam had taken over. He could feel himself transitioning already out of the training role and into search-and-rescue mode. His attention would no longer be divided and he could perform at his peak performance. He nodded to the group and strolled toward Bob and his truck. Before long, he and Bob were rearranging gear from inside the truck cap.

Paul watched Jack out of the corner of his eye, as Sam lead them back to the van. He was not sure of what to make of what was happening, and the reporter in him was surveying his actions, sizing up what he was going to do next.

The rain was torrential now, driven hard by strong gusts of wind that hardly abated. When walking into the wind on the way back to van, they had to face its blasts, making it hard to see. They were grateful to climb into the relative comfort of the old van. It was not luxurious, but it was dry and considerably warmer than out in the wind driven rain.

Once settled into their seats, Sam reassured the group that Jack was an expert in his field. "We've worked on many situations together; lost hunters, fishermen, campers and children. We've been involved together in every possible rescue you can imagine. Jack is solid in his experience and I can promise you that if you are straight with him, he'll do the same for you. He'll give you his best and it's a lot more than most people will do. He'll go out on the line for you.

"Now, what I need from you is a complete picture of what happened up there, no details left out or added, just what happened. Any changes to the story and it can throw us off and waste time." He looked each in eye, one by one, ending with Paul. Paul was uncomfortable with this emphasis, as though Jack had told him that he was holding back somehow.

"So who wants to begin? We need to start from the beginning. How did you decide to come up here?"

This started an intensive questioning session. The more Sam knew about the details of the motivation for the trip, the better he could get to know the group and understand their actions. A good history saved time every time and he knew the drill well. When you follow procedure precisely, things just work. Today they needed everything to run smoothly because the weather was working against them.

The clouds collided, while the air pressure tumbled, moisture gathered, and winds escalated. It was all in the plan. The evil entity within this storm drew energy from these conditions and created them at the same time. It fuelled itself and moved downward, pushing itself on those below. The excitement was in its unpredictability, the changeability moment to moment. It kept these mortals guessing and wondering, off guard. What could be more tantalizing than watching these fools mount their preparations only to find them inadequate compared to the forces unleashed on them. And what could they do against this might? No army or navy could stop it once it was set in motion. They could merely watch in horror until it ran its course. What delicious satisfaction it brought to the ogre, knowing they were all at its mercy. And mercy, well, it had none.

Headline: North Carolina coastline: Devastation beyond compare.

The news reports were starting to filter in gradually. All power was disrupted to the area, so were telephone and cell-phone capabilities.

Any available power was supplied by generators at this point. Water was fouled and undrinkable. The flooding had reached unthinkable levels in some areas and was only beginning to recede, so far inland did it penetrate.

Any residents who remained in the area and had survived the ordeal were in shock and horror. Rescue crews hardly knew where to begin their efforts; such was the demoralizing scene that presented itself before them.

The shoreline was unrecognizable. Stately mansions were reduced to shells and often rubble. Some sailboats were on top of houses that miraculously were still standing.

Many compared the scene before them to what they would expect if a nuclear bomb attack had just taken place. An air of hopelessness and grief surrounded them. How could one reassemble the pieces of lives shattered here, where, in so many instances, there was nothing to put back together or gather to take elsewhere? These were people beaten and mortified by the attack of unexpected proportions.

The call for help was loud and long. An urgent plea went out for all available agencies to bring assistance with all life sustaining supplies and equipment. Hospitals were damaged and often barely functioning. Casualties were mounting by the minute and there were not enough personnel or supplies to handle them. They could not begin to convey the critical nature of the appeal. Life and death was on the line for many survivors.

Cape Fear had fulfilled its name this day.

Sol and Hildy had managed to get back to their house unscathed and quickly set to finding all available shovels and picks and other gardening implements which might prove helpful. Sol picked up the chainsaw and an extra gas can in case he should need it. The way the weather was rapidly deteriorating, he thought he could expect almost anything.

"Sol, maybe we should bring some garden stakes and cloth to tie to them to warn other vehicles before they drive right into the hole. However well we try to fix it, you know it will only be temporary if this rain doesn't let up. What with the visibility being so bad, they'll probably drive right into it before they even know it's there!" Hildy commented as she headed to her garden supplies.

"Sure thing. So you'll take care of that while I get this stuff loaded?" he called to her. "No problem," was the last thing he heard before she disappeared into the house to retrieve the cloth from her sewing stash.

Sol had gathered most of their tools supplies when Hildy returned from the house. "In case this goes on longer than we hope, maybe you should throw in the portable generator and lights. We've got room in the back of the van, so it won't hurt to throw it in. It would be a pain to have to come back again later."

"It's not a big deal to come back here and it takes up extra room in there," Sol protested.

"Look, Sol, given the road conditions, I think it could be a big deal, so humor me will you and please just put it in?" Hildy was insistent and Sol realized that there would be no arguing with her about it. How much frustration did he want to cause himself? He quickly decided that disagreeing with her was more work than moving the tools he had already packed into the van to make room for the generator.

"So are we all set then? Any last-minute details?" Sol was used to being almost out of the driveway and having to stop to do some extra errand Hildy insisted on adding.

"No, I threw in some extra first aid supplies in case we need them. That should about do it. Let's get going before that road erodes anymore and we have more work to do!"

Sol shook his head. Hildy had a way of talking as if it had been his idea to pack the extra things and cause the delay. However, after thirty-two years of marriage, he knew better than to comment on it.

Hildy climbed into the van beside him, buckled up and Sol put the van in reverse. Once out of the security of the garage, the winds and rain engulfed them again. Sol put the wipers on faster, only to realize that he needed them on full speed. Even then, it was hard to see more than a few feet in front of them. They were forced to creep along the road or risk hitting some hazard. It was proving a treacherous trip to the mountain.

"You know Lacey, I realize you want to get back to Jack right away, but do you mind if we stop into see Nan and Horace? We go right by their place on the way. Nan has had her hands full lately with Horace and I just want to make sure they're alright given the conditions." Eli had spent considerable time over there recently, helping with maintenance on their place. Horace could not do anything constructive and Nan had to devote most of her time to Horace and keeping him safe.

"No problem, Eli. Let's stop in and make sure their house is all secure. It shouldn't take long to do anyway," Lacey responded thoughtfully. They were the one couple in the area who could have serious problems in a situation like this. If Horace were to get out wandering in this weather, especially after dark, the events on the mountain would be the least of their worries. Horace would not last long with his mental status.

They crested a hill and pulled into the driveway of an elegant property. Nan had always prided herself on her lovely gardens, although now it was Eli's job to keep them groomed. Nan was particular about the appearance of their property so she paid Eli well for his work there. She did not want shoddy workmanship and made sure Eli spent enough time manicuring the lawn and weeding the gardens to her specifications. Hers was not the only property that Eli worked on, but it took the most time and kept him well supplied in groceries.

The house itself was a ranch-style wooden structure with a large porch out front. Colorful hanging baskets of pink and purple petunias swayed in the wind, battering the posts to which they were attached.

Eli noticed that Nan had managed to pull in the cushions from the lawn furniture on the patio by the side of the house, but the furniture itself was in danger of blowing away. He immediately headed to the chairs and stacked them and leaned them over by the porch railing. Though the chairs were metal, the wind was so strong that it would not take much to send them flying on to the lawn. He unhooked the porch swing and secured it where it would not blow away. He then took down the hanging baskets so they would not do more damage to the posts. Nan heard the commotion outside and came to the door. She was a full-figured woman in her eighties with stunning white hair pulled back into a clip at the back of her head. She was sharp mentally and willing to do any project you set before her. It was frustrating to her at times that Horace had become such a full-time job to care for, as she was always used to being involved in, not only her gardens, but also the local community activities. She was devoted to her husband of sixty-plus years, and however disabled he became, she would be at his side caring for him as he had for her all their married life. Eli realized that these people were stuck like glue to each other and it would take the grave to separate them.

"Thank you so much Eli. I would've tried to do that myself but I didn't want to leave Horace that long. You know how he wanders when he can't find me," Nan said as she opened the door.

A voice piped up behind her. "Who're you talking to woman? Is that the milkman? Tell him the last milk was sour yesterday!"

"Don't worry, Horace darling. I'll take care of it for you. It's Eli come to help us with the garden furniture. And Lacey is with him!"

"Not one of his better days I see," Eli commented.

"No, it seems when the weather closes in like this he loses it earlier in the day or maybe he's just plain losing it altogether lately. I'm starting to worry about him, you know," Nan sighed glancing toward him with a furrow in her brow. "The doctor said that the medicine would help for only so long and well, he's getting up there in age now. Come on in out of the rain. Can I get you some iced tea or coffee?"

"No, no. Nan we can't stay. We were just on our way to help Jack Davidson with some of his students, but wanted to make sure everything was secure over here as we were driving by."

Lacey smiled at Nan and added, "Nan do you think that it might be an idea to have Gertrude come over and stay with you during the storm? It would give you someone to help with Horace if you need to attend to something, or Gertrude could do it for you." Lacey realized that Nan and Horace were vulnerable under the circumstances and it made sense to have help with them until things were calmer. She kicked herself for not thinking about it sooner.

"Well, I would enjoy the company considering everything that's going on. I have her phone number by the telephone and can call her," Nan said after a moment's consideration.

"Nan! Nan, are you there? Where did you go now? You are always leaving somewhere when I need you, woman!" Horace yelled from the living room.

Lacey intervened, "Nan, you go help Horace and I'll phone Gertrude for you. No better still, we'll go over there now and ask her to come over and help her get here if she agrees. We'll be right back."

"Thank you so much, Lacey. It would be a great help," was Nan's reply as she took off down the hall toward the living room where Horace was rummaging by the bookshelves, looking for goodness knows what.

Gertrude was Nan's next-door neighbor. Being twenty years her junior, she could do many things that Nan was no longer capable of tackling, but Nan did not like to burden her with many things. She supposed that Gertrude had retired up here for peace and solitude and not to take care of a cantankerous old man. She had tried to keep the relationship a friendly neighbor basis and not overstep her welcome. However, Lacey realized that extraordinary circumstances allowed for special requests.

Eli and Lacey walked the hundred feet to Gertrude's small blue bungalow, bowing against the wind and the rain. The rain felt like piercing needles against their faces. They knocked at Gertrude's door and it was immediately answered by a short squat matronly woman with gray curly hair. "Lacey, what brings you here? Is there anything wrong?"

Lacey smiled and answered quickly, "No, Gertrude. We have a favor to ask of you if you don't mind. We were wondering if you would mind coming next door to help Nan with Horace during this storm. We would feel better if they weren't alone given the weather, you know. Is everything okay with your place, by the way?"

"Oh, everything's fine here. I got it all secured and put away when I heard the forecast yesterday. It has sounded progressively worse. This time they might be right about it for once, although unfortunately on the bad side of things. I'll just grab a few things to take then I'll be ready to go. Come on in out of the rain while you wait, I won't be long."

Lacey and Eli stepped into the entry way. A coat stand stood close to the doorway, a tray with a variety of footwear by its side. An ornament cabinet stood a few feet on down the hall, arrayed with knick-knacks that Gertrude had purchased on every trip she had taken since she retired from teaching. From the look of the collection, Gertrude had taken many excursions. As she looked at the objects, Lacey was happy they were all in Gertrude's house and not hers because she wouldn't want to dust them all.

Gertrude returned with a craft bag in one hand and a load of groceries in the other. "This way I'll have something to do and snacks that I like. I don't want to impose on Nan. She has enough to do, goodness knows."

Lacey smiled as Gertrude put on her raincoat and boots, tossing her slippers in her craft bag. They went outside and Eli helped her lock the door behind her, doing a final check that everything was safe before she left. Soon they had her over at Nan's house and settled in to keep each other company. They said their good-byes and assured them that they would try to check them, weather permitting on their way back and if not, by phone.

"I hope that the phone holds out with the storm though," Eli said as they got back into his truck. I suppose that it's something to add to the Prayer list.

"It would not hurt to add anything you think will help. Nan and Horace need a special Covering, I think. They are especially at risk in this type of situation. Well, we had better get back now. Jack will be wondering where we got to."

Evangeline lay still for what seemed like eons. She had no true concept of time down there in the dark. There had been no more scratching sounds for quite some time and she began to wonder if it had all been her imagination running wild. However, she just had been too terrified to try to move; too tired and sore to even contemplate it.

Slowly, she was able to focus on the muffled sounds she could hear outside her cloistered surroundings. She listened for a few minutes and finally decided the rumbling had to be from thunder and it seemed to be increasing in intensity. There had to be a big storm out in the real world. The trickling of water was louder and now sounded like an actual stream. In the recesses of her brain, it had a calming effect on her emotions. Her mind wandered, allowing herself to listen to its soothing flow; relaxing her apprehensions; until the cold hard rock began to dig into her leg and its chill began to penetrate her bones.

She tried to shift her position only to be met once again by a sharp pain in her knee. *At least this time it was localized in my knee. My back seems to have eased since I untwisted.*

Her thoughts were starting to glue together into coherent trains of reasoning. Previously, everything was so random and disjointed, based merely on sensation and emotion. She tried to focus her eyes next. The light was so dim that it made it difficult to make out any shapes.

Remembering the backpack she had removed, she scanned side to side trying to locate it without moving to any great extent. She was afraid of twisting her leg and starting the pain again. It was no use. She was essentially useless lying in this position. Her mind started to question her situation. *It doesn't seem like anyone is coming to help me. Where's Paul? Why hasn't he come to help me? Is he hurt too?* She contemplated her options, one tumbling forth after another. *Should I yell for help? No, wait, that scratching sound. I thought it was an animal! I don't want to call attention to myself if I'm not alone down here. What if it wasn't an animal, maybe it was Paul . . . or maybe someone else?*

Now her mind began to race again, filling in the gaps with all sorts of possible explanations for this predicament. *What kind of person would use this kind of place to hide out? Only some twisted sick-o that's for sure. This is getting altogether too strange. My mind is going crazy.* She closed her eyes again, the old reflex returning, but somehow it was slightly reassuring. *Okay, now breathe slowly. Focus on what you do know, not what could be.* She opened her eyes once again, straining to see her surroundings. It definitely appeared to be some sort of cave, mostly rock and some dirt, and then there was the water. Was her imagination playing tricks on her or was that getting louder now?

Suddenly she startled. The water was pooling around her now. It was cold and she was lying in it. *Oh no, no. This place is filling with water. It must be runoff from the storm. Oh no! What should I do now?*

Chapter 13

Flashback:

She had decided to quit fighting the 'companion'. It was not worth the struggle any longer. A quiet acceptance had crept into her soul, a resignation of destruction. She no longer had the will to continue the combat. There had been too many compromises along the way, too many disappointments and twists of misery mixed with the ecstasy. She had long forgotten joy. It was such a distant memory, like a fable in her mind. Ah, the mind. What a cruel battleground that was. One day it seemed so clear and logical, then next it was in chaos and disaster. Thoughts of defeat always were waiting whenever she imagined that she could be brilliant and triumph again.

Why try anymore? What prize was worth the constant presence of the 'companion'; none that she could muster. The prize was no longer a lure. Like a defeated boxer at the end of a bout, she was beaten, bloodied, discouraged and left drained of life. Her compromise of ideals and morals were complete now, at least by her almost forgotten standards. What had led her to this low, low state? How could she have thought it was worth it all, selling out all she once held dear?

Now what could make her believe that continuing was worthwhile? What could bring light into this bleak darkness that invaded her soul? Questions, only questions raced through her mind, but slowed their pace as the resignation in her soul settled in. Why was she here? The ones she had long tried to please did not care a lick about her or her work. She no longer had any relationships. She had burned too many bridges with coworkers on her way up the corporate ladder to have what others called friends. She had used them as much as they had used her. She knew their dirty little secrets and too many of them knew some of hers, enough of them to distrust anyone with any of her heart in friendship.

Who had time for a life outside of work? She had given her last ounce of energy for that job only to realize that it was not the prize in life. It could never be the goal. It never had the power to lift her and put joy in her heart or soul. It was a leech sucking life from all who entertain it. She, like so many before her, was now barren and dry like dust in the desert, blown about and lifeless. How could she have been so stupid, duped? She had been deceived into thinking that pleasing the corporate gods would bring satisfaction and fulfillment, when instead this job had robbed her of all her peace.

Now, what to do about it? How could she show her face back home, with former friends or her family? Her despair was complete. The humiliation was enormous. Why bother? Who would care she left their lives now? Despair loomed large before her, ever growing, consuming her mind, her feelings and views.

Thoughts of desperation mixed in her head, but desperate for what? Life? Was she caring about life anymore or yielding to self-pity and sorrow? Confusion ruled, a muddle of chaos now, spiralling downward in a chasm of misery. Tears gushed like rain on a dark night. Tears until no more tears would flow.

She was left with resignation and emptiness. But strangely, once the fall was complete, the emptiness searched for filling. It was not content to stay barren. In a moment she realized she was now a blank canvas ready for new paint, a new identity. But who or what could be the painter in this new movement in life?

There it was again, where those memories ended. Why this flashback from the recesses of her brain? Why now, of all times was it here again? With all this going on, why now?

Sam looked directly into Paul's eyes making sure he had his attention. He wanted to be sure he heard his explanation of what he was about to do and that he did not take it the wrong way. "Paul, I understand that you are a newspaper reporter, is that right?"

"Yeah, I do investigative and character pieces."

"Okay, I need to do something you're familiar with for a little while. You know how you interview people for your stories? You ask a lot of questions trying to understand the hows and whys of people you are writing about, right?" Sam asked.

"Sure, I understand what you're getting at, but I don't see how that's going to help find Gel. You guys just love to stall, don't you?" Paul was starting to wind up again and it no longer took much to light his fuse.

"No, no, wait, Paul. It's important to get my mind around what Evangeline is like-or Gel as you called her, may I use that name?" Sam was attempting to establish a rapport with Paul, however slight it might be at this point.

Paul nodded but still looked skeptical. "Sure. Whatever works for you."

"Okay, I need to understand what Gel is like and how she thinks, what she likes and doesn't like, how she might react if she found herself in a strange situation. You know the stuff I mean. The 'how', 'where', 'what', 'why', 'when' of the matter. That's your expertise. I need you to help me do the reporter digging now. I need to get inside her brain a little so I can predict some of her responses out here. It will guide me know what to look for. It will help us all know how to help her. So I need you to focus and help me out," Sam continued. He felt he might be making some headway with him.

Paul was starting to see the logic of Sam's thinking. It made sense, after all, wasn't it what he did when he was on the trail of a good story. When the scent of a lead exposed itself, Paul was like a hound dog flushing out partridge. If it was there, he would find it and he didn't rest until he had finished. Gel often said that it was better that he went out on the road and finished hunting down his story than have him restless at home at those times. He nearly drove her nuts when pursuing leads.

This he could understand. Paul was warming up to him. *Maybe he isn't as much an idiot as I first thought. I might be able to work with him if he does things as I do.* "Okay, I see your point now. If it will speed things up a bit, I can help you out."

"Just remember, don't get too annoyed with me if you think I'm asking redundant questions. You may see them as pointless, but I have my reasons for them. I'm sure sometimes people you interview get offended at your line of questioning too. So stay with me, okay?" Sam realized that it wouldn't take much to send Paul off like a rocket at this point, so he needed to gain his cooperation.

"Sure, let's just get things started. Times a ticking," Paul said, his eyes watching Jack unload gear from the back of his truck.

"Why did you decide to come up here and take this training?" was Sam's first question.

"It was a gift from the guys at work for my birthday. They thought it might get me out of the city for a while; be a change for me," Paul replied.

"So how did you decide who was going to come along? Was the trip for one or two or more?" Sam was trying to pry more information from Paul.

"Well, it was for me, but the course was for two, so I guess they assumed that Gel would come along. We talked with Mac and Sarah. They thought it would make a good vacation for them too."

Sarah interrupted, "I don't know whether this helps, but Gelly was reluctant to come unless she had some female back up. I think she phrased it like, 'I don't want to be stuck in the middle of the forest with a bunch of macho guys that I can't keep up with.' I agreed that it would be fun especially if we made it a 'couple thing'."

Paul gave Sarah an odd look, like this information was new to him. He quickly averted his glance, filing this information for later use. Sam thanked Sarah for her information. "So I gather that Gel is not a camper or used to the wilderness?" was Sam's next question.

"Nah, she likes her comfort. Her idea of camping is a big motor home in a nice secure campground, preferably away from wild animals. She's come with me at times, but it's more to humor me than anything else, I think. She likes to lug everything she owns with her if we do go. She likes her hair dryer, if you know what I mean," Paul answered with a sarcastic tone.

"Is Gel from the city herself?"

Paul answered, "No, she came from a small town about a hundred miles from the city. I just think she grew to like the city better, with all the facilities and extras that urban living can provide. She likes the luxuries that we can afford now. Her philosophy is: 'why rough it when you can afford not to?' She doesn't get stupid about it, but she prefers to do things with the least inconvenience to her. She likes to dress up and you can't do that here," Paul commented.

Sarah piped in at this point. "Well, she did live out on the West Coast for a while. I don't know much about that part of her life. We weren't as close during that time. She was working hard and travelling a fair amount. It didn't sound as though she had much time for vacations in the wilderness while she was there though. Do you know much about that, Paul?" Sarah was hoping he did and would explain it. It was the one side of Evangeline's life about which she was tight-lipped. Maybe it was different with Paul. He was her husband after all; surely she had confided in him.

Paul shrugged and said, "Well, she preferred to keep that to herself. She wasn't happy about that period of her life and I didn't press her on it. Whenever I did, she accused me of trying to interview her for a story so I backed off. She can be funny about things like that. It didn't matter. I mean, there are things I probably haven't told her either; that don't matter anyway. I've seen a bunch of stuff when I've worked on stories that she doesn't need to know about. I think it's better that I don't bring that home. So it doesn't bug me when she says she'd rather forget it."

Sarah was disappointed with what Paul had revealed. Gelly was hiding something about her past and was good at stuffing it away. At least it was a relief that Gelly was not keeping anything from her that she might have divulged to a good friend. She obviously was not ready to deal with it yet. It just piqued her curiosity a little more.

Sam looked at a list he had in front of him and jotted down some notes. "Has she any previous wilderness experiences to draw from?"

Paul shrugged and answered, "Sure, when she was a kid, her family used to go to a cottage. I think they did the basics. You know, campfires, canoeing, swimming, some hiking. I think she was up there with male cousins and they didn't do stuff she was interested in most of the time. Some of it must have rubbed off on her though. She's a logical thinker and can follow the stuff I talk about when I've gone camping with the guys. She knows about it. And she was doing well with this course until . . ."

Sam slowly added another question, "Other than that, do you know if there's any occurrence in the past to make her dislike coming into this type of environment? Any rotten experiences that she wants to avoid?" Sam wanted to probe deeper into Evangeline's motivations and lines of thought.

"There might have been, but she didn't open up about it with me. I kind of figured that the cousins were probably teasing her a bit. You know the tricks guys play on girls with frogs and snakes. It probably was a little much for her. They were a few years older than her and it freaked her out sometimes. I know she's never liked bugs; so that may be part of it." Paul was stretching his memory and imagination to recall this much. It was starting to occur to him that he knew more about some people he interviewed than he knew about his wife. She did not offer the information and he had not asked. *I wonder why. Maybe I just was tired of asking questions all day.*

Sol and Hildy arrived back where they left John Wilson and his gray Honda. Two more vehicles were waiting for them. Everyone was surveying the damaged road and suggesting the best way to fill it in.

"Well, welcome back. I guess we'd better get down to work here. What did you bring with you?" was John's greeting.

"We emptied the garden shed. Take your pick or should I say shovel or hoe? What do you think? If we move gravel back into it, the hole will be back in twenty minutes. I'd say we'd better move as many rocks into it as we can find. Short of that we might add a few branches but I'd rather stay away from them if possible because they can break or wash away too considering the flow we have going here." Sol opened the back of the van as he spoke. John grabbed a shovel as he did it.

"Do you think there's a way we can divert the water off the road?" John asked.

"Unfortunately, there is not much of a ditch here. That's probably why it chose to flow over and through the road. Let's see what we can do with what we have." Sol grabbed a shovel himself.

"Oh, by the way, as you see we have a couple more sets of hands here. Chuck, Jim, this is Sol. Choose your weapon and let's get started."

The men began digging and moving rocks. It was slow work considering the weather. It was not pleasant labor on the best of days, but the rain made it miserable. The rocks were slippery and hard to get a firm grip on and a few times they dropped their load partway across the road. Hildy busied herself with making flag markers to warn motorists of the danger. Then she used the hoe that remained in the back of the van to deepen the shallow ditch by the side of the road.

"Well, that looks at least passable now. I'm not sure how long it will hold but I think it's the best we can achieve. Maybe the diversion we created in the ditch will improve it for at least awhile." Sol stood surveying their work, his back already starting to ache from the manual labor. Three other men agreed that they should all be able to get their vehicles through now.

"It sure didn't take long for the road to erode. The road crews probably won't fix this for a few days. After all, we don't often see them around here on a good day. No wonder it eroded so quickly." Sol always had a few words to say about the way his tax dollars were misspent.

"Who wants to try it first?" John asked.

"Well, your car is first in line. If you think it's safe, why don't you try it? I'll stay out here and watch and direct you to the shallowest part to make sure your car isn't damaged going through," Sol offered.

"I can do that. Thanks for the use of your tools. We wouldn't be going anywhere without your help." John commented as he put the shovel back into the van. "I'm afraid that they're kind of muddy. It might make a mess in there."

"That's why Hildy has me cover the carpeting with plastic. She knows how I work," Sol answered.

"An ounce of prevention saves me hours of work!" laughed Hildy as she brushed off her hands. "I'm no fool!"

John got back into his car and eased it toward the partly repaired gully in the road. The dip had been reduced to about three or four inches and was passable. John waved as he drove off. Chuck followed close behind and Jim came last. Sol climbed into their van quickly and he too was through the breach as Jim's taillights disappeared in the distance.

"We're a little behind schedule. Lacey will be wondering whatever became of us!" Hildy commented as they got under way. "It's amazing how a short drive to the mountain can take so long when other forces are at play."

"Remember, we're Armed and Dangerous. You already said it. No one got hurt and nothing will stop us. You agree?"

"In the Name of Jesus, I sure do Agree!"

Evangeline realized that with the pooling water her situation had radically changed. She no longer had the luxury of lying there to await a rescue. The tables had turned. She now had to move by herself; how far she did not know, but at least to higher ground that was sure. Adrenaline started to course through her veins as she understood how critical it was to get moving. Even if the water just flowed through where she was, it was cold and uncomfortable and would soon lead to hypothermia. She knew that from the first responder's course she had taken at the high school.

Evangeline gingerly tried to sit up. If she did not jerk her leg, she found that the pain was bearable. She felt light headed with waves of nausea, but managed to get herself at least partly erect by propping herself on her elbows. She closed her eyes until the dizziness went away. Now that she was up this far, she decided to grope and try to find the knapsack. She was sure that they had packed flashlights in each bag. This morning she had thought that it was overcautious, considering that it was the middle of the day and they were on such a short trip. Her perspective had changed dramatically as she understood that it could make the difference between life and death.

How far could it have rolled? I don't think I flung it that hard. It must be here somewhere. She leaned on one arm as she reached out with the other hand, slowly sensing with her fingers what lay beside her. It was a delicate balance between her terror at the notion of touching some creepy bug or snake or imaginary creature and the idea that the knapsack and its contents might mean her survival.

Come on, you can do this. Where is it? Her frustration was beginning to mount. Finding nothing with her right hand, she switched positions and reached with her left. *A little further. You can do this, Gel.* As she leaned further left, she let out a yelp as pain shot through her left knee. Immediately, she laid back down sobbing. *It's so useless. What am I going to do? Oh! It hurts so much.* She tried to quiet her breathing, relaxing as best she knew how.

When her knee had settled into a throb she sat up again. This time she was determined to find the bag. *I won't twist my leg as I do it, I'll try to roll over as I go. That should work better.* This time her reach was further and she bumped into the knapsack on the first try. The next operation was dragging it over without rotating her leg. She decided it would be easier to drag her body to the bag, so inch by inch she managed to get there. Sobbing, she collapsed on the backpack, like it was her newfound friend. Relief flooded her being.

The water was getting colder by the minute. It was no longer a trickle. It had increased velocity and now she was convinced it was now a bit deeper. Her situation was getting more urgent by the minute. Now that she had the bag, she determined that moving out of the stream was the next thing she must do. *I'll get the flashlight in a minute. I'd better try to move before I get any wetter.* She grabbed the strap and looped it around her arm. Reaching out more bravely now, she tried to determine which area was driest. It was drier to her right, so inched in that direction.

Ow! What was that? It must be a stone, it is so sharp. Aw, I cut my hand open. Great! Now I'm bleeding there too! This time she was more careful to feel her way before putting her hand down. It seemed to take forever to move first inches, then a few feet. Inch by inch she maneuvered herself to the rock wall, out of the water. *There, at least now I'm dry.* Exhausted from the effort she leaned against the granite, panting and groaning from the throbbing pain in her knee. She would just have to wait a few minutes before she could explore the contents of the bag. It satisfied her that she had managed to move herself into a safer position.

Sam had been questioning Paul, Mac and Sarah for close to fifteen minutes now. He was starting to get on delicate ground. "I understand that the two of you had a disagreement about something on the mountain. Can you tell me more about it?"

"It was about nothing. Gel had been in a mood all morning. I think she might have been nervous about the exercise. She had been complaining that I was walking too fast and she couldn't keep up. I have longer legs and it was easy for me to walk down the slope. She had trouble keeping up with me. She slipped once, then she got angry with me."

Sam needed to probe a little more. "So you helped her up?"

"Well, not exactly. She got up on her own and started to follow me again. We were doing well until we hit the ridge." Paul looked out the window of the van. His teeth were clenched. He continued to watch as Eddie helped Jack sort through the gear.

Sam could tell he was on touchy ground here. "What happened when you reached the ridge? How did you attack the problem?"

Paul gazed back at Sam, then looked away again. "Well, I looked at the drop-off in the rock and thought that we could negotiate a way down. I figured that we might save some time."

"Was there a set time to do the exercise?" Sam knew that there was no time limit built into the course itself. He just wanted to get a picture of why Paul was in such of a hurry. He could guess at it but it was better to see if Paul knew why himself.

Paul shook his and answered, "None that Jack had given us. But the weather was getting lousy and it was better to get it finished."

"So what happened next? Did you agree on what to do at that point?" Sam asked.

Paul sighed. It was inevitable. He had to admit what happened. He would look like a jerk, but there it was. He just had to spit it out. "No, we didn't agree. Gel didn't like the idea of going down the rocks. She thought it was too dangerous."

Sam continued, "So what did she want to do instead?"

"She wanted to follow procedure and go further down the ridge till we could walk down easier, more safely."

"And you didn't agree?" Sam probed deeper.

"No, well, it looked as if we could negotiate it. I offered to help Gel down; that we could do it together. But she flatly refused to try. She didn't want to get stuck partway down. She just wouldn't do it," Paul said with disgust in his voice.

Sam was getting closer to truth of the incident now. He needed to get the rest of the information from him before he bolted. He knew Paul was watching Jack intently and would be on his tail soon. "But you pressed the point?"

"Well, yeah, I thought it could be done and I did do it, so it was possible," Paul said with growing irritation.

"So what did Gel do at this point?" Sam asked.

"She said she was going down the ridge, the way we were taught. We were going to meet at our mark; a specific tree," Paul answered flatly.

"What did you do next?"

"I started down the rocks. It was difficult, but possible," answered, a defensive edge was now in his voice.

"Did you watch Gel go? Do you have any idea where she went at this point?" Sam needed this piece of information more than any other.

"The last I saw her, she was walking along the top of the ridge going west. I started down the rocks and had all my attention on that for the next few minutes because I almost got stuck getting down." There it was out. He had admitted the difficulty of the descent. He hoped they would not dwell on it. The point was that it could be done.

"What did you do when you got down?" Sam asked.

"I went to our mark, the tree with the gash in it and waited for Gel, but she didn't come. I waited a long time too. Then I radioed her. She didn't answer me."

"How long did that take? Sam was trying to establish a time frame.

"Look, I don't know. Maybe ten minutes, fifteen at the most. I didn't check my watch.'

Now Sam needed additional detail and inquired, "Did you hear anything while you were climbing down or waiting for her? Anything unusual?"

"Jack asked me the same question. You always hear birds on the mountain. I might have heard a squawk that I assumed was a blue jay or something. That's about all. I'm stretching to say even that much."

Sam needed to get any other pertinent details he could from him now. Some of his squad had just started arriving and Paul's hand was now on the door handle. "So what did you do at this point?"

"Look, I called Gel on the radio to try to convince her to come down. I thought she might be playing a trick on me or playing hard to get because she was still angry at me. It wasn't like her to stay mad though, especially in this kind of situation. I would have expected her to do her thing and just come back. We'd meet and go on down the rest of the way and that would be the end of it. But she didn't and here we are."

Sam realized he could not hold Paul much longer so he got to the point, "Did you check for her, follow her?"

"Yeah, Eddie met me, then we went down the ridge but saw nothing. That's about when Jack came up the mountain and got involved. You know the rest. Look Jack's getting going and I don't want to waste more time with this stuff. I'm getting out of here. If you think of anything else to ask me later, just find me." With that, Paul was out the door and slammed it behind him before Sam could respond.

Sam looked back at Mac and Sarah, who shrugged. Mac was out the door behind Paul, leaving Sam and Sarah alone for the moment.

Calvin and Jan Talbot had made it down their access road and on to the highway in their black Jeep Rubicon. As Calvin negotiated a curve in the road and they came to Butlers Creek, he slowed to a crawl. It no longer looked like the lazy little creek that ran under the road at this point and beside it for a mile or two. This seemed like a river about to explode its banks. The bridge spanning the creek was barely high enough to pass over it now. The waters were turbulent and brown from the runoff.

"It's serious business, Jan. If that creek rises much more, we're all in trouble here. There won't be any getting back to the house today if that happens. You got all you need for a while?"

"Well, I always pack extras. Goodness, you always give me enough grief over the amount I pack and you know it! It'll have to do. We're filled to the gills in this vehicle. Whatever I'm missing, I'm sure Lacey will be able to supply. We shouldn't waste time on it now. It's important that we get there before it floods, from the look of that creek."

"Yeah, I agree. We'd better get there soon or that woman will be in serious trouble."

They rode the rest of the way in silence. Jan was muttering Prayers under her breath, partly for Evangeline's sake and partly for their safety. Calvin was not usually a cautious driver and she often wondered if she would arrive at their destinations alive or in one piece. He had raced stock cars in his younger days and did not seem to care when there was no visibility when driving. It irked her but no amount of nagging had changed his driving habits. It was something she just learned to live with. She was regretting telling him to get there quickly. She had earned every gray hair on her head married to Calvin Talbot!

Jan grabbed what she called the "Lord, help me" bar on the frame as they rounded a sharp S-turn, much faster than she thought they should. Somehow, Calvin always managed to keep the vehicle on the road. He always knew how far he could push it before it was too late but it did nothing to settle her nerves. Every ride was like a road rally adventure with him and was especially wild with the wipers beating as fast as her heart at the moment. She let out a long sigh and another Prayer of thanks when they finally pulled into the clearing by the base of the mountain.

By the number of parked vehicles, they realized that the Rescue Squad had arrived. Calvin pulled off the road in the front of the clearing to make room for more of the Squad or an ambulance should it become necessary.

Calvin and Jan got out of the truck pulling up the hoods on their raincoats as the rain began to pepper their faces. The wind caught Jan's door pinning her between the door and the frame of the vehicle. She winced in pain as she pushed the door open again, reached in and grabbed the backpack with their immediate essentials in it. It was not a good start to the day.

Jan surveyed the scene. Organized chaos is what it looked like to her. She was sure that they all had a job they were doing, but it looked like disordered running around for nothing at first glance. She had helped at enough of these situations to know that these people were professionals and knew exactly what to do and when to do it. It just always looked a little confused at the start of a search as they set up their gear and established their base camp.

It looked like both Sam Fowler and Jack Davidson were present, so she wondered who was going to be in charge today. Both had held that position depending on the circumstances or who arrived first. They worked well together and it rarely mattered to either one who was in charge; neither had egos when it came to rescues. But today might be different; it was Jack's exercise gone bad, not Sam's, so she wondered how it might play out.

As she walked from the Jeep toward the hub of activity, another thing arrested her attention. It was intangible, nothing you could see or touch, but real, nonetheless. It was similar to what they had encountered back at the house, only more intense. It enveloped her as she walked, stopped her and wrapped itself around her shoulders. A chill suddenly made her shiver and she knew she had felt this specter before. A wave of revulsion washed over her and took her by surprise.

Eli and Lacey pulled into the clearing, arriving from the opposite direction from Calvin and Jan. Their trip had been uneventful once they left Nan, Horace and Gertrude. The roads were slick owing to the rain, but there was no apparent damage in that direction yet. Several vehicles were parked along the side of the road also, including Bob Fisher's so Lacey knew he must have returned.

They got out of the Eli's truck and walked over where Jack was preparing gear in the clearing. They arrived in time to overhear Sonya Countryman talking with Jack about her cousin, Tucker Warley. "I don't know whether Tuck will make it, Jack. He was pretty wasted when he came in this morning. It was morning already when I heard him crash into his apartment at the back of my place. He woke me when he tripped over the trash can on his way in. I looked at the clock and it was 3:20 a.m., if I recall correctly. I rapped on his door before I came out, but he hollered some obscenity at me as I left. I think he may be a little too hung over to be any good to us anyway."

"So are you saying that there won't be a party at his place tonight?" Jack chuckled.

"Are you kidding, Jack? If he tries it, his hangover will be the least of his worries! I have to work tomorrow and I need an early sleep. There'll be no parties at our house tonight!" Sonya snapped.

"From the look of this weather, we might all be working most of the day, and night too, holding this area together. Once we finish here, I'm sure there will be lots to do down toward Lofton and Moulton. I'm not so sure people took this thing seriously. We don't usually get hurricanes this far inland!" Jack answered.

Sonya pulled a box of ropes from the back of Jack's truck and replied, "Yeah, you're right. Wasn't the last bad one back in the '50's? I wasn't born yet, but my mother talked about all the damage it caused. They were isolated up here in those days at the best of times, but it took out most of the bridges on the East River, making it impossible to get back into the city. Smaller roads were washed out and there were some landslides or something, too, I think. There wasn't nearly the population up here at the time so most fatalities were lower in the valley. But it was awful for them anyway. She still talks about it, though she was just a kid when it happened."

"I wasn't in this area when I grew up. We travelled around a lot with the military, you know, but my dad did talk about it. The military did come in and help clean up the mess and rescue people."

The two turned as Lacey and Eli approached. "We just got back. Any news on Evangeline yet?" Lacey queried.

"Nothing to report. We haven't been back up yet. We're about to set out. Sam's been with the three of them trying to get a history and assess the events." Jack turned in Sam's direction just in time to see Paul bolt from the truck and head his way. "Well, speak of the devil!" Right behind Paul, Mac followed as well.

Lacey and Eli looked at each other at the use of that phrase. Lacey took that description seriously and did not like inviting that evil entity into anything. Jack put his game face back on and greeted him as pleasantly as he could. "So you guys finished with Sam then?"

Paul looked like a caged animal just released from captivity. He was obviously more than ready to attack any available prey. "As finished as I'm going to be. So are we ready to head back up the mountain now?" he asked impatiently.

"We just have to organize into teams now. We'll be assigned team leaders and sectors to investigate. When Sam has finished and I talk to him, we should be set to start. Let me introduce you to Sonya Countryman. She'll be supervising you with Eddie."

Sonya gave Jack a look of annoyance. Why did she know that was coming? Jack knew she was good with interpersonal skills and would bond well with Sarah under the circumstances. She just wished she could move up the ranks a little and be more in the leadership core. It frustrated her that she was often relegated to these jobs, even if she was good with people.

Jack returned her look with a grin and tilted his head in apology. She knew he would make it up to her later, but the frustration still nagged at her. She got along well with Jack; maybe, better than just well. She had an inkling lately he had been hanging around with Tucker and the guys this summer just so he would be around her place. He had helped her wash her car again last week in that hot, humid weather. He said it was to cool down with the hose, but she suspected he was more interested in her than her car or the hose.

Sonya smiled back at Jack as she picked up the storage container of ropes and carried it over to the central supply depot. How he got away with toying with her emotions she did not know. He was just too good looking for his own good. *How many more girls did he have on the hook already*, she wondered as she walked away.

Chapter 14

Sarah remained in the van. She sensed that Sam might want to ask her more questions and she did not want to be around Paul's erratic behavior at the moment. It was dry in the van, and she knew the howling winds and rain would be miserable outside. She wondered whether she was being selfish but did not move anyway.

Sam was scribbling notes as he asked quietly, "Are you close to Gel?"

Sarah paused before answering, considering her words, "I've always thought so, but there are a few things she doesn't share and I don't press her on. It's like that in any friendship, I guess."

Sam nodded and continued to write. "You think she gets along okay with Paul. There's nothing more I should know about their relationship, is there?"

"As far as I know, everything is fine between them. He works hard and travels a fair bit, but they get along okay. You know, they have their squabbles, but, doesn't everybody?" Sarah said with a shrug.

"Yup, we do. You can ask my wife," was Sam's reply. "But sometimes girlfriends confide in each other, saying things that she might not tell her husband. You know, girl talk."

"I know there are things she finds hard to share. Things that have been difficult for her in her past, but even I have a hard time cracking the shell she puts up around those memories." Sarah sighed as she said this. It made her realize that maybe she had not made it easy for Gelly to be open with her. Sarah had been disappointed when she took the job on the West Coast and blamed the move on their drifting apart for a period. A cloud hung over that part of their friendship.

Sarah continued, "I know she had some relationship difficulties when she was out West before she married Paul. I don't know with whom or over what. She once said that she made some bad decisions, but wouldn't elaborate." Sarah paused a moment, fumbling with a tissue in her hands. "I don't like to break confidence over this."

Sam turned in his seat and faced her. He looked her square in the eye and said flatly, "If there's anything you might know that could affect her behavior or relationship with her husband and explain what happened here, you need to let me know. It could mean the difference between life and death in this instance. I'm not gathering information for gossip. I'm just doing my job here and trying to save a life before the weather makes it more complicated. Do you understand?"

Sarah looked down and tears welled up in her eyes. The stress began to overflow, as a tear escaped and trickled down her cheek. She was torn between keeping a confidence she swore to Gelly she would never tell anyone and the practicality of helping her friend. She closed her eyes and muttered, "Forgive me, Lord." Then she opened her eyes and stared back at Sam, "You have to swear to me that this goes no further. It's just between us, and is only about this rescue; because if it goes any further, I will never forgive myself."

"Look Sarah, I am just trying to do my job and you may hold the key to understanding what happened here today. Just please trust me to use the information appropriately."

Sarah looked down and began, "I don't know what happened out West and it probably has no bearing on anything. But I do know that Gelly has a few insecurities. She realizes that Paul travels a lot. A lot! She has sometimes suggested that she wonders who he sees while he's away. You know what I mean. Like, if there are temptations with other women. It made her feel as if she had to be someone she's not to keep him interested. His writing is so important to him that sometimes she feels as though she takes second place or maybe even third."

"In her weaker moments, after they had a spat, she wondered what he saw in her. So coming on this trip might have been a way to prove to Paul that she was attractive and courageous, you know, desirable. It's not her area of interest. I think maybe she was in over her head. She was trying so hard to fit in. But it seemed to be bringing stuff up for her. I could tell she was nervous about something, maybe just the environment. But something was wrong and bothering her. I just didn't get a chance to talk to her about it."

Her tears began to flow like a spigot that had just been turned wide open. Sam was never comfortable when a woman who cried. It just made him feel awkward, so he always just tried to be calmly compassionate and professional. It was his way to handle all he saw on this job. He quietly said, "I'm sorry it upset you to share that but it might prove important. Can you think of anything else that might be pertinent?"

Sarah pulled at the tissue, dabbed her eyes and blew her nose. Thoughtfully she said, "No, not now. I'll let you know if something else occurs to me. Thank you for helping me share that information though. It has been bugging me all afternoon since this all happened. I was wondering if not letting her talk about it might have caused what happened."

"I doubt that it has any bearing on it but telling me might help us find her. You've done a good thing. I think it's time I join the rest of the gang. You coming?" he asked.

"No, I think I need a moment to myself first. I won't be long," Sarah murmured, staring at the tissue in her hands.

Sam slid out of the van, adding as he left, "When you're ready, come over and join us."

The evil force that dwelled within the storm took pleasure in touching down, skimming over the surface of the Earth. It poured itself over the trees, branches, rocks and weeds, ripping at whatever it touched. It aimed to destroy as much as it could at each pass. It had an insatiable need for destruction that drove it onward. Soon gliding over top these surfaces was no longer enough to feed its malevolence. An unquenchable lust desired to pierce the dust of the Earth; to go deeper and darker to devastate from inside. Downward it pushed and drove in its tentacles. Deeper it pressed into every crevice and cranny, seeking blackness, ever away from the light.

The forces of darkness delighted in this union with the wicked power. The two entwined themselves, uniting to form a bond of viciousness. Ferocious might railed against any remnants of light, drawing darkness ever downward, whipping winds in the explosion of their bonding. Mankind had never looked into the heart of this monster, nor seen the pure evil of its intent.

Evangeline sat along the wall of the rocky cavern. The stream of water had increased, so had the pooling. It was getting deeper and closer to her by the minute and with it, her predicament was getting more serious. She realized she needed to find the flashlight now. She no longer had the luxury of resting and waiting.

She felt for the bag and tried to trace the flap and find its clip. She fumbled in the darkness, feeling clumsy and foolish. It angered her that she seemed so inept doing such a simple task. Finally, she located the buckle and grappled with the release. She almost had the clasp open when it slipped from her fingers and she nearly dropped the backpack in the pool of water. She caught it at the last instant, somehow managing to regain control before the sack and its contents submerged. Again, she sat there trying to regain her composure.

Come on, come on! You can do this! She was getting frustrated now. *Get it together. This isn't helping. What would Paul do now? Focus!* With the thought of Paul, tears welled in her eyes. *He would never have gotten himself into this predicament, would he? But, if he did, what would he do? Think . . . He would calm himself and just get on with the task, wouldn't he. Yes, that's it. Calmer. You can do this.*

She grabbed the bag again, finding the clasp more easily this time. She tried to slow her breathing and finally managed to open it. *Okay, that's the first step. You did it. Now, the next step: find the flashlight.*

She slowly felt through the contents of the bag, trying to recognize each item by feel alone. The task was made more difficult by her quivering hands. Was it the chill in here or the fear that was mounting in her chest? It was palpable now, like a presence she had felt before, years before. *Just do it. Ignore it. It doesn't change things. Didn't Paul say that when he encountered those terrible events when he was covering a story, he just forced the fear away? At least until he was through, then it was gone anyway. So do the same thing.*

She groped inside the bag again. First, she recognized the granola bars in a zippered storage bag. She realized that she might want them later, but now she was facing something far more frightening than hunger. Next she felt one of the water bottles; another item that would be useful, but not now, not yet. Her frustration was beginning to mount. *Come on. I know I packed it in there. It must be under the sweater I stuffed in on the bottom. I know it has to be there. Aha! That feels like it!*

Although initially was the right shape, she soon understood that it was merely the other water bottle. As she was about to give up completely, her fingers curled around what could only be the flashlight.

Relief flooded her heart. "Thank God" was all she could muster, not as much a call of gratitude, as a habitual phrase she used. However, the fear dropped a notch and she could now begin to think. She clasped the light as though it was a life source, knowing she could not afford to drop it in the rapidly rising waters. The sound of the gurgling stream was ever louder, a constant reminder of her dire situation.

Okay, what are you waiting for? Turn it on. She hesitated a moment, as though she feared what she would do if it did not work, or even worse, what she would do if what she saw in the light was more frightening than the encapsulating darkness itself. *Okay, it's time to do it.* She fumbled with the switch, first pushing it in the wrong direction. A brief flicker of light gave her; then it went out. *No, no, don't do that to me! Stay on. I need you to stay on.* She was trying to will it to cooperate now. She struggled to figure out how the switch worked. This time it came on, but was dim. *Why would he give me such a lousy flashlight? I need a good one! Come on now. Calm down. Some light is better than no light, right? That's right. Look at the positives. What can you see?*

She shone the light around her rocky prison. Rock and water was all she could see in the dim light, except the occasional patch of dirt. She moved the light to her left but it would only illuminate a meager few feet. She would have to move to see anything more. She snapped off the light, realizing that she needed save what little power that remained in the batteries.

Lacey and Eli left Jack to talk with Paul and Mac. They turned in time to realize that both couples, Calvin and Jan and Sol and Hildy, had arrived. They did not see any others of their group milling among the crews, so she assumed that they would have just their six to do the job. Better to have half of them, than none of them. They needed two or more for agreement in Prayer, so six fit the description well.

She and Eli headed to the other four, leaning directly into the wind as they walked. The cool rain cut against their skin as they plodded along, forcing them to hold their hoods and turn their faces away from the wind. They walked in silence as the intense gusts of the wind now made talking an effort. They greeted one another and Lacey signaled them back to Sol's van to shelter them from the wind. She filled them in on the status of the missing student.

"Her name is Evangeline Montgomery. Her husband is Paul Montgomery, the fellow who writes for *The Journal*. They came up here with another couple, Mac and Sarah Donnelly. Evangeline disappeared on the way down the mountain doing their final navigation exercise.

"There's her husband over there, the man standing beside Jack. You can't tell with the rain gear on, but he's athletic, not as tall as Mac, maybe 5'10" with light brown hair. Mac's more the tall, dark and handsome type. Mac and Paul play squash together, so they're in good shape. Mac is a business consultant and Sarah and Evangeline are teachers. They've known each other for many years. Do you want to go over and meet them? Then we can get out of this miserable rain and discuss things."

They walked toward Jack who was holding court with Paul and Mac. Paul seemed distracted as Jack spoke to him. He kept looking around at the Rescue Squad, sizing them up and assessing their capabilities. Mac was listening more intently to whatever Jack had to say. They glanced their way as they approached. Jack looked relieved that they had arrived, cutting the tension for him.

Lacey introduced her friends to Paul and Mac as Sarah wandered toward the group. Lacey noticed that her makeup was a little smudged and she assumed that Sarah had likely been crying. She was not surprised considering the stress that had been hanging over them all afternoon.

As Sarah reached the gathering, Lacey put her arm around her and gave her a compassionate look. She introduced the group to Sarah and said, "We usually give support to the rescue crew. They have their jobs to do and if needed, we can help with the search. We all have at least basic training. But sometimes we just provide support at the base camp if they have enough crew already.

"We also supply a different kind of support as well. We are all members of a Prayer group that meets regularly. We usually do Prayer backup for the search-and-rescue expeditions when we are notified. We have worked together for awhile and it works out well for everyone. We thought you should know why we're here. I am not sure how Jack and Sam will use us today, but considering the weather, some of them may be called away to other incidents, so we'll be available in whatever capacity is necessary."

Paul was polite with them but disinterested. Mac and Sarah smiled and seemed more responsive, especially Sarah as she nodded and relaxed a notch. Lacey sensed that she might be grateful for some Prayer at some time today.

Lacey added, "I just wanted to introduce everyone to you before things got too busy, so we'll leave you for the moment to take care of our own business. Remember you're in good hands; so is Evangeline. You've got the best people working for you here. They don't come any better than this crew."

The group shook hands and Lacey gave Sarah a hug before leaving. A rapport had been established and that was all Lacey had hoped to achieve. It also forged a link that would be helpful in Prayer for the group.

Then the six Prayer warriors retreated to the Penfield's van to escape the buffeting winds and rain. They had serious Work ahead and needed to get started.

Evangeline willed herself to reason through her situation. *Okay now, think. Were there more batteries in the supplies you packed this morning? Yes, I'm sure I saw some. But were they in my bag or Paul's?* A momentary stab of anxiety welled up inside her as she thought she might have given them to Paul to carry. She closed her eyes trying to remember what she had done. *Well, I had better see if I have any because I'm sure I'll need them.*

Evangeline started to rummage in her packsack again, more calmly this time. She felt more self assured now that she had found a working light, however faulty it might be. Something was better than nothing. Strangely, it t seemed like company in this dank dungeon.

Suddenly she heard the scratching noise again, but this time it seemed louder and closer. Evangeline froze, forgetting her task. She held her breath, listening. Now she heard no sound save the running of water. Slowly she allowed herself to take a breath, shallowly at first, as though the sound would attract whatever was the source of the scratching.

Was it merely her imagination? Or perhaps it was just debris in the runoff falling into the cave? These questions hung in the air, unanswered, yet pressing in on her consciousness. Breath by breath her heart rate slowed, but the terror remained, unresolved, waiting to rise again. It anticipated her every move and it looked for ways to take her unawares. She now felt its presence like a mist in the early morning, light and wispy, hardly tangible but creeping into all crevices around her like an unwelcome odor.

How long she sat there, back pressed against the rocks she could not tell, nor did she care. Her mind was temporarily paralyzed. Gradually, the sound of the running water came back into focus, enabling her to think. *Backpack. Flashlight. No light. Batteries. Oh, yes, batteries. That's what I was doing. I have to find the batteries before it's too late. Too late for what? Before the light dies. Before my hope dies.* She was now fighting against despair. Hopelessness was attempting to drape itself over her. *No, I have to do something, anything. The bag. I have to find the batteries, now.*

She grabbed the knapsack as though her life depended on the light it could bring. She struggled as she reached inside, panic making her fingers stiff and nearly useless. She took the flashlight and tried to turn it on, failing on the first try, then finally succeeding. She directed the feeble light into the bag but its weak glow was hardly any help. Again she decided to save the little energy left in the batteries for more important uses and switched off the light. Again she stuck in her hand to try to feel her way around the interior of the sack. This time she hit it. It had to be. Drawing out her hand with the prize clutched tightly, she used two hands to make sure she did not drop it; her hands were shaking so much.

She sat back and savored her success for a moment, trying to calm her overactive heart. Previously, the sound of the water had been calming. Now it meant danger. The flow was becoming alarming, threatening.

The package in her hands, her reward, needed to be used to be worthwhile. She had to open it. Could she manage it in the dark? How many times had she done this at home? It should be simple. She ran her fingers over the edges of the packaging, looking for a seam, a weak spot, a place to tear it open. It was far more difficult with no illumination; mere shadows met her eyes. Her hands were cold and stiff and uncooperative. *Focus, Gel. It's a basic task. A child can do this; so can you. Paul could do this. Oh, enough about Paul! He's not here. Just do it.*

Once more, she fumbled with the package, finally, finding a loose edge. She gripped it and pulled, her fingers slipping and nearly dropping the pack. Managing to juggle the precious parcel, she caught it and tore into wrapping. At first it would not budge, elevating her frustration another notch, but finally it gave way and loosened. The wrap fell open and she could feel the valuable reward inside.

She carefully placed the batteries on the bag, in her reach, dry and away from the water. She now shifted her attention to the flashlight. She had to determine how to open it. *Most flashlights are the same. I'll unscrew the top and it should release.* She twisted it with no results. *Okay, is it just too tight or did I try it in the wrong spot?* Again, she attempted to open the casing. Again, it would not budge. *What am I doing wrong? Maybe if I try turning it further down. Maybe it opens differently.*

This time she grasped it differently and used every ounce of remaining energy she could muster and nothing happened. Despair began to rise once more. *Hold on now. Use your light to see if you can make out how it comes apart.* Switching on the light, it was difficult to make out the lines of the flashlight because the beam pointed away from it, but it was just enough to give her comprehension of what she must do. She turned it off quickly to preserve the remaining power in case her efforts were not fruitful. It was still her sole light source.

This time she changed her grip altogether and twisted. Although tight, it gave a little under her fingers. This small sign of hope made her heart jump and she smiled for the first time since awakening in this hellish hole. Again she twisted and the casing opened in her hands. She then felt along the batteries taking careful note of their orientation in the case before she removed them; one battery out; then the other one. She put the old ones to the side, not wanting to get them mixed up in the dark. She removed a new battery from the package, gingerly feeling for the positive end and dropped it into the flashlight case.

Then she found the second battery. As she removed it from the package, her fingers slipped and she started to drop the fresh battery. *No! No!* A quick grab and she scooped it up before it had a chance to roll into the water nearby. That would have been a disaster and she knew that she could afford no such mistake.

Grasping this power source like a precious gem, she inserted it too into the casing. Lining up the two parts to screw it back together was a frustrating challenge, with her cold stiff fingers. But finally it caught and started to work into place. It seemed to drag and stop. *Okay, is it back together or it cross-threaded? Just try to turn it on, you fool. Then you'll know.* She turned the switch and nothing happened. Darkness remained.

She reopened the casing and realized that the resistance that she felt under her fingers meant that she had it cross-threaded. She was more careful this time, turning cautiously until she felt it align and grab under her finger tips. She turned it until it was secure and surely had made a good connection with the contacts.

This time she was rewarded with a good powerful beam of light. Her spirit soared with elation. How could such a small event cause her to be so jubilant? It felt as if she had just crested Mount Everest and it was just a flashlight. She sat there staring at the light in her hands, delighted in her ability to overcome the challenge, a silly grin on her face. *At least I can do this. Maybe the rest will be easier.*

Her celebration did not last long. As she began to point the light around her rocky enclosure, she heard it again. This time there was a scratching sound with what she thought was a faint grunt. Time froze. She was sure if she looked at her watch, it would have ceased to function. Her thoughts backed up and smashed into one another. *Not alone.* It was the only coherent thought that she could muster.

Chapter 15

Few customers had ventured out on this miserable afternoon. John Brompton did not care much. He had made more sales in the last two days than he probably made all last week. Most locals had been in buying supplies to prepare for the storm. He had to send Art Prescott into the city to bring up more stuff from his suppliers, who made the trip up this way only once a week. He had sold out of most of that new stock too.

Now he had another job on his hands. He had spent most of the afternoon placing and emptying buckets to catch the drips from a leaky roof. It never seemed a problem before, but the wind had driven the water into every crevice in the store. He would have closed the shop long ago but for the six steady streams of water leaking from the ceiling.

The bell on the door sounded as a tall lanky man hustled in out of the wind. A cool blast of air followed him as he pushed the door shut. It took a fair amount of effort owing to force of the wind opposing him. John sized up the man as he strolled back to the counter from the freezer section. He was a stranger to him. He thought he had to be about forty-five years old and a little winded from the exertion of walking outside in the storm.

John greeted the fellow, "Hello there. Braving the weather, are you? I didn't expect to see many customers today. I was just thinking about closing."

"Well, I'm glad that you didn't. I drove down from Chuck and Sylvia Matthews' place. My name's Stu Wheeler. My wife and I are visiting for the week. A tree came down on their porch and took out the phone and power lines. The way the lines came down, there are live wires dangling and it looks dangerous. I left Chuck to deal with the house but I was wondering if there was any way to contact the power company to shut off the juice so nobody gets electrocuted."

John raised his eyebrows. "That does sound like a bad situation. Here, I have the number to the power company handy. Uh. Yes, here it is. Go ahead, use this phone. No one was hurt, I hope?"

"No, we were all at the other end of the house at the time. Good thing, though, because it was huge tree. It's one of the original trees on the property. It wasn't planted since they've had the place. It's a shame. But it sure has done a lot of damage to the porch. It will have to be completely rebuilt. I guess the next call will have to be to the insurance company. I figure they'll be busy today though."

"No doubt the insurance companies will be working on the damage from this storm for days, even weeks. It's the kind of day an insurance company dreads, I'm sure. It's nasty out and getting worse by the minute," John replied.

Stu connected with the Power Company and talked with them for several minutes. "They're swamped with calls. I was afraid it might be like that. They suggested we evacuate the house until they can make their way up here. I won't hold my breath on that one. We'll have to see if the neighbor can accommodate us. They seem like nice folks. Let's hope they have room for four more people!"

Stu was about to leave when he stopped short, "Oh, I almost forgot one of the reasons I came here. Do you have any batteries left? We thought we had spares but they've been around so long, there isn't any juice left in them."

John held up his hands in response, "Aw, no, I'm sorry. I sold out of them this morning. There's been a run on supplies with this storm."

Stu looked disappointed, "I thought it might be too late to get any, but I had to try given our circumstances. Well, I'd better get back and help Chuck take care of things."

"You be careful driving back there. You already know how deadly the trees can be if they come down," John warned as Stu headed back out the door.

"Don't worry, I will. And thanks for the use of the phone!" And with that he was out the door; the bell jangling as he pulled the door shut behind him.

John watched as he ran back to his car. By the time he reached it, he looked like someone had dumped a bucket of water on his head. John shook his head. He flicked on the television to grab the latest news on the storm. Channel 8 News headlines came on. A highlighted banner ran across the bottom of the screen. It was giving warnings of high winds and rains. Police were warning people to stay off the roads. Flood Warnings were being issued for most counties in the region, and evacuation orders had been issued for several communities along the East River." John stared at the pictures being aired by the news station. They found the worst of the worst to report on, that was certain.

"First they say stay off the roads then they say they are evacuating people. They'll have to be out on the roads with that. Aw, I hope they're the only ones out today, except the emergency personnel. They'll be making lots of overtime for sure," John muttered to himself.

John sauntered back to the freezers. It was time to empty the buckets. *I should've changed those shingles earlier in the summer as I said I would. Yeah, but the fishing was too good to pass up. Now I'm paying for it.* John shook his head and set about to his task.

The Penfield's van seated seven so the six Prayer Warriors fit reasonably well. With all their rain gear on it was not as comfortable as Lacey's great room, but it would do under the circumstances. They were about to begin when they recognized Bert Lawson's Ford van as it pulled in, parking behind Eli's truck. Lacey smiled as she watched him get out of the vehicle and scan the area for his fellow Believers.

Sol got out of the van quickly to signal their location to Bert. He hustled over as well as he could in the driving rain. Both men got into the van as swiftly as they could, grateful to get out of the downpour. Bert had not taken time to put up his hood so his salt and pepper hair was plastered to his head.

"I don't know about the others, but I'm glad you could get here! We wondered if the roads were impassable, because we didn't think you want to miss this," Calvin exclaimed.

"No, I sure wouldn't. We encountered some problems with a washout in the road, but it looked like someone had done some of their own work on it. It was partly filled in with rocks, but it had started to washout around it. I stopped with a couple other guys and filled in more rocks to make it passable. It probably won't hold together much longer though, but it got me here, at least."

A snicker from Hildy could be heard in the rear seat as she said, "Well, that roadwork was partly Sol's handiwork. We faced a crater about a foot deep earlier on our way in and had to do some quick fixing to make it passable too. We wondered how long it would hold; obviously, not long in this weather. Well, at least it got you here. I'm sorry you had to finish our work for us!"

"I might have known you folks would have had something to do with it. Hildy, I thought I recognized that material on the warning flags as one of those shirts you made for Sol."

"Well, the material was bright enough. I suppose that's why Sol refused to wear the shirt much. It might have been a bit too gaudy for him!"

They had a good laugh over that comment. Then the mood soon turned serious again. Lacey filled Bert in with the little information that they knew. "It doesn't make any sense why she would wander off, especially given the weather. They lost her trail on the ridge itself, so more careful exploration needs to be done. I think Jack wanted the students off the mountain quickly so any evidence wouldn't be messed up by all the tramping around. The husband was starting to get agitated. I'm sure Jack wanted to contain him in case he wanted to go looking for her without supervision. He mobilized the troops when they couldn't find her immediately."

"Are there any other things that we need to know, for the search and, of course, for Prayer as well?" Bert asked thoughtfully.

"There's not a lot that we know about, except that there was some tension between Evangeline and Paul on the way down the mountain. We don't know the root of it yet, but it might have something to do with her discomfort in the wilderness setting. I sense that there is more to it though. It's probably something that they brought with them in their relationship or some history. It's hard to tell, on the surface of things, at least. That's not something they're going to blurt to a bunch of relative strangers, even under these circumstances. I sense we might get more from listening to God than from them at this point," Lacey responded thoughtfully.

"Is there any possibility that she just got completely fed up with him and just walked off? Could she have just headed down the mountain another way and hitched a ride back to town?" Bert questioned. "I don't suppose it is possible she is sipping a soda at the Eagle's Rest Inn by now, feeling a tad guilty about messing up the weekend?"

"Well, we did check back up the roads around the scene immediately after she went missing. Bob ducked back into the bush the other way along the route she might have taken and there was no sign of her that he could find. I suppose it's possible that she might have hightailed out of there quickly if she were that angry, but I think she would have left some sort of trail behind her if she did. They couldn't find anything," was Eli's response.

Bert began the session, "So we're here for a purpose then, aren't we? When people go missing, they call out the Search-and-Rescue squad. Our intention is to supplement and pinpoint those efforts more effectively. Agreed?"

Murmurs of agreement could be heard. Bert continued, "Let's break this down to concerns we need to consider before we begin. First, if it is alright with you, I'd like to just open in a Prayer for Wisdom and Protection from The Lord. Then we can set forth the specifics and do some Directed Prayer. It never makes any sense to go into a search without some good Guidance.

"It might not be a recognized policy of the Rescue Squad to include our assistance, but I do think that we have been accepted by them. They've been okay with our participation so far. After all, results speak for themselves. They seem to have been happy when our gut 'intuitions' have panned out for them. But we need the proper Preparation for our participation here. When we finish Praying I'll go out and fulfill my job as chaplain and Pray for the group. So we had better get started so we don't hold up the crew."

A solemn atmosphere could be felt in the vehicle. Each knew their role well, having done it many times before. They had never yet set out on a search and rescue without Prayer and would never consider doing it any other way. As each member of the group bowed their heads, the only sound that could be heard now was the constant beating of the windblown rain against the van's exterior. It was a grim reminder of the seriousness of their mission. Time was against them and the clock was ticking down.

Evangeline sat motionless for a few minutes after hearing the noises. She was certain that she had heard not merely scratching but also a grunt this time. It could have been her imagination running wild but she doubted it. Was it an animal or a person? She did not know, nor did she want the answer. She waited a few minutes more with no more ominous sounds. It seemed safe again.

Now that she had light, Evangeline let her spirits rise. She felt far more courageous than when she was completely in the dark. She panned the torch around her rocky enclosure. First she directed it to her left, inspecting the rocks, dirt and water flow. The cavern extended some twenty feet but narrowed dramatically, as though the passageway ended where her light vanished. She then continued to scan the rocky sides of the cave, realizing that there was no exit directly above her.

Continuing to sweep along to her right, she saw a break in the rock, perhaps twenty feet above, but more than eighteen feet to her right. Beyond that, the passageway narrowed dramatically into what looked little more than a crawl space. She stopped and gazed at the rocks above. Could this be an opening and escape route? Her heart skipped a beat as she considered this possibility. She continued to stare at the gap in the granite. *It could just be an optical illusion. How can you tell from this angle any way? You'll just have to get closer to be sure.*

Now Evangeline faced the task of willing her impossibly sore body to move closer to the gap in the boulders. She then did a wide sweep with the torch again, assessing the velocity of the waters that continued nonstop into her stony prison. *It must be my imagination. That stream seems to have risen dramatically. It couldn't have been more than five minutes since I turned on this light. How could it be so much deeper?*

Her thoughts began to race. *Why is it rising so fast? The storm. Yes, that's it! A storm was predicted. A hurricane or something, but why here? Hurricanes don't come this far north. We aren't close to the coast. That's just ludicrous. Not a hurricane.* Logic tried to intervene. *But why the rising water then? It must a soaking rain!* This thought was followed by more anxiety. *If it doesn't stop raining, the water will continue to rise, won't it?* Her mind jumped into panic mode again. *How did I get here? Where's Paul? Is he okay? Why isn't he here? Why isn't he looking for me? Doesn't he care?* She collapsed back as tears welled up and spilled down her cheeks. Her fears were giving way to self-pity.

The sound of the rushing waters echoed in her rocky chamber penetrating her thoughts. It was picking up intensity now, minute by minute. *My mind is playing tricks on me. All I can hear is that water. Why is it so loud?* Again, she played the light around her surroundings. It was not her imagination running wild. The water was streaming through every available crack in the rocks now. The wet walls glistened in the strobe of light. New rivulets were forming through the fissures in the boulders, tumbling down like cascading waterfalls. Her heart almost stopped as she now realized that her feet were now rapidly being consumed by the pooling waters. The water seemed to have no outlet and was rapidly filling the cavern like a bathtub, but this water was not warm and comfortable; it was cold and ominous.

State officials had declared the Cape Fear region of North Carolina a disaster area. The devastation extended northward along the coast some fifty miles and a similar distance south into South Carolina. The summer tourists could recognize little of what remained of their vacation playground. The beaches were littered with every kind of debris imaginable. Extreme erosion from the pounding waves had washed away much of the plush sand leaving exposed rocks, shells and sludge from who knows what source.

Those evacuated from the district were being directed not to return yet, to allow emergency personnel to work unrestricted. Many roads were made impassable by rubble and the illogical placement of sailboats and even parts of houses. The rising waters had lifted entire homes, transporting them often hundreds of feet down the road, where they then crashed into other buildings that had somehow remained fixed in place.

Evidence of the incomprehensible intensity of Hurricane Igor lay everywhere, flung away like undesirable toys in the hands of a petulant child. This storm had murderous intentions and the darkness of its heart was manifested in the destruction it churned along its path.

FEMA officials had meetings with state and local representatives to determine the best search-and-rescue plan and how to get emergency supplies into the region. Despite their experience with Hurricanes Katrina and Rita, there were not enough resources to handle this emergency quickly. However many mock scenarios these agencies had used for preparation, no one had expected the extent of the devastation that Igor had delighted in inflicting.

Authorities determined priority of resources. The first efforts were given to saving lives and transporting victims to higher care facilities. Make-shift triage units were springing up at strategic locations, determined by the density of casualties. Hospitals were straining beyond capacity, attempting to cope with the extraordinary influx of patients and were already finding themselves depleted of supplies and personnel. Some casualties came from within their off-duty staff who had attempted to aid friends and neighbors. It had moved the crisis from merely an external event to one that affected the very bones of the emergency response system itself.

Roads were impassable in most areas, so it became a logistical nightmare to transport necessary supplies into the regions of highest need. Personnel were making astonishing human efforts to respond to the crisis but it was becoming abundantly evident that it was not going to meet this astonishing need.

Reconstruction was the furthest thing from anyone's mind at this point. Mere survival had become a priority; as well as reaching the most critically injured and those in need of medical care for preexisting ailments. The weak, frail and elderly who had determined not to leave the familiarity of a longtime homestead were most at risk, but children were also high on the minds of emergency workers. Little could be provided for many of these people because access was so limited. Even locating the greatest need in the shortest time was a problem in itself, because most traditional communication technologies had been disastrously affected. It was quickly beginning to be a nightmare on a scale few in this area had encountered.

Igor smiled as it looked back on its trail of destruction. The fear it generated refueled the storm, intensifying its efforts to maim and destroy. Seeing these simple human beings fighting desperately for survival brought pure pleasure to the core of the storm.

Jack walked slowly with Sam Fowler as they discussed his take on the matter at hand. It disturbed him that Jack could not find a trail to follow, considering it was Jack's field of expertise. He was stymied and he felt sure that no one on his staff was more capable than Jack.

Sam listened as Jack explained, "Look, Sam, I had an irate husband on my hands at the time and the rain was moving in rapidly. I may not have been as careful as I normally am. I was feeling pressured to deal with a situation that was rapidly unwinding. I didn't know what part Paul had to play in the events and wanted to get him off that mountain as fast as possible. Maybe I missed something. But I don't think so. I'm thorough and you know it. I guess I didn't like that it was happening to one of my people, of all things. I take a lot of care to ensure things don't get out of control. You know that, don't you?"

"Hey, Jack, I have no doubt in your abilities. You've found people my crew would have given up on many times. That's what perplexes me so much, because if you couldn't see anything, with all this rain, I have concerns that we won't find anything either; at least, not until it's too late. Let's try to strategize. We both know standard procedures like the back of our hands, but let's try to think like these people, get into their minds. What would they have done under the circumstances? Our logic may not be theirs."

"Yeah, I know. Gel isn't the outdoorsy type, that's for sure. She might panic easily and not think rationally given unusual circumstances," was Jack reasoning.

Sam nodded as he said, "I got the sense from my discussions with these guys that something might have been eating at Gel; something that she brought up with her. I can't pinpoint if they were having marital problems; maybe she just thought that Paul was doing stuff on the side, if you catch my drift. Sarah seemed to think that Gel had something to prove to Paul on this trip. She seemed stressed to do well in the course to keep him interested."

Jack chuckled and agreed as Sam continued, "Well, she didn't do that, so that's gone out the window now, hasn't it? So where does that leave us then? I think we can rule out the husband doing anything off-color. I don't think he had time to do anything to her and dispose of a body, so he's probably telling the truth."

Jack snickered at that remark. "Sam, you've been watching too much television. When was the last time we had a murder up here?'

Sam shot Jack a look and replied, "Look, you already implied that this didn't fall into normal limits. I'm just reviewing all possibilities." Sam shook his head ruefully and added, "And you know that Wally will try to bring up the possibility if it comes to a police investigation. He's been itching to pin some serious crime on these city folks for some time. If there's even the hint of that suggestion, we have to erase it. Better still, let's just find her and eliminate his involvement. He's become a big fish in a little pond lately. Too bad he's coming up for reelection as sheriff this year. He would love a big bust to boost his votes."

Jack shook his head in disgust and grimaced. "The last thing we want is to have Wally in on this. I just hope he's got his hands full down in Moulton. That's where most of his votes come from anyway. There'll be enough rescues in the valley that will give him newspaper coverage today. He probably travels with *The Moulton Sentinel* photographer in the backseat of a patrol car!" Jack never did have a good feeling about Wally Truscott at the best of times but now he wanted him on the other side of the county.

"Okay, then we'd better gather the troops, share the strategy and get started. There's Bert Lawson coming over now too. He'll want to be involved. I wonder what his take on this thing is going to be," Sam remarked as he waved Bert over.

"Whatever it is, we probably could use his insight about now. Any ideas could be helpful under these circumstances. If this rain gets any worse, we'll have to be careful we don't lose our crew to injuries. The sooner we get this done the better," Jack remarked.

"I couldn't agree with you more," was Sam's observation. He grabbed a clipboard from his truck and walked toward Bert, ready to start the search. "The sooner we get this under way, the better. I never did like searches in weather like this."

Hurricane Igor was being dubbed the worst storm of the century by the press. It had old tracks to follow and slowly attempting to penetrate as much territory as it could along the way. It enjoyed the terror it was creating as it scrubbed the surface of the Earth. The longer it pounded these mortals, the more horror it could induce and more energy on which to feed. These human beings were naïve enough to think that it was produced merely by pressure differences and warm and cold fronts clashing. They neglected the possibility that unseen elements fuelled this malevolent monster.

Yet, this tempest was not yet satisfied with the mark it had made scouring the terrain. It had yet not pushed further than any other storm. More complacent mortals lay in its path for devastation. Most laughed at the ludicrous idea that they were vulnerable this far inland. They did not realize that the storm's insatiable lust to whip up fear had not been filled. Still further it would push, squeezing every possibility to destroy along the way. Punishing the land was easy, pushing these people to despair was fulfilling and changing the landscape was marvelous. The hurricane desired to carve and shape the land as once was done by the Creator Himself. After all, is that not the ultimate ambition? To be like the Most High God; oh, the delight it brought at the thought! And humanity could not stop it, could they?

Evangeline desperately panned the light around the rocky enclosure. She thought there might be an opening in the rock above. She briefly turned off the illumination, to see if there was any daylight coming through the apparent gap. She hated to turn off the light as she craved the comfort it gave to her, but she had to be sure that there was a possible means of escape. She thought there might be a slight glimmer of light above her. She then turned the flashlight back on. Panning down the wall on the other side of the cave, she recognized the streaks of dirt on the rock that marked her less than graceful entrance as she had catapulted down the sharply sloping rocks. Oh, yes, that was how she fell into the cavern; she was certain.

It all was beginning to make sense. She must have somehow stepped into the hole that formed the entrance to this cave. It looked so small above her, but she was not a large person. Her backpack must have slid up her back and followed her into the gap, because she was sure there was no room for both her body and the sack. No wonder she was so twisted up in the straps when she awoke.

How she fell into the hole, or why, was lost to her. That part was fuzzy and could not be retrieved, at least not now. It made no difference, considering the urgency of her predicament. She had to move out of her current location. Her escape choices seemed limited. She could go back up the rock wall to the opening or explore deeper into the cavern for another exit point, if there even was one. Would the passage just end abruptly? And those noises seemed to come from that direction. *I just don't want to meet whatever was making those sounds. They didn't seem human. I don't need more problems than I already have. I would rather tackle the problem I can see than the unknown lurking down that cave.*

The water was coming in from all sides around her. Every crack oozed water. *It must be a horrible storm up there.* It just seemed that the ground above was supersaturated and was now pouring out into any available crevice. The water level had risen dramatically in the last few minutes alone. *Why doesn't the water just keep running down the mountain? Why does it stop here? This must be a low point in the cavern. If it can seep into the cave, why doesn't it go out too?* She searched around with her light to look for outlets for the water. Although there were cracks above her head, she found none below. Surely, if it could pour in why would it not drain out too? *Does it have to fill completely before it will run out? This won't be a good place to be for long! I just have to get out of here.* Her breathing began to quicken as she realized her dire predicament.

Evangeline attempted to stand but searing pain shot through her left knee. She cried sharply, then collapsed, panting to regain her composure. *What am I going to do?* She sat there for a few more moments, but soon realized that the waters had risen so rapidly that there was not even a little high ground on which to sit. She had to stand now or risk being drenched and cold.

She would have to find some way to put less weight on her left leg and try again to rise up. Gingerly she shifted her weight to the right. It was manageable but barely. Any rotation of her left knee caused extreme pain. She then tried to carefully push up on her arms, leaving her left leg extended and taking her weight on her right knee. Looking around her, she tried to find anything grab to help heave her body into an erect position. This would be difficult at the best of times with help, but alone, it seemed an insurmountable task. Evangeline then gathered her backpack and pushed it against the rocks to form a make-shift step. It was not that high but might give her some leverage.

It was a toss-up; which she feared more, the rushing waters or the thought of causing that horrible pain in her knee. Then she heard it again; the scratching sound followed soon after by several deep grunts. Evangeline froze and held her breath. *What is that noise? Is it getting closer or is it my imagination?* She remained motionless for a few more minutes, listening for any hint of a sound over the rushing waters. No additional noises met her ears and she slowly exhaled. *That must have been loud for me to hear it over the water. Could it be it's someone coming to help me?* She was momentarily hopeful. Then she had the chilling realization that it was a likelihood that an animal that had taken refuge in the cavern away from the rain. She did not want to even contemplate what type of animal that would make such a sound.

Her mind started racing, sorting through her options again. She had to get out of there and fast. But going toward that noise was frightening at best, terrifying at worst. It brought her no solace, so she immediately eliminated it as alternative. *Go back up the way you came into the cave. It seems up is the only practical direction. But how am I to do it?*

She took a long heaving sigh and willed herself to start to move again. It was clear that she had to raise herself first, before she could do anything else. Leaning her forearms on the backpack she could elevate herself a little but she then needed more purchase to hoist herself the rest of the way. She grabbed the rocks above her, hoping for any handhold she could find. Fortunately, the surface was not completely smooth and she soon located a small ledge on which to grip. With one mighty effort she soon found herself standing precariously on her right leg, leaning to one side and swaying, trying to find something to grab before she toppled.

Evangeline managed to take hold of another rough piece of rock in time to steady herself. At this point, she was not sure whether she should celebrate or cry in pain. However, the possible presence of a wild animal down the cavern was enough to silence her. She stood there allowing herself to whimper softly as the throbbing in her knee gradually subsided.

She was then able to turn slightly, allowing herself to lean against the rock wall. She enjoyed this new perspective. Somehow, being upright, made things look differently. She felt more power over her circumstances, less vulnerability. This satisfaction allowed her to process the possibilities of her predicament.

She played the light over the cavern wall until she could see the exit point. It looked impossibly steep at first glance, but on further inspection she soon realized that with an intact body, one might be able to climb. Ledges were visible; enough to make climbing reasonable. That posed a distressing problem for her, however, for she knew her left knee was neither stable nor reliable at the moment. And the pain, well, that was excruciating. *What can I possibly do to get out of here?* The problem before her seemed insurmountable.

Chapter 16

The crowd of rescue personnel gathered around Jack and Sam. Bert Lawson and his group joined them as well. It had been determined that Sam would head up the expedition with Jack as second-in-command, partly because Jack was so close to the problem Sam had felt his emotional investment might be a distraction. Jack had protested vehemently earlier, but had reluctantly conceded to Sam that he would have insisted on the same thing should the tables be turned the other way.

Sam had just finished briefing everyone on the details of the disappearance as they understood them at this point, the methods they would use and special precautions given the present conditions. "Remember, safety is the primary consideration as always. We are likely going to be busy for the remainder of the day with other rescues, so we need everyone in good shape. I don't want to hear about any foolishness going on here, okay?"

Sam scanned the group, looking each in the eye except Jack and Paul. Jack was glancing down at the ground, avoiding Sam's gaze and Paul was fiddling with the zipper on his backpack. Sam was not even sure that Paul had heard a word he had said up to then, although he was not surprised. He had seen many family members far more distracted under the same situation and he realized he was probably more 'together' than many people. He just had a bad feeling about this guy and thought he would be almost as unpredictable as this weather.

Sam studied Paul out of the corner of his eye, not wanting to make it obvious what he was doing but trying to gauge what he was thinking at the same time. *Maybe it was the reporter in him. He's probably been in on the periphery of other 'searches gone bad'. I'm sure he's seen his fair share of ugly circumstances in his line of work and it's been his job to look into the nastiest of details. Can't say I envy him. He's likely thinking about everything that could go wrong and wants to be sure we don't screw things up this time. Still, he could be a 'loose cannon' around here. I just don't need him becoming rescue number two or putting my guys in more danger than they are already in, given the conditions.*

Jack was his best friend. He could trust him with his life in any set of circumstances, and already had several times. This rescue was a little different because Jack was in the middle of it. Like quicksand, it had given way under him suddenly, without warning; much faster than any other situation they had ever handled. If this could happen to Jack, whom he had almost idolized, then what were the chances of any of them handling it any better? It was strange the way it had all happened. But no one could have predicted that the weather would begin to cascade like it had. *I'm not going to start doubting our abilities to handle this. Jack will have some ideas what to do. He's a rock and he taught me much of what I know about this business, the stuff that comes from the gut, instincts. If anyone can pull this off, he can. I'll just have to watch his back.*

"Are there any questions?" Sam asked. No one offered anything, obviously eager to get going before the storm was completely out of control. Paul continued to avert his gaze. He obviously had a lot on his mind and this meeting was beginning to fray his patience. The sooner they got under way, the less agitated he might become.

"Bert, have you got some words of wisdom for us?" Sam asked respectfully.

"I won't keep you guys long. By myself, I don't have the Wisdom we need, but I do know Someone who does. We've already been Praying for everyone while you have been gathering the gear, so I'll just add a group Prayer.

"Dear Heavenly Father, as much as the conditions may raise some doubts at times in the minds of some, I know You have this situation under control. We rely on You as we embark on this rescue and we stand on the Authority You have given us to perform in Your Son's Mighty Name. We thank you now for Your Holy Spirit and Mighty Miracles and Wisdom that does not come from mankind. I ask you to release your angels to provide Protection and Guidance on this mission to each person involved. I thank You for Safety and a good result that will again show Your Wonderful Working Power in our lives. I know that You mean only Good for us and have full Confidence in Your Ability to see us through this expedition with a quick extrication of our lost lady. I thank You that you are Empowering Evangeline to be sustained and energized to facilitate her rescue. I especially ask that You give to her Healing for any injuries that she might have received that may be keeping her from being located. We ask that You give her Ability beyond the norm to make it easier for us to find her and bring her home safely. I thank You for a successful rescue mission, in the Name of Your Son, Jesus, the Christ, the Annointed One. Amen"

Quiet 'Amens' could be heard around the group. Sarah looked straight at Bert, with her mouth slightly agape. She had never heard so powerful a Prayer by anyone, certainly not from the pastor of the church they sporadically attended. Evidently, this rescue crew was used to hearing Bert Pray, as they were now preparing to break into their individual teams as though it was just another day at the office. She, on the other hand was stunned by what had happened. She felt as though Bert was talking to his Wise Father, with whom he had a comfortable relationship. He seemed to Trust his very soul to Him. Somehow he had bold confidence approaching with certainty of results. Something about this man urged her to want to know more about him. Either he was different or the Father he talked to was not the One she thought she knew about.

Mac squeezed Sarah's hand and yanked her out of her thoughts. She glanced up at him and he nodded. He had read her thoughts and was agreeing with her. Sarah suddenly felt a rush of peace amid this raging tempest. It was so out of place given that it took all her stamina to resist the howling winds around her. How could there ever be a pint of pleasantness in the middle of these swirling demons? What was the origin of this sense of serenity? Or perhaps, it did not come from a source with which she was familiar, at least not to the degree that Bert Lawson was.

The rock walls around Evangeline glistened in the beam from her flashlight, wet with the runoff pouring in off the mountain through every available gap. The stream was continuous and increasing in intensity, escalating the dread Evangeline felt in her chest.

Banged and bruised, every bone in her body ached and combined with the rapid beating of her adrenaline charged heart, she was overwhelmed by the circumstances in which she found herself. Despair was rising within her at the impossibility of the task at hand. How could she scale such a steep slope with her injuries? Standing with the majority of her weight on her right foot eased the throbbing in her left knee only marginally. She dreaded the thought of trying to walk, much less climb. On a good day, she had found the task of the rock-climbing wall at the outdoor center to be exceedingly challenging. Now, faced with a seemingly insurmountable obstacle, the thought of what lie before her seemed ludicrous. How could she pretend to think she could do it by herself, miserably ill-prepared and with merely one good leg on which to stand?

She heard what sounded like thunder outside, loud and long, reminding her of the urgency of her circumstances. Judging from the streams of water spraying into her rocky prison, the storm was not easing but growing in intensity. Not only were her shoes now covered in water but it was now rapidly rising up her shins. Shivers made her shudder, startling her out of her useless pondering. She realized that she needed to take stock of her situation.

If I'm getting cold, how long can I stay here? Even in warm weather, people have died of hypothermia. How long have I been here already? I don't even know how long I was out cold. Cold, that's appropriate, isn't it? As her mind focused on her body temperature, she began to shiver again, causing her to hug herself trying to conserve body heat. It was a futile maneuver, as she soon realized that the clothing under her raincoat was already damp from her slide into the cave. The water was spraying from every pore in the rocks around her and it was not making it any better. Without dry clothing, she would not be able to stop her heat loss. Her only hope was to get moving to generate body heat and find a way of escape. *Talk about being between a rock and a hard place! Now I know why they coined that phrase.*

Evangeline realized that she was now running out of choices. If she attempted to move further into the cave, she faced uncertainty. She did not know whether there indeed was a feasible escape route or a dead-end and the fear of the unknown was daunting. Then there was the animal or was it an animal? *I just am not willing to go exploring. I know what my task is right here. I have to climb out of this pit. Going back further could be far more dangerous. I'm sure those sounds were real. I might not hear them now, but I am certain it wasn't my mind playing tricks on me. It's probably still there, just masked out by the sound of the water. I just don't know what I will be facing, literally, if I go further into the cave. Anyway, I just can't waste time exploring. I just want out of this hellhole now!*

Panic began to rise again. Going up seemed equally absurd but the more reasonable alternative at the moment. She could, at least, see that option, but how she could achieve it was lost on her. *I just have to move now. I don't have a choice. Doesn't anyone know where I am? Where is that radio I had? If only I still had that radio!* Evangeline panned the light around the cave looking for any sign of the radio, but soon realized that if it were inside the cave, it was likely submerged in the rapidly rising pond. Any electronic equipment would not survive in such conditions. *Do I dare call out for help? What if there is an animal back there? I just don't want to attract its attention. I don't even know what it is. Paul made fun of me with the raccoons last night. How could I handle something bigger and more dangerous and without a weapon? I just can't take a chance. What could it be anyway? What type of animals live this far up the mountain?*

Seconds passed and turned in to minutes. She gazed at the opening above her. Thought evaporated. She just stared at the same spot, not thinking, just looking at it. Her mind was numb, jumbled, exhausted. The longer her eyes locked on her target, the farther it seemed to move from her; twenty, fifty, then a hundred feet higher than her head. Confusion settled into her brain, fuelled by the cold. She felt her heart beating in her ears as the fear fought for control of her soul. She held her breath until she felt she might pass out. Was this how she would die, alone, forgotten and abandoned?

Sonya Countryman walked to Eddie. "I guess you and I are partnered up today. Bob gets to stay with Jack to help him out on top of the ridge. We have to take the three musketeers up the mountain. It should be quite the experience, given the husband's attitude. I figure that he'd like to tear Jack apart right about now."

Eddie grimaced at the thought. He and Jack were friends and he was loyal to him. They had worked together many years and had been through many situations during that time. They had dealt with various types of people coming through Jack's courses, some strange and some good. Never had he seen Jack lose it with any of them. No matter the challenges they faced with these people, he had always been professional, honest and fair. Eddie was not the sort to express his feelings about Jack's friendship, but as far as he was concerned they were tight and anyone attacking Jack would be just as much going after him too. He hoped that it would not come to that today.

"It's about the way I read it too, but we'll just have to keep them under control, won't we? Actually, we've probably got the hardest job of the day, considering," Eddie commented.

"Considering? Considering what?" was Sonya's question.

"Well, considering Paul is a reporter and all. We sure don't need any bad publicity," Eddie half grunted.

"You're right about that. We'll have to treat him carefully; you know, watch what we say with him so as not to set him off. I don't think that it'll take much to trigger him at this point. I'm not sure about Mac though. He seems a little more level, but you never know. He seems pretty tight with Paul so anything that's a problem for Paul might be just as volatile for Mac too."

"You think I don't know how to talk to these city folks? I know more about these woods than they know about their city. They're on our turf now and I think they know it. I don't think they're about to do too much nonsense given the weather and all. They're kind of dependent on us out here anyway. After all, we do know what we're doing here. We just have to prove it to them." Eddie was getting a bit too defensive for Sonya's comfort.

"Whoa there, Eddie. I didn't mean to get you angry. I agree with you. Sure we're the experts here, but Paul is the unpredictable element in the game plan. We just have to make sure he doesn't foul things up or cause another rescue. I'm sure you'd agree that it'd be the last thing we need today on top of everything else. Let's just go up there and show these city dwellers that we're professionals. That's the best publicity we can get." Sonya wanted Eddie on her side and knew he would be protective of his turf. This might be a double balancing act, keeping Eddie and Paul both in check. *I guess that's why they pay me the big bucks.*

"Well, let's get going. We might as well get them outfitted before this storm worsens. Man, I hate this kind of weather. It just complicates things and compounds our problems. There's just so much more to factor in. I just hope these guys are cooperative or this could be a nasty long day."

The trees above them were groaning under the strain of the wind. Both suddenly came to attention as a large branch snapped and came crashing down about thirty feet up the hillside. Sonya and Eddie looked at each other, understanding the added danger of this expedition. They were now going to have to be looking up for safety as well as down on the ground for clues to Evangeline's whereabouts. Danger was now a prime feature. Rescue missions often involved painstaking and boring searches, mixed in moments of sheer excitement or terror depending on the situation. This one might prove more of an adrenaline rush than any of them cared to have.

Jack and Sam went over their final details of the search plan. Although the method was 'routine', the execution was obviously not going to be so easy. The wind and the rain were making it difficult to hear valuable clues in the environment. Footing would be a problem with the wet terrain and steep grade. Visibility was now beginning to be compromised and would be more of an issue as the day progressed.

"Your radio working okay? I think we'll have to rely on these things more than usual," Sam observed as he finished fastening the buckle on his backpack.

"Yeah, don't worry about my gear. I've checked it three times already. I don't want more foul-ups today." Jack shook his head in disgust. He still could not believe the turn of events. The grim look on his face reflected his emotions. He was determined to find Evangeline and no mechanical or electronic glitches were going to get in the way.

Sam surveyed the current conditions of the mountain and took a deep breath. His sandy colored hair was matted by the rain. He had pushed back the hood of his jacket so he could hear Jack. The constant beating of the pelting rain was annoying but there was a price to pay for the action; now he was drenched. He clenched his jaw as he heard the falling branch. Each man acknowledged the other's gaze.

Jack let out a heaving sigh and said, "Look Sam, we don't need anyone hurt today. Maybe we should keep Paul and the others down the mountain and just put our people up there. The weather is closing in more every minute."

Sam shook his head in response and answered, "Jack, I understand where you're coming from but I don't think Paul will buy into that for a minute. It would be more trouble to keep him down here than to let him go up well supervised. Eddie and Sonya are good at what they do. I trust them to put those three to good use but keep them out of trouble at the same time. Maybe getting up on the mountain will help Paul's memory about what happened and lead us to something useful. If you stay on his flank, then you can intervene if you think Paul and Mac are getting into too much mischief. You know him better than I do. It just might be better not to be directly in his group so you can do your job without worrying about babysitting those two."

"Okay, enough said. I agree. Let's get going now. You ready?" Jack answered as he lifted his pack on his back, effectively cutting off the conversation. He knew what had to be done, but just needed confirmation that they were making the right decisions. Though he had years of experience, it was one scenario he had never encountered, but he hated to admit it made him uncomfortable. His training and experience had always been enough to succeed in any situation in the past and this should be no different. Any good plan just had to be approved by all in command, as in the military. Once accepted, the plan just needed to be implemented. Now his focus was moving into execution mode.

Sam donned his pack and stuck his radio inside his jacket. The two men leaned against the raging wind and walked toward the other teams. Final instructions were given to the personnel and they all headed for their appointed search perimeters. Jack hung back for a moment to speak with Paul, Mac and Sarah. He fell into pace with them as they followed Eddie and Sonya.

"You guys all set?" Jack asked them as a group.

Paul nodded, not looking at Jack. His face was set on his target above him. He looked down at his compass, taking a bearing as he walked. He knew where he was going and nothing would stop him now. Jack realized that he must have taught him something right as it seemed he was putting the course material to good use. *I just hope it's enough for today.* "So you know how to search your grid?" Jack attempted to break the silence.

Sarah replied, "Yes, between your instructions and what Sonya reviewed with us, it seems straightforward. I just hope there's something easy to find that will lead us to Gelly soon. Is there anything in particular that you want us to be on the lookout for? I just don't want to miss anything important."

Jack waved toward the ground in front of them as they walked and explained, "Anything can potentially be a clue if you know what to look for; any tracks or scrap of clothing or something she was carrying. Stuff like that. Broken branches are always worth assessing. Sonya and Eddie can tell if they are fresh or old ones. The problem will be the rain. It will be rapidly degrading anything we might hope to find, so be extra vigilant in what you are looking for. Anything unusual is something to check. Just watch out for yourselves and one another. It's the buddy system up here. No one is to go out of reach of anyone else. That's partly to make sure we don't miss covering all the ground and partly to keep everyone together and safe. You got that?"

Mac piped in, "No problem. You're the boss here. We'll follow your lead on this one." He didn't want to give Paul a chance to make a wise crack about losing people. He sensed that Paul would like to light into Jack given the opportunity, and had kept himself in check until now only so it would not slow the progress of the search. His patience was wearing thin and he could lash out easily now.

"Okay, you're in capable hands. Go to it." Jack nodded at Sonya and Eddie and veered off to join his team.

Paul watched him go for a moment, saying nothing, but the expression on his face was intense. He was relieved that Jack was out of reach for the moment because he did not trust his responses at the moment. He was not sure how far he wanted to trust Jack any longer. Although Jack initially seemed capable in his knowledge and experience, with events having spiraled out of control so quickly, he was beginning to doubt his skills under these circumstances. His wife's life was now at stake and nothing, not even Jack Davidson, was going to stop him from being part of her rescue. He would see to that.

The water was colder now, making Evangeline's feet ache. She sighed and forced herself to think. Though muddled, her brain fog had allowed her to realize that if she did not move now, she might not be able to soon. The chill was rising throughout her body, settling into her core. Her body temperature was beginning to plummet and that she knew could mean disaster. Not only would her body not respond to her commands but she would no longer care if she even did move out of the looming danger.

She willed herself to try to move, although it took all her remaining concentration to convince herself of the need. Had there been some dry ground, she would have just as easily lay down and rested. But the water continued to pour in around her, rising perceptively like the filling of a coldwater basin. Days earlier, when the temperature soared back at home in the city, she would have done anything to find this cool retreat. How sharp was the contrast in her viewpoint now! This place was rapidly becoming a death trap and she was the prey caught in its snare.

Unsure of the stability of her mangled left knee, she gingerly leaned a little weight on her foot. It was more bearable than a few minutes ago, perhaps owing to the numbing effects of the cold environment around her. She did not have the energy to analyze the reasons, she was just thankful for it. *If I can at least do that much, maybe I can start to move. I'll just have to use the wall for support until I get closer to the outlet.*

She awkwardly leaned into the side of the cavern as she gingerly moved her leg forward, taking an apprehensive step while holding the flashlight and backpack. She managed to put weight on her foot gently at first, then, gaining more confidence, she allowed her leg to support her a little more. *Well, that may be a baby step for most, but it was one of largest ones I have ever taken.* She paused to catch her breath, having held it for the last couple of minutes. Small victories were precious, so she savored this one. *If I can do one, perhaps the next one won't be so bad.*

Venturing forth once more, she leaned against the rock wall like a child leans into its mother for moral support in an uncertain situation. She moved another few inches onward, then managed a yard further. She continued to move gingerly, feeling with her feet on the uneven stony floor.

She permitted herself to put weight on her left foot again, and as she did, she could sense there was something under her foot that shifted as she applied pressure to it. Suddenly, she found herself toppling, grappling for support on the sheer rock wall. The flashlight swung wildly with her body jerks as she fought for control of her balance, panning eerie, gyrating beams of light around her. Her knapsack began to slide from her hand, so she grabbed for it just before it fell into cold dark waters. Managing to hold the flashlight, she stumbled against the rock face with a terrible thud, banging her right shoulder, arm and side of her face in the process. She slid downward just managing to stop herself before she completely immersed herself in the now frigid waters.

She cried loudly with the searing pain that first shot through her left knee, then arm and face. Panting, Evangeline, leaned precariously to her right side, her arm awkwardly bent, holding the flashlight up and out of the pool, her forearm supporting her torso. Her left leg was extended with her right knee bent and bruised. Somehow she had the presence of mind to preserve her sack and light, her two lifelines of security. She cried, long rolling tears flowing like a fountain too long pent up and pushed by an unstoppable force.

Great sobs convulsed her body in rhythm with the beat of her heart, keeping pace with the throbbing of her body. It all seemed so useless and hopeless. How could she have thought she could do the impossible in such a miserable prison as this? Frustrations and fear flowed from the core of her soul, sweeping over her miserable body, trying to pull her into the waters around her. Devastation threatened to overwhelm her. Clinging for balance in this hellish dungeon, she hovered between despair and the last shreds of hope that were rooted in her inner being. Darkness threatened to wash over like the incessant flow around her, drawing her downward. Heaviness pushed against her making it difficult to breathe.

A presence had swept into the cave with her. It was evil, dark and malicious, taunting her to let go, to quit. She felt consumed in its grip and smothered by its swift attack. She teetered between life and death; with each second, life's hold on her seemed to wash away.

Chapter 17

"Is this the spot?" Sonya asked Paul, as they neared the bottom of the ridge.

"The spot for what?" Paul responded irritably.

"Sorry, I meant, is this near where you and Evangeline separated? I was lost in my thoughts. I should have been more explicit. I just wanted to pinpoint a good starting point for us."

"Yeah, close. Uh, maybe a little more east, closer to that pine over there. But she was on top of the ridge. She headed west while I climbed down the rock face about here." Paul responded as he started to walk toward where he descended the rocky incline some time earlier.

"Whoa, hold on there, Paul. Just stay put until I scout out the terrain here. I don't want to scuff up footprints or anything. We have to be careful how we walk. Just give me a second, okay?" Sonya called loudly over the sound of the wind and the rain. She motioned to Eddie to follow her. "You guys stay put for a second, okay. Just let us check it out."

As she said this, Paul stopped short. He watched warily as Sonya and Eddie pulled in front of the trio. Mac and Sarah came up beside Paul and waited. They could see Jack and his group above them on the ridge, a little to the east. Sam and his group had arrived just to the west, also above them. They had blanketed the surrounding area, making sure no territory was missed.

The skies had darkened markedly making these woods gloomy and gray. The rain was steadily increasing as the winds raged above them in the treetops. The mixture of aged deciduous trees and tall pines that towered above them offered little protection as they strained against the push and pull of the intensifying squall.

Mac and Sarah watched Paul shift his weight from foot to foot. Not as obvious as pacing, it was Paul's way of expending his pent up energy as he waited. It was not lost on them however as they knew their friend's habits and recognized the agitation he was feeling. Not that Mac would have reacted any differently had Sarah been in the same situation as Gel. He would do anything he could to find her and set anyone straight who got in the way. It was the uncertainty that wore them all down. No one had offered any concrete possibilities, much less answers to their questions. It just did not make any sense to anyone, especially the three friends. It was so unlike Gel to behave like this, they had a foreboding sense about the possible outcome about to unfold before them.

A sense of urgency drove them up this mountain, yet at the same time there was a fragment of reluctance in case they made a terrible discovery. They remembered some of Paul's most memorable and award-winning pieces and they often involved shocking crime stories and human dramas. Few had happy endings, too few.

Etched in Paul's memory were scenes behind yellow police tape that would make most readers recoil in horror. Several times he had embedded himself in the neighborhoods that spawned the most violent crimes. Attempting to understand the raw savagery that motivated the daily headlines, he had found himself in the line of fire as those crimes were committed. Occasionally, he interviewed families with heartwarming stories, but these were sporadic at best. Being this close to these unfolding events gnawed at Paul's psyche, rousing emotions he long ago tried to contain and extinguish. He had rationalized many times that he could not be effective in his job with erratic emotions hampering his objectivity.

Sarah was concerned about Mac and the possibility that he may be motivated to do some heroic deed beyond his capacity or experience. Part of what troubled her was the possibility that Mac might have to intervene should Paul's frustrations get the best of him. They were good friends, but even pals have known to come to blows when pushed beyond human endurance. The conditions were conspiring against them and the scene might spiral suddenly out of their control. Dread hung heavily on her heart as she watched the figures around her examine useless bits of debris on the ground. It felt as though they were all moving in slow motion in a surreal drama playing out before her eyes.

Mac scanned the forest above the ridge, hoping to pick up some still unnoticed clue to Gel's whereabouts. *There has to be some logical explanation that has been overlooked here. People don't just vanish. We must have missed some obvious point. What did I see on the way down? Sarah and I travelled the ridge too. There must be something that we saw that we just haven't recalled up to now. But what is it?*

Bert watched the various teams ascend the hillside as he pondered their alternatives. "What do you think the best approach is here? I sense we've missed something obvious and it's nagging at me"

Lacey glanced over at him, barely hearing his question over the sound of the drumming rain on her jacket. She nodded slowly. "Yes, this isn't what it seems. I think . . . we should Pray again. We haven't Heard well enough from The Lord here. I feel He's got more to say on this than we understand. I have a check in my spirit too. We have to get Armed with more than we have so far before we head on up there. A few extra minutes might save us several hours in grief and frustration. Let's get out of the rain for a few minutes. The van will work well for that." Lacey was already moving before she finished the sentence.

No one argued with Lacey. They just followed closely behind her and quickly piled into the warm interior of the van. A united spirit bonded them in an expectation of Hearing their marching orders from their Commander.

No idle chatter could be heard just Prayer for further Wisdom and Direction. It was serious business; lives were at stake and they knew it. They had participated various times in these rescue expeditions, but never had there been a situation involving Jack directly. Usually Jack had been called in as an external adviser to assist the rescue squad. He was a mentor to most team members, respected for his expertise in these matters. Never had he been the cause of the search. Something did not sit well with them about it and it extended beyond the circumstances.

Having asked God for further Insight into the circumstances, they sat in silence, Listening in their spirits for responses from their Father. The sound of the beating rain might have distracted most people from their purpose, but this group was focused on a needed Answer. Not even a viscous hurricane could dissuade them from Hearing from God. God wanted to Speak and it was their job to Listen.

A blast of thunder broke around them, attempting to invade the semblance of Peace of the moment. The sound reverberated through their bones, like a direct hit overhead. As loud as it seemed in the van, they could only imagine how it sounded on the mountain above them. Malevolent forces were gathering around them, trying to distract them from God's Purposes. It impelled them to pinpoint their efforts against the unseen force assaulting the mountain.

Bert broke their silence, "Satan, get behind us. We bind you in the Name of Jesus! That is enough of you, now! You will not stop what God has put us here to do."

Murmurs of agreement rippled throughout the group. Each Praised God for His Sovereignty over the situation and resumed their stance of Listening. Minutes ticked by, then they slowly opened their eyes and sat in silence, assimilating what their spirits had heard.

Lacey was the first to speak. "You were right, Bert. We have missed something. We all know what's at work here and it's up to no good. I've never felt such an evil presence on this mountain before, have you?"

Jan nodded as she replied, "Calvin and I sensed the presence earlier at home. It was like, well, I can hardly describe it other than a mist invading the lake and surroundings. It was strange, but real, nonetheless."

"I have to agree with Jan. It seemed like it was seeping into every crack in the house. Sort of like a mist or smoke, I'd say. It is pure evil. There's no doubt about it," Calvin said grimly.

Lacey nodded as she looked at each of the team. "I haven't experienced this since the day Warren had his accident . . . if you can call it that. I will never forget how it felt. It's the same today, but worse, I think. Yes, worse. It will not win this time, though. We're more Prepared. We aren't naïve and ignorant of his devices this time, are we?"

Lacey paused as the others nodded their agreement. They knew what she was talking about and knew the gravity of what was happening. The spirit of death was hungry today, but it had a Fighting force to contend with this time. They were trained for this. They had been studying and preparing for this moment for months. This time they were not going to be taken by surprise and their arsenal of Weaponry was full and ready for use. They lowered their heads once more and moved in to engage the enemy 'full on'. A Mighty Battle had just begun.

Evangeline leaned into the rock face, clinging to its steady support. Waves of despair flowed through her, threatening to dissolve any hope that remained. Heaviness choked her being, making it difficult to breathe or think. Senseless images drifted before her mind's eye, drawing her downward into helplessness.

She felt a war raging inside her; opposing forces drawing her toward them. Fear mixed with hopelessness, grabbed at her heart. Then simultaneously, she heard an inner voice softly calling her name with tenderness. How could such opposing sensations clash in her being at the same time? Back and forth they pulled and battered, fighting for the upper hand. It was intense combat deep, deep inside her, beyond thoughts and images, into the chasms of her heart. She could do nothing in the wake of it. Paralyzed by conflicting sensations, like a bizarre drug induced hallucination, she could merely cling to the rocky wall for support, waiting for it to pass.

She could hear the blood coursing through her vessels, pounding in her ears. It roared as it flowed through her body. What was happening? Was she losing grip on reality? Darkness threatened to enclose her. The taste of bile rose in her throat. Her breathing came in short shallow bursts; shallower, shallower, making it harder to extract the needed oxygen. It squeezed her chest; it weighed itself against her throat. Gasping now, she felt her surroundings graying out even more. Blackness was grabbing at her being, drawing her downward into an unknown oblivion.

A crazed voice in her inner recesses beckoned her into the darkness, tempting her to let go, stop resisting and slide into its waiting arms. She was suddenly so tired of trying, fighting to save herself. It seemed easier to release her grip and go to that voice. Why not? What hope remained here, in life, in existing?

Chapter 18

Thunder boomed overhead, sounding like the mountain might split from the force it unleashed. The wind lashed at the branches overhead, straining their fibers to their limits; then releasing them, only to do it again. Back and forth the boughs whipped in a hideous dance. The rain cascaded from the blackened skies, loosed from turbulent clouds to flood the Earth below.

Sarah looked up with the last crash of thunder and shuddered. This storm was nothing like any she had witnessed before. It threatened to fray her already taut nerves. One more explosion like that and she might lose what little composure she had remaining. *What more could go wrong? I never like storms, but this one is worse than normal. It sounds like the atmosphere is about to detonate. What kind of weather is this?*

Sonya had paused in her investigation of the terrain at the last earsplitting sound. It was far worse than she expected from the forecast. This storm had moved in so quickly, it had taken even the most seasoned professional on the mountain by surprise. It was not like any other weather front that had hit the mountain in her time here. This seemed to have an urgency that defied expectation. But why now, when they needed time on their side? It just was not good.

She could not see any tracks that could belong to Evangeline. The rain was making it nearly impossible to discern anything anyway, but what she could see was probably the result of Paul and Eddie tromping about in their initial search. It was going to be a miserable experience if they did not soon find some sort of clue. They would need a better break than they had already had so far if they were to make much headway.

Sonya sighed and straightened, motioning the others to join her. They immediately moved toward her, eager to get going and participate. "I don't see anything that will help us much here. Did you guys, walk along here when you were looking for her?" Sonya asked Paul and Eddie.

Eddie looked uncomfortable and replied, "Yeah, well, you know, when she didn't show up, it didn't occur to me right away that we might have to do a search. We've never lost anyone up here. It was the last thing on my mind to preserve the sight."

"That's okay, Eddie, I probably would have done the same thing under the same circumstances. This thing has been kind of weird from the start anyway," Sonya answered. Then realizing how this comment might sound to the three extra members of their party, she added, "This storm has us all a little off guard." The last thing she intended to do was to give Paul or the others any fodder for an argument. She needed to keep everyone calm and on task.

Mac shrugged at that exchange, but inwardly, he had to agree. This day had suddenly crashed in on them like the rain that now poured on them. He had never witnessed a more bizarre set of events before in his life. The speed of how the events had disintegrated was unnerving and showed him that even the best planning could come apart in a matter of seconds. One would think that outside forces were conspiring against them. The thought had been nagging at him for some time and it was something he could not shake. He wanted to believe that it was just natural weather patterns and coincidence, but something deep inside him was off-balance. Pressure was building, twisting inside his gut; something was not right but he could not grasp it with his mind.

Paul was studying the spot above him where he last watched Gel march off before he turned to climb down the rocks. From this vantage, he mentally analyzed Gel's possible path. It looked so straightforward. *What would she think? Sure she was mad at me, but she wouldn't just run off into the bush. It makes no sense, especially with the squall moving in. It's just not like her. She just has to have encountered something beyond her abilities to stop. It's the only sane answer here.*

Eddie followed Paul's gaze and realized that he was replaying the earlier events in his head. He, too, had done a similar thing as they reached the rocky outcropping above them. It had been probably the strangest scenario he had ever encountered. If Jack had devised it in a training exercise, he would have laughed him off the mountain. It just seemed ludicrous, but here they were just the same. "So where do you want to begin, Sonya?"

"Okay, let's start over by that rendezvous point at the tree you picked out then we will head west. Let's not get too far apart so we don't miss any clues and if anything, we should overlap a little. I'll take the upper end. You guys space yourselves below me at equal distances. Eddie, you take the bottom. That way we are on both sides of the group and can keep everyone on track. It's easy to veer off course when you are looking at the ground around you. Does that suit everyone?" Sonya was setting up a strategy for the greatest effectiveness while keeping her charges under control. The last thing she needed was to lose someone or have one charge off without her knowing it. Paul was her greatest concern. With Eddie stationed below Paul, she hoped he would be able to head Paul off should he do something stupid.

Sarah nodded agreement. She was eager to begin but also wanted to be as helpful as possible, without obstructing the search. Mac nodded and said, "Sure, whatever works best." Paul just shrugged and wandered toward Sonya, thinking that he would be closest to the base of the ridge where they might see some evidence that might explain things. He wanted to be close to where the action might be, not too far down slope to be of any reasonable help. Sonya had suspected he would do this, almost expecting him to want to be on her high side and take over the investigation. At least they were now about to make progress.

Chapter 19

Lacey and Bert were the first to get out of the van. The looks on their faces expressed their feelings without words. The remainder of the group slowly followed them. One by one, they caught their breath, standing wordlessly, lost in thought. It would take a few minutes to assimilate what had just transpired in the vehicle. Lacey looked up the mountain side, eyeing the forest above, slightly nodding her head,

"There's no doubt about it, guys. I recognize that evil. It feels the same. What a difference a few years make though. It's time well spent. It's been hard at times, but worth the effort. Hmmm. Yes, I think we're ready this time. Okay, then. Are we agreed on the target?"

Each looked at the others in silence. From outward appearance they did not look like much, but this cohesive group was now as fiercely focused as any trained military unit. Although Bert and Calvin did carry rifles in case of a chance encounter with the bear, their greatest Weapons were not obvious to the casual observer. What they heard in this Prayer time was Powerful. Armed with Knowledge that did not come from their heads, they were about to mount this hillside, knowing that their enemy was not visible to the normal eye.

Each carried a Weapon far greater than guns or artillery against an enemy more cunning than those discernable to the eye. They were about to undertake an assault on an unseen and unwelcome intruder to Seeley's Mountain. Timing needed to be exact. Stealth was necessary. Their aim had to be precise. This search was not just going to be for Evangeline, but for an uninvited presence that few realized was even there. It was time to eradicate this thing before more damage was done. Now that they knew what they were up against, time was now of the essence. Each of them knew the stakes were high but they were now an Armed force, one their enemy needed to take seriously.

Bert broke the silence. "You know the drill and now you know more about what we're up against. Just stay tuned. We can't proceed without it. It could prove deadly. We should fan out, but in sight of one another. We want to cover as much territory as we can, but without getting separated. Does everyone have their radios on?" Bert watched as each checked to make sure they were on the same frequency. "If any of you hear anything we need to know, share the information immediately. It doesn't matter how inane it may seem to you, just share it with the rest of us. Someone else in the group might have Insight into its meaning."

The group touched hands and said, "Godspeed." They started to separate, when Lacey added, "Remember where our Strength comes from. We're going up the mountain in His Strength and Authority. It's time to Pray as never before!" A chorus of agreement murmured through the group. Purposely, this trained search group strode forth up the mountain. Though separated by a distance, not one was alone in their job.

Evangeline closed her eyes tightly as vivid images danced in her head. *No! Stop it.* Confusion barreled through her mind's eye, violently rattling her thoughts, grabbing at her resolve to continue, to try to survive. Pain bombarded her body from her head to her toes, savagely eroding any will to live. Panting, she struggled for breath and a coherent thought. Sulfurous fumes assailed her senses starving her of oxygen, threatening to suffocate her.

She froze, hallucinations threatening to consume her. Images of dark shadows and tentacles danced before her eyes, hideous faces taunting her to let go. Her vision grayed out and her ears now buzzed. She realized she was about to pass out.

She grabbed the wall trying to regain hold of reality around her. She could no longer see her surroundings but could feel them. Words flipped through her mind. Sensations were heightened. She strained to breathe and felt herself slipping downward, ever nearer the cold waters.

No! I can't go like this. Not now. Not yet. Hold on, hold on! Help me! I can't surrender. She sobbed. *Help me! Please, please, help me!*

Slowly, she opened her eyes, faint images before her came into view. Bit by bit, her vision returned; fuzzy images gave way to sharper focus. She was now able to look around her and see that her surroundings were real, concrete. She stared at the small beam of light from her torch. *What is this? Why can't I think?* The battle in her brain slowly surrendered to her will. The crazed images dissolved into lucid thoughts. Racing emotions quelled, allowing her mind to regain control.

Evangeline gingerly moved into steadier footing, easing her battered body into a stable stance. She wept deep soulful sobs. Wave after wave of emotion collided into one another. Slowly, she gained control. Questions overwhelmed her soul. *What happened there? I know I almost fell, but what went through my head? That was hideous. It was awful and . . . evil. What was that? Was it just because I hit my head or is something else in here? And what is it?*

No answers came to her mind. She panned the light around her to be sure that nothing else had changed. Her brain was playing tricks on her. Exhaustion and pain were wearing her away, no doubt. *What was I doing?* Straining to think with purpose, Evangeline leaned into the rock wall as she looked at her environment. The granite walls were unchanged, and evidently, neither had her situation.

Sense gradually washed through her mind. She remembered her dilemma. *Oh, yeah; the climb.* She shook her head at the thought. There seemed little use in trying to climb when walking was impossible; when catastrophe seemed so near, when she seemed consumed by this evil lurking in the darkness. *I need some help. I just can't do it alone.* "Paul, where are you when I need you?"

The question hung in the air. No answer came.

He can't help you now. She was startled at the thought. *Where did that come from? Was that from me? It seemed like a . . . voice.* Evangeline played the light around her to be sure no one was there. Nothing. No one was with her. *Now my mind is messed up.* She swallowed hard and tried to slow her breathing. Her heart pounded in her chest. *It's just too weird. I must be losing it completely. First those images, now a voice.*

Water was now trickling down her back as she leaned against the rock wall. She shifted uncomfortably. Looking down, she now saw that the depth of the pool was now gathering above her knees. *Did I black out that long or is the water filling the space that quickly?* Shocked at the mounting danger around her, she pointed the flashlight above her to the entry to the cavern, then slowly down again to the waters around her. *I have to get out of here!*

No, you can't.

Where did that come from? That wasn't me! Evangeline wildly moved the beam of light back and forth, hoping it was someone coming to help her. She had not said anything aloud, so how could it respond to her thoughts? It did not make sense. It must be her mind playing tricks on her. *Do people go crazy in confined spaces like this? Maybe I hit my head harder than I realized. I have to get out of here before I lose my mind completely!*

She forced herself to focus on the task before her. Evangeline straightened her body, trying to establish a more erect posture. She realized that her footing needed to be solid, but she could not see clearly into the dark waters. She would have to feel her way to the other side of the cavern. It was a painful process, inching her right foot forward to take a step, while feeling if there were any loose stones underfoot. She did not want to take any chances of slipping again. She now had to let go of the support of the rock wall and venture across the pool unassisted. It was nerve-wracking to think that her left knee might suddenly give way, but determination rose in her. *I just have to do this. No one is here to help me. I have to. Paul would do it. I'm sure Jack would too.*

The space remaining was a little more than ten feet across but it might as well have been a mile. Each careful footstep caused shooting pains in her knee. Her head was throbbing. Her hands were numb from holding the flashlight and backpack, but she had no choice. She had to reach the base of the rocky entranceway. *It better be there. I didn't imagine that hole. If there was a way in, there has to be a way out.*

The opposing wall was in her reach now. It felt as though it had taken an hour to move less than ten feet. She reached out to grasp the chipped granite. The stones she had slipped on earlier must have come from the walls of her rocky prison. Years of freezing and thawing during the winter must have opened crevices, allowing the pieces to break free. How much more of the wall was unstable? Was it useless to think she could climb the slope?

She leaned into the rough wall. It might not be comfortable but it was reassuring to have its support, while she regrouped her thoughts. *I thought I was in better shape than this. How could such a small effort take so much out of me?*

Evangeline lifted the flashlight to shine above her. No doubt remained in her mind. An opening, small as it seemed from her vantage, was barely visible. Below the gap, the wall sloped slightly, making it a less than vertical climb. However, it would be challenging to scale the wall under ideal circumstances, much less in her injured state. *It'll tell you what you're made of, I guess. Now, think. What do you have to do to make it safer?* Evangeline relaxed a moment, allowing herself the momentary satisfaction of having made it across the cave and willing herself to forget the hallucinations that had gripped her mind just minutes before.

Collecting her thoughts, she began to plan her attack. She soon realized that she would have to somehow strap the flashlight to the knapsack so she could have both hands free to climb. She looked inside the bag and found some spare shoelaces. It would have to do. She busied herself with tying the torch to the sack. Her hands were awkward and stiff from the wet and the cold. Twice she thought she had it secured only have it slip as she adjusted the pack. Both times she had managed to grab the light before it tumbled off into the waters. Frustration was mounting. Time seemed to tick away before her eyes and she had achieved nothing toward her goal of escaping.

Slow down, Gel. You can do this. Take a minute to regroup. You can do it.

What if you can't?

She drew in her breath and stopped what she was doing. *Oh, where did that come from? I didn't say that or even think it. I just don't know why I keep hearing these things.* "I can do it!" she yelled, anger rising within her.

What makes you think you can? You're injured and useless. You can't do that. It's ludicrous to think you can.

Chills made her shudder. Was it the voices in her head or was it the cold?

Evangeline closed her eyes for a moment, trying to regroup her thoughts. When she opened her eyes again she sensed a shadow in the periphery of her vision, moving, hovering above the water. How could this be? She felt fear gelling deep within her. Time stood still for a moment as her heart skipped a beat. She now knew she was not alone. Panic gripped her throat, choking her. Suddenly, she could no longer breathe. The image grayed out at the periphery of her vision, threatening to blacken out completely. A sulfurous odor gripped her senses.

Lacey stopped abruptly as she crested a steep section of the mountainside. Bert glanced her way as he spotted her action. He knew Lacey well enough to recognize the body language. He too stayed where he was, Listening, less to external sounds and more to the stirring in his spirit. Something was afoot. It was not good, but what was it? Bert caught Lacey's eye and saw a strong resolve forming on the soft creases of her face. He knew that Lacey tried to discourage those lines, but when facing such a battle in her spirit, the creases often pinched with her effort for control. *This must be significant for that look to be there.* He motioned for the others to stop.

Each of them in turn signaled the next person to stay still and Listen deeply. It did not take long for each of them to realize what was going on around them. It was not visible. It was not tangible, but it was there, nonetheless. They were not alone. Something was watching their movements, hidden from view.

Each marked their spot and moved toward Lacey and Bert. When the group was gathered, Bert remarked, "we aren't alone up here folks."

"Yeah, that's obvious. Any idea what we are dealing with?" replied Eli.

"Not exactly. It could be many things, but I'm sure that it won't show itself to us. It's watching though," Bert answered. "Lacey, what do you think?"

Lacey did not look up as he spoke, she seemed lost in thought. She held up a finger to ask for a moment of silence from the group. The forest was not quiet though. Winds were raging above them in the tree tops, while the rain escaped the canopy to splatter down on their hooded heads making a constant pattering against their ears. They could just make out the voices of those above them as they examined their terrain.

Each head bowed to concentrate on an inner Voice not heard around them. What they needed to know came not from human understanding, but a greater Wisdom than each or any of them had. It was not a time for egos. They needed Information that no eye could see nor ear hear from the clues surrounding them. Lives could be lost. Significant danger surrounded them, but it was not clear what it was. No doubt the bear could be nearby, but it might not be the only source of peril.

Each person, one by one, placed hands on Lacey's shoulders, entering communion with the Wisdom they sought so desperately. They could not afford doubt or fear, just unity in spirit and quest. It was so beyond their understanding that they needed to surrender to the Knowledge they so urgently needed.

Lacey was the first to look up from their Prayer. Each, sensing an Answer of sorts, followed her lead and surveyed the bush around them.

"That bear may well be still on the prowl, but I think we have more to contend with than just that." She shook her head slowly. "I think we have multiple threats here. The bear still is a problem obviously, but it has company if you know what I mean."

Sol scanned the group, taking note of the rifles that Calvin and Bert held. It was slightly reassuring to know that they had protection from what they might see, should it decide to come into the open, but what could not be grasped by sight was far more dangerous to them now. A hungry bear might be desperate enough to attack, but likely there was enough noise on this mountain to discourage even such a creature. The other entities were not to be trifled with by any novice and there were many on this hillside with them now. It upped the danger quotient to be among a group so ignorant of the menace creeping around them.

Solemn realization of what they might face settled into each group member. Jan squeezed Calvin's free hand as they started to Pray quietly, each in turn. A tiny island of Peace settled on the territory surrounding them. The Battle lines had now moved up the mountain. They were prepared to regain lost terrain and, in the process, souls. It would be a Fight to the death, but the death of what or whom?

Evangeline stood frozen, terrorized. Her vision was shadowy. She dreaded moving, afraid to catch the attention of anything that might be with her in the cave. Afraid. A fear so fundamental it came from a deep, deep place within her, permeating her cells and controlling her very core. Her thoughts dashed about, erratic images played before her mind's eye. The presence was on every side, above her, near her, pressing in on her, body and soul.

She closed her eyes to force the images to stop, to will the sensations to cease. Gasping for breath she gripped the rock wall for support, sensing she could collapse at any instant.

Slowly the wave of panic ebbed and she struggled for breath. Tears rolled down her cheeks in rivers as she sobbed. Such terror; it threatened to suck the life right out of her. It was pure evil itself.

Moments ticked by. No sound but the streams of water pouring into her surroundings. The fear eased and receded. She slowly opened her eyes, realizing that her vision had returned. She blinked scarcely daring to survey her surroundings for the presence she felt watching her.

She stared into the waters gathering around her, trying to make her mind work again. Was this presence she felt and saw actually there? Was her imagination merely playing tricks on her eyes?

She held her flashlight, pointing the lens away from the shadows she thought she saw. Nothing was visible in the gloom beyond her, nothing obvious anyway. Slowly she directed the light over in that direction, but saw nothing but wet rocks and water. *It must have been my mind jumping to conclusions.*

A rumble seeped into the cavern above her with the rush of water, and with it, a vibration. She felt the noise more than heard it. *What's going on above there? It must be the storm. Thunder, I guess. That shook the place. What kind of storm shakes a mountain?*

Evangeline played the light around her again, then above her head to the opening in the rocks. *Great! First danger around me and vibrations above. What next?* Water was rushing in every opening in the rocks, like the mountain was opening around her. New waterfalls appeared before her eyes, adding volume to the pool around her. The intensity of the rushing sound echoed, reverberating off one wall, then the other.

Urgency was building in her. It threatened to overtake her. No, it was not mere urgency. It was a growing sense panic now. There it was again, the presence, that evil entity. Something was here with her. She could smell it, like an animal sensing its prey. Only that was wrong. She was the prey here. Trapped; caged with something staring at her. Primal survival instinct started to surface, fuelled by raw fear. Rational thought escaped her; her mind was jumbled and chaotic as images crashed into one another.

Slowly she was aware of a low growl coming from the darkness beyond the illumination of her flashlight. Then it stopped. She strained to hear over the rushing waters. There it was again. Low and angry, the growl made her shudder. It was not her imagination. There had to be an animal close by, there was no doubt now. *Bears make that noise.* What could she possibly do against a bear in this cave? What possible defense did she have? Her breathing was becoming fragmented like her thoughts. Trapped, injured; she sensed the presence pressing in nearer.

She leaned into the rock wall feeling that she was beginning to crumple under the pressure of the unseen entity. The shadows wavered and danced around her. She was certain she heard a low snicker from the darkness beyond.

"Whatever you do, continue in Prayer. We move on, but we Pray," Bert said gravely. "We can't let up."

Each member of the Prayer team locked eyes and nodded. They now knew in their hearts that what they were up against was far more dangerous than anything that one could be seen with the eye.

They wandered back to their original positions and resumed their search, looking on the ground and around them. Separated by twenty feet or more, they slowly made their way up the slope, making a wide sweep below the search and rescue teams. Silently, they whispered declarations of God's Word to blanket the mountainside in Faith.

Focus, you fool! You'll die if you lose it now! She closed her eyes; her breathing came in shallow gasps. Waves of terror threatened to engulf her.

What was it that Sarah had said the other day? Thoughts crashed over her, spilling into emotions, tripping over and piling up against one another.

Think! She said something about her Faith or something. God. Prayer. Oh, what was it? She was groping in her mind for one coherent thought, desperate to extract what she needed from the swirl of sensations barraging her psyche.

Tell him. Yeah, that's it. Tell Him, she said. Tell him what?

What a fool you are.

There it was again; the voice, in her head. No, it was in the cave; in the cave with her. "Who's there?"

The waters splashed about her; the sounds escalated in her head until it cascaded into a voice of laughter. Snickering echoed in the darkness.

Who is that?

No response, save the crazed echoes of water rushing around her, squeezing in on every side now. No answer, but it was there, nonetheless. She knew now, there was something else in here with her, pressing in on her like the rising water. It was real.

Slowly Bert's group advanced up the mountain, closer to where the rescue squad scoured the ground for clues. Solemnly, they moved up the mountainside, Words of Prayer emanating from their lips.

Each member of the team sensed the change in the atmosphere. Every movement was an extreme effort. Oxygen was sucked out of the air around them, replaced by an evil mist. Their breathing was strained with every step.

Their mission was under siege by a menacing unseen force.

What makes you think you can escape?

Evangeline's eyes darted around her surroundings, trying to see what was there. Nothing firm met her eyes. Just a shadowy haze seemed to hang beyond the periphery of her vision.

I'm not alone!

You think. That's your trouble. You think too much.

I'm not alone! Evangeline bit her lip at the thought.

Yeah, it's an animal alright! Bears attack, don't they?

Evangeline put her hands over her ears, willing the voice to stop.

What can you do against a bear?

Again Evangeline pressed her hands harder over her ears, shuddering in convulsive spasms. Hideous laughter assailed her senses. Awful, evil snickering echoed around her.

What makes you think you can fend off a bear? And . . . then you have me to contend with too, don't you?

Evangeline tried to swallow, her throat seemed to constrict as she did. She bit her lip again, this time drawing blood. She groaned at the questions. What could she respond? *What did Sarah say about her Faith?*

Again, Evangeline sensed the snickering reverberating through the cavern around her. It seemed to come from various directions at once, surrounding her.

Remember, Faith.

Hideous laughter penetrated her head followed by a sulfurous odor.

Faith.

"Who . . . are you?" Evangeline surprised herself to say.

You don't want to know.

The voice stopped, but she felt its presence around her, just beyond her reach.

Quite the dilemma, don't you think. A bear, the unknown. Which would you rather deal with?

"Who are . . . you?"

Do you really want to know?

The question hung heavily in the stagnant air, drifting around her, as the sulfurous odor wafted about her nose.

Laughter warbled, fading, changing directions as it echoed off the stony walls. Hallucinations, hideous images molded themselves in the shadows, shifting, challenging, and surrounding her. No longer just hanging around her, they morphed into grotesque sinister colors. She could now taste it and sense it like an electric charge.

A low growl built in intensity. The animal could sense the presence too.

Evangeline wheezed, her breathing shortened, her chest was constricting. The presence pressed in on all sides now. She could no longer lift her head, so intense was her terror. She was cornered now, so was the animal. *What do bears do when they're threatened?*

The growl was louder this time. The bear sounded closer, angrier and ready for a fight. It let out a roar that reverberated off the rock walls and into her every nerve ending. She was bound in terror now; with it came nausea, bile rising in her throat. She stopped breathing altogether. Losing the will to stand, she slumped lower on the rock wall. Images of translucent dark hues swirled before her eyes, threatening to suck the life from within her. She leaned forward and retched pure dark bile, heaving to get a breath and whimpered a slow, long, painful moan.

The Prayers were spoken aloud now, audible and defined. They purposed in their hearts to speak forth the Faith they had in God's Word and the Protection He Promised. They knew their enemy, but just as much did they know the Source of their Help.

Jan fell to her knees under the spiritual pressure she was bearing. Her soul was bombarded by monstrous images that flashed before her mind's eye as she struggled to utter God's Word in response. Calvin moved in closer to her and was immediately knocked to his knees by the sense of an unknown presence. Resolutely, he continued in Prayer, slowly returning to his feet. He helped Jan regain her composure and together they moved onward, up toward the ridge.

Fight!

Confused, she whimpered under her breath, "How?"

Sarah told you how.

Sarah?

Sarah said it.

Sarah?

The voice came at her loud and sharp. *NO! Don't listen to that!*

The growl seemed closer this time.

See you're trapped!

Softly she heard, *Sarah said it.*

It won't help you! You are wretched and useless!

A small voice again. *What did Sarah say?*

The presence pressed in closer again, *No! It's too late. We have you.*

Sarah said she leaned on something.

Not here! Not now! You're such a fool!

Sarah said something about Faith.

Just nonsense!

Hope.

Don't listen to that!

You have nothing to lose. You have nothing else.

Don't do it!

The stench choked her, penetrated her pores, like a clammy drape blocking all reason.

Lacey stopped in her tracks, eyes closed, concentrating on a solitary Voice deep within her, drowning all outside resistance. Barely able to breathe she whispered Prayers, Declarations of what she knew to be True.

You can say it.

"No, I am not a fool!" *Where'd that come from; surely not from me?* Stunned at her words, she waited for her foe to attack. How dare she be so bold!

Of course, you are. You are stupid and useless!

Just say it!

Oh, what did Sarah say to me? Stop thinking so hard, just say it. "Lord Jesus, Help me!" It just blurted; its source was not a formed thought. It just gushed like the fountains from the rocks surrounding her.

She leaned back into the rocks; eyes squeezed shut, waiting for an ugly response from the voice. Nothing. She waited still further, expecting the next assault.

None came; just stillness amid the gushing waters. Seconds elapsed, then minutes; still no reply. Slowly she allowed herself to breathe, welcoming the intake of oxygen. Her cells, starved of vital nutrients, were about to collapse in exhaustion. Weak and dizzy from terror, she dared not move lest she drop into the rising pool of chilling water around her.

Breathe now.

Focus.

Breathe.

As she leaned against the wet granite wall, her senses gradually returned, now aware of her environment. The presence had retreated. The smell of the thing, sulfur, lingered in the air, but now dissipated with its withdrawal. It was not gone, she knew that, but it had stepped back; why she did not know.

What did I say? What happened? My mind must be playing tricks on me. No, that was real; as real as the rocks around me. It was and it's still here, just waiting now. Something made it move back. What though?

Slowly, Evangeline's breathing regained rhythm, feeding her body, energizing her. She listened and heard nothing but the streams of liquid pouring in about her. No voice, no bear, nothing. She felt the blood coursing through her arteries as her heart rate slowly returned to normal. Her brain started to engage. Thoughts passed in a flurry, straining to explain what had just occurred, with no coherence or structure. This surpassed normal experience. It was real but not 'real' at the same time. What lurked in the shadows defied her experience, her intellect. This thing played by different rules and she did not have time to learn the game before she escaped. She needed to leave now while she still had the chance.

Lacey lifted her head and opened her eyes, surveying her surroundings. Bert was on her right as he had been minutes before, but it could have been hours to her, such was the intensity of the spiritual attack they had just endured.

Lacey looked directly at Bert as he nodded back at her, acknowledging the burden he too had suffered. She took a deep breath and murmured, "Thank You, Lord."

Each person resumed their Prayers, sensing that their enemy was moving, shifting its strategies; searching for an alternate assault.

Chapter 20

Jack's group inched along the top of the ridge, analyzing all available clues. Broken branches and twigs showed direction of movement. Footprints were hard to see given the effect of the rain, but at least the canopy of trees above had given a little protection to forest floor for the first while. Now, any clues were rapidly eroding owing to the runoff. Little rivulets had formed where none had been before. The steep angle of descent accelerated the flow, etching paths as it traveled down the mountainside.

Painstakingly, they moved along the rocky outcropping, Jack above the crag, with the rest of his crew scattered above him in case Evangeline had moved up the hillside as she proceeded west. Nothing unusual was visible, much to Jack's frustration.

He had hoped that he had missed something the first time he had climbed the hill. He glanced toward Sonya and beyond her to Paul. They, too, were examining the ground for clues, checking the undergrowth and low hanging branches for signs of movement. However, they were not having any better result than he was in his position.

They were all nearing the end of the steep portion of the ridge now. Jack hoped that this area would show something he had missed before. If not, well, he did not want to contemplate that next move yet. He just returned to the job immediately before him for the moment. Better to be extra careful about what he had before him and not miss anything was his philosophy.

The storm slowed its movements, enjoying this new territory. Its energy was newly fuelled by the arrival of the cold front from the west. It was especially satisfying, as forces crashed above and descended below. Fingers of evil intertwined their way down toward the dirt below. The terrain was easy to penetrate and people were so unprepared for an event of this proportion. Yes, they thought it was merely nature at work. So naïve, they were; so ill-suited to defend themselves. The demon had lulled them so well into slumber about their abilities. Few had an inkling what could slow or stop the advance of this monster. So easy was this operation, so delicious the terror it incited.

The small number who exercised their Authority against it, merely were an irritation this time, like bumpers to deflect its course. So little hindered its flow. How pleasing this must be to the tyrant; how much fuel these creatures provided. The rising fear escalated the movements of this menace. They did not realize that they were increasing the danger they faced by their responses to this storm. Emotions bounced around these human beings, spiraling out of control, up into the surging monster, providing a defined path for it to follow. The greater the terror, the more it grew and curled into their midst. What easy pickings these mortals had become.

The sound of the creaking branches above them was beginning to unnerve Sarah's resolve to be on the mountain. Little had been achieved so far. She watched as Sonya had stooped occasionally to examine the peaty ground, looking up and around to sense the direction of movement that the disturbances of the ground indicated. Often she frowned as she stood again, evidently dissatisfied with what she had found.

Paul was about six feet down slope from her position, looking sullen and increasingly moody. His brooding expression was not lost on Sonya. She sensed the gathering frustration that Paul was feeling. She was not a stranger to this emotion, as she had often felt the same thing when she first worked these rescues. So often, a search was unproductive, with no hint of satisfaction, when suddenly a crew member radioed an important clue and redirected the search to a different position with a good result.

The key was to wait it out and keep your eyes focused for any slight variation in the expected terrain. No evidence was too small to overlook. But that patience came with experience because emotions can easily distract and sway your discernment. Sonya had enough practice now that she could see footprints in this peat, where the typical untrained eye would see nothing.

Jack had been her teacher for that. They had spent hours analyzing various soils and surfaces in training sessions. She admired his penetrating eye and had learned so much from his experience. However, Paul did not have this keen eye and his roiling emotions were simmering under the surface and blinding any effectiveness he might have. Only an obvious sign would strike him as noteworthy at this point, she guessed. That was why she put herself closest to the base of the ridge. If anything was visible, she was available to pick it out, if she could keep Paul out of her way.

Then she saw the change in Paul's expression and she knew trouble was about to explode.

Bert, Lacey and their party paused in their ascent. They had chosen a path perpendicular to the rest of the crews, trying to catch any other possible descent path that Evangeline had taken. At the same time, they spread their Prayer blanket as broadly as possible from below. Bert was slightly ahead now and radioed a request to stop for a moment. They were on an alternate radio frequency from the rest of the rescue crews, so as not to interrupt their progress. Their methods were different and could cause confusion to the other groups.

Bert asked for a check from the other members. One by one they conveyed what they had seen, sensed and discerned both from the physical environment and the shifting spiritual atmosphere. They had no doubt about what they had just felt. Their enemy was not visible yet was palpable to their trained spiritual senses. It lay like thick smog, draped over the mountain, lurking, waiting for a chance to attack.

They agreed on their plan, each standing, renewed in resolve, clothed in unseen Armor and speaking words unfamiliar to most of those above them. It was a Fight as well as a search, gleaning Wisdom beyond the obvious. Their methods of operation were precise, calculated for superior effectiveness, but using the least effort. They were trained and experienced in ways few would suspect.

They realized the nature of the enemy they faced on this mountain. They knew its source and its goals. It was evil to its core and had to be dealt using rules the world did not understand and would disregard. This group understood the character of the efforts used against them and knew the stakes were higher than the others realized. Lives were at stake here and not just Evangeline's.

The swelling surge of water descended the mountain carving new trails, pushing obstructions out of its way. The steep grade provided momentum for its advance toward the valleys below. Obstacles were lifted and displaced to make a smoother descent, more efficiently than any mechanical excavator. The hands of nature were more effective than human-made equipment at reforming the terrain. The efforts of humanity did little to slow its relentless pursuit lower and deeper into the Earth. The storm had a life of its own. It moved and pushed and chased a path prescribed by physical forces and demonic entities. Some people were taken by surprise; some ran for their lives out of the way in its menacing race for lower elevations. Some were the unfortunate recipients of a beating beyond human endurance as trees and vehicles and even buildings were uprooted and carried along by the pulsing maniac as it coursed to the valley.

It was just the beginning. What began above would end at a destination below. This demonic force could not remain in the upper atmosphere for long; it was no longer its place to be. No matter, better pickings came in the lower strata anyway.

Evangeline panned the flashlight again around her surroundings and saw no obvious intruder, although felt the remnants of its presence. Thoughts tumbled forth, one after another. *I have to get out of here.* The light beam gyrated as her hands shook uncontrollably. She swung the light side to side, up then down again. *What do I do? Where do I go?*

Again she shuddered at the memory of the hideous voice. Not trusting that it would not immediately return, she shone the light back and forth, looking for the presence lurking in the darkness. *What do I do? Up. That's the way out. I can't go back. That thing is back there. I have to go up. But how? What am I to do? I have to get to the hole in the rock. Now!*

She leaned against the rock face trying to calm herself; her thoughts reeling. Painfully she forced herself to breathe and think. She pointed the light above her, focusing on the cave entrance, her only avenue of escape. Her thoughts began to align as her pulse slowed. She closed her eyes and fixed her mind on the task at hand. *What was I doing? I have to get out of here. What do I do next? The flashlight; I have to secure the light!*

Fumbling, her cold fingers grabbed the bag and the shoelace again. Awkwardly, Evangeline managed to secure the torch so it would shine above her shoulder as she climbed the wall. But that would make it impossible to see into the inky blackness below her once she started to climb. *What if it follows me? What if it traps me on the wall? What do I do then?*

She shook her head. The thing seemed to have retreated for the moment. She was not sure why it had stepped back away from her words. Yes, that is what she felt had happened. Her words had repelled the presence for the moment. How long it would remain quiet she could not guess. The time was now; she had to commit herself completely to the task.

Oh, how can I do this? It's impossibly wet and steep. No, just do it; don't question it. The alternative is . . . is what? That voice! What is it? Where did it come from? Don't think about it; just do it!

Evangeline turned her body, slowly easing herself around, so as not to twist her knee, looking for the source of the voice. She had to force herself to put her back to the intruder. She was completely vulnerable to attack now. In her weakened state, her resistance to the stabbing pain in her knee was low, causing her to cry out involuntarily. She did not want to expose her weakness to the entity that waited in the shadows, but she knew it was already aware of her state. It had mocked her abilities already; it knew her emotions.

She faced the rock face now. Placing her hands above her, she groped for a handhold on the rough surface, anything to give her leverage to raise her. Her hands were so wet and cold now that the sensation in her fingers was dull and tingling, making it hard to tell what she was grasping. Finding a ledge to grip, she realized that she now had to climb.

But which foot should she try first? If she used her good leg to find higher footing, she would have to put all her weight on her twisted left knee and she knew the pain that it would cause. If she stood on her stable right leg, what good would her left leg be to her climbing, levering her body up. *How can I do this?*

As she draped herself against the wall for support, she felt the fear rising in her again. It started as an uncertainty and quickly rose to a pinch in her chest. Her pulse quickened and her muscles tightened. The calm of a few minutes ago was ebbing and the presence in the shadows moved toward her again. She felt it; she smelled it, stronger this time. She sensed its presence, its noxious emanation yet felt its delight at trapping it prey. It enjoyed watching her panic. It was a game to the thing. It was like the way a cat plays with a cornered mouse, batting and pawing away at it until it succumbs.

What do I do? What do I do now? Calm yourself. It wants fear. Settle down. How? How do I not fear? The question hung in her mind, burning in her for what seemed eons.

A quiet whisper within her spoke gently but firmly, "*Trust.*" She swallowed hard. Trust. A single word. It sounded so simple, but seemed so hard. *Who do I trust? Me? Paul? Jack? That didn't work before, did it? Look where it got me!*

Evangeline pressed her head into the rock wall in front of her as if the hard surface would push her mind to comprehend the thoughts passing through it. If she did not move, either way, the thing behind her would win; she would surely be defeated and die waiting for rescue or be attacked by whatever was in there with her. Climbing was an impossible task. She let out an involuntary laugh. *Now I really am between a rock and a hard place, aren't I? What worked before? What gave me the courage to climb?*

Her mind was playing tricks on her and could not be trusted. She froze for a moment and her heart took over, the only thing functioning at this point. "*Trust Me.*" She heard those soft words again. *Who? Trust who? That thing? Whose voice am I hearing now?*

You can't tell, can you? You are foolish and silly and useless and you know it.

No, I'm not! I can do this.

Well, just try, then. Then we'll see, won't we?

Determined to climb, Evangeline shifted her weight, testing her legs as she braced herself against the rocks. It was going to hurt no matter what, she realized, but she had to move or be overtaken. This presence was pressing closer to her, emboldened by the darkness, fuelled by her rising dread.

She rose on her right toes, putting her full weight on her good leg, as she reached above her to grab the jagged edges of the cut rock. With no gloves, the sharp surfaces cut into her manicured fingers, making her wince, but she knew that it was nothing compared with the pain she would endure should she use her left leg for support. She had to move now. Having secured a handhold, she used her upper body strength to pull her body up as she swung her left foot upward, feeling for a place to rest her foot. However, the rock was sheer: slippery, smooth and wet. *There has to be somewhere to put my foot! Come on. Find it now.* Precariously, hanging by her arms, she felt her grip slipping and panic wanted to twist into her Heart.

"Trust now!"

Hanging like a kite stuck in a tree, she grasped at whatever would support her. Trust? It was all she had now. "Ahhh! Okay, I Trust you! Just help me!"

The panic subsided again. Her foot found a ledge, out of nowhere. She was sure it was not there a second ago. At the same moment, the pain shot through her knee at lightning speed, ricocheting into her brain. "Ahhh!" Sobs loosed from her mouth, echoing throughout the cavern. It took several moments for her brain to register that she was off the rocky floor and on the wall, one small step closer to her destination. As the pain lessened slightly, she could focus her thoughts again.

It was impossible. I couldn't do that. I was so sure, I couldn't without help. Was there help? What happened here? Who was here? Who talked to me?

Uncertainty swam in her reasoning. Here she was a foot off the ground, one foot closer to the entrance above her, but so many more feet yet to go. Slowly, she realized that the other voice was now quiet. It had retreated. Where did it go and why?

"Okay, whoever you are, I need your help now. If there ever was a time to Trust someone, something else beyond me, it's now. Oh, Jesus, I need you now. Sarah said that you are Real, so I have no choice but to Believe You now. God, help me. I have nothing to offer You, but Help me now!"

"Trust Me."

It was soft, simple and quiet. Just a Voice from somewhere that differed from the taunting voice she heard before. Encouragement was in this Voice; a quiet Strength sure of its Power.

Evangeline looked above her to the gap in the granite that imprisoned her. It looked distant and dark in the dim light from the torch. She shifted her position slightly to illuminate area above her, to see if she could visualize a path to follow. It was awkward to use the light in this manner and she could see so little. Every movement caused jabs of miserable pain in her knee.

How can I go where I cannot see? How can I trust my leg to support me? What was I thinking? I can't possibly do this.

"Don't trust your leg, Trust Me. Follow the Light."

Evangeline was about to protest that the light was weak, so was she, when the rocky expanse above her seemed to brighten slightly. A dull glow emanated from the granite that seemed dark and foreboding a second earlier. Slowly it became brighter and brighter. What was happening, she could not fathom. She wondered if she had lost all sense of reality now. Was she drifting into the insanity of this prison?

Paul looked up at Jack directly above him on the ridge. He had reached the end of his patience. With no sign of Gel anywhere, Paul was annoyed with the charade unfolding around him. He wanted to confront the 'expert' and challenge his training. The circumstances were utter nonsense.

Sonya recognized the change in Paul's stance and turned to face him directly. Although there was a rocky cliff between them, it looked like Paul wanted to bolt right up to where Jack stood above him. She was the only thing between him and this insane urge and she did not like the odds. She knew she could not stop him if he were to charge. She had seen men do stupid things under similar circumstances. It made no sense, but in these situations sometimes guys were driven by caged emotions that were about to explode.

"Paul, can you tell me the color of Evangeline's backpack? I want to be sure I don't miss small fragments if I see them." Sonya's strategy was to distract Paul with a question to break his pattern of thinking. However, she realized that if he were motivated by emotions, it might be too late. She kicked herself for not having kept a closer eye on this guy.

"Uh, black, I think. Maybe some red on it. Did you see something?

Where?" was Paul's disjointed reply. He had not taken his gaze off Jack above him.

"No, just wondering, you know; just in case. Have you seen anything resembling tracks or a trail of any sort?" Sonya was trying to use any type of question at this point. She also pressed the call button on her radio to attract Eddie's attention. Unfortunately, it would call the rest of them too, but it might break the tension for a moment; long enough to diffuse a brewing problem.

"No, don't you think I would have said something if I had," Paul responded irritably. He jumped when the radio chirped at him.

"Oh, sorry that must have been me, by mistake. I didn't mean to do that." Sonya covered her ruse. Eddie looked up immediately and caught on to what was going on right away. He casually wandered toward Sonya but he knew that trouble could be brewing.

"You got a problem with your radio, Sonya?" Eddie commented as he passed Paul.

"No, no problem, just fumbling fingers, I guess. Did you spot anything of interest down there?"

"Nothing much," Eddie replied. He lowered his voice and added, "Mind you I did spot some old bear scat, so it has been on this side of the mountain in the last day. You got any other concerns you need to let me know about?"

"Perhaps, keep yourself available. He's volatile now," Sonya whispered. Aloud she answered, "I'll put my radio in my pocket so I don't to make that mistake again. You keep your eyes open for boot prints. If she took off down the mountain, she might have crossed paths about where you were positioned. I just don't want to miss any signs."

Paul glanced at them suspiciously. She was not sure that she had fooled him, just aroused his curiosity. The reporter in him would see through most things she did to distract him, but at least it might have stopped him for the moment and that was all she cared about now.

Eddie meandered back down the hillside to his original position. He kept one eye on the terrain around him and the other on Paul in his peripheral vision. *Nothing worse than babysitting supposed grown-ups!*

"Let's get back to business, okay guys?" Sonya motioned everyone to resume the search. Paul stood where he was, still staring at Jack above him. Sonya shook her head knowing that a confrontation was about to erupt and there was little she could do about it now. She only hoped that the rock face would keep it verbal and stop any physical contact from happening.

"Hey, Jack you see anything that can help us up there?" Paul called.

Jack stopped what he was doing and stooped to the ground. "Just examining the last of the prints that I think are Evangeline's. The others are probably yours or Eddie's. They're too big to be hers. They seem to end around here though. I think she probably backtracked along the rock face. I am going to check along there to be sure." Jack was trying to remain calm and not be suckered into an argument with Paul. He would be far more effective conducting the search than ducking this guy's questions about now.

Mac moved from his location, realizing that Paul was getting agitated. He was his best friend and could probably hold him back if necessary. Sonya was grateful at the gesture.

"Look, Jack, you lost her trail the last time you were up here, what makes you think you can find it this time?" was Paul's response.

"I didn't take the time to check as closely the last time. This time I`m doing a more thorough examination of the evidence." Jack regretted his use of that word the moment it came out of his mouth.

"What do you mean, evidence? You think there has been some crime or something?" Paul was looking for any kind of thread to grab to start a fight at this point.

Jack slowly stood and shook his head. "Paul, it was a poor choice of words, that's all." Jack breathed a long sigh and pressed his lips together. He searched for the right words to say that would not set Paul off completely. "Look, Paul, I'm just trying to do the best job I can for you. I want to be thorough, not miss any small stuff, you know." Jack wanted to add that he could help things a lot more by not hindering him at what he did the best. It was his expertise. He had done it for more years and in more miserable situations than he cared to share. However, he held his breath and did not add anything more. His frustration level was mounting as well and he did not want Paul to stir up his emotions.

"You think maybe Sam should take over for you here? Seems like you could use the help," was Paul's loud reply.

At that last response, Sam appeared from behind Jack and stood beside him, both towering above Paul, side by side. The message was clear: 'you mess with Jack; you have me to contend with too'.

Mac had moved in beside Paul from below, just close enough for him to know he was there but not so close that it made him feel cornered. Paul looked at the men above him then over at Mac. He felt like a caged rat under inspection. He wanted to escape and charge after someone or something. He just did not know what. He yanked off his knapsack and threw it past some underbrush. The explosion startled Sarah and made her jump. She let out a small shriek. She had never seen Paul so explosive.

Mac turned to face Paul and blocked his path to Jack. Paul reached toward Mac, realizing at the last second that it was his friend and not Jack. His sight was blinded by rage fuelled by frustration. He grabbed Mac's arm and was about to throw him aside. Mac held him fast and diffusing the energy of the blow. Paul began to reel as Mac stood firmly planted to the ground. The momentum of Paul's movement sent him flying past Mac on the ground. In a heap, Paul breathed heavily and closed his eyes.

"Easy, Paul. You're among friends here; remember? We're here to help too." Mac said as he regained his balance. He reached out his hand, offering to help him up.

Paul looked up at Mac and shook his head. "Sorry," was Paul's reply. He continued to shake his head. He closed his eyes again and looked down. "Look, I, uh, I didn't mean to hit you. I just . . ."

"Sure. No problem. I understand. If it happened to Sarah, I don't know what I would do. We're all upset here; none more than you. Look, this isn't how it was all supposed to go down this weekend . . ."

Paul opened his eyes and nodded, "No, it sure wasn't. And it wasn't supposed to storm this bad either. It's all like one bad nightmare after another. How much worse can it get?"

The question hung in the air. Everyone listening knew one way it could get worse but dared not say it, especially in front of Paul. The events could become far more disturbing and they knew it.

Chapter 21

Lacey called on the radio. "I think something is going on up there. It's not just about Evangeline now. Get to work, guys! I don't know what it is, but we need to support them now!"

Contrary to what one might expect, they stopped in their tracks. Not moving toward the confrontation, they stood still. They looked above them and called for Wisdom and Intervention from sources unseen. Theirs was an intense Battle, yet not a physical one. They directed their energies toward a different enemy, one with an army bent on the destruction of every person on this mountain today and more if it could achieve it.

It made no sense to put their efforts in confronting behaviors or emotions. They were merely the aftereffects of strategies of demonic forces. Their efforts were directed toward the source of the problem and the only Power effective against it. They did not want to get into the fray or cause more tension up there. That would neutralize their effectiveness. No, each held their Place and Purpose. Their Weapon was Prayer. Each remained steadfast in the Support they provided on this mountain. It was a struggle, a fierce Battle being waged for their souls in this storm. It was a visible storm waged on land, but a spiritual hurricane in the unseen realm.

Evangeline had hung on this ledge for far too long. Stunned by what she thought she saw, she seemed unable to move until she had processed her thoughts. But what could one think about such things? It was beyond understanding, at least understanding as she knew it. *What is this?*

She stared at the rocks above her. Sure enough, a glow had appeared. She was certain that it had not been there before. How could it illuminate by itself? It made no logical sense. But then, had any of this experience made sense up to now? There were those voices, one inside her head; the other one, well, who knows where it was from.

I'm standing on a rocky wall contemplating voices. Whoa. Okay, so I have to climb to escape. Keep your grip on reality here, girl. Do what you did the last time. Lean on your good leg and reach up. Grab onto the rocks above you. Pull up. Follow through with your other leg. You can do this. You have to do this! "Oh, God, help me!"

She reached above her, grabbing for a rocky ledge, then pushing up. Miraculously she found purchase and control. Again she repeated the procedure, somehow achieving a new level. Agonizing pain followed as she twisted to gain purchase on the rocks. She cried in pain and she almost lost her grip completely, but suddenly leaned into the rock face with what felt seemed like a slap on the back.

The pain was beyond endurance, making her mind go blank and blurring her vision. She thought she might vomit. She could not understand how she maintained her position. As she hugged the granite wall, she became conscious of a calm surrounding her that she could not explain. Gone was the fear. It was just her and the wall now. She felt plastered to the rock face now; secure in her position, but unable to move up or down. It was as though some force was pushing against the rock, holding her in place. *What is going on here? That glow on the rock, this pressure on my back. It is surreal. I can't understand it.*

Paul sat on the ground, shaking. Mac let him go, knowing he needed time to decompress. "I'm sorry, man. I don't know what came over me. I just . . ."

Jack watched from on top of the ridge. He could understand what happened. He had seen it before. He had experienced it himself. He had been in training and was under so much pressure to perform that he had cracked one day with a member of his unit. Blind rage was a terrible thing. He knew it and he swore it would never overtake him again. He had been disciplined over that incident and was fortunate that they had not kicked him out on his butt. *Second chances. Yeah, they're a good thing. I can give this guy some space. Been there, not going back.*

Sol and Hildy slowly proceeded up the hillside with the rest of the group. Hildy was on Sol's right side as they ascended. The slope was getting much steeper at this point. With the rain, the footing was getting more precarious. The winds whipped the treetops above their heads causing them to twist in a tormented dance. An eerie roar and whine could be heard as the gusts of wind wound through the branches, causing a demonic symphony above their heads. It was not a place that they would want to be, given different circumstances. They had ventured into the den of evil and it was not for the faint of heart, physically or spiritually.

Most people on this mountainside were completely unaware of the additional dangers that were faced this day. They saw merely the tangible effects of this hurricane. They saw rain, the trees bent to their limits, the sounds of the wind in the trees, felt the cold and the wet. But what they missed was far more ominous and insidious and penetrating. It had far deeper implications than the physical damage caused this day, but the remnants of fear it seeded in the soul was lifelong and corroding. That was the enemy they faced on this slope this day and the Prayer group knew it.

Although it was a formidable foe, they had the Tools to handle it. They were Equipped and they knew it. Experiences and study had cumulatively prepared them for this day, as this one as would prepare them for the next Battle. That was the way their Commander worked with them and Trained them. He was Patient and Kind but Honored their Obedience with increased Responsibility and Knowledge.

Both Sol and Hildy were in excellent physical shape, hiking and swimming in the summer and skiing in the winter. They took full advantage of the terrain for their leisure activities and could out-climb most other parties on this slope. The weather made it a miserable hike today, however, and the grave consequences of their mission weighed heavily on their hearts. It was not an amusing trek up Seeley's Mountain; their enemy was greedy for death and destruction today and they knew it.

The group with Sol and Hildy was now making slow progress to the ridge. It appeared that something was amiss as everyone in that area was standing around waiting–for what, they could not tell.

Bert veered to Eddie's position. "What's going on here?" Bert questioned.

"Ah, just letting off a little steam, you might say. Paul's getting a little antsy about the situation. Not that I can say I blame him. But he kinda wants Sam to do most of the work. I think he's had enough of Jack about now."

"Mmmm. Okay then," was Bert's noncommittal reply. Bert wandered back to Lacey and the rest of their assembly had gathered. "Looks like Paul's about reached his limit. I'll have a little chat with him, but you guys need to back me up as I do."

Bert ambled to Mac and Paul. He put his hand on Mac's shoulder. As Mac turned to him, Bert nodded to him, like a father offers his help to a son. Mac smiled weakly, appreciating his support. "Anything I can do to help here?"

Mac turned and took a few steps away from Paul who was pacing a few feet up the grade. Bert followed close behind him. Mac leaned into his ear to be heard over the roaring wind, "Look . . ." Mac paused to gather his thoughts. "Paul's under a lot of stress here and could use some support. You seem to have a handle on Prayer, and . . . well, I think we could use some about now, you know."

Bert smiled at Mac again, "Mac, let me assure you, we have been doing that all the way up the hillside already."

Mac looked at him with a puzzled look. "You've been Praying all the way up the mountain, not just earlier? I hadn`t thought of that. So you guys aren't just here to help with the search while you're climbing?"

"Let's just say that we search and provide support in varied ways. Sometimes these situations require more Wisdom than the obvious clues might provide and we think that having a continuous pipeline to the Father helps at times. The rest of the squad has learned to appreciate an extra set of hands for the search and to respect our methods, though they can be a little different. We don't get in their way and they obviously don't hinder in what we do. We stay more to the periphery unless we feel we have something concrete to offer," Bert explained.

"Mac, I don't know where you are coming from, Faith-wise, I mean. But we're a group who have a comfortable relationship with our Heavenly Father and His Son, Jesus. We trust the Holy Spirit to provide what we need in any situation and this type of event sure needs extra Wisdom.

Let's say, we provide physical and spiritual support. We tap into Help that is beyond our physical ability. It has supplied surprising results at times and that is what has garnered us sufficient respect among the other members of the squad so they not only permit us along on some of these rescues, but they`ve asked us to participate."

Mac stood there digesting this information. He had not encountered anything like that before. Where he came from, church was confined to the church walls on Sunday. Sure people went to Bible study groups sometimes but Faith was mostly private. It was something they drew on within themselves and did not talk about with others and usually was reserved for the big crises in life. What he witnessed was not that kind of Faith. It was much more dynamic in nature; more practical and every day.

"I think that Paul could use more of that Prayer now. He's at the end of his rope. I don't pretend to know everything that is going on in his head but I think he's seen too many nasty situations to have a clear view of this one. He's not religious, you know. He might not receive it all that well. It's a part of my life that we don't discuss. He has blown me off when I've talked about it in the past, so be careful how you approach him."

Bert shrugged and replied, "Don't worry, we've encountered this before. I don't even have to go to him just yet to Pray for him. I usually ask the Holy Spirit to open the way first. It isn't my job to do that. It's just my position to look for the Leading of the Lord to act. He'll work in people's lives to offer them the opportunity to turn to Him. I'm merely his hands on Earth to do the work when Assigned to do it. I thank you for the information, though, because it makes our Praying easier when we know more about what happened." Bert put his hand on Mac's shoulder again and looked him in the eyes. It was a kind but penetrating gaze. "We'll Pray for you too, if that's okay with you."

Mac was riveted by the depth of Bert's eyes. They were not just looking at him; they were looking into him; not in a fear inducing way, but with compassion and sympathy. He deeply cared and it stunned him. He did not know him, yet he seemed connected with him. He had never encountered that before. *Oh, those eyes.*

Mac hesitated for a moment, not because he did not want to receive Prayer, but because he was digesting what he was seeing. "Yeah. Yeah, that would be good. Do it for all of us. Gel needs it the most at the moment. But, yeah, I'd appreciate that." Mac turned and walked back to Paul, head down, considering the conversation.

Bert turned back to Lacey and the others who had gathered and watched the interchange between the two. Jan was the first to speak, "So . . ."

Bert pursed his lips together and replied, "Paul is having problems with all this. It's to be expected. It deserves attention though. I just suspect that it may be a distraction leading us away from the essence of the issue. We'll add it to the list, but not eliminate the primary target here. We've been through this before as you know. Our adversary doesn't devise new tricks, does he?"

Lacey nodded. She knew all too well what Bert was talking about. The day Warren was killed, she was off course in her understanding of the enemy's tactics and lost big time. That would not happen again if she had her way. It was also too easy to become emotionally involved and lose sight of the root problem with disastrous consequences. It had taken her years to forgive herself for her lack of Insight the day Warren had died. It was a hard lesson to learn. Lacey and Bert's eyes met in understanding. He was one of the few who understood the pain that this had caused her and he was protective of her as a result.

Calvin added, "We must be getting closer to finding Evangeline if he has stooped to these tactics. Make sure that your radar is tuned. You never know what is about to happen. It had better be soon, because I think this storm is intensifying, if that is even possible. It sure is getting darker up here." Calvin had to shout to be heard at this point. The trees above were strained to their breaking point by the screeching wind. It sounded like some demonic creature crying from the pit of hell protesting their appearance on the hillside. A loud snap could be heard on their right side, followed by the fall of another large branch from a tree overhead. "That was too close!" Calvin exclaimed.

The radios crackled to life and each in the squad heard, "Is everyone alright?" It was Jack's voice. Responses came over the airwaves confirming each group's safety.

"Keep your eyes and ears open guys. We`ve got a lot of dead wood ready to come down with this wind. Some of it is big and it can do some serious damage. Stay alert. Stay tuned for updates," Sam added.

Jack and Sam both knew what updates meant and they were hoping that Paul did not. Sam meant that if the conditions became more dangerous, they might have to pull people off the search. It was the last thing that Paul would want to hear, so he was careful to phrase it so he would not spark another incident. He hoped it would not come to that and they would find Evangeline sooner than later. It was not a decision he wanted to make.

Sarah watched as Mac walked back to Paul's side. They talked for a moment then Paul glanced to where he had flung his backpack. Sarah was closest to where it had landed and started to stride toward it. Lacey was close by and fell into step with her. "What are you up to?"

"I just thought I could retrieve Paul's bag for him. He threw it over there in his fit of anger a while ago. I'm just glad I wasn't in the way. This event has made us all doing stuff we'd rather forget, I think," Sarah answered.

"Let me help you with it. You have your sack to carry," Lacey offered as they made their way over past the clump of bushes. Lacey had to yell to be heard over the wind. The rain dripped from her hood onto her cheeks as she stooped to grab the bag. As she did, she stopped midbend. Sarah looked at her and asked, "Are you alright? Did you hurt your back or something?"

Lacey straightened with a puzzled look on her face. "No, I'm fine. But . . ." Lacey paused, thinking, searching.

"What's wrong? You look troubled. What can I do?" Sarah was worried for her.

"Nothing. Just give me a minute, would you. I have to figure something out. We've missed something and I don't know what it is," Lacey responded, holding up her finger to indicate she needed a moment's quiet.

Sarah's mind raced. What could they have forgotten or missed? What could she possibly mean?

Chapter 22

Evangeline felt completely stuck and useless, plastered against the wall and unable to move up or down. She was waiting for something; but, for what? Wouldn't it make more sense to move up toward the entrance than halfway between the pool below and possible rescue? Every time she tried to move, she felt herself starting to slip.

She had called out again in frustration to the mysterious Voice, but there was silence. Deep inside her, she sensed *"Trust Me"* was the only response she would get. She was getting a little frustrated at this point, however. What could she possibly gain by staying where she was? "Trust You to do what? To leave me hanging like this?" Evangeline yelled.

Silence from the Voice. The sound of water rushing in around her was all consuming now. Streams flowed freely from every crevice in the rocky prison. The level of the pool below her was rising dramatically again making a descent out of the question. Fear began to creep back into the darkness below, slowly rising like the waters. She could feel its entrance. Trust. Fear. Both had staked ground in this cavern. Both were beckoning her allegiance. She was not sure which would win. She realized that Trust had gotten her up this rock wall this far and fear had threatened to consume her and kill her. What did she have to lose by Trusting an unknown Voice, when the alternative was death?

"What are you waiting for? I Trust You, okay?" she yelled, to make a statement to herself and to the presence of panic creeping ever closer. "I Trust You."

Lacey pressed the button her radio, signaling the rest of her crew. Mac became curious when he saw Eli, Sol, Hildy, Jan and Calvin join Bert as they approached Lacey. *Sarah is with Lacey, so it must concern Gel.* He strode to the other group. Everyone had a quizzical look on their faces. No one had any idea what she was up to.

When they had all assembled around her, she said excitedly, "Look, I don't know what this means, but I sense that we have missed something. It's . . . over here, I think. I have this feeling there is something here. Look for yourselves."

Lacey reached down to pick up the backpack and as she did, she saw it. A small fragment of material was caught in the bushes. It was so tiny that it would probably have been missed it had she not felt led to look in that specific spot. "What color was Evangeline wearing or the knapsack she had?"

Sarah answered immediately, "She had on a blue jacket with black trim but her bag was black with red on it. Red's her favorite color. But she also had the rain slicker. I don't know. What do you see? I can't see anything."

Lacey walked to the clump of bushes. Deep in the branches, on the side closest to the rock face was a minute scrap of red material; no more than a half inch across. Sarah exclaimed, "That's the same color. How could you see that? It's so small, so . . . hidden!"

Lacey did not respond. She was immediately joined by Bert and Eli as she pushed her way into the bushes. They were dense and hard to penetrate. Mac came to help hold the bushes open as they pushed them aside to reveal the base of the rock wall. The ground seemed loose and spongy along the rocks. It looked to be an area that was pulled away from the granite revealing what could be a small opening. Scuff marks along the base of the boulders could have been made as something scraped along the lichen on the rock face.

Lacey's eyes flashed brightly in the gloom of the dwindling afternoon light. Mac's foot almost slipped into the opening as he moved in for closer inspection. "Whoa, that was close. Do you think she's somehow down there? I mean, it's such a small opening. How could she?"

Lacey looked him in the eyes directly and spoke clearly. "Call Jack and Sam and Paul over here now. They need to see this, now!"

Mac turned to look over where Paul had been a minute ago, but saw that he was already on his way over, pushing through the group. Jack and Sam had run down the slope of the rock wall to join the crowd.

"What have you got there?" Jack yelled to them as he darted down the shallow rock face.

"I'm not sure but it looks like a hole in the rocks. It's small, but Gel is small herself. She might have slipped through the hole, I don't know. Come look for yourselves," was Mac's reply.

Paul beat Jack to it, pushing his way past Eli and Bert; he scrambled to get a closer look. "Where is she? Have you found her?"

Mac pulled him back for a moment. He didn't want to get his hopes up unnecessarily but he too could hardly contain his excitement. "Look, we don't know. It's a small hole. But she might have slipped through. Give Jack a chance to look at it. Okay?"

"Are you kidding me? Let me in there to see. I've got to get closer," Paul said he tried to push past Mac.

"Paul, let him check it out . . . if she's not in there, there may be clues on the ground we might miss up if we charge in there," Mac countered. He wanted to be sure they weren't acting rashly or making things harder for Jack and Sam.

Jack made it to the base of the rock and squatted on the ground. He felt the loose peat and gently pulled it aside to expand the opening. He took off his backpack to find his flashlight, only to be handed one by Sonya. "Beat you to it. I had the same thought," was her comment.

Jack grabbed the torch and turned it on, pointing it into the small space. "I can't see much. The rocks curve and block my view. I'll have to get in somehow if I'm going to see anything."

"Are you kidding me, Jack? There's no way you're going to fit in that hole! You're way too big. If Evangeline is in there, she must have squeezed herself like a rabbit to get through. You must be twice as big as her," Sonya laughed as she bent to get a better look. "The only people small enough to get even close to that space are me and Sarah. I'm calling this one. I've got the training here to do it."

Jack pulled back from the hole and turned to look Sonya squarely in the eye. Sonya smirked at him and added, "If it is okay with Sam, after all, he's the situation leader here."

All eyes turned to Sam, who was already preparing ropes to secure her for her entry. "Sonya, you have the assignment."

Evangeline could hear muffled sounds from above her, but nothing distinct. The rushing waters around her obscured most other sounds.

Okay, is this my imagination again? I can't take more disappointment. This better not be my imagination. Let this be real!

"God, You said, "Trust Me," and I did. Please come through this time," Evangeline said aloud.

She tried to adjust her position to get higher but started to lose her tenuous grip on the stony wall. Desperate to get the attention of whoever might be above, she mustered as much breath as she could to call out. "Help me! Can you hear me? Help me!"

She waited for a response, but heard nothing more than a muffle from above. "Come on, now. You've got to hear me." Then she tried again with all her remaining strength, "Help me! Paul, is that you. Come and get me!"

Lacey kneeled near the opening in the rocks as Jack and Sam helped Sonya don her gear. She pulled down her hood and listened carefully. She thought that she heard a voice inside the rocks. She held her breath as she strained to listen. "Evangeline, can you hear me?" she yelled into the opening.

Paul ran to Lacey and got as close to the opening as he could. "Gel, are you in there? It's Paul. Can you hear me?"

Evangeline listened with her eyes closed, trying to focus. Although muffled, she was sure she heard a woman's voice, then her heart almost stopped. She was sure that it was Paul's voice. She would recognize it anywhere, under any circumstances. "Paul, Paul, I'm down here. Help me now. Help me!"

She attempted to look above her again. This time she was sure she saw a small reflection of light, this time from a flashlight. A directed beam from a flashlight, not some supernatural glow from above! It was real and from someone, not something.

Evangeline's heart began to pump again, now on overdrive. She had nearly given up all hope they would find her. Now she realized that Paul knew where she was and had come to get her. She was dizzy with excitement. It did not, however, change her predicament of being stuck on this rock wall. That was something Paul would have to figure out when he found his way in to get her. It just mattered that he was there. Surely Jack could figure out a way to get her out.

Okay, hang on, girl. Help is actually on the way!

Jack and Sam ushered Sonya to the small rocky cleft. Paul was on his stomach reaching the flashlight in as far as he could put it and yelling to Evangeline, "Hang on, honey, we're coming down to get you. Are you hurt? Are you alright?"

Lacey tapped him on the shoulder and said, "Paul, give her a chance to answer you. Can you hear what she's saying?"

"Barely, it is kind of distorted. Wait, I think she said she's okay. Uh, no, maybe, not so okay. I can't hear distinctly." Paul shifted his position; reaching in as far as he could manage until his shoulders stopped him from entering any further. "Gel, are you okay?"

A small voice met his ears. It could have been the sound of angels to his ears, when this time he could make out her voice and knew it was hers. "Paul, I thought I'd never hear your voice again! Oh God, thank You! Thank You! Paul, you have to get me out of here soon. I don't know how much longer I can hold on!"

"What's wrong? Hold on to what?" was Paul reply.

"I'm stuck on this wall. The cave is filling with water and I'm stuck. Help me quickly!" was her answer.

Paul responded immediately, "I can't see you, but help is on the way. We're sending in someone to get you. Hang on till Sonya gets there. You can do it. I know you can. Just hang on a little longer!"

Sam moved into where Lacey was kneeling and put his hand on Paul's shoulder and said, "Paul, Sonya's ready now. You have to move to let her in. It's time to get her out."

Paul yelled down to Evangeline, "Gel, I've gotta go now. Sonya's on her way in. Give us a minute to change places and she'll be there to help you."

The weak response came back, "Good. Hurry. Please, hurry. I need help soon."

Paul backed out of the hole. He was on his hands and knees and up to standing in one swift move. He grabbed Sonya's hands and appealed to her, "Just hurry as fast as you can. She sounds desperate. She said something about being stuck on the wall. I don't know what she meant, but she sounds as if she can't hold on much longer. She said the cave is filling with water. We have to move fast."

Sonya locked eyes with Paul and replied, "Paul, I will do everything I can to make this work. I want to do it safely for Evangeline, so let me work as I need to, okay?"

"Sure, whatever you need to do, just do it. Go! Go now. We have to get her out now!" Paul was on the edge of panic at this point. The stress had built to a fine point and was about to explode from inside him. He was eager to have it all take place quickly; petrified they would not get her out in time.

Paul stepped back out of the way and let Sonya take his place. Mac and Sarah came over and stood beside him as they watched Sam and Jack help Sonya make her way into the hole. It was a good thing that she was so petite. Paul had doubted her abilities earlier in the day when he first saw her, thinking that anyone so small could not be any good on a rescue detail. He changed his attitude as he watched her slight frame slip into the minute hole in the rocks. Ropes attached to her safety harness held her from falling into the cavern as well. She was wearing a helmet equipped with a light and microphone system to communicate with the rest of the squad.

Jack talked to Sonya as she inched her way into the dark recesses below, "What do you see? Where is she located?"

"Give me a minute to round the corner. The rock slopes then drops off suddenly. Ah, okay. I have her in view now. She is partway up the rock wall. She must have tried to climb to get out. Hold on. I'm going to talk to her for a moment. Evangeline, my name is Sonya Countryman. I am member of the Rescue Squad. I've come to help you out of here. Are you hurt?"

"Thank God, you're here. I am kinda stuck here. I can't seem to climb any further and I keep losing my grip. I don't know how much longer I can hold on. I hurt my knee badly. I hit my head, my shoulder, my arm. I can't climb any further. Just help me, please. Oh, please, please, help me."

"No problem, Gel. Do you mind me calling you Gel?" Sonya asked her.

"Sure. Whatever; just get me out," was her breathless response.

"Okay, Gel, I'm going to talk to the folks on the surface now for a moment. Just hang on a little longer and we'll get you up and out of here as quickly as we can. I need to back out and get some gear to pull you up, but I'll be right back. I won't leave you alone for long. Keep talking, okay?"

"Yeah, I'm getting tired though. I don't have much strength left."

Sonya asked to be pulled up again and was soon out of the cave. "She's climbed partway up the wall somehow. I'm not sure how she did it though. She said she hurt her knee and her shoulder. It must have been some miserable climb for her to have gotten that high on the wall. Guys, quickly, I need another harness and ropes to secure her because she won't be able to help herself much from the look of it. We have to work as fast as we can. I don't want to leave her alone any longer than necessary because it looks as if she could easily fall back into the water. Surprisingly, she managed to climb a fair distance up, but that means she has a good fall if she loses her grip. "

A scurry of activity followed as gear was gathered and packaged compactly to make it through the narrow opening in the rock. In a few minutes Sonya was making her way back into the hole, feet first this time so she could rappel down the slippery granite wall and get beside Evangeline to secure her properly.

Evangeline did not know whether she should be relieved. She realized that if she relaxed she might not be able to maintain her position on the wall. She had felt all along that there was some force pushing her against the stony façade but she was not willing to test her theory and risk a deadly fall into the rocky pool below. She just waited for Sonya to make her way to her level. *Lord, You said to Trust You. I have to give it all to You now. I can't move and I can't help myself. I can just wait. Wait and Trust You. You got me this far. I'll just wait.*

As Sonya moved in by her side, she spoke softly to her, "Gel, how are you doing now?"

"I'm not sure. I'm glad you're here. Where's Paul?" Evangeline whispered.

"He's outside the cave. You fell through a tiny hole and I am the only one small enough like you to get through to do the job. He's waiting for you above. Don't worry; he's fine and wants to see you too."

Tears welled up in Evangeline's eyes as relief flooded her system. She added, "Good, I'm glad he's there. Is he mad at me for getting lost?"

"No, Gel, he's just worried about you and just wants you safe. I think he loves you and just wants you back up there with him. He's not mad," Sonya reassured her.

"Good, I'm glad. I'm happy you're here now. You don't know how relieved I am to see someone. I was so scared. I thought I'd die here. I was just so frightened."

"I can imagine you were. You did a good job here. You almost did our job for us. You came close to rescuing yourself. Now, Gel, I am going to carefully put this harness around you so you cannot fall. The ropes are attached securely, so once the harness is on you can relax a little. Then I am going to take your vitals to see how you're doing. Okay? Do you understand?"

"Yes, I really want that harness on because I am sure I can't do this much longer. Just do what you have to do," Evangeline answered as her tears spilled down her cheeks.

Sonya leaned herself against Evangeline to brace her as she put the harness around her body. It was difficult to achieve as she was lying flat against the steep rock wall. Any jerking movement might cause her to slip and fall and that was the last thing that Sonya wanted at this point.

"I'm just going to talk to the rescue squad now, so give me a moment. Jack, I have her secured so make sure the ropes are taut. I want her to be able to relax her grip now. You copy?"

An affirmative reply came back to her from above. "Gel, you can gradually let go now. Do it slowly to ensure the harness is holding well enough."

Evangeline tried to release her grip but to her surprise her fingers did not want to move. She seemed to have a death grip on the rocks now. She had maintained the position so long that her fingers seemed permanently welded onto the rocks. "I can't move them. My muscles seem locked."

"That's okay, Gel. You don't have to do anything. I'll get the guys to lift you a little and that will release the pressure for you. Jack, could you raise her just a few inches? It will help her ease off the ledge she's on."

"Roger. We're lifting now. Six inches. Is that enough?'

"Affirmative. Whoa. That should do it. Hold her there until I give you the signal. I want to check her vitals before we go any further."

"Roger. We'll hold until we get your signal. Jack out."

"Gel, I am going to ease your arms down now. Just relax your muscles. The harness is doing all the work now. That's it. Let me help you. You're doing well. I'm going to take your pulse then I'm going to put this blood pressure cuff on you to see how you're doing. You look great under the circumstances. How do you feel? Any pains other than your knee and shoulder?"

Evangeline hesitated before answering, "No, no, I don't think so. I am so cold though. I can't tell."

"That's okay. We'll have you out in a jiff and get you warmed up."

Sonya took Evangeline's vitals and realized that although she had injuries, she was in stable condition and ready to extricate.

Sonya talked gently to Evangeline, "Gel, it's time to get out of here now. We're on our way up now. Just do as I tell you and we will be out of here soon. I might need your help getting you through the opening because it is small, but for the trip up, you just enjoy the ride."

Evangeline gave her a weak smile and said, "I just want to go home now. Can we go home?"

Sonya smiled back. *It might be a while before you get home, but I sure will do my best to get you to safety.* Sonya was not optimistic about their chances of getting any further than the local access road. From the reports that were coming in earlier, the roads were rapidly being washed out and impassable in all directions and the conditions were deteriorating quickly. It was going to be a rough night even if the rain were to stop now. It had not shown any signs of abating and the forecast was grim for the overnight period.

Chapter 23

Hurricane Igor had been downgraded from a level 5 storm to a level 2 by now, but its collision with the cold front from the west had refueled and restored its fury, ensuring its devastation inland. Its winds whipped to a frenzied dance, demonic and insane. Its swirling lashes overtook the landscape allowing it to entwine itself into the most fortified structure. It took delicious pleasure by taking these mortals unprepared. They were the spoils of victory. The panic it induced replenished its waning energies. Vehicles and dwellings that stood in its path were never a match for its rage. Restrained from this territory for so many years, its welled up fervor had to be unleashed in a cataclysmic discharge, like the horrific damage inflicted by a cat o' nine tails pounding repeatedly on human flesh. Only this would satisfy this hideous demon.

At the mouth of the cave, Paul waited anxiously with Mac and Sarah and the others. It was difficult not being able to help with the rescue, just waiting for the efforts of one other person. Mac and Sarah, arms draped around one other, silently supported Paul. No words were necessary; they knew what the other was thinking. They listened intently for any communication on the radio, trying to snatch any fragment of news before it could be taken from them. They hardly dared to breathe.

Bert and Lacey and their group sat on the sloping rock face above the unfolding scene, also listening, but Praying and engaging the enemy in unity. They were not passive as they watched. Their waiting was different; Active and Purposeful. They knew the stakes were high, the extraction would be difficult and the instability of the victim could increase dramatically once she knew she was being rescued. It was a juncture of extreme vulnerability and Prayer was essential and needed to be continued, not stopped.

The extra members of the search team were called down from their deployments on the mountainside. Some lingered as they packed their gear, but they now knew that their services would be needed in other venues beyond the mountain. They realized they could not stay to savor the victory with the others. Their services were increasingly needed at lower elevations where the conditions were becoming increasingly dangerous. It was not an evening to sit back and enjoy a job well done. They had to move before the roads were impassable, locking them into this area, unable to provide the services for which they were expertly trained. Their window of opportunity was rapidly closing. Reluctantly, they dispersed to the areas where they would be most crucially needed.

Vehicles began to pull out of the clearing below, their headlights barely visible through the driving rain. Only those essential to this extraction remained. Anxious words were spoken among the support personnel as they attempted to obtain an ambulance unit for Evangeline. None was immediately available; all were engaged on calls down the mountain in the valley below.

"Is your patient stable?" was the radioed message.

"Yes, for the moment. But she is injured and will need transport soon. We are concerned about hypothermia and latent shock once extraction is complete, besides her other stated injuries. Over"

"We are overwhelmed with higher priority calls at the moment. You know the drill. Execute it. We have to triage and prioritize accordingly. We're handling heart, blood loss and airway issues first. We don't have the personnel and equipment available at the moment. We'll get back to you if things change. Use the equipment and training at hand until our status changes. Over."

"Copy that. Our resources are thin at the moment, but we will make do. Don't forget us. We'll continue to contact you for updates. Over."

A convoy of vehicles descended the mountain. They headed toward the lake then beyond through Lofton and into Moulton. What they would encounter on their trek, they did not know, but they were prepared to face any challenges. Fortunately, the Rescue Squad had traveled in SUV's equipped for the rugged journey they were about to encounter. They had chainsaws and other gear necessary for navigating treacherous conditions. It was a band of men and women dedicated to tackle the situations that most others would go to lengths to avoid. Their training and endurance would be taxed to the limit tonight.

"Okay, Gel, I need to know whether you can help me. This opening is small. Somehow you got in wearing a backpack. Without it on, it should be easier, but I won't kid you, though you're tiny, it's a tight fit."

"I think I had the straps on loosely after putting on the rain slicker. I think I forgot to tighten them again. The pack must have slipped over my head as I slipped down the opening. It all happened so fast, I'm not sure. I don't remember much. But my arm was sore afterward, so I think it must have been yanked above my head as I slid in," was Evangeline's response.

"That sounds logical. I'm going to cut the pack off you now. It will make it easier to maneuver," Sonya continued to talk her through her procedures.

"I have stuff in there that I don't want to lose. Don't junk it! Please, don't throw it away," Evangeline reacted in tears.

"It's okay. I'll secure it to a rope and we can pull it up later, okay?" Sonya responded calmly.

"That's good. Thanks. I think I can squeeze through the opening if you help me. My leg is useless to push with though," Evangeline offered.

"It might be better if I package you for transport and have the guys pull you through the opening," Sonya said as she planned the extrication.

"No! No, please, let me try to do it. I don't see how that would be good. It looks awkward and I think I'll end up more bruised that way than if I try to do it myself. At least let me try. You said that my vitals are stable, so it shouldn't be a problem. Just a bit painful," Evangeline pleaded.

"Okay, I think it is worth a try, but let me know if you experience anything that might be a sign of problems; any dizziness, undue pain, difficulty breathing. Promise me, now," Sonya conceded.

"Okay, guys, we're coming through the opening. Gel is coming first. Keep her rope taut and follow my instructions. Don't just yank on her because we have to negotiate the curve in the rock and find a way to squeeze back through. Okay?" Sonya radioed up to the surface.

"Copy that. Talk us through it. Over."

"Gel, can you get your arms over your head and skinny yourself as much as possible? Yeah, that's the way. Okay, guys pull nice and easy now," Sonya instructed.

They continued to inch Evangeline up, slowly and painstakingly she moved to the narrow opening until her hands poked through the soil above. Inch by inch, they were now able to move her shoulders through until finally her torso was now visible. Gradually, they continued to pull her hips and legs through the small hole.

Sarah was amazed that such a tiny opening could swallow a human being. Seeing how difficult it was to extricate her, it seemed impossible to have occurred in the first place. Evangeline's situation had been unexpected and her location would baffle the team for the rest of their rescue careers. This scenario was one for the training videos!

Sarah stood as close as possible to watch as they gently lifted Evangeline the final few inches. The group applauded as she was carried to a spot a few feet from the opening.

Lacey grinned at Bert as she watched them bring Evangeline out into freedom. "Praise, the Lord. Thank You, Jesus! You Did it again," she said.

Bert nodded and replied, "Thank You, Father, for Your Help. Thank You."

Lacey replied, "Amen."

Sonya was the next one to slowly emerge from the cavern's small entrance. Jack was on the ropes as they pulled her the final few feet and he lifted her as she struggled out of the minute hole. She smiled when she realized it was Jack. She then made sure that Evangeline's beloved backpack and its contents were brought up behind her. She and Jack walked to where they attended to Evangeline, to assure themselves that she indeed was stable.

The EMS personnel permitted Paul a brief kiss on the forehead before they attended to Evangeline. They had set up a make-shift shelter as a first aid station using a tarp to shield them from the rain. It flapped violently in the wind but did provide basic protection in which to work.

Paul hovered as close by as the staff would allow. Evangeline was busy answering questions and could merely smile weakly at Paul as he stood impatiently on the periphery nearby.

Jack turned to Sonya as she began to remove the safety harness and said, "Good work. That was a tight space to maneuver through. You seem to have gotten her out in one piece."

"Well, I know you would have preferred to be the one to go in, but sometimes we small and mighty ones can get the job done you know. Maybe I'll command a little more respect from you guys in the future." Sonya was just teasing Jack and he knew it but decided to play along.

"Just because you did one good job doesn't mean you've hopped up the promotion ladder yet," he teased.

"One good job? Hah, you know that I'm better at what I do than half the guys on the squad!" Sonya retorted with a laugh.

"Ah, don't let the others know I said this, but you might be right." At this point Sonya realized that he might be flirting with her. That was high praise from Jack Davidson.

Mac and Sarah stood behind Paul watching as the medics worked with Evangeline. They were relieved that she was found and now free to receive care. Mac turned to Sarah and gave her an embrace. "I am so glad she is alright. If it had been you . . . well . . ."

Sarah looked at him seriously, "I know. I kept thinking what I would do if you had disappeared like that. So many strange things pop into your head when it seems so inexplicable. I was thinking the wildest things . . . why it had happened, where she was, nasty outcomes. It was awful. I'm so relieved that it had such a good ending."

"I agree, but you know we still have to get her to a hospital to be checked. I never heard an ambulance arrive, did you? Mac commented.

"No, come to think about it. I had all my attention on the rescue, I wasn't thinking about an ambulance. Those medics are part of the field rescue team, aren't they? Where's the paramedic unit?" Sarah asked.

Mac looked into the growing gloom of the forest below them and realized they were too high on the slope to see any vehicles from their position. "I don't think there is one yet. They may be held up by the storm."

Mac scanned the area and confirmed that the two medics were

part of the original squad who arrived with Sam earlier. "It looks like we might be going it alone. She's stable, for now anyway. Once we get her down to the road, they might have better idea of what needs to be done."

Sarah observed the steep hillside below them and realized the next hurdle would be difficult as well. "Yeah, but first they have to get her back down to the road. It doesn't look as if she's in any shape to walk. I'm sure they said she'd hurt her leg. Carrying her down on a stretcher will be treacherous."

Mac hugged Sarah again and gave a peck on her wet forehead to reassure her. "We'll see what they do. They probably have some first aid gear in their vehicles. If it's serious enough, they'll drive her out, I'm sure." They stood there watching for a few more minutes, then Mac realized they would soon be preparing to move down the hill. He added, "Let's see if there's anything we can do to help get her back down. If nothing else, we can gather the gear."

Mac and Sarah joined Bert and Lacey's group who were already packing some extrication equipment. Mac pulled Bert aside and asked, "What happens next here? Is there a way we can get her to a hospital to get checked out?"

Bert frowned and explained the position that had been sent from the EMS dispatch office. "I think it's going to be hard to get far tonight. If she is as stable as she appears, we might be better to make it back to Lacey's house tonight for shelter. She has a large house and it's well equipped for a storm like this. We might cause another crisis if we venture further in this storm. They're reporting deteriorating road conditions and some flooding. We'll do well to make it back to Lacey's."

Mac shrugged and realized that circumstances were dictating their next move. His heart wanted to move back to the safety of the city but his head soon acknowledged the foolishness of this thought.

The medics had now allowed Paul to move in beside Evangeline. He gave her a gentle kiss as she said, "See, honey, I'm just fine. Twisted and bruised is all."

Paul turned from her to face the medics. "So is she giving me an accurate report? Just twists and bruises?"

The medic closest to him replied, "Essentially, but she needs to get out of those wet clothes soon. I'm concerned about hypothermia under these conditions. The sooner we get her off this mountain, the better. We'll monitor her condition to be sure nothing else crops up. We'll have to splint her left leg. She has a nasty gash on her head that makes me suspicious of a concussion or neck injury so we're going to keep a collar on her to be sure. If you could let us get her ready, we'd sure appreciate your cooperation. The sooner we get her down this mountain, the happier we'll be. None of us need to stay here any longer than necessary with these branches flying everywhere. There's no sense taking any chances of anyone else getting hurt!"

Paul nodded his head and gave Evangeline another gentle kiss as he backed out of the way to allow the medics full access. He stood watching their work but never took his eyes off her.

The convoy of SUV's wound their way down the mountain, stopping occasionally to remove limbs and entire trees obstructing their path. The road was completely washed out in two locations alone before they hit the highway. Only vehicles like theirs, with off-road capabilities, would be able to negotiate the terrain at this point and not for long either. It was fast becoming obvious that those still up the mountain would be locked into their location until the worst of the storm dissipated. They also realized that the runoff that caused these washouts would soon be causing increasing difficulties down in the valley. Stream and rivers were already overflowing their banks, so the priority was moving toward evacuating homes to prevent any loss of life in the low-lying regions. It was going to be a long and perhaps terrifying night ahead.

Sam, Jack, Sonya and Bob were in the throes of packing the larger equipment boxes as Eli wandered over. They were discussing the cave that had swallowed Evangeline. "Did you know that there were caves on this side of the mountain?" Sam questioned.

"Not that I was ever told about. It hasn't been my interest to do cave exploration, so I've never looked into possible sites before," Jack explained.

Bob interjected, "Well, I think we all knew that there were caves over on the western face of the mountain. Heck, we used to explore them as kids. We even found some artifacts in them from the old days. We were mad when our parents took them away from us and gave them to the museum in Moulton. There were some spooky ghost stories that cropped up as a result. But no one ever talked about any caves on this side though. I'm sure that I would have known about it if they'd been discovered. What are the chances of us finding them this way though?"

Sam wound up a rope as he added, "It's often kids playing or hunters who discover these things. I would just rather not repeat this experience though. It's been a rough one. It could have ended a lot differently had we not found her when we did." Sam stopped his winding and frowned. "So who exactly thought to look there?"

Sonya paused as she put her harness in the box, "I think Sarah and Lacey went over there. Yeah. They went to retrieve Paul's knapsack. Something must have caught Lacey's eye over there."

Jack helped Sonya put the lid on the harness box and remarked, "I guess I'll have to ask her what it was. But you know Lacey; she has her hunches that don't always make sense. This one panned out at least." He shrugged and returned to loading up the gear.

Eli nodded. He knew about Lacey's 'hunches'. Most would call them intuition or luck or superstition. Eli knew the Holy Spirit prompted Lacey to look where she did and He had nothing to do with luck. He was certain she would tell him more about it later. There might be a time to share the information with these fellows soon enough. All in God's timing though.

By the time Jack's group had their gear stowed and ready to take back to the vehicles, the EMS staff had Evangeline fitted with a brace each for her leg and neck. They had already transferred her to a litter to carry her down the slope. It would be a slow task owing to the steepness of the terrain and slick footing. They were trained to do it, but did not want anyone to injure themselves on the way down, much less what it might do to Evangeline should they drop her.

Dusk was now descending on the mountain, amplified by the low brooding cloud cover. Rain continued to drum down on their hoods as they made their way down, taking deliberate steps to avoid slipping and jerking their precious cargo. By the time they broke out into the clearing by the road, the full blast of the wind hit them at once almost knocking them over. They had not appreciated how much shelter the trees had given them until they were out in the open and unprotected.

They picked up speed as they neared the vehicles. It was decided that they would try to use the Bob's van. Bob and Jack jumped in the back and flipped a seat down to make a flat surface to receive the stretcher. They eased her in and the medics hopped in with her. Bob closed the hatch behind them to give them shelter from the rain. He then moved quickly to the front and climbed in to start the engine to provide lights and heat.

Jack moved around and climbed in the passenger side, shutting the door against the raging wind. "Whew, that's better," Jack said breathlessly

Bob nodded agreement, rubbing his hands together to try to get some warmth into his frigid fingers. "The temperature dropped in the last while, didn't it?"

Jack agreed as he turned toward the medics, "So what do you think our best plan is here?"

Larry Walters looked up from his work with Evangeline and said, "I don't know. I was hoping by the time we got down that the ambulance would have been available and here, but obviously we're on our own. Let's see what Sam has to say."

Jack looked out the window of the van in time to see Sam arrive and yank open the side door. He jumped in and slid the door shut. "Okay, what's your assessment, guys?"

Larry nodded at Parker Johnson, his partner, and Parker responded, "All vitals are normal at present. We have to get her warmed up, that's a priority now. The other injuries would best be assessed in hospital but I don't think we're getting back-up here, are we?"

Sam shook his head slowly, "No, doesn't look like it's going to happen. All units are tied up and the roads have deteriorated significantly. They can't risk losing a vehicle with all the calls down the mountain. Believe me it doesn't sit well with me, but with the budget constraints lately, it doesn't surprise me either. So do we take her down now ourselves or do you think it can wait until the worst of the storm is over?"

Larry and Parker looked at each other and shrugged. Larry answered, "Under normal situations I wouldn't hesitate to have her checked at the hospital. But you know as well as I do what we are dealing with and under the circumstances, I think she can wait till morning. Her vitals are all stable. Her injuries are painful but don't seem life threatening.

Getting her warmed up is the most important thing at the moment, which can be done locally. The trip into town might do more damage than good at this point, especially if we find the roads are impassable."

Sam looked at Jack and asked him, "You think you can handle it from here?" Jack nodded and said, "Sure, no problem."

Larry asked, "Where do you plan to go; back to your place?"

Jack nodded and said, "It's probably closest to my place than anyone else's, so that would be the plan." Jack paused and added, "If Lacey will agree, I think her place is probably more comfortable for Gel. I doubt she'll have any problem with it."

Parker then asked, "Anyone check if the roads are still passable that way?"

Jack shook his head and said, "We'll head out in a convoy to assist one another in the event anyone runs into trouble."

Bob agreed, saying, "This old van has seen a lot of bad road conditions and come through it all. We'll make it, don't you worry."

Sam looked at the vehicle and thought that it looked like it had too. *If they stick together, it should be okay.*

Sam nodded and slid open the van door. He got out quickly closing the door behind him. Jack jumped out and followed him toward Sam's vehicle where Sonya was waiting for Sam.

Sam unlocked his truck and turned to speak to them. Knowing that both would want to go down with him to help handle the growing number of emergencies that were being faced by the rescue squad, Sam decided to address the issue head on. "Jack, my friend, I have to head back to town now to check things out down there. You need to get some rest. You've been going all day on this thing. And Sonya, you did the extrication, so you are officially off-shift and need to get some rest too. I'd like it if there was a trained medic with Evangeline, so could you accompany her to Lacey's?"

Both started to protest, but Sam would not hear of it. "Look, you'll be no good to me if you're all worn out. Jack, you have a responsibility to take care of those folks and you know it. And don't you go laying any guilt trip on me about helping tonight! Get some rest and if everything is stable up here, you can always follow down on the four-wheelers in the morning. I have all available personnel pulled on-shift for this thing. We can manage without you two for tonight. By morning, you'll be rested and by then we'll need more help as all the flooding hits the river."

"It probably has already started from the sounds of the reports that trickled in earlier," Jack protested.

"Jack, I insist that you get some rest and food into you. You're too valuable a commodity to take a chance like this. You take care of your charges and I don't want to hear another word from you. Sonya, it's an order from your superior. Keep an eye on him to make sure that he does! " Sam waved them off as he started for his vehicle.

Jack followed him. "Hey, Sam!" Sam turned and gave him a look as if he did not want to listen to more protests. "No, Sam, I just wanted to thank you for all your help up here. It wasn't the way I expected the day to go down, you know. You shouldn't have had to come out here and bail me out when there's so much else going on."

Sam shook his head and said, "Look, you're like a brother to me. You call and I come. No questions asked; no explanations necessary. It could have happened to any of us. It was a freaky incident. I know you would've done the same for me and have lots of times before. Go get some rest and food and I'll talk to you later. I'd better get going with the remainder of my crew. There's strength in numbers under these conditions. Gotta go now! See ya."

He did not give Jack more opportunity to talk about it. He climbed into his SUV and shut the door. Jack waved him on and turned to his group.

Chapter 24

Paul climbed into the van with Evangeline and was ready to go. It was decided that Eddie would accompany Bob in the van while Sarah and Mac would stick with Jack and Sonya in his truck. Lacey and Eli and the others would meet them all back at the house.

They packed the remaining pieces of gear and soon were carefully making their way back toward Big Rock Lake. The visibility was negligible as they crept along the road. Fog lights did little to illuminate their path in the driving rain. Although there were some washouts along the road, the route was passable. However, everyone was relieved as they turned in to Lacey's parking area.

They backed Bob's van as close to the house as they could then set themselves to carefully moving Evangeline into the house. Lacey was the first through the door. She flicked the light switch but found that the power was out. "Well, I can't say that's much of a surprise considering the extent of the storm. We've lost power in far less than this. Okay, it's a good thing the generator is in good working order and I have lots of fuel for it too. Always pays to be prepared up here," Lacey commented.

Jack and Paul followed Lacey in, carrying Evangeline. Despite her protests, they had elected to keep her on the stretcher to minimize the strain on her bruised and battered body. Lacey directed them to take her to the large couch in the great-room so she could be close to the fireplace. Their priority was to warm up her core temperature to more normal levels. Lacey also pointed out that they could keep an eye on her more closely than if she went into the back bedroom.

Lacey brought out several blankets and pillows and a warm robe to wear and with Paul's help, Lacey and Sonya set out to make her more comfortable.

Paul asked her, "How's the pain, Gel? Did they give you anything for it?" Paul was starting to fuss over her. If she were feeling better, she would have loved the attention. Now it was almost more than she could bear.

"I'm fine, Paul, really I am. They gave me some good meds and I feel kind of spacey. I'm just cold and wet. If I can get out of these wet clothes, I know that I'll start to feel better."

With that, Paul and Sonya helped her remove her wet attire and change into the dry robe. Soon they had her settled with pillows to support her left leg and head, covered her in layers of warm blankets.

"It feels good to lie on something soft. It's so much better than that cave . . ." she murmured. She began to frown at the memory.

"It's okay now. You're out and safe. You were good at hiding though. It took us a long time to find you. You can thank Lacey and Sarah for spotting the place where you fell in. I don't know how, but they did."

Evangeline said weakly, "I'm just so glad you got there when you did though. I couldn't have lasted much longer." With that, Paul pulled the blankets around her more securely.

With Evangeline settled, Mac and Sarah headed out the door to go fetch their luggage from the cabins, hoping they still had a dry change of clothes for all of them. Jack was already outside talking to Bob and Eddie before they left. "Thanks for all your help today guys. I appreciate it. Sorry it didn't go the way we planned."

Eddie shook his head and said, "Look Jack, uh . . . I'm sorry I lost her so quickly. It was my job to keep track of her, but . . ."

Jack cut him off before he had a chance to say more, "Hey, dude, there was no way you could have predicted that one. How many sessions have we done without trouble? Nah, I'm just glad you were there to back me up. It would've been five times worse trying to handle that by myself."

Bob and Eddie turned to get back in the van as Jack added, "You guys don't take any chances on the way back. If you want, you could stay here."

Bob cracked a smile and answered, "Jack, if I could get this old van over here, I can get it back to Eddie's then to my place. You go tend to your people." With that, he backed out on the road and headed away from the house.

Jack watched their taillights disappear quickly into the driving rain then turned to help Mac and Sarah. He hoped they had remembered to close the windows in their cabins before they had headed out in the morning or there would be no dry clothes to change into tonight.

Calvin handed Sol the matches as the two worked to get a fire going to warm up both the house and Evangeline. Meanwhile, Jan and Hildy busied themselves with gathering any food that was leftover from the supplies in their vehicles. Although, they had made it available to everyone, most members of the squad had left in such a hurry that few had time to grab a sandwich before departing.

Lacey brought out lanterns and distributed them between the kitchen and great-room, while Eli and Calvin went to the back porch preparing to start the generator. Until they got it going, they had to make do with lanterns and the light from the fireplace.

An especially strong gust of wind sent a whine through the house as the windows vibrated. They looked out the window in time to see a garbage can fly by.

"Did you see that? I wouldn't want to be in the path of that thing!" Hildy remarked as she stepped away from the window. "This has to be the worst storm I've seen. I've been around for a few years, although we don't have to comment on how many."

"This one may hit the record books. I imagine it may even surpass Hurricane Hazel in magnitude, though they have dubbed this one Hazel II," Sol remarked as he rubbed his hands together to warm them up. "All I know is the temperature sure dropped dramatically when the storm hit. That old mountain sure wasn't very friendly today. You guys will have to come back when it's hot and sunny. You'd get a vastly different impression of the lake."

Paul chuckled at that statement. A return visit was not high on his to-do list at the moment. His chief concern remained how he was going to get Evangeline off the mountain to be checked at a hospital, not returning for a holiday. *I guess he means well, but I'm not sure Gel will be game for the return visit.*

Mac and Sarah entered the cabin that Paul and Evangeline shared the night before. They checked if the room had managed to stay dry with all the wind and rain and were amazed to find that it was. They repacked most of their belongings into their overnight bags and moved to their cabin to do the same thing. Again they found the little cabin dry and intact.

"Whoever built these cabins must have done it to hurricane standards. It's amazing how they have withstood this storm. Everything's dry. The roof isn't even leaking. I wish we could say the same thing about our house," Mac quipped.

"We'd better get this stuff up to Evangeline to see if she wants to change her clothes," Sarah observed as they prepared to leave their cabin.

They lugged the bags up to Jack's house as he was just locking the front door. They piled into his truck for the short ride to Lacey's house.

"So how's your house? No damage I hope." Mac asked as they pulled away from his house.

"You know, in all the years that I have rented from Lacey, we've never had any damage from any storms that have blown through here, summer or winter, come to think of it. I don't know how she fairs so well." Jack steered the truck into Lacey's yard and parked as close to the front porch as he could.

They piled out toting the luggage with them. Jack had already changed into dry clothes when he was over at his house. He had grabbed a few extras for the other men so they could get dry as well. An especially strong gust of wind hit just as they entered the house, ripping the door from Jack's hand as it forced the door open with a bang. They piled in as fast as they could. It took Mac and Jack combined to be able to shut it again.

"Whoa! That's a strong gust. That wind's something else! Just listen to it in those trees. It sounds like the whole mountain behind us is going to come down on us. Those trees sure sound eerie in a storm!" Sarah cried excitedly. "You sure don't get those sounds in the city."

They brought the suitcases into the foyer as the generator rumbled to life. Lacey plugged some lamps into an extension cord and the great-room was well illuminated, "That's more like it. We can use the generator while we get cleaned up and get some food going. We should use it sparingly, because we don't know how long it will be until we get power back. But I think we need to start with some electricity," Lacey announced.

Sarah went to the couch where Evangeline was resting. She stroked her head above where they had applied a bandage to her gash. "Are you feeling any better, Gel? I brought you some dry clothes if you want them. Those cabins were dry. Can you believe it?"

Evangeline smiled gratefully and answered, "I think I'm okay in this robe but I'd like to use the bathroom if that's possible. I think I'll need some help getting there though."

Paul looked at Sonya and asked, "Is she alright to get up?"

Sonya nodded her head and said, "If she thinks she feels well enough We'll keep a close eye on her and help her walk with the splint on her leg."

"Wait a minute. I think we have a cane in the cupboard from the time I sprained my ankle a few years ago. Give me a second and I'll get it for you." Lacey returned promptly with a cane. "Now I know why I kept this thing. We'll get you in there and by the time you get out, the fire should be blazing and it will be warm and cozy for you."

Lacey had everything under control and she did not seem fazed by events of the day. It was as though she had to do this every time Jack had a group up for a course. Mac shook his head as he watched Lacey and Paul guide the limping Evangeline into the bathroom down the hall. "Lacey sure knows how to normalize a miserable situation, doesn't she?"

Bert brought a load of firewood in from the back porch and remarked, "You might as well make everyone comfortable than fret about what you can't change. It's a big storm, so we can make the best of it and help one another out. It's about attitude, I guess. Stewing about it won't help us any."

Mac pondered that for a moment. He had seen a lot chewing over situations over the years, especially in the business world. That was a refreshing attitude, so different from what he had to endure at work. "You know, I think you're right. I wish that you could have a talk with the guys I do the contracts for!"

Bert laid down the firewood and turned toward Mac and said, "It's been my experience that if I want someone else to change how they deal with things, I have to be the first to change. If I respond differently, so will they. It took me many years to realize that and messed up a lot of situations before I started to get it right. I still forget sometimes, although less often than before. It's all about attitude and perspective."

Mac pondered his statement as he picked up Sarah's suitcase to bring it down the hall to her so she could change. *I kind of like these folks. They sure have a different viewpoint on life; maybe it's because they live away from the city. It must be easier to be here away from the dog-eat-dog atmosphere back home.* Mac disappeared down the hallway without saying a further word.

Sam Fowler made it into Lofton and was on his way toward Moulton, where he found the bridge on the back road into town was already unusable. The waters were lapping over the surface and threatening to take it out at any minute. That would leave the main highway bridge and the longer route ten miles back still intact. It was not a good situation. It would completely isolate the communities above this point and if the other bridges became similarly compromised, it cut off all access to the hospital and medical care.

He helped the local road crew set up barriers to stop vehicles from approaching the bridge. He knew that this would hardly stop anyone from trying to drive around the barriers but unless they had enough personnel to guard the bridge, it was inevitable that some sort of incident might happen.

Sam turned his vehicle around and headed to Moulton. The normally sedate Butcher Creek that flowed along the highway was filled with turbulent brown water threatening to flood the road and had already spilled over the road surface by six inches in spots. The water was rising quickly and it was going to pose a threat to the homes downstream by morning if not sooner. With the power out in the area, it was going to be a difficult door-to-door task to warn residents of the impending danger.

Sam drove by the building that housed the branch office. The attached garage area looked empty as he knew his personnel were already out attending to calls. Soon he doubted that many would even be able to make calls out because the phone service would not last much longer. He decided to drive on to a likely hot spot. It was going to be a long, tiring night; that was for sure.

Chapter 25

Once everyone had a chance to change into dry clothes and the fire was crackling in the fireplace, the mood improved in Lacey's house. The aroma of food being prepared on the propane stove in the kitchen soon wafted out into the great-room. Hildy and Jan's leftovers made good appetizers while Lacey and Bert heated the goulash that Lacey had made earlier in the day. They served it up with hastily prepared salads and crusty bread.

The group sat around the great-room with plates brimming with food. Bert interrupted the conversations to say a Prayer over the meal. The first thing he did was to thank The Lord for bringing Evangeline back to them with few injuries. It was followed by a murmur of agreement from the gathering. He then Prayed a Blessing over their food and asked for God's Divine Hand on each of them for safety in this storm and especially for those who were out working on it this tempestuous night.

Every scrap of food was consumed by this hungry bunch, most of who had not eaten since the morning. The only one who did not eat much was Evangeline, who just nibbled at a sandwich then chose to take a nap. They continued to check her periodically to make sure they could rouse her, a routine procedure following a head injury, but she insisted that she just was exhausted from the day's events and her injuries. Sonya checked her vitals periodically as a precaution, but her condition continued to be stable. Paul sat close by on the floor, watching over her like a hawk as she dozed off to sleep.

The group gradually became more relaxed as the evening progressed. Cups of hot coffee and tea finished the meal.

"It's amazing how a full stomach can change one's point of view, isn't it?" remarked Calvin as they were clearing away the dishes.

"It almost makes the moan of that wind bearable," commented Sarah. "It hasn't dissipated much since we got here."

Hildy nodded as she reached for her coffee cup. "I expect that it'll continue through the night from the sounds of that forecast. I hope by morning it will have passed through." She paused and added, "It's the rain that concerns me though. The river may be the biggest problem with all that runoff. We have trouble with it at the best of times in the spring, but with this much volume in such a short time, it's bound to cause a lot of flooding. We'd better be prepared to be stuck up here for a while if the bridges don't hold. Still, we should go out tomorrow and check this neighborhood."

Jack spoke up and said, "I agree, but, I might just head down sooner than that to see if Sam and the guys need help. I can take the four-wheeler down to Lofton and maybe beyond."

Sonya put up her hand to stop him, saying, "Jack, I don't think that's a good idea. You'd be exposed to all the falling branches on a four-wheeler. They already have a lot of personnel available for the Rescue Squad tonight. Get some rest as Sam said and we'll go down in the morning. I understand that you're eager to get going to help, but believe me, there'll plenty to do tomorrow. The guys will be glad to have fresh legs by morning. We've had enough experience to know how accidents happen in these conditions when you're tired. It'd be foolish to go out now."

The group agreed with her argument. Sonya quickly reminded him of Sam's orders. "Yeah, but he's your boss and just my friend. I don't take orders from him," was Jack rebuttal.

Sonya gave him a warning look and added, "Jack, what he said made a lot of sense though. Think about it." With that, Jack reluctantly agreed to stay there for the night.

The generator was turned off after the meal and the group huddled around the fireplace, finishing their cups of coffee and tea by the crackling fire. It created a comforting atmosphere. Evangeline awoke, this time more alert and able to listen to the conversations around her.

The discussion rolled back to the day's events. Jack asked Lacey why she had gone over the clump of bushes instead of just grabbing the backpack. “What caught your attention over by the cave opening?”

“It wasn’t what I saw so much as much as what I felt, Jack,” Lacey replied. She paused, looking for the right words to say. “It’s sort of hard to explain. When Bert and the rest of us go up to help you on a search-and-rescue mission we operate in a different way than the rest of you, as you know. You’ve seen how we hang back a little. I don’t know whether you realize what we do while we are waiting.”

Jack murmured, “Well, I guess I assumed that you were Praying or something.”

Lacey smiled, “Yes. We do Pray, but not just asking for a good result. This little group of ours has a deep dynamic Faith in God. We have a Trust relationship with Jesus and the Father that through the Holy Spirit He’ll provide us with all that we need. We Pray, not just for Protection, although, that is part of it. We also Pray for the Information that we need to be Effective. It takes active Listening skills. In this case, my ears were tuned to Hear His leading to look over there. It’s just that simple. It’s like having my radio tuned to the right frequency.”

The hair on the back of Evangeline’s neck raised on end as she heard Lacey use the word ‘Trust’. Memories of the cave flooded back to her mind and she gave an involuntary gasp. Lacey glanced over at her as she did, but the others did not seem to notice.

“So why aren’t others able to Hear as you do? Is it some special talent that you have?” Sarah inquired. “Mac and I go to church and we rarely hear about people who get that, maybe the pastor, but that’s his job, isn’t it?”

“Anyone who Trusts in The lord and gives time to developing this gift can experience this. Think of it this way. If you have a radio that is on but off the station, you don’t receive the signal very well. A lot of the times you get interference from other stations that overlap. Life can be like that for us, causing static that hinders our ability to Hear clearly. The signal is still being transmitted, but our ability to hear it is not there. As a group, we’ve just yielded ourselves to learning how to tune our radios to the right station. Anyone can do it.”

The silence was heavy in the room for a minute or two while this statement was digested. Sonya broke the hush, repeating Lacey’s words, “You’re saying that anyone can develop this skill?”

“If you have turned to Trust in Jesus with your life, yes, you can. He’s waiting to Talk to all of us,” was Lacey’s answer.

It was followed by another pause. Evangeline was looking troubled. She drew the comforter up under her chin and stared at the fire.

Sonya continued the line of thought, “Let me get this right. You're saying that God told you to go over there and look for Gel?”

“Well, sort of. It wasn't as if I heard this Voice from Heaven say to me to go over there. It was more like a gentle nudge that I shouldn't leave before I investigated it more. My Lord is a gentleman. He doesn't shove me or yell at me to do anything. He's good at gentle persuasion. It's up to me to obey or to not obey. It's my decision once I feel the leading. I'm also capable of tuning Him out completely. Life easily provides distractions that can drown His Voice. It's a decision we make to determine to Listen amid a crisis. It's sometimes not that easy. That's why during a search event we stay back awhile and Pray, once everyone else has already left, to use that time of quiet to tune our Hearing and ask for the Lord's Guidance. When it's quieter, it's easier to Hear even when you're used to doing it.”

No one ventured a comment as they pondered this concept. The only sounds that could be heard over the wind outside were the sharp crackling of the fire and the occasional hiss as the fire consumed some sap in the burning wood. The light from the flickering flames danced across the room, twirling and landing gently on the faces of those gathered before the fireplace. The glow reflected a curious mixture of expressions from those faces, revealing the jumble of emotions these words had conjured. It was a new notion for many in the room. Most were struck by the peace that the idea brought with it. It was so foreign to them, not the way of thinking in which they had been schooled.

Evangeline broke into their thoughts this time, “You're saying that God was Leading you to me. He was Helping you find me, to get me out of that hole . . . because you Trusted in Him?”

“Yes, that's part of it. Trust is essential in any relationship. It's no different with a friendship with God.”

“Friendship? I never thought of it that way. I sort have always thought of God as the Big Boss and we have to obey or get fired!” was Sonya's response.

Lacey laughed at her analogy. “That's a common notion. Our Father has taken a bad rap for many things over the ages. Misconceptions are spread easily by those who don't understand His Heart, His extreme Love for us. He's always been willing to do anything it takes to get us back into a Loving relationship with Him,” Lacey continued.

"How do you explain this storm then? Why would he send this storm on us?" was Paul's question.

"Well, this may take a long explanation. Are you ready to hear me out to the end of it?" Lacey responded. She looked around the group to get their agreement.

Paul replied, "Sure, we're willing to hear you out." He momentarily glanced at the others as he spoke for them. The reporter in him was curious at this point.

Lacey continued, "I don't look at it as God sending the storm, Paul. I have a different view of why rotten things happen. It's more about the decisions each of make each day. They influence the eventual outcomes we experience.

"Bert and the rest of our group would agree that God created this Earth with a set of physical laws, like the law of gravity, the speed of sound. He also set forth some Spiritual laws for us. One is the law of confession or speaking words. Another is the law of Blessing and cursing, or good and bad outcomes, if you will, depending on the words we speak and our obedience. He let us know what the consequences of specific actions would be if we did or said particular things and not others. They're just natural consequences that take place for things we do and say. On one side we have the Blessing, the power to do well, and the curse, the empowerment to fail, available on the other. He said we could activate the Blessing if we speak and act on His Word, and the curse, if we speak and act on our own ways of thinking. Usually our ways of thinking are influenced by the world around us. He gave us this basic precept to operate these laws and make daily choices. It's in our hands to choose."

Paul interjected, "So you're trying to say that we choose these catastrophes?"

"Well not the specifics of the calamities, but indirectly we often open the door to them. You see God also gave each of us the free moral will to choose what we'll do each day. Most of us, these days, have not been taught about these principles or laws of operating, so we aren't even aware of the Spiritual laws we are turning on when we do or say certain things. From the beginning, God gave us the Authority on Earth to operate these principles. They are activated by the words we speak and our Faith in those words. Just as God created the Earth and man and all the materials for all the things you see around you by speaking Faith

Words at the beginning of time, He also gave us the Authority to speak Faith Words and rearrange and change our environment."

Lacey paused for effect and continued, "If we truly Believe in our words, those words will eventually happen. If we Believe in and speak God's Words, then those Words are already full of God's Faith and they will come to pass if we continue to speak them over time. So if we hook up with God's Faith Words, we can change our environment and circumstances for the Better. But if we attach to negative words, full of doubt and unbelief in God's Words, then we open the door to those negative results."

Paul held up his hand to slow Lacey's narrative, "Bad things don't happen every time I speak negative words."

Lacey nodded and continued, "Well, the kicker is that our negative words don't usually materialize immediately then we forget what we said over time. Then when bad things happen, we wonder how it could have occurred. We see no connection to our words and those events. We are good at blaming God for things that we ourselves have spoken into our lives; phrases like, "I was blown away", as in this storm or similar expressions. They're idle words spoken frequently enough over time that they become ours, part of us and finally part of our experience. Sometimes it is a combined effect of words spoken by many people, bringing a large calamity, hurting many people at once, without them even realizing they participated in it all. And, of course, those negative words are so fuelled by fear."

Paul frowned at Lacey's words, trying to comprehend their meaning. This concept was way beyond his normal thinking and he was trying to catch up to her explanation. As a wordsmith himself, he knew the power of the pen, but spoken words changing his environment? That was new to him.

Lacey smiled and looked into the fire as she added, "The Truth is that God put us on this Earth to be like Him and speak His Words to create our reality, not our own words and not those of Satan. Using words, we shape our end point in life. Words put us on a road that takes us to a specific place over time, sometimes to places we would rather not be.

"And like my garden outside, He gave us the ability to plant seeds. We can think of words like seeds that can be planted. Then, as in nature, we can watch over the seed during the growing season, over a long period; then we get a harvest of the same plants in the fall. If you plant words and keep them in place and tend them over time, you get a crop in your life eventually, good or bad."

Paul stared at Lacey in astonishment, "So you're saying that this storm is the crop from our words?"

Lacey replied, "It's not that simple, but essentially, our words have power in a Spiritual sense to release the forces of nature or to hold them back. Words that are connected to our fear release negative consequences; while words connected to Faith and God's Power release the outcomes that God Planned for each of us. This storm is such a big one; it's not the result of just one person's actions. We have allowed our words to rain over this land in such a negative manner for so many years, there's no telling what evil or cursing and connections to fear we have unleashed."

"Lacey, you believe this stuff? You think we have some sort of power over the weather and negative events. What about all the good people who have horrible things happen to them? God just lets people get hit by disasters?" Paul retorted.

"Paul, it`s not that God just let it happen. He gave us the ability to create and change things and we haven't done it. Most don't even know that they can. God just permits us to choose our words, and thus, our outcomes. If we continue to speak negative words, it's just a natural consequence of those words that occurs. The problem is that we've pushed God so far out of our society that few even know these principles exist, let alone act on them. Most have no Faith in Jesus to hook into it, so they don't know about His Faith Words. They have mostly, by default, just hooked into the fear that has been injected into our society," Bert interjected.

"So it's all about becoming some Jesus freak?" Paul replied defensively.

Bert continued, "Paul, I'm sorry, we forgot to mention an essential component to God's Love story toward us. When God first put man on this planet, He gave him the Authority to speak words, to tend and expand the garden He put him in and thus shape his environment. God also intended to have a relationship with man, to Teach him about this ability. He wanted to come with his man to walk and talk with him each day, to Teach him at His pace, until the man could understand it.

"He gave the first man, named Adam, a simple rule to obey; just one. He told Adam that he had all the food he could want, that he could eat of any tree in the Garden but one, the tree of the Knowledge of good and evil. He didn't want him to eat of that Knowledge before He had a chance to Teach him about these things Himself. He came to talk to and Teach Adam daily. All Adam had to do was just follow God's lead in what He did and wait for God's Teaching.

"However, there was an evil entity named Satan who enticed him to make a wrong decision and to go against God's command. He lured him into thinking he could bypass the Teaching and get immediate Knowledge. Satan wanted Adam to think that God was holding out on him. So, Adam ate of that tree anyway, an act of disobedience that opened the Earth to the Knowledge of the evil and all that goes with it, essentially a system of pain and hurting. And that horrible decision effectively allowed Satan to move in and manipulate and taint that special Authority and to separate man from God and His Wisdom. Sin is destroyed in contact with God's Perfection. Because Adam's decision was disobedient, God considered it sin. God could no longer be in close contact with Adam because His Perfection would consume him and he would die. Satan had caused a wedge in God's relationship with man."

Paul shook his head and said, "So, if God is God, why didn't He just toss Satan out and take it all back from Adam and Satan and just start over?"

Bert nodded, anticipating this question and answered, "God had set up the laws and given man the Authority to administer them. He wouldn't violate His laws by yanking that Authority back from him. It was now Adam's to right to choose how he dealt with it. If God had just taken it back, He would be disobeying His own laws of operation. He chose to allow the consequences of that decision to unfold as He had set them up. None of this took Him by surprise mind you."

Paul grunted and shook his head, obviously unconvinced but willing to listen while Bert continued his explanation. "Unfortunately, when Adam made his wrong choice and thus gave up his Authority to Satan, it set up a cascade of consequences and negative events. One was that man died Spiritually that day and fear was unleashed on the world. And since God is a Spirit, man lost his Spiritual link with God. He was now separated from the One Who Created him and Breathed Life into him. That disobedience made it impossible for man to come in close relationship with a Perfect God anymore. It was devastating for both man and for God. They were now disconnected from close contact. It was always God's desire all along to maintain a close relationship with us because He Loves us that much. As you can see, it posed a dilemma for God. Man was now more linked to Satan with fear than he was to God through Love and Faith."

Paul frowned at Bert, trying to follow the logic of Bert's dialogue. He held up his hand for Bert to stop for a moment and said, "Wait a minute, Bert, you said that God knew all this would happen. Why didn't He just teach man how to fix it?"

Bert smiled and continued, "Well, God did just that. But now it was a much more complicated affair because of the loss of the Spiritual connection and the separation from God. He was so in Love with His mankind, that He spent years and years finding people who would Listen to Him. Then He Taught them through these people the Ways that they should live, giving them opportunities to do it Right and thus be able to come closer to Him. Normally, such sin would cause them immediately to die physically in God's Perfectly Holy Presence. Instead, God provided a system of atonement, through offering unblemished animals. Their blood would pay for man's sins. Instead of the man dying in God's Perfect Presence, the animal's death and blood atoned or covered man's sin in God's eyes so they could approach Him. This had to be done daily, weekly, year after year because man just continued to sin. This went on for centuries."

Paul shook his head and said, "That doesn't seem like an effective solution to the problem, given that you say we're so imperfect. Why did He let it go on so long?"

"Well, God is infinitely Patient. It was probably because mankind was, and still is, thick in its thinking. It took a long time to persuade us to Listen. As I said before, the problem was that people, and that includes men and women like us, just kept doing things that were not Perfect and Right. God didn't want them to have to continually do blood sacrifices repeatedly to pay for their sins so they could have a relationship with Him. Man kept failing and they had to do the sacrifices again and again to cover up their sins. At the same time, God continued to want to get closer to us. As you see, it was not a Perfect system and God had planned something infinitely Better."

Sarah leaned in closer to hear what Bert was saying, reaching for Mac's hand as she did. Mac glanced at her and nodded. They knew that he was about to tell the good part now.

Bert took a sip of his coffee as he paused to see if Paul was still willing to listen. Paul stared at Bert, waiting for him to continue and prompted him by saying, "So obviously it doesn't end there. What's the rest of the story?"

Bert smiled slightly, realizing he had Paul's interest now. "God sent His Son to grow up as a man on Earth, but also as a perfect example of how to operate in God's System of operation. He learned God's Word from an early age and spoke things from God's Words that He truly Believed in His heart and those things came to pass. He showed us how to live and change our environment and circumstances through pure Faith in God and speaking His Word.

"He lived a sinless life. Then, when the time was right, He put Himself out as a perfect pure Sacrifice, shedding His perfect Blood for us, so we don't have to continually offer animal blood sacrifices. He became the final, complete and perfect Offering to God that satisfied all the conditions of His covenant relationship with man. So, now, if we Believe that what Jesus did by Offering Himself up on our behalf has paid the final Price for our sins, God now Forgives of all our sins and our spirit comes to life again. We now have that necessary Spiritual connection with our Father and we can enter into a relationship with Him permanently. He no longer sees our sins when He looks at us. He sees Jesus' Blood and us as Cleansed of all our sins and mess ups. We can now be close to Him as our Father, transformed and made alive Spiritually by the Blood sacrifice Jesus shed for us."

Paul frowned as he heard this statement, trying to make sense of it compared to his knowledge of the world. It was obvious it stretched his thinking to the very core and he was trying to keep up with Bert's message.

Bert's face now shone with the glow of the fire as he continued, "But you haven't heard the best part of all. Jesus died to shed His blood for us so God could permanently Forgive us of our foul-ups in life, which is wonderful. But while Jesus was dead, he also invaded Satan's territory and took back that precious Authority that Satan stole from us. Then, our Father accepted Jesus' Blood Sacrifice on our behalf and brought Jesus back to life. Jesus appeared back on Earth and handed back that Authority to all people who would Believe in Him and His Sacrifice. Then He left us in control of Earth again and returned to sit with His Father in Heaven. Just think of it. Jesus did what was necessary to restore the Authority to speak God's Faith Words back into man's hands. He reconciled our close relationship with God our Father and as a Believer in the Name and Authority of Jesus Christ, He gave us back our right to speak God's Faith Words into our lives and our land!"

Bert leaned back in his chair and smiled as he readied for the finale of his teaching, "And now Jesus sits with His Father in Heaven, being our mediator or go-between with our Father. He is constantly reminding our Father about our good points and showing Him that because we Believe in His sacrifice, the Price was permanently paid for our indiscretions forever. Through Jesus, we can go to the Father each day and talk with Him and ask Him about our lives, His plans for us, how to get out of and prevent difficulties. And the most exciting part about it now is that if we realize that we have messed up, and goodness knows we have, we just go to our Lord directly and confess those errors and He Forgives us of them. Nothing should keep us from having that relationship and fellowship with Him anymore . . . if we Believe, have Faith and Trust in Him."

Not a word broke the silence in the room again. Bert took a sip from his coffee. He just let this information digest. Only the sizzle and snap of the fire broke the silence.

Finally, a dry small voice ventured a comment. Paul spoke one word, "Why?"

"Why what?" Lacey asked quietly.

He asked the ultimate reporter's question, "Why? Why bother with man if he had made such a mess?"

Lacey nodded at that question and said, "Why, indeed." She paused a moment longer, then took a deep breath. Her voice was filled with emotion when she finally answered, "It seems so illogical. Then again, God is Love. He doesn't just Love. He *is* Love. He *is* Light and Good and Life and Truth and, above all else, He *is* Love. Love is the very essence of What and Who He is. Love is His very character and nature. Love is what motivates His every Word and action. Love is Who He is."

Lacey took a deep breath and continued, "Love doesn't always make sense. He is so beyond our human love. He is unconditional, run you over with Goodness kind of Love. He is looking for opportunities to Bless you and give you Favor and Mercy and Kindness and Grace and Forgiveness and Protection and Healing and anything you need, if you will let Him; if you will hook into His Love. If you will connect with Him, through Faith in what you can't see, His Spirit."

Lacey inclined her head as she looked around the group and added, "If you are willing to receive His Love, what He did for you to bring you back into a pure Love relationship with Him through Jesus Christ, then He is so willing to pour out His Love on you. He is Love and Love looks for a willing recipient of that Love. Anyone willing to truly Receive His Love is a candidate. It's free, a gift He made available for us, not based on what we can do to earn it. We don't deserve it. Nothing else is necessary; just willingness to Believe He did what He did out of Pure Love, to restore His relationship with you. Accept it, Believe in Jesus and His Love Sacrifice and enter into an indescribable new Life."

No one ventured further into the discussion, even Paul. He did not look convinced, but he had heard enough.

Chapter 26

The quiet in the room was suddenly broken by an intense gust of wind which flew over the house, rattling any loose structure in the building. It sounded like a jet plane had buzzed the dwelling, such was the roar overhead. All eyes looked up then to one another.

"Okay, that was big. That's about enough excitement for one day. I, for one, am ready to see this storm end! Enough Satan! Be still in the Name of Jesus Christ! It's time for you to go," Calvin announced to the group.

Murmurs of agreement could be heard around the room. No further blasts followed. "What do you think? Is anyone ready to head off to bed now?" Jan asked. "Lacey, how do you want to arrange us to sleep?"

"I think it might work better if some of you join me over at my house," Jack answered first.

Sleeping bags and blankets were pulled out of storage with the extra pillows scavenged from the cabins. It was agreed that Sol and Hildy and Calvin and Jan would go to Jack's house, while the rest would bunk out at Lacey's place. They felt that it was a good idea to stay together in groups should any crisis arise. Mac and Sarah decided they would stay at Lacey's to be near Evangeline and Paul, taking one of the upstairs bedrooms, Bert and Eli the room next to them. Sonya would remain close to Evangeline so she could check her condition.

Jack was about to turn to leave to take his group to his cabin, when he saw Sonya collecting stray cups by the fireplace. He walked to her side and said quietly, "That was quite a day. You get some good rest.

Tomorrow may prove worse than today. You did do a great job today, you know. I wasn't just saying it earlier, I meant it."

She smiled softly, cocked her head and whispered, "I bet you say that to all the girls."

He leaned over and gave her a kiss on the cheek and mischievously said, "But I don't give them all kisses." With that he turned and walked to the door, picking up a sleeping bag on the way.

Sonya stood where she was with a smirk on her face, following him with her gaze. She nodded to him as he waved good-bye to everyone, taking the two couples with him. Sonya continued to stand there for a moment, lost in thought.

Lacey walked by and whispered in her ear, "Looks like Jack might have designs on your time, my dear. Be careful where you tread. A Heart is a tender thing to play with."

Sonya smiled more broadly and replied, "It depends on who is playing the game. Perhaps I like the pursuit."

Sonya carried the mugs into the kitchen. Lacey commented, "We'll leave these dishes for the morning. We have no pump with the power being out so, consequently, no water until we start the generator again. Just find a place to bunk down for the night and we'll try to sleep as best we can with that storm raging. You might want to try the couch in the study, because it's close to where Gel is sleeping."

"I'm going to check Gel before I do. I want to make sure that she isn't having any latent effects from her ordeal today. You have to be careful with concussions."

Lacey put the last of the mugs in the sink and said, "That's true. Is there anything I can find for you or that you need for her?"

"No, I think I'm all set. Thanks anyway. You gave us a lot this evening already and a lot to think about. I'm ready to sleep though. I feel tired."

Lacey finished her rummaging in the kitchen. Evangeline had elected to stay on the large wide couch that she lay on all evening. Paul had a sleeping bag set up on the other couch but was upstairs with Mac and Sarah at the moment. Sonya checked Evangeline and then moved into the study so the great-room was now quiet, save for the occasional crackle from the fireplace. A single lantern remained to illuminate the room leaving a cozy atmosphere. Lacey went to say goodnight to Evangeline before retiring.

"Are you sure that you're comfortable enough on that couch? I told you that you could have my bed you know. It's cozy in my room," Lacey offered.

"No, no. I'm fine here. It's so comfy. I am already used to it. Lacey, about what you were talking about earlier, you really Believe that, don't you?"

Lacey stopped and sat on the coffee table. "Yes I do, with every fiber in my being, I do."

"You used the word Trust. Is it so significant?" Evangeline asked.

Lacey answered, "Yes, it's all entwined with Faith and Love. It is something you develop in relationship. The more you know God, the more you learn to Trust Him and the more He can Trust you with things too. Yes, I would say it's significant. Why do you ask?"

"It's just something that happened while I was in the cave. I don't know how to describe it. I know that Paul wouldn't understand it. It was really . . . weird," Evangeline confessed.

"Believe me, nothing would shock me after some of the experiences I've had over the years. I'm sure that you could tell me if you feel you would like to," Lacey replied.

Evangeline smiled weakly and replied, "I imagine I could. It's just that I thought that I was going mad down there, alone, hearing things and . . . voices and . . ."

"It must have been frightening for you," Lacey encouraged her.

"Oh, you have no idea. When I was in the dark and no flashlight at first, well, it was just awful. But that's not when it was the worst. When the water started to fill the cave and with the noises further down the cave, it was just horrible. I was so afraid. I just know there was some animal in there with me, and maybe . . . well, something else too. I don't know what it was. If I tell you, please, don't tell Paul. He just wouldn't understand this."

Lacey leaned forward and took her hand in hers. "You have my word. What happened to you down there?"

"Well . . ." Evangeline hesitated. "I think . . . I know . . . that I heard voices in there. Sort of like what you talked about, you know, like someone talking to me." She paused and took a long breath. "There, I said it. Now you probably think I'm crazy or something."

Lacey squeezed her hand and reassured her, "No, Gel, I take this seriously. What kind of voices?"

"Well, there seemed to be one voice . . . it was so evil . . . it was trying to get me to give up, to stop trying to do anything to save myself and telling me that I was useless. It was so awful. I almost did. I thought I was losing my mind. I was so terrified. It . . . it . . . even smelled disgusting and was so suffocating. Then I remembered some things that Sarah had said about her church and Faith and . . . I . . . I called out for God, you know, for Jesus, to Help me and . . . "

"Go on, I'm still listening."

Evangeline hesitated then said, "And . . . I think He spoke to me, too. I think He talked to me about Trusting Him . . . to Help me, I think."

Lacey smile broadly and answered, "That sounds like Jesus. He'll extend His hand to Help you anytime you ask Him to. It is easy to get His attention, if you Trust Him. He will grab onto any hand that Trusts Him."

"I think it was what He was trying to say to me. He just didn't say much, just a few words, about Trusting Him. I told Him that I did . . . and well . . . that's when it got even stranger."

"Stranger? How so?" Lacey asked. She leaned in as Evangeline began to whisper now. "Well . . . I started to climb and it hurt so much. Well . . . it was as if I got some Help. The more I tried, the more Help I got until I got halfway up and it seemed as if I couldn't move."

"You found it too hard?" Lacey asked.

"No, I mean, like . . . I was being held there in place so I couldn't fall but also so I didn't climb any higher. It was as if . . . something was Protecting me from going beyond my capabilities and falling back into the water. I was locked against that wall. It was . . . well . . . bizarre! Then there was this glow or light or something. I just can't explain it."

Lacey lean forward and said, "You, my dear, were Graced with the Love of God in action and there is nothing more foreign to our understanding than that. It makes no sense to our human worldly understanding. But it is, nonetheless, Real. You call out for God with a genuine Heart and He comes running. It is simple but that complex."

Tears began to roll down Evangeline's cheeks. Lacey reached for a tissue from the box on the table and handed it to her. "I'm sorry to blubber like this, but it's all been so overwhelming. I thought maybe the knock on my head had damaged my perceptions of reality. I just didn't know what to think."

Lacey touched Evangeline's chin lightly to get her to look into her face. "No I have no doubt that what you went through down there was dreadful. You had a taste of Satan's taunting; that seems obvious. It's what he does and it's terrible. I won't dispute that, but you've been given a wonderful Gift amid that confusion. You had what I call a 'God Encounter'. You had a Heart to Heart talk with Jesus and He came when you called. You told Him you Trusted Him and He Responded. That . . . is so beautiful!"

Evangeline paused to consider Lacey's words, then said through her tears, "I guess, when you put it that way, it is. It may take me awhile to really understand it though. Especially, with all the things you talked about tonight. I think there's a lot of stuff I need to learn, you know, about God and why He did this for me. It's all so overwhelming."

"Just take it a little at a time, my dear. Don't try to understand it all in one day. God is a very big God and no one yet has taken Him all in, and especially not in one day." Lacey smiled. "Any questions you might have, ask me. If you want to share this with some of this little group, I'm sure that they'll be happy to answer to the best of their understanding. Just remember that each of us is a 'work in progress,' and we learn and understand in stages as in school. Some of us have different Insights than the others depending on our experiences. No matter what anyone of us tells you, you can always check it out with God's Word to confirm it. We can help you with that. The best way to learn more about God is to read His Words to you. I have a Bible that I can give you to read. Look at it as God's Love story to you. We can help guide you if you like. The bottom line is, Gel, it's all about Love, Real Love."

Evangeline looked down at her hands and fumbled with the tissue she was holding. "Real Love. Well, I could use a little of that now. I have no idea how I would ever share this with Paul. You heard him tonight. I don't think he'll be receptive to it."

Lacey reassured her, "I'll Pray for him as well as you if you'd like. Is that okay?"

"Yeah, that would be really okay."

Paul could then be heard coming down the stairs and as he entered the great-room he said, "Looks like everyone is ready to hit the hay now . . ." He paused when he saw Lacey sitting beside Evangeline. He saw that she had been crying. "Is there anything wrong?"

Lacey stood and replied, "No, I think things are good now. Gel was just finding things a little overwhelming and some girl talk helps getting it all out. It's hard for us women to hold it all in, you know."

Paul came to her and responded, "I just wanted to thank you for your hospitality here. Opening your home to all of us has been great. We appreciate it a lot."

Lacey started to walk toward her bedroom picking up a spare flashlight and said, "No problem in the least. I hope the next time you visit there won't be hurricane to greet you. You both have a good sleep now. If you need anything, just knock on my door and I'll find it for you." With that, she was down the hall and disappeared into her bedroom.

Hurricane Igor was losing strength now. Tiring of the game it was playing in this region, it decided to proceed north. Moving along at a painfully slow pace, it continued to dump a tremendous volume of rain on the populations below. Streams became rivers, rivers became swiftly flowing lakes and lakes rose beyond their boundaries. The appearance of the countryside was transformed and reshaped. If one were to hover over the landscape, the former topography was now unrecognizable.

The winds slowly abated overnight to gale force then to irregular gusts. The rain slackened to a steady shower. The worst of the storm itself had subsided. But the new fun for the storm was watching these mortals deal with the aftereffects of his terror. This made the pounding it produced below so worthwhile. It did not end with the tempest.

Chapter 27

Early next morning, sleepy bodies began to drift into Lacey's kitchen one by one, having awakened to the aroma of bacon and coffee wafting into their rooms. They looked like a ragtag bunch dragged off the back street.

Paul was already sitting up, drinking coffee, beside Evangeline as Bert and Lacey cooked in the kitchen. The generator was humming away in the back porch providing electricity for all their luxuries.

"Help yourself to pancakes, hot off the grill and coffee. We have bacon crispy and what Lacey would term, partly cooked. If you ask me, she likes her bacon frazzled. But that's just a friendly disagreement we have!" Bert quipped as he started to pass plates across the counter to interested customers.

Mac accepted a coffee gratefully and took a sip. "Oh, that's hot, but so good." Mac stretched and added, "I haven't been up this early on a weekend for a long time, but I feel rested. It must be the mountain air, or should I say, hurricane air?"

"Looks like Igor decided to leave us overnight," Paul observed. "It's just drizzling and looks like the sun is trying to break through."

"Isn't it always the way, it's beautiful the day after a storm? There are a few trees and branches down, but your house fared amazingly well last night," commented Sarah.

"I think this house could withstand a bomb blast. I guess you could say that it was 'overbuilt'. It doesn't hurt that I have regular maintenance done by Eli. He keeps me well protected," Lacey replied with a smile. "Gel, how are you feeling today? Did you get any sleep?"

Evangeline answered quietly, "I slept a little until the pain meds wore off, then Paul gave me more and I dozed on and off until the next ones kicked in. It could have been worse. I suppose I was the only one who kept track of the storm overnight. It started to wane shortly after I awoke in the middle of the night. The wind wasn't so vicious and I think the rain started to subside as well."

Paul commented, "I hope that means that the storm just kicked itself out altogether and didn't just move on to another area. Surely it won't last much longer; it moved so far inland as it was."

Sonya interjected, "Has anyone checked Jack's place to see if they're okay, too? I should see if Jack wants to head down to help handle the flooding problems."

Lacey answered, "I haven't been over there yet, but the house seems intact from I can see from here. If you want to make sure, maybe Mac can go with you, in case you need help."

Mac looked up from his coffee and agreed. Sonya grabbed her rain slicker and headed to the door before his cup could hit the counter. "Guess that would be my cue to leave," he chuckled. They were out the door before anyone else could comment.

"I suspect that her concern for Jack's wellbeing goes beyond a professional interest," was Lacey's comment as the door closed behind them.

Bert looked up from the pancakes he was cooking and chuckled as he said, "Yeah, I'd say you're onto something there."

Sonya and Mac walked to Jack's house with Sonya in the lead. Large pools of water lay across the parking area making it look more like a small pond. Taking the long route around the water, Sonya still beat Mac to Jack's door, even with his long strides. Sonya was about to knock when the door was opened by Jack. "Saw you coming through the window. Come on in. I used the portable propane stove to make coffee. Would you like a cup? Well, I might have to wash out a cup, cuz I ran out of clean ones already this morning."

"No, it's alright. We've had some over at Lacey's. Everything's okay over here? The house wasn't damaged?" Sonya asked brightly.

"We had a few things blow around a bit but we're all in one-piece,"

Jack answered with a boyish grin. Dressed in jeans and a T-shirt, his unshaved face and the natural unruliness of his wavy hair added to his rugged appearance.

Sonya approached him and returned his smile. She was eager to start work and asked, "What are your plans to get down to Lofton? Do you want to take the truck or the four wheelers?"

"I think we might want to scout things out first with the four wheelers, to see how bad the roads are. I don't think taking vehicles down there would be a good idea yet. If everything's clear, we can always come back for the truck."

Sonya agreed that it was a good plan. "When do you want to leave?"

"Just let me make sure everything is secure and I'll gather a few things and we can leave. How's Gel doing? Is she okay to leave for a while?"

Mac answered that one, "She's having a fair amount of pain, but isn't complaining much. I'm sure she's probably feeling a little worse than she's letting on. I suspect she's a little embarrassed about causing all the commotion yesterday. The sooner we get her to a hospital, the better."

"Well, that's a good reason to go check the roads. So let me get my stuff together and I'll meet you over at Lacey's." He turned to his houseguests and added, "I hope that you understand that I have to leave."

"Sure, no problem. We understand. We'll clean up for you," Sol remarked.

Mac and Sonya left Jack's and started to return to Lacey's house, as Mac looked over at his silver Mustang parked down by the cabins, he groaned, "Oh, no, don't tell me. Aw!"

Sonya followed his gaze and immediately realized what caused his response. A large branch lay across the trunk. "Ooh. I bet that's going to cost something to repair."

Mac stood there uncertain that he wanted to look at the damage, but finally decided to go and look. As he walked over, he could not believe what he saw. Although, from a distance, the branch seemed to be lying on the car, it was caught on another branch. It rested a few inches above it and had not even made contact. Mac shook his head in amazement. *What's the likelihood of that happening?*

Mac strode back to Jack's house and knocked on the door. As Jack answered it, Mac exclaimed, "Guys, you have to come see this! I think I need your help with it."

Jack, Calvin, Jan, Hildy and Sol all piled out the door to see what all the excitement was about. As they looked at Mac's car, there were exclamations of dismay as they too thought the Mustang was surely smashed. However, they stopped short as they neared the vehicle, dumbfounded at what they saw.

"What are the chances?" was heard repeatedly.

"You took the words out of my own mouth," was Mac's reply. "I thought I was imagining it at first. I guess we have some work to do to get this thing off there before it does hit the car. It looks pretty tangled there, but I am not willing to leave it there."

"Well, buddy, you've seen your second Miracle of your trip," was Sol's response.

"Second? What was the first?" Mac asked.

"The first was getting off that mountain yesterday with only one person with injuries. There wasn't much chance of that yesterday given the conditions. Actually, it probably was the third miracle, because the chances of Gel falling in that small hole, getting found and coming out alive were slim as well," Sol responded.

"You're right. I guess I've been so taken up with the events it hasn't had time to sink in," Mac said as he shook his head again in amazement.

Hildy piped in, "When you've been involved in as many situations with the Rescue Squad as we have, you see some strange turn of events. I must admit yesterday's was different for us. It all happened so quickly that it took all of us by surprise."

"I'm just glad it turned out as well as it did. Thanks to you people. A lot of those folks who helped yesterday are volunteers, aren't they?" Mac asked.

"Oh, probably about three quarters of them are. There aren't many paid to do it in this area. It's a good community to live in. They're good folks, you know," Jan answered.

"You don't realize it until there's a need for them and we sure needed them yesterday. We don't know our neighbors as we should back home. We're all so busy travelling and working, it's hard to have that sense of community. I've learned something about that from this trip though," Mac observed.

"That's a good thing. The trick is making lifestyle changes once you go back into your regular, everyday existence. Daily pressures can rob your peace and determination to change," Calvin added.

Jack had been quiet up to now just listening to the conversation. "I'll go grab some ropes and the chainsaw so we can get this thing off the car. It would be a shame to see it damaged at this point."

"Thanks. Jack, if you want to give us the stuff to work with, we can do it, I'm sure. It sounded like Sonya was eager to get going soon," Mac offered.

"Could be, but I'll at least help get you started with this. It looks like it might be tricky to get it off without it dropping something on the car," Jack observed as he sprinted off toward his shed.

"I'll go to Lacey's house and tell them what's going on. With this many people, we'll surely devise a good plan. There's a lot of brawn and brain in this group," Jan declared.

"Maybe too much! It'll be interesting to see if they can create a single plan that works. " Hildy laughed.

John Brompton entered his store and left the closed sign hanging. He knew that there would be some damage, it was just a matter of how much. He had left buckets set up before he left and did not know what to expect when he opened the door. He was surprised at how little water there was on the floor as he entered the store. It did not make sense to him until he realized that the old building had enough holes in the floor to allow it to drain into the crawl space below. It was like trying to fill a bathtub with the drain open.

He went to the back of the store and saw that a tree had fallen, sending a branch through the window. *It's a good thing that wasn't one of the big trees on the other side of the parking area. This whole building would be a wreck.*

John grabbed the bucket nearest to him and dragged it outside to empty. As he did, the sun poked through the clouds. He then realized that a full, beautiful rainbow had appeared across the sky. He smiled and dumped the bucket then went back in to get the next one. It was going to take awhile to clean up this mess.

Lacey and Sarah stood back watching the men devise a plan of attack to remove the branch from the Mustang. They were laughing and guessing whose plan would win because they had at least two, if not three ideas.

The rain had dissipated and almost stopped. The sun suddenly broke through the clouds and a rainbow materialized in the sky above them. "What a sight!" Sarah exclaimed. I didn't expect to see that this morning. Isn't it beautiful?"

Lacey agreed wholeheartedly. "Do you know what a rainbow signifies?"

Sarah paused then said, "Yes, that was the sign that God gave Noah that He wouldn't flood the Earth again and kill all mankind. But He has flooded the Earth again, hasn't He?"

Lacey shook her head. "Floods have occurred but not to the degree that happened in Noah's day. Noah's flood annihilated all mankind and all the animals. That's why Noah had to build the ark to save his family and the animal species to repopulate the Earth."

Sarah nodded her head. "That makes sense. I've just heard the story from a Sunday school perspective. I guess I never looked at it that deeply before."

Lacey added, "God Promised to work with us and not wipe us out in the future. He must have had full confidence that He could achieve something through us or He wouldn't have made that Promise. He's lived up to His end of the Bargain."

"Yeah, I guess He has," Sarah replied pensively. "But He's put hurricanes on the planet."

"Hurricanes, and other disasters, are not God's Best for this planet. He permits them to happen, like the floods, because we have chosen not to use the Authority we were given and Jesus got back for us. There's an evil force that exists and we've given him permission to manipulate our lives without restraint. There aren't many people, including Christians, who know that they have the Authority, in Jesus' Name, in Faith in God's Word, to speak to those storms, those mountains and events in their lives, and command them to depart. Unfortunately, we have let Satan walk all over us for too long. It has taken me many years to learn this," Lacey declared with passion.

"So why didn't you speak to this hurricane and tell it to leave this place?" Sarah asked.

Lacey raised her eyebrows and stately flatly, "Oh, our small group has been Praying for a while now about a lot of things. But this storm was really large and had picked up a head of steam by the time it reached us here. It would have taken exceptional Faith for one person alone to divert. It was fuelled by a lot of fear as well. That would take a united effort of tremendous number of people with a whole lot of Faith to counteract it. I sure would love to get enough Believers together to achieve something of that enormity."

Lacey paused, contemplating the possibility then added, "But I did Declare Safety and Preservation for what was mine. That car was an example of that. It was on my property and I had spoken God's Word over it. The enemy tried to take that car out, but The Word stopped him. God's Own Words contain enough Faith to bring that to pass, if I Believe It when I Pray and speak It in His Name."

Sarah was puzzled. "How did you learn this? I've never heard that before, at least not where I go to church. What makes you think you can do these things?"

Lacey looked down for a moment then straight into Sarah's eyes and answered, "I had good teachers who led me to read and understand what The Word Said. God is The Word. The Bible isn't just a history book, It's a Person, It's God Himself Speaking Promises and lessons to us. It's God's Love toward us. I've learned to Know Him and His nature and character through some wonderful teachers, but most of all, through His Words to me. No matter what, I always go back to God's Word to me. He Said those things in the Bible for me . . . and for you too.

"I think religion has often stolen the Power of The Word from us trying to explain why it doesn't work for some people. Being afraid that it won't work sometimes, has made us afraid to use it anytime. Therefore, we've just stopped trying, or we've done it without Believing that it will Work, so it doesn't. Just saying the right words is not enough. God said we had to Believe It in our Hearts for our words to affect our lives. We connect our Faith with the Faith of the One Who spoke those Faith Words and Power can be released. The trouble is we believe failure more than God's Promises."

"This goes counter to anything I've heard in church. I've thought that it was mostly about being good. You know, 'do unto others as you would have them do unto you.' Our pastor has rarely even mentioned anything about Satan, except in the Garden of Eden," Sarah replied pensively.

Lacey sighed. "Well, you can't teach what you don't understand. If he didn't have it explained to him in these terms, he wouldn't know to teach it, would he?" Lacey answered.

Sarah looked at Lacey and slowly nodded her agreement.

Lacey continued, "Unfortunately, God's Word has too often been reduced to a history book with good morals added for good measure, instead of being explained as our Manual of Power. The Bible is God's Love toward us. He's done all He needs to do to give us back the Authority through Jesus' Sacrifice and Resurrection and Ascension. He restored back to us the Authority to speak His Words. We're now His ambassadors on Earth and we need to understand our designated Authority in His Name to speak His Words.

"We also so need to understand the Power that's released when we speak His Faith Words. When we truly Believe His Words, we are connected to Him. He is The Source of True Faith and the Power. It's that Faith connection that allows His Power to flow on our behalf. So . . . as we speak His Faith-filled Words, that Faith and Power can be Released into our situation."

Sarah stared at Lacey shaking her head and frowning. She commented, "It seems such a responsibility to do that. How do we know the right things to say?"

Lacey looked up toward the sky and replied, "Jesus is at God's right hand now making a clear path for us to the Father, so we can go to Him at any time to Ask Him His Advice and Counsel. We've been given the Holy Spirit within us, if we have accepted Jesus as our Lord, to Help in what we do here to accomplish God's Plan for us and others. He's not left us alone to do the things He Teaches in His Word."

Sarah was not convinced yet. "You make it sound so simple, but life isn't like that. Tough stuff happens to us all. Look at this storm for example. How many lives have been destroyed through it? Is that God's Will?" Sarah mused.

"No, it isn't God's Best for us to have to experience that. And, well, God didn't intend to make it complicated either. He gave us a few simple Principles that He expects us to use in making our life decisions, big and little, so we can avoid trouble. And if we mess up, we can go to Him and Repent and He is Faithful to Forgive us. Then He'll help us turn things around again. He allows us to choose to make mistakes and He allows us to choose to change. And all the while He Loves us and Strengthens us amid our disasters."

Sarah nodded and said, "Yeah, I sure was glad He was with me yesterday. It was so hard with the storm and not knowing where Gelly was. I just had to lean on Him to get through it all."

Lacey replied, "You were brave. It was good you could Rely on God to get you through. It's just a shame that it often takes a crisis like this to get us to turn to Him."

"I'll admit that I don't think about Him as often as I should. We're all so busy. I know it's just an excuse, but Lacey, it's all so foreign to us. It isn't how people live these days."

"Yes, I know that all too well. But, you know, people had different stresses on them in Jesus' day. Life wasn't that easy. Jesus was our example on Earth of how to live no matter what the era. Did you notice how He lived was most often counter to how others lived and thought then? It's still opposite to how we live today, too." Lacey countered.

"Well, He did challenge the current thinking about life then and, I guess, now, too. In His day, there were so many rules, but now anything seems okay." Sarah chuckled, "Our cultures have gone in opposite directions in that respect, haven't they?"

"You might say so, but Jesus tried to bring it down to one simple Principle, as exhibited by His life among us. He said that all we do must be guided by Love. We must Love God above all else in our lives, even above our life itself, and Love others as ourselves. If we base our decisions on an outward looking perspective, instead of how it will benefits us, life would be better for most people. It would accomplish God's Best for us, too. Jesus understood this and walked the Earth as our example of it," Lacey stated.

Sarah countered, "Yeah, but . . . Jesus was God's Son. He could do that, couldn't He? We're human beings."

"Ah, yes; the 'yeah, but . . .' We all cease in our Faith when we hit that 'but'. It's like hitting the stop button," Lacey said with a twinkle in her eye.

Sarah turned to look at her with questions bouncing about her head. "What do you mean by that 'but'?"

Lacey continued, "It was an expression my husband used to use. He meant that when I used the word 'but', I was erasing everything that came before in that sentence. It was a word that signified that I had hit the end of my Faith and begun my doubt. Like saying,' I can believe this much, *but* anything else is beyond my ability to grasp and use'. He loved to remind me that I had to stop my 'butting', so God could do His part."

Sarah creased her brow as she asked, "What if it doesn't make sense?"

"Sometimes we have to look past our limited reasoning that causes the 'but'. God understands His Word, we don't always have to. We do need to let God do His part and what He wants to do through us. We have to stop limiting God with our small thinking."

Sarah's mouth opened slightly as though she about to speak, then stopped a moment longer as she tried to process this statement. "But . . . Oh, there I go again. Oh my, I see what you mean. It's so beyond what I've been taught. I see that it'll take some processing to understand and grasp what you've said. It's a habit, isn't it?"

Lacey smiled at her. "You might say so. It sure took me awhile to unlearn the habit. Warren used to catch me in it when I was new at it. It was good that he held me accountable to retrain my thinking. Nothing is impossible for God or to us through Him if we line our thinking and actions to God's Word and Principles of operation."

Sarah pondered Lacey's words as she stared at the puddle before them.

"It does take time. You have to exercise your Faith muscle like any other in your body. It takes time to develop," Lacey explained. "And to answer your other question: yes, Jesus was God's Son, but He didn't operate on Earth using His Divine Powers. He did everything He did as a man born into Earth, Annointed by God and Guided by the Holy Spirit. He was like us, but Guided all He did according to what God's Pure Intent was in all that He was trying to teach mankind to think and do. He filtered through the rubble that we had added and just lived His life according to the underlying Plan of operation that God had given through His Word during the previous ages."

Sarah eyed her, wondering how this could be. Lacey smiled back and explained, "He studied the Word for Himself. They said He had superior Insights even when he was only twelve years old, even beyond those of the rabbis who listened to Him speak. He just focused on what His Father wanted Him to understand from His Word and lived His life according to those Principles. It was all laid out for Him in God's Words already and He had only the Old Testament to study. And just look at what He accomplished that way. He said that we could do the same and more than that too. We just have to focus on what He actually said and not add man-made layers added to it."

Lacey looked directly at Sarah. "Jesus did everything He did as a man Anointed by God. We can do the same things in His Anointing and guided by the same Holy Spirit. It's available to each of us through

Faith in Him. He tried to make it simple for us," Lacey finished as she could see she was beginning to lose Sarah.

Sarah's facial expression mimicked the confusion inside her as she replied, "Mmm . . . simple perhaps, but so contrary to what my mind can grasp. This has thrown my thinking on its head. It seems complicated to me. It's just jumbling about in my brain. Maybe there's just been too much going on in the last couple of days for me to keep it straight. You might be right. I need time to digest this. It's difficult for me."

Lacey put her arm around Sarah shoulders and consoled her, "Don't be so hard on yourself. You can't unlearn years of training in one morning. We all have been indoctrinated into a system of living. It takes effort to retrain habits and thinking. You have to give God time to Help you Understand it all. If you give Him your attention, He will gladly oblige you."

Lacey gazed at her house and added, "We should get back to the house and organize things so we can move Gel into town if we're able. She must be wondering what's going on out here." Lacey said as she turned back toward the house. She was moving in that direction before Sarah could gather her thoughts.

Sarah stood there for a moment, transfixed to the spot like her thoughts. Her mind was in a muddle by what Lacey had said. Slowly she looked up again as the rainbow began to fade and realized God had been talking to her through Lacey. *I guess I'll just have to ponder this awhile. Better that I deal with the little I do understand right at this point and I do know Gelly needs my help.* Sarah hurried to follow Lacey as she headed up the path.

Jack returned with the necessary gear to extricate Mac's beloved Mustang from the clutches of the tree branches. The men had produced a workable plan of attack and they quickly secured ropes on the tree to prevent any slippage that would scratch the car's silver paint. Before long, they had raised it sufficiently for Mac to ease the Mustang away from the tree. Mac then parked it twenty feet beyond the tree line to be sure of its safety. As he opened the door to get out, he glanced over just in time to see the heavy branch crash to the ground as the men released their grip on it. Mud splattered in all directions and the men jumped back to avoid being hit by the branches.

Mac walked over, amazed at the size of the limb, and commented, "That was even larger than I originally thought it was. It was a heavy sucker, wasn't it?"

Jack looked up from his work as he was attempting to release the rope from under the branch and said, "Beats me how that thing was hung up there by those other smaller branches. It makes no sense. Nature can be funny sometimes, I guess. It just seems to defy the laws of gravity though."

Mac's raised his eyebrows as he surveyed the scene. He wandered back to the vehicle to check his paint job. He ran his fingers over the shiny surface of the car to confirm that here was no damage. He shook his head in wonder as he could not find even a scratch. "Everything looks fine here. You're right. It doesn't make sense, does it?"

Bert's face betrayed a look of satisfaction as he glanced at Sol and Calvin. Eli looked their way as he prepared the chainsaw to cut the tree limb. They nodded at him, knowingly. Bert replied quietly, "It is amazing what can happen in the middle of a mess, when you put Faith to work." The trio agreed with him and continued their work.

Mac was busy talking with Jack and did not hear the comment. "Jack, why don't you go and see if the roads are passable. I'm sure Sonya is eager to get going by now. We can handle things. You'll need to fill Paul in on the plans for the morning so you can coordinate your efforts. I think he'd like to get her to a hospital soon to check that she doesn't have any further injuries. She's been in a significant amount of pain overnight I think. I know that he was kind of worried about her condition."

Jack headed back to his house only to find that Sonya had repacked the necessary gear from the truck so t it would fit securely on the back of the four wheelers. Jack arrived just in time to help her lift the first bundle. "Let me help you with that," he said as he strode up to her side. He easily took the weight from her hands.

Sonya smiled at him as he grabbed the load with his strong, muscular arms. "Well, that timing was impeccable. I could have done it myself, but why should I if I have you to help. I'll gladly let you do the other pack too. Since I assembled the gear, you can secure it. That's my idea of team work."

Jack glanced back at her without saying a word. His broad smile was enough to convey his thoughts. He was enjoying working with Sonya more than he liked to admit. He had sometimes been a loner up on this mountain. His business of teaching tracking and survival had taken up most of his time and energies and only left time for hanging with the guys. Sonya's presence lately had changed his perspective of things and he found himself liking it.

"You know, when all this settles down, in a few days, maybe we should get together to . . ." Jack began to say.

"To do what?" was Sonya's reply. She started to tease him a little. ". . . to go over rescue strategies?"

Jack cocked him head at her and gave her a look. "You aren't going to make this easy for me, are you?"

Sonya smiled coyly at him and answered, "Nope. Jack Davidson, I'm not. You spell it out for me. I'm a little dumb about these things."

Jack tightened the pack on the back of the ATV with a grunt and said, "Okay, you want me to be straight with you. How about we get together and go into town and see a movie or dinner or something? I'll even put on some respectable clothes if you want me to."

Sonya put a finger on Jack shoulder and grinned as she cocked her head, "Now, that's more like it, my friend. I think I could handle that, especially if you spiffed yourself up a little. A shower and a shave might be nice."

Jack played with her, "So I don't have to put on the nice clothes then?"

"Aw, you know what I mean. The clothes are part of the package. I'll even put on a dress if you'd like, too," Sonya quipped."

"Sounds like you've just sealed the deal then. We'll figure out a time . . . after this all over . . . you know, when you don't have to work and I don't have a course," Jack went on.

"Don't tell me going to make this difficult to arrange. You're not backing out because I asked for you to get dressed up a little?" Sonya asked.

Jack started to sputter, "No. Don't put words in my mouth. I was just . . ."

Sonya added, "That's okay. I'll hold you to it. I won't let you forget it. But now we'd better get on our way or Sam will think that I've taken a vacation day in the middle of one the worst situations there's been up here in years."

Chapter 28

Paul was sitting beside Evangeline on the couch. "Are you sure you don't want to get up and get cleaned up? It might make you feel better."

"I don't know. I suppose that with the generator on, there would be water, but I don't think I want to bother," Evangeline murmured.

"I could help you if that's the problem," Paul replied.

"No, I just don't feel like it. I still have that headache and I'm light headed. I'd rather save my energy for the trip back home. If you get me a cloth, I might be able to do a hand wash, if you think I need to."

Paul looked at her more closely. It was not like Evangeline to not worry about her appearance. She must be feeling sick to not care. "Is there something you're not telling me? How do you really feel?" Paul questioned. He was starting to be concerned about her condition.

"It's nothing. I just want to rest. I'm sore and tired; that's all," Evangeline answered weakly.

"Sore? Where? Just your knee and shoulder, or other places too?" Paul asked with mounting unease.

"It's my side. Maybe I twisted my back or banged my ribs or something. It's been aching since early this morning. I think I was hurting all over so much before that I couldn't tell what hurt the most. I'm so cold too. If I rest here a bit, maybe it will get better. I just don't want to get up anymore than I have to. Going to the bathroom has been enough of an ordeal already." Evangeline replied with her eyes closed. *I hurt so much and I feel so confused about everything that happened. It's just so overwhelming.*

Paul let her lie back and said, "Okay, you just catch a nap then. I'll let you rest and see how the others are doing. Call me if you need anything. I'll check you periodically," Paul said as he rose from beside her on the couch. He started to think that the extent of her injuries may be worse than they first thought. He reached over and pulled the blanket over her shoulders to tuck her in more comfortably.

Evangeline opened her eyes and gave a weak smile. She grasped the blanket and snuggled into it. *If I rest, maybe it will all make more sense to me. And maybe the pain will go away.*

Paul glanced over at the kitchen and realized that the women had gathered there to do the cleanup. He walked to the group and said quietly, "You know, I think it would be good if we could get Gel back to town soon. I'd feel better if she were checked by the doctors there."

Hildy and Lacey exchanged glances as Paul entered the kitchen. "Do you think her injuries are worse than we first thought?" asked Lacey.

"I don't know, but she's complaining of pain in her side, she's cold and she has no interest in getting cleaned up. That's just not like her. It has me kind of worried. I've never known her to turn down an opportunity to get cleaned up and put on makeup before. She must be feeling lousy," was Paul's reply as he toyed with a coffee cup on the counter.

Jan and Hildy put down their dish towels and turned to him. Lacey pulled the plug from the sink, grabbed a towel to dry her hands and declared, "Well, we'd better make plans then, because traveling might be a significant problem. Maybe we can catch Jack before he leaves with Sonya and tell him that things might be more urgent than we originally thought."

"I can do that, if you want to do what needs to be done here to get her ready to move, if we can," Paul said as he headed toward the door. "I'd like to get going soon."

"No problem, do what you think is best and we'll get things ready here." Paul was out the door before she finished the sentence. Jan took a deep breath and said to Lacey and Hildy, "That man is even more worried than he's letting on. We'd better get moving. Lacey, how about you check Gel and we'll prepare some supplies for the trip?"

Lacey nodded and went to Gel's couch. She kneeled before her and placed her hand gently on her shoulder and said a quiet Prayer. Evangeline stirred as she felt Lacey's touch and slowly opened her eyes.

She managed a weak smile as her eyes focused and she realized it was Lacey.

Lacey smiled back and quietly said, "You're not feeling that great, are you? You can be honest with me. There's no need to hide anything. We need to know what's happening, so we can do what's necessary."

"I thought I was feeling okay, but now I don't think so. Maybe if I can rest a little longer. . . ." Evangeline whispered as she closed her eyes again. A small tear trickled down her cheek as her lip trembled.

Lacey spoke reassuringly, "That's okay. We'll take care of you. We should prepare to get you to the hospital though. This might require more assessment and care than we can give you here. Just get some rest and we'll work out the logistics. Jack and Sonya have the expertise to work it out. I'll ask Sonya to come in and check you out before she leaves."

"Whatever you think is best," Evangeline mumbled as she pulled the cover higher on her shoulder. "I'm cold. Is there another blanket?"

Lacey brought her another blanket, gently placing it over her. She frowned as she looked over her; then glanced out the window as she heard the four wheelers approach the house. A moment later, Sonya entered the front door with Jack on her tail.

"Do you have concerns about Gel?" Sonya asked as she entered the great-room.

"I think you should check her before you go. I'm not sure what's going on, but she's having more pain in her side. It could be some sort of internal injury or her back," Lacey recapped the problem.

"I'll have another look. Don't worry, we'll take care of things," Sonya said in return.

"Worry won't help. I already Prayed over her. That will help on one front. You take care of her physical needs," Lacey answered.

Sonya went to the couch to tend to Evangeline with Paul a couple steps behind her now. He went directly and sat on the coffee table leaning in to watch what Sonya was about to do. It was obvious he was not going to leave her alone as he did yesterday.

Lacey turned to Jack and asked, "How hard do you think it would be to get her down to town and to the hospital? What about the roads and the river?"

Jack shook his head a little as he ran his hand through his hair. He looked down at the floor pondering the problem. "Experience says it could be challenging. It also depends on the extent of the injury. If it's internal that is one thing, but spinal is another. She didn't complain of tingling or numbness, did she?"

"No. Nothing like that, just pain, I think," was Lacey reply.

"That's good, sort of. Maybe it's internal. Not that it's good, but maybe easier to deal with than the possibility of a spinal injury," Jack said as he sighed. The weekend had already been full of unpleasant surprises and he did not need more.

Sonya wandered to where Lacey and Jack were standing near the door, leaving Paul to watch over Evangeline. "I don't think there are any spinal injuries. It's more likely either bad bruising or internal injuries. I can't tell anything more than that without getting her to the hospital. They can do the necessary diagnostics there. It's the reason we need to get going and scout out how we might get her there. I think she's stable enough till we get back, but we had better get going now." Sonya caught Jack's eye as she moved toward the door. She slipped her boots back on and quickly laced them up. As she straightened she spoke to Lacey, "Take care of her till we get back. We'll have the radios on. You might want to say more of your Prayers just in case though. I just don't know what we'll find. I don't imagine it'll be good."

Jack glanced over his shoulder at Lacey as he opened the door to leave with Sonya, "We'll be back. I promise you, we'll come back to get her."

Lacey watched the door close behind them. She moved to the large window as they drove off on the four wheelers. Her lips were already moving in a quiet Prayer that the Spirit urged her to Pray. She nodded moments later and a small smile creased her face. She was now sure the pair would not be alone on their journey down the mountain.

Nan leaned over the table to dab Horace's chin with a napkin. Breakfast consisted of cereal and fruit because there was no power to cook with but they were well fed, nonetheless.

They had been up early that morning, relieved to see the break in the storm. The wind had pounded the house all afternoon and night till they thought the rafters would lift from the walls. The creaking and groaning of the house and the trees was eerie and disconcerting, rattling even Nan's strong nerves. Gertrude had proved helpful in settling Horace as the night wore on. He had grown increasingly confused with all the strange noises and the power outage. Sitting by the light of lanterns had cast odd shadows on the walls and combined with thunder and lightning, the elderly man had slipped into old memories of the war and bombings years before. Had she been alone, Nan was sure that Horace would have been too much for her to manage with his erratic behavior. It was a concern she would have to address later, once the power was back on, the yard cleaned up and life was back to normal, whatever that meant these days.

Nan leaned to get a better view of the yard. Her wonderful garden looked like it had been battered and beaten. Branches were littered about, not only on the lawn but across her petunia and geranium beds. She groaned inwardly as the thought of all the work to clean it up. *Thank goodness that Eli will be by soon enough to help with the jobs. I just don't know what I would do without his help. It's just so hard these days with Horace. Whatever will I do come winter?*

Gertrude passed the dish of fruit her way and rerouted her attention. It was better to live in the present anyway. It was the only thing she could control at the moment. She was out of the rain. The sun was even to show itself. *What else can I do?* Horace then reached out to grab some fruit from the bowl, knocking over the jug of juice. Nan closed her eyes for a moment. *Yes, what else can I do?*

Sonya followed Jack down the roadway toward Lofton. Her red four-wheeler soon was unrecognizable under a thick cake of mud that had splashed from the sodden track. The road was washed out and impassable to all but four-wheel-drive vehicles in many spots. The water rushing down the mountainside continued to etch deep grooves, searching for the path of least resistance. Streams had become rivers, overflowing their natural courses and new streams were evident everywhere you looked. The ditches beside the highway were useless as they were clogged with debris in many locations causing dams that created ponds and small lakes in low-lying areas. Fortunately, there was sufficient slope in most places to keep the water flowing downward. However, the road had become the new streambed in some spots and it was starting to erode the pavement in others as they moved closer to the village. Both Jack and Sonya realized that the tremendous volume of water would drain into one location: the East River.

Jack looked over his shoulder to be sure Sonya was close behind him. He did not want any problems. He would be certain that he did everything according to proper procedure. He knew Sonya was a professional, but "stuff" happened when you least expected it. He did not want it to be today.

Sonya nodded back at Jack, acknowledging his diligence. She was in her element now. It was what Sonya was trained to do. She did not look forward to disasters but she was ready for them, nonetheless. It was reassuring to know that she was on this trek with Jack. She knew whatever they found before them, he probably had some experience with similar events during his time in the military or survival training. She could not think of anyone else she would rather be paired with at the moment. She was beginning to realize that being with Jack was what she wanted to do, period.

The two continued to negotiate deeply carved gullies where the road was completely washed out. Sections of the blacktop had been ripped away from the road by the eroding waters. Some segments had collapsed down sides of hills into the bushes and trees below.

It was quickly becoming evident that no normal vehicle would negotiate this route. Off-road vehicles were the only reasonable means of transportation today and perhaps for an extended period until repairs were made.

They rounded a corner and found an overturned blue van halfway off the road smashed into a tree close to the soft shoulder. They quickly parked their all-terrain vehicles to check if there was anyone still in the vehicle. Although it was empty, evidence remained of the work the emergency personnel had done earlier. Jack shook his head as he said, "That couldn't have been a good outcome. Someone must have been trying to outrace the storm in the dark. These roads are bad in the dark and the rain at the best of times. That would have been downright foolishness. Looks like the crews were busy last night."

Sonya nodded feeling a little guilty she was not out with them. "There'll be enough for all of us to do today though. I haven't seen runoff like this in all my years. You do know what that means about the river, don't you? I don't know if the bridge in Moulton will hold with this kind of flow. It might even surpass the bridge. It doesn't look good, does it?"

"You're probably right, but we'd better go a little further down to see what we might encounter. We should meet some crews soon. They may be able to give us more information," Jack replied.

"I'll be right behind you. Let's get going." Sonya agreed.

They travelled a half mile before they came across with another four-wheeler driven by one of Sonya regular crew mates. Danny Laurence slowed his vehicle as he saw them approach. He was headed down a bush trail by the side of the road. They stopped and took off their helmets. Jack was first to speak, "Hey, Danny. Good to see you, man. What's the status downstream?"

He frowned and answered, "I was just down there and was taking a shortcut this way to check things further up the road. Things are not looking good further on down. The river is rising rapidly and they're working on evacuating homes at risk. Some stubborn old codgers don't want to leave their possessions. I don't know what they think they can do against a raging river, man. It's not as if they can save their houses if the river decides to take them. It's hard to persuade them to save their lives and forget their dwelling. People can be some stupid at times!"

Sonya and Jack agreed with him. Jack answered, "Don't we know it. They can lose their brains in a crisis. It's not as if they can take their possessions with them. If they stay, they die. So what happens to their stuff when they're gone?"

"So how's it up the mountain?" Danny asked.

"There's a lot of water to come down. There's significant flow in areas I've never seen it before. The roads are gouged out and nonexistent in spots and other areas look as if they may slide soon. It's not a good situation. The only thing we can hope is that a lot of people left before the storm hit. At least there aren't as many people up the mountain. Most weekenders only stay while the weather is good. The other residents are hardy folks and know how to handle themselves in nasty conditions; not that we've had too many storms like this one recently. Those left up there will have to stay put for a while though. I hope that neighbors are checking one another, because there aren't enough of us to do it now," Jack replied.

"There's no doubt about that. Are you able to help us down here? Or do you have your hands full with people up your way?" Danny asked.

"Ah, we have a situation of our own. The woman who got caught in the cave yesterday needs to get to hospital. She seemed stable and okay to wait out the storm last night but now we're concerned about possible internal injuries. We're just checking out how we might get her down to town to the hospital. What do you think? What would be the best way to get her out?" Jack replied.

"Ooh. You'll have to get her down on your own, I think. We can't spare anyone. Once you get her down, we'll see what we can do to take her off your hands. I can't be sure if you'll be able to use the bridge though. I don't know." Danny ran his hand through his hair. He shrugged and shook his head.

"That's okay. Just let the guys know that we're coming, so they'll be ready for us. Whatever they think is the best method of extrication is what we'll have to use. I trust you guys to be ready when we get there," Jack countered.

Sonya added, "We'd better get going. It'll take us awhile to get back up there and even slower when we have her on board to bring her down. We don't have time to lose. I'm just glad we met you so you guys are prepared for us. Remember what Sam always says. Stay safe. Don't take any unnecessary chances."

Danny smiled at Sonya and nodded as he put his helmet back on. "Don't worry, I know the drill. As he always says, you're no good to anyone if you need to be rescued yourself. I'll see you down there soon. We'll be waiting for you. I just can't guarantee what you'll find when you get there, that's all."

"Don't worry. We'll cross that bridge when we come to it. Sorry, maybe that was a poor choice of words! Safe travels, my friend."

They climbed on their vehicles and started back down the road. Sonya and Jack had to take their time due to the deteriorating conditions and the often steep grade. It was not going to be an easy day.

Chapter 29

Lacey and Hildy busied themselves rounding up supplies for the trip down the mountain. They were not sure who was going to make the trip or how but they wanted to prepare in advance so they would not waste time once Jack and Sonya returned.

Jan and Calvin came into the kitchen as Lacey said, "We have to Trust God that He has this under control even when it doesn't look good. How long have they been gone now?"

"I've lost track of the time. Let's see, at least an hour, maybe an hour and a half. They must have gone a long way, unless they are helping someone else along their route," Lacey answered.

"I'm sure they'll be along any minute. How's Evangeline doing?" Jan asked.

"She's resting now. The pain meds have kicked in. Paul hasn't left her side since she started to complain of the increased pain though. I think he feels responsible for what happened. He probably won't rest until she's safely down in the hospital," Lacey replied, glancing back into the great-room. She set the knapsack she was packing down on the counter. "I think we'll all feel more peace once she's been taken care of, to be frank with you."

"I can't argue with you about that. This storm has put us all on edge," Calvin replied.

Bert walked in the front door looking disheveled. "Well, the car is safe. The branches are sawed up and stacked. A few trees have a fair amount of damage, but the branches are too high to get at. The next big wind might dislodge them but, meanwhile, we'll just have to be careful not stand under them. It could have been far worse around these grounds. I hate to think what most of the area looks like though. I know you did some heavy-duty Prayers of Protection over your property here, Lacey. We all did our part too, but so many don't know to do that. It'll be a big cleanup after this storm."

"Bert, go back outside and shake that sawdust in the yard! You look like you took a bath in the stuff!" Hildy exclaimed as she walked into the room.

Bert glanced down at his jacket and realized she was right. "Sorry, ladies. I'll be right back," Bert said as he backed out the door.

Hildy and Jan laughed at the sight of the man. He returned soon after, straightening his jacket and smoothing his hair. "Is this more presentable?"

"Yes, Bert. Sorry to be on your case like that but you were about to bring it all in the house. It would have been such a mess," Hildy replied.

"Well, I wouldn't want to do that to Lacey's house, now would I? After all, you've been so gracious to open your home to us all," Bert commented.

"Bert, you looked like a mountain man as you came in. It becomes you, no matter what Hildy says," Lacey smiled with a look of true affection in her eyes.

"I think we should have a short meeting in the library. We should get Sol and Eli in with us too. We'll want to gather our thoughts and resources before any of us embark on the next adventure. I expect the trip into town may be demanding. We need to be of one mind about things," Bert said, ignoring the attention from the women.

The group quietly went into the library together and closed the door behind them so as not to disturb Evangeline as she rested.

Paul looked up and watched them go into the library one by one. They did not say a word to him, but he gathered that they needed privacy to Pray. He did not understand their Faith or how they thought. It was such a contrast to his philosophy of life. He had always worked by his wits and intuition about events and the stories he followed. It had served him well over the years and he had become successful and respected in his work. These people just seemed to fly against conventional wisdom, but they also seemed so at peace amid this turmoil. *How do these people operate? Do they actually tap into some unseen Resource? It just doesn't make sense. But somehow they do have a sense of calm about them. I guess everyone has his crutch to lean on. These people just use God for theirs.*

Paul leaned his head back into the couch and took a long sigh. He was tired; bone weary. It was not how he had imagined this trip to play out. If he had written it in a story, no one would have believed it. But here he was living it. Things kept getting worse and he had no control over it. It just kept moving and he could not stop it. *How could things just fall apart like this? It's been such a disaster. It could have been so good too. How did things just get so out of control?*

The meeting broke up in the library and each person quietly left the room one by one. Paul was resting on the couch opposite Evangeline's. Bert whispered to Lacey as they walked on to the veranda, "That is one tired man. I wish I knew what was going through his mind. It would make approaching him a little easier. He looks as if he's got it altogether, but I think he's one troubled soul."

"I think you're right about that. I've been asking the Lord how to Pray for him. The only response I get is that we need to concentrate on what moves him on from one story to the next. You know, what drives him. That's probably what gives him the most fear. That's what to Pray for him. You find the fear; then you find where you need Faith the most."

"That sounds like our Father. He isn't into Band-Aid fixes or just covering the symptoms. He wants to find the root of the problem and pour in His Love and Power and Word into that. Anything less is ineffective," Bert replied quietly.

"God isn't into window-dressing. He wants a complete makeover. He Loves him too much to leave him that way. He cares deeply about Paul. I sense it. I think the Lord allowed me to see Paul's pain. I think it's deeper than a ruined weekend trip. I don't think it's just Paul, though. Gel is covering a world of hurt as well." Lacey commented.

"You could be right. If you're receiving it from The Lord, I know you are. The question is what do we do with this Information?" Bert asked.

Lacey thought for a moment and answered, "You know, I think it is a God appointment. They're supposed to be here for a reason. I just don't know what it is yet. Give me a little more time in conversation with The Father. I have confidence that the Holy Spirit is up to something and

He'll let us know when we need to. Better to say little now and let it all play out as He wants it to."

Bert agreed, "I know you're right. You have a lot of Wisdom within you, Lacey."

Lacey responded quickly, "Bert, it doesn't come from me. You know that. We do need Patience. It's difficult to walk out sometimes, but I know that's the Answer now."

Bert gave Lacey's hand a squeeze. She gave him a quick smile, the kind of smile that conveys deep agreement and understanding of the other person. It was true friendship.

The sound of approaching vehicles changed the mood quickly. Mac and Sarah walked across the yard as Jack and Sonya drove around the curve and into the parking area. They were both a sight as they wore as much mud as their four-wheelers. They cut their engines and pulled off their helmets.

"So what's the story down there?" Mac asked as he strode over.

"The roads are bad and deteriorating as we speak. A lot of water still has to make it off these mountains. Most creeks can't contain this flow. New streams have formed everywhere. The existing creeks and ditches are overflowing and gouging out new paths. We encountered new gullies where the road has just given way. If the water finds a way under and erodes the ground enough, the road above just collapses. That's happened both on the dirt road and the paved route. The only thing that'll make it down successfully would be a vehicle with off-road capabilities. We may be stuck with the four-wheelers for now," was Jack's reply.

"Well, we'll just have to make do, I suppose. But there's no way you're going to be able to put Gelly on the back of an ATV with the way she is," Sarah mused.

Sonya dismounted her vehicle and pulled off her helmet, revealing a human face, the only part of her not splattered with grime. Sarah laughed despite the grim situation. "What's so funny?" Sonya asked.

"Well, the two of you hardly look human, all covered in mud like that. Your clean face looks out of place," Sarah answered. "Sorry, I didn't mean to laugh like that."

"That's okay. We all need some comic relief at the moment. I can take it. How's Gel holding up?" Sonya smiled as she replied.

"She's been resting with the pain killers. Maybe that's a good sign that things are easing off a little. I hope so. I don't imagine that we'll know exactly what it is until she gets assessed at the hospital," Sarah answered. "It so hard just waiting here when I want to get her to the hospital. It feels as if we are wasting valuable time."

"I understand where you're coming from there, but we had to make sure we can get there safely. We don't want to incur more casualties. We found one vehicle overturned on the way down and we wouldn't want to end up like that. I especially don't want to cause Gel more injuries than she already has," Sonya responded, her smile now evaporating.

Sarah took a deep breath and tried to collect her thoughts. "You're right of course. It's just my impatience coming out. It's hard waiting when I would like to be doing something constructive. At least you got to go down and scout the route. Wondering is the hardest part of waiting."

Bert and Lacey had joined the group by this point. "Patience. That's hard for most of us. We like to charge in and do something, anything. Holding back until the timing is right and the plans are set, now that takes maturity and training," Bert commented as they reached them.

The four turned as Bert and Lacey arrived. "Spoken like someone who has charged into a few situations and learned from his mistakes," Lacey added.

"Oh, yeah. That would be me in the past. I've changed a lot over the years, I hope," Bert replied. He set his jaw as memories collided. "Yeah, I made a mess of a few situations in my day."

"But nothing that couldn't be fixed. After all, you're still here with us now and we're benefiting from your experience and wisdom," Lacey countered.

"I'd like to think so. If I can help a few people avoid some mistakes I've made, maybe they weren't all for naught," Bert concluded.

Sarah patted Bert on the back and added, "I've learned a few things on this trip from you and I appreciate it. Maybe you can help us out with our current dilemma. It looks like the roads are impassable to conventional vehicles. We're trying to figure how to transport Gelly down without causing her more injury than she already has. The only off-road capable vehicle I know of is Calvin's Jeep."

Bert was quick to answer, "Oh, Calvin loves to go off-roading when he has a chance. He even goes to the rallies, so he knows how to handle himself in these conditions. Jan goes with him but doesn't do much of the driving. She just enjoys the adventure and people. They're a great group to hang out with, you know. I've gone a few times with them. No doubt about it, Calvin is the man for the job."

Jack responded, "Yeah, I thought he did some off-roading. He should be able to manage those roads then. It won't be a smooth ride for Gel but riding on the back of an ATV is obviously out of the question."

"I'll go in and talk to Calvin about it. I'm sure he'd love to help," Bert said as he turned to go back in the house.

"Great! We've overcome the first obstacle," was Jack's reply.

Mac caught Jack by the arm, "Jack, is there a way Sarah and I could get some four-wheelers as well to go down with you and Paul to take Gel to town? I know Sarah wants to stay with her if possible."

Jack stopped and turned to him. "Yeah, there are a couple down at Eddie's place. I'm sure he wouldn't mind lending them to us under the circumstances. Are you sure you want to make the trip. It'll be hazardous. Have you ever ridden one before?"

"Yeah, no problem. Sarah and I went to her uncle's farm a few times last summer. They had tons of trails on the farm. We had a blast riding them over all kinds of terrain. We might not be as experienced as you guys, but I'm sure we could manage."

Jack looked down at the ground as he considered the possibilities. The question was did he want to risk having a couple of newbie's on the trip. He had enough on his plate without putting additional factors into the equation. Mac could see the hesitation in Jack's face. "Look, we can start with you. If the trip gets too hairy, we can just turn around and go back. I think we could surprise you. We're athletic and can manage something like this. Sarah is a lot stronger than Gel is and can do this."

Jack thought about it for a moment longer and replied, "Okay, you can give it a shot on one condition. We don't need more accidents. If I think it's beyond your capabilities, you'll have to agree to turn back."

Mac nodded, "I don't need anything to happen to us either. I know we can do this and it would be better for us to stay together under the circumstances. That way I can be there for Paul and if you need help, we'd be there for that too."

Mac had Jack convinced, so they set about packing safety gear for the trip while they waited for Bert to retrieve Calvin. Soon enough, Calvin came out of the Jack's house, followed by Jan, close behind.

Calvin walked to Mac and Jack and asked, "You need the Jeep?"

"It sure would make things a lot easier. You okay with us using it under the circumstances? It could get rough down there," Jack replied.

"You haven't seen the courses they have had us do in those rallies we go on. It couldn't be much worse than that. They set up some unlikely scenarios for us. If we can do those, we can handle whatever we might encounter down there. It's exactly why I have the Jeep anyway. That thing can get through most anything," Calvin assured them.

"Okay. We'll need to pick up two more ATV's from Eddie's place first if that's okay, then get back here to load Gel up for the trip down. Mac, are you ready to go get the ATV's?" Jack said. He was moving into action mode. "And Calvin, thanks."

"Glad to be of service. So are you ready?" Calvin said as he slapped Jack on the back as they turned to get in the Jeep. Calvin was itching to get going as much as Jack. "The sooner we leave, the sooner we can be back. So let's get moving," was Calvin quick response.

Eli looked out the window of Lacey's great-room. He turned to see Lacey coming out of the library. "Lacey, I think it's time for me to go and see how Nan and Horace and Gertrude are doing. I don't think you need me now, do you?"

"Of course not, Eli. You're right. They're vulnerable. Nan will have her hands full with Horace even with Gertrude's help. If you want to check back here later, that would be okay. I think the road is still intact enough down that far. With your new truck, you should make it no problem. I don't think it would handle it where the road is out though."

"I'll look in on a few more of the folks along that road while I'm at it, especially those who are at risk like Nan and Horace. It concerns me that they are out of power like this," Eli added.

"Go ahead. We're under control here. We'll get Gel organized to leave until Jack's ready to go. Let us know if you need any of us for anything though," Lacey added.

Eli was out the door before she could say anything else. *There goes one keen young man. We are all itching to move out and do something. It feels as if we're trapped up here. We want to be useful in a crisis and to be stuck here doesn't feel right.*

Lacey walked quietly by the couch where Evangeline lay, hoping not to disturb her. Paul was sitting on the couch opposite Evangeline staring at the coffee table. He looked up as she walked by, then stood and approached her.

Lacey looked expectantly at him as he came near. "Is there anything that I can get you, Paul? "

Paul shook his head. "No, that's okay. Bert said that they were going to use Calvin's vehicle to take Gel back to town. I just wanted to thank you again for helping us out and opening your house to us all. You seemed prepared for this ordeal. Sort of like you anticipated us being here. Are you always this ready for disasters?"

Lacey chuckled. "No, only when I get advance notice. I've sensed something might be afoot and have been stockpiling a few supplies."

"You mean, you heard the forecast and brought in some groceries?" Paul asked.

"Sort of. But I've sensed something big was going to happen. I've been putting aside some supplies for a while now. You know, nonperishable items," was Lacey's response.

"What are you saying? You knew it was going to happen?" Paul asked, skeptically.

"I don't know how to describe it to you Paul. It is all tied up in my Faith. I have an open and continuing conversation with the Holy Spirit. He tips me off when I need to know things; like this happening. Let's just say, I wasn't completely surprised by it. I didn't know the details of it. You know, who or when or why. Just knew to be prepared with supplies. I just knew there would be a need for it, someday."

Paul stood staring at her for a moment with a furrowed brow. He slowly looked away and through the window overlooking the lake. "So let me get this straight. You claim to have an extra sense about future events? And you get this from communication with God?"

"In a manner of speaking; yes. I get prepared for things that will happen, when I need to," Lacey replied, choosing her words carefully. She was painfully aware that Paul was a reporter and could take things out of context and change the meaning of what she said.

"When you need to," Paul repeated.

"Yes, when I need to. When my participation in an event makes those preparations necessary," Lacey answered, offering no extra information.

Paul's reporter instincts were kicking in now. "Okay, then. So why didn't you get more information that could have prevented Gel's accident?"

Lacey raised her eyebrows. "That's the million dollar question, I guess. I would suppose that it wasn't my job to do that. Events are brought about by a series of decisions. I would presume that my participation would not have altered the outcome. I can't be responsible for other people's decisions, just mine. I just have to be obedient to follow the Instructions I am given, for my decisions. I can give others information to base their decisions upon, but I can't make the decisions for them. I think God knew that anything I might have done wouldn't have changed the outcome for the better."

Paul stared at her, trying to assimilate her statement into his concept of how life worked. What she said had a modicum of logic to it, but still his basic impulses fought to make a counterstrike. The reporter in him wanted to debate her theories. "Are you intimating that we would have been too pigheaded to listen to reason?"

Lacey licked her lips before she responded, mostly to slow her response, "Well, think of it this way, Paul. Suppose I did have advanced Information that your wife would fall down a hidden hole and get swallowed by that cave and be missing and injured amid the tail end of a hurricane, would you have believed me? Or would you have nominated me for admission to a mental institution?"

Paul stopped where he was, mouth slightly agape, processing her statement. "When you put it that way, I see what you are saying. So did you get all that advance Information?"

Lacey smiled and shook her head. "No, because obviously it wasn't necessary for me to have it and it wouldn't have changed the overall outcome. I only received instructions about what my part in this event was. I knew I had to prepare for a big event; something beyond the normal up here. I just did what I knew I had to do, that's all."

Paul pondered this again. "So is that all you know. Or is there more to it than this? Not that I buy into this communication with God and all that. But if there's something you know we need before we leave, I think I would listen to you; at least hear you out."

Lacey turned from him and took a breath. *Lord, what do you want me to say to him?* Still holding her breath, she looked up to the ceiling. She closed her eyes and slowly blew out the air she was holding.

"What is it? Do you know something about the trip?" Paul asked, pressing further.

"No, Paul, not about your trip. But there is something you need to know before you leave." Lacey walked to the library and grabbed two books. "These may answer some of your questions if you care to investigate it further. 'Remember, it's about choices. What will you choose?"

Paul looked down at the books she was handing him. One was a Bible. The other one was a novel. He turned it over and saw that Lacey McCrae was the author. "You wrote this book?"

Lacey chuckled and replied, "Not the Bible. But yes, the other one is my work, well, with God's Direction. It might lead you on a road of discovery that could open a few doors to you and answer some questions."

Paul turned the Bible over and flipped through the pages quickly, "Why the Bible?"

"All the Answers you will ever need are contained in the Bible if you spend enough time searching and asking the right questions. Just ask Jesus and He'll Answer you. If you let Him into your Heart, He can Talk to you there through the Holy Spirit. Go beyond your head and let Him into your Heart and you'll be amazed at what you'll find. He'll lead you to the right questions to ask," Lacey answered, appealing to his investigative nature.

Paul stared at the books in his hands and said, "So it always comes down to the Bible with you people?" There it was; an emphasis on 'you people'.

"No, Paul. It isn't my idea. It's God's. If you have a bone to pick with someone, talk to Him. It's His Idea, not mine or Bert's or Eli's . . . It's God's. Do you think it's easy for me to talk to you like this? It isn't my idea. You've been set up by your decisions and God. He knew how you would respond to every event this weekend, but He Loves you so much he Provided a buffer zone for you and Gel. You can respond to it in anger or you can choose to Listen to Him for once in your life," Lacey said with a slight edge in her voice. It was the first hint of irritation Paul had seen in her all weekend, yet it had pushed a button in him.

Paul could feel his face getting red as his anger stared to rise. *How dare she talk to me like that, as if she knows me, my feelings? I've never seen her before this weekend. How can she pretend to read my thoughts?* "What do mean? Listen to Him for once in my life? How do you know He's even been Talking to me?"

Lacey paused and looked uncomfortable. *How far do you want me to push this, Lord?* Lacey then turned to face him squarely. "Paul, I'm sure that God has been Talking to you for a long, long time. You've been running from Him; running from a lot of things you don't want to face. He did the same thing with me. It's not a weakness to turn to God."

Paul looked at her skeptically. "So, if God has been Talking to me, why don't I Hear Him?"

"What frequency do you have your radio tuned to, Paul? Has it been God's or the stuff the world takes you to each day? How much time have you given to Him?" Lacey lowered the tone of her voice. "He often talks in whispers. Can you hear the whisper?"

Paul was obviously confused, "The whisper? What do you mean; a whisper?"

"Paul, right now He's talking to you in plain English. Can you hear it? It's more than a whisper. Can you hear it? Or do you just hear me speaking to you?" Lacey responded with a question.

Paul stood there, furrowing his brow. He closed his eyes and rubbed his temples. Suddenly, he opened his eyes and stared straight into her eyes. "You're trying to get me to believe that God is speaking to me now; through you?" He let the rest of the question hang there, incredulous that God would use a mere mortal to talk to him.

Lacey shrugged, "Sorry to disappoint you, Paul. Sometimes he uses people like me to be the delivery woman. No grand entrance, no shining angels; just a person like me."

Paul continued to stare at her, ready for a rebuttal but no words came to him.

Lacey paused for emphasis, "Paul, can you Read between the lines, Hear what isn't said? Listen from your Heart. Just stop and Listen to what isn't said. Just Listen."

Paul stood there dumbfounded. He did not have a word to say; not a word came to mind. He stood speechless before her. His eyes darted around the room, looking for an 'out'. None came. Even Gel continued to sleep despite the conversation beside her. *Why didn't she awake at the noise?* He felt cornered like some animal with no escape. *What's your answer?* He turned away from her, not wanting to be forced to say anything. Her words hung in the air.

Slowly, he turned to her, narrowing his eyes, he said, "Okay. I'll take the books then. I'll think about it; do some research into it. I can do that."

Lacey allowed a small smile to creep into the corners of her mouth. It had been a big risk, this conversation. *Obedience doesn't always have to hurt. It just makes you squirm a little sometimes. I sure didn't want to do this one, Lord.* Lacey sighed inaudibly. *You know best, Lord. You know best.*

Lacey pointed to the books in Paul's hands, looked him in the eye and said, "You won't be sorry." She then walked out of the room down the hall to her bedroom.

Paul stood there, arm still extended, books in hands; staring at the Bible she had pointed to last, wondering what it meant.

Evangeline slowly opened her eyes, feeling drugged and disoriented. She saw Paul standing between the two couches with books in his hand. She tried to gather her thoughts, but felt woozy. She slowly closed her eyes and sensed Paul moving to the other couch. Slowly she reopened her eyes and realized Paul was shoving the books into his backpack. *I don't know what that's all about, but I don't care at the moment. Nothing matters a whole lot now. I'll ask him about it later.*

Paul looked over at Evangeline and saw that she was awake. "Good nap?" he asked.

"Good enough, I guess. I think it's the drugs you had me take. What's going on here? How are the roads?" she asked groggily.

Paul sat beside her on the edge of her couch. "The roads are washed out in spots, I'm told. But they have devised a plan to get you into town anyway. Calvin drives a four-wheel-drive Jeep and he's experienced in navigating difficult terrain. He's going to be our chauffeur. It might be an exciting ride, but we'll get you there. Jack and Sonya met someone from her crew and they are expecting you. They'll get you to safety from there. It's all coming together."

Evangeline smiled and said, "I knew it would. I Prayed last night, you know. I knew it would."

Paul gave her a sideways glance and said, "You too? It seems as if they have everyone Praying around here."

Evangeline smiled even broader, "I guess it's contagious."

Paul shrugged and gave her hand a squeeze. "You sound better than you did earlier. I'm glad to see that. You rest awhile longer. You'll need your strength for the trip home."

Evangeline snuggled into the blanket, "I think I will. A little longer; sounds good." With that, she drifted off to sleep again. Once she was obviously asleep, Paul slipped outside for some fresh air and a new atmosphere. He needed to clear his thoughts. Too many conflicting words were confusing his thinking.

Lacey heard Paul leave and wandered back out to the kitchen. She spied Bert out on the back veranda and decided to join him. He turned when she closed the door behind her and sat on the porch swing. Patting the seat beside him, he said asked, "Care to join me?"

"I suppose that there's no harm in taking a rest. There doesn't seem anything more to do at the moment." She sat and let out a long breath.

"That sigh said something. Penny for your thoughts," Bert commented.

"Oh, I just had one of those God conversations with Paul. I didn't intend to speak to him, but God kind of opened the door to that one."

Bert tilted his head, ready to hear more, "Ooh. I suspect Paul wasn't too happy to hear what you said either."

"Oh, it ended well enough. It just was the part before it that was a little stressful," Lacey admitted.

"So it was between you two, and God of course. It's not for repeating?" Bert inquired.

"Not for repeating. All I can say is God might have opened the door to that private place in his Heart a little. Paul may be slightly more likely to hear His Voice in the future. He has a Bible now, at least, if he does Listen to Him," Lacey remarked cryptically.

"Well, that's progress. I don't know how you manage to do these things, Lacey. You're able to get the most unlikely folks to at least consider that God might be waiting to Talk to them," Bert said admiringly.

Lacey patted his hand and responded, "Bert, my dear sweet friend, you should know by now, that it isn't me doing the Doing. I just Listen and follow His lead."

Bert took her hand and said, "You keep reminding me of that. You're just good at Obeying that lead."

Lacey looked away for a moment and her eyes narrowed, "Speaking of Listening, I just had a bad sense about what they may encounter in town."

Bert's expression darkened and asked, "How so?"

Lacey cocked her head, Listening to the Leading inside her and answered, "Now, don't get alarmed. I don't know what it's about, as usual. It's just a leading to Pray again, that we've missed something." She shook her head in frustration. "I don't know, I just want to Pray for Jack especially, and Sonya too."

"Well, then we'd better do it and get more Guidance, oughtn't we? We'll just do what we do well," Bert stated matter-of-factly. He had learned to go with many of Lacey's leadings over the years.

Lacey agreed with him and said that once the group on its way, they would gather everyone for more Prayer. They may be missing Eli, but they would do what they needed to do with whom they now had available.

Jack and Mac soon returned to Lacey's with the additional four-wheelers. As they dismounted their vehicles and Calvin got out of the Jeep, they saw Lacey and her group coming out of the house. Paul rounded the corner of Jack's cabin from his walk as they assembled.

"So are we ready to move?" Jack asked. "How's our precious cargo?"

"She roused again when you arrived back with the four-wheelers. I think she's ready to leave this place. A good snooze helps a lot, I guess," was Hildy's observation.

"Jack, I hate to bring this up now, but do you think you might want to call your sister before you go. I don't know if the phones are working yet, but you might want to try. You can use my phone if you want."

"Yeah, thanks for reminding me. I guess I could try but I doubt the phones are working yet," Jack said as he turned to go in to the house. "At least I could try to call my folks too. See if they've heard from her."

Sol commented, "You know, if the landlines aren't operating yet, maybe the phone in my van would work. It operates off satellite. We might have more success with that."

"I didn't think of using that phone, but that's a good idea," Hildy responded.

Jack came out of the house quickly confirming that the house phone was dead. They then suggested he try the van phone.

Good idea. I've got the numbers here. Mind if I go try your phone before we head out?" Jack asked.

Sol volunteered readily, “No problem. Let’s get to it before anything happens to distract us.”

The men headed to Sol’s van. “Jack’s sister’s in Wilmington with their aunt who’s in hospital. It was in the direct path of the hurricane. It seems so long ago that they got hit. So much has happened to us in the last couple of days,” Lacey explained.

Sonya looked concerned. “I didn’t realize that Laurie had gone to Wilmington. They were getting hit hard the last I heard on the television. That can’t be good.”

“Let’s hope he gets through to someone to see how they are. The hospital was a good place to be in the storm. They might have power where no one else would. They have generators, don’t they?” Bert observed.

“That’s true. But during Katrina, the hospitals were hit too, weren’t they?” Hildy answered.

“Yes, but that was Katrina. Maybe they’re better prepared this time,” Lacey responded.

“While he’s doing that, let’s see how we can move Gel out to the Jeep. We should be ready to move when Jack gets finished,” Calvin reminded them.

The group split up, some checking out the Jeep and some moving into the house to prepare Evangeline for transport.

As expected, Jack could not connect to the hospital phone number that Laurie had given him. He heard a recorded message saying that all the available circuits were jammed and to try again later. They suggested calling state authorities for instructions about communicating with loved ones in the affected areas.

On a whim, Jack punched in the number for Laurie’s cell phone. It rang, but he heard a similar message. He was about to give up, but Sol reminded him about calling his parents to see if they had heard from her.

Jack nodded, “Good idea. They’re probably worried about me up here too, given the path of the storm. My mother most likely won’t sleep till she hears my voice for herself.”

Jack called his parents’ number and it was answered on the first ring. “Hey, Mom. It’s me, Jack. You answered quickly. I suppose you are sitting right beside the phone.”

His mother's worried voice came through clearly over the speaker, "Jack! I'm so glad to hear your voice. I tried to call your numbers but neither of them was in service. I suppose all the phones are down. But, then, how are you calling me now?"

"We're using a friend's satellite phone service in his vehicle," Jack replied.

"I'm glad you got through. I'll put you on the speaker so Dad can hear you too. How is it there? The news reports sounded like there was a lot of damage and flooding in your area."

Jack said, "Hi, Dad. We're okay here. We're managing. Lacey has a generator and we have the basics covered. It'll just be an inconvenience for a while."

"I heard there was flooding in the region. You're up too high in the mountains to be affected by that, but how are the roads?" his father questioned.

"Oh, the roads will take some time to repair but we'll get by. That's when we use the four wheelers," Jack answered easily.

"Yeah, I suppose you do. How about the flooding, though?" his father asked.

"Yeah, there's been a fair amount. I am headed down to town soon so I'll get a look at how bad it is there. Have you heard from Laurie yet?" Jack inquired.

Jack's mother piped up, "We heard from her before the full brunt of the storm hit. She said she had talked to you. But we haven't been able to connect since the hurricane made landfall. The news reports on the television look bad, Jack. Even hospitals that have been badly damaged. It worries me that Laurie and Liz may be at risk," his mother answered with an edge of concern in her voice.

"Well, Mom. They'll give preference to the hospitals when restoring power and phone. They're essential services," Jack reminded her.

"You're right, Jack. It was probably the best place to be in a disaster. Laurie's smart and she's a nurse. She'll know how to handle these situations. I just can't help being a mother, you know."

Jack nodded and said, "That's okay, Mom."

"Jack, you take care of yourself too. Don't go taking any unnecessary chances. I know you are trained too, but . . ." her voice trailed off, not wanting to finish the thought.

Jack was quick to reassure her, "Don't worry, Mom. I won't do anything stupid. If you hear anything about Laurie, leave a message on my cell phone. I'll eventually get somewhere that has service and pick up the message."

Jack's father answered, "We will, Jack. You do what you need to do and take care of yourself. We'll be in touch soon."

Jack's mother added, "We love you, Jack."

Jack thought he'd better respond, "I do too. I'll talk with you soon."

With that, Jack disconnected the phone. He looked over at Calvin and said, "Well, no news is good news sometimes."

Calvin nodded. "Yes, we'll have to assume that everything's okay. At least you have settled your mother's nerves a notch."

Jack chuckled. "Yeah, I don't know how she survived my stint in the army with the way she worries."

Mac and Sarah were headed out the front door of Lacey's house as Jack walked from the van.

"Heard you were trying to call your sister. Any success?" Mac asked.

"Nah. But I did get through to my parents. They haven't heard from her either. The news reports sound bad out of her area and the phones are still down. They may be for a while from the sounds of it. She's a resourceful lady, and a good nurse. I'm sure that she's fine. Aunt Liz wasn't doing well before this all started so she's another matter. But they haven't notified my mother of any problems with Aunt Liz so I have to assume it means that she's okay too."

Mac nodded, "I bet you made brownie points calling your Mom though."

"Oh, yeah. Good thing Lacey reminded me or I would've forgotten with everything going on. It's not that I don't care. It is just that I've had my mind on so many other things in the last couple of days. I feel kind of useless trying to help Laurie from this distance anyway. At least there's something concrete that I can do right here," Jack replied.

"Your sister's a nurse?" Sarah asked.

Jack nodded, "Yeah, she has intensive care training and trauma experience from the military. I wouldn't be surprised if they've put her to work down there anyway. She's not the sort to sit around if there's work to be done, even if she is on leave from her job. She's just that kind of person."

"My mom would have worried herself for days if I'd not called. I must admit though, I'll feel better when I hear from Laurie myself. Mom said that Wilmington was hit dead on, full force by Igor from the sound of it."

Sarah added, "I don't think any area that was hit by that storm could have gone without significant damage. You might as well assume that Laurie is part of the aid crew down there now. She sounds like a capable woman."

"So, is Evangeline ready to go?" Jack asked, changing the subject.

"Sonya is just finishing checking her and getting her ready to move. I think they're rigging the stretcher to carry her out. She wanted to walk but Paul wouldn't hear of it. He offered to carry her, but Sonya thought that a stretcher would be better," Sarah answered.

As Sarah finished speaking, out came the group carrying the gurney. They stopped in front of the Jeep as Paul opened the passenger door. He lifted her off the stretcher and into the Jeep in one swift movement. Evangeline winced as he fastened the seatbelt tightly around her.

Paul hesitated, "Sorry, honey, but with the roads as bad as they are, I have to make sure you don't get tossed around. Here are some pillows to make you more comfortable."

Evangeline touched his arm in apology and responded, "It's okay. I'll manage. We both know I have to wear the seatbelt. Don't worry about me."

He kissed her cheek and closed the door then threw his knapsack in before he climbed on the seat behind Evangeline. Jan, who was coming to keep Calvin company for the trip home, climbed in beside Paul in the back and Calvin closed the door after her. He then hopped into the driver's seat and began to buckle his seatbelt.

Jack, Sonya, Mac and Sarah mounted their ATV's and they were ready to head down the treacherous trip into the town below. Bert stopped them only long enough to say a brief Blessing over the venture and they were off with hardly another word spoken. Each knew many unknowns lay before them. They did not want to discuss it further in front of Evangeline.

Each rider donned their helmets, fastening the chin straps securely. Jack nodded to Sonya and the rest of the group as he started his motor. As it roared to life, each of the other vehicles in turn did the same.

Calvin was the last to start the engine of the Jeep as he looked directly at Bert. Bert slapped him on the arm and nodded as Calvin put the vehicle in gear.

First Jack pulled out on his four-wheeler, followed by Sonya. Mac and Sarah put their units in gear, moving tentatively at first, then more quickly to catch the other two. Calvin steered the Jeep slowly after them.

Lacey, Bert, Sol and Hildy watched as the group motored out of sight. "So our Work begins again in earnest," Bert said solemnly.

"Yes, it surely does," Lacey agreed. Sol and Hildy nodded as well as they walked back into Lacey's house. "The hard Work starts now."

Chapter 30

It didn't take long for the group to encounter the first washout in the road. Although rough, the road surface had been passable until now. The area of road that had posed the problem to Sol and Hildy on their way yesterday had completely eroded into a two-foot ditch across the road. Water still flowed freely across this trench making it difficult to see how deep it was.

Jack was the first to go through the trough, followed by Sonya. Calvin could judge his track from watching the other two before him and easily crossed with minimal jostling. Mac and Sarah followed through behind the Jeep.

"Sorry for the shaking but there isn't much I can do about it, Gel," Calvin said.

"I'm okay, Calvin. It wasn't so bad. I've got these pillows, that'll help. You do your job," was Evangeline's quiet response.

They drove on carefully dodging potholes and divots along the road. It was slow progress while they were still on the gravel road. The water had worn grooves and created streams, sometimes running across their path; other times the length of the road depending on the topography, always moved by gravity.

They swayed this way and that as Calvin carefully maneuvered the vehicle showing his years of driving experience. "Calvin, you've obviously done a lot of this kind of driving before. Did I hear them say you make a hobby of off-roading?" Paul asked.

"Yeah, it's something I do for fun these days," was Calvin's answer as he carved a turn through another shallow ditch.

"You seem comfortable driving in these conditions. Have you been doing it long?" Paul continued to inquire.

"Oh, I've been off-roading a few years now; I don't know maybe nine, ten. I've been doing rallies for most of that period. The courses they set up are challenging and good experience. It's monitored and all-in-all is fairly safe. They don't want anyone hurt and no one wants their vehicle messed up, you know. It's a weekend sport, not professional or anything," Calvin responded.

"So, Jan, do you drive too?" Paul added.

"Oh, not like Calvin. I leave most of that to him. It's his passion. I come along for moral support, doing some driving, but mostly I just go for the fun of it. It is great group of people to hang out with. When you have something in common like that it brings you together. We have had to help out and save a few vehicles on countless occasions, so you really get to know one another. We have a blast with everyone. There always are a few characters in the bunch, like any other group, but we have a good time together. The party after the course is just as fun. You know; lots of laughs," Jan answered. She grabbed for the frame as Calvin hit a particularly deep groove in the road.

"So you just got a notion to go off-roading or would there be more to the story?" Paul asked. The reporter in him was digging for more information.

Calvin kept his eyes on the road and eased around the rut, answering, "Nah, I raced stock cars for about twenty years before starting with these babies. I was drawing near to fifty and had a bad wreck with a few broken bones. It took me a long time to recover; a lot longer than it used to when I started with the cars. I used to wreck a lot when I was younger. But when it took the stuffing out of me the last time, Jan kind of suggested it was time to put my helmet on the hook with the stock cars."

"So what did you do for a living that you got into stock car racing? Did you work as a mechanic or something?" Paul's investigative instincts were kicking in. He wanted know more of Calvin's story now.

"Oh, no, no. I was an investment banker back in the city," Calvin chuckled. "No, I wasn't a grease monkey. I learned what I know about engines by hanging around the pits at the races for years before I started racing. I had an interest when I was a kid, you know. I hung out with a few guys at the races in my teens. I worked my way through school and finally started working full-time and making good money. But the stress would half kill you if you let it. I needed something as a distraction. I started going back to races and hanging out on weekends long enough that someone suggested I get one myself. It didn't take too much convincing, because I had the money at that point," Calvin continued.

"So did Jan drive too?" Paul asked.

Calvin chuckled, "Nope. That wasn't her thing, but she did make for a gorgeous pit crew."

"Did you get your hands in there and work on the cars, Jan?" Paul continued his interview.

"I wouldn't say I messed with his precious engine, but I did know my way around the tool box. I'd say that I was the mechanic's helper more than a mechanic. I knew how to do an oil change, but let Calvin and his crew set the timing and the critical stuff. I also knew when it was better to get my butt out of the way when things weren't going well," Jan chuckled.

They had a laugh over that statement. "Did you win much?" Paul probed more.

"I won my share. I have a few boxes of trophies in the cellar and on a couple of shelves in the study. But trophies don't pay for the gas to race, you know. I wasn't any Dale Earnhardt or anything. It was just Saturday night at the local dirt track. We had fun, it was a great stress release, and well, I liked the people too."

Jan added, "I think he liked the competition a little, if he's honest with you."

Paul was digging for more information, looking for that angle in a story that made it all tie together and let you into the depth of a person. "What were the guys in the pits like, the racers and crews?"

"Now, they were a good bunch of guys or I wouldn't have stuck with it for so many years. They came from a broad range of backgrounds, as in anything else. They could be rough around the edges at times and we had our share of rednecks, but they were a good group of guys. Well, I'll correct that. We had a few girls into it and some were good racers too. But the vast majority were men, like it is today," Calvin concluded.

"Was there serious competition or was it low key racing?" Paul dug further.

"It could get really competitive at times, but it was all in how you approached it. I just did what I did and tried my best at it with the time

I had available. I wanted to stay away from the nonsense that the others were trying to make of it. Oops, sorry, Evangeline, I didn't mean to let my tire go in so deep into that rut," Calvin apologized as he saw her grab the door frame then let out an involuntary groan.

They reached the paved section of the road in a few minutes and travelled uneventfully for a distance. Soon Jack held up his hand to slow the convoy and stopped to assess at the road ahead. He walked back to the Jeep and said, "It looks like the water has eroded the roadbed under the pavement. The surface is all broken up and I don't trust it not to give way under our weight. I think we'll put all the four-wheelers over it first to see how it takes the weight and maybe pack it down a little before you go over it."

"Whatever you think is best. I'll just follow your lead then," Calvin responded.

All four ATV's proceeded through the questionable section of roadway one by one with no catastrophes. Calvin put the Jeep in gear and carefully moved forward over the broken pavement. The surface sank about six inches under the weight of the Jeep. You could feel the stress climb in the Jeep as Calvin slowly moved the vehicle forward, carefully gauging his advance. The pavement held as the back tires moved into the depression. The front tires soon grabbed the intact pavement ahead and they were safely across the hazard.

"Good thing Jack had his eyes open. It could have been far worse than that," Jan commented.

""Yes, Jack's a good man. He won't let us down," Calvin responded as the tension eased in the Jeep.

Again, they travelled along intact blacktop and made good time. Water still rushed down the creek beside the highway, hopping and splashing over fallen logs and sundry obstructions. Occasionally, streams of swiftly flowing water gathered over the road surface causing rooster tails as each vehicle drove through them.

"It's good those guys are wearing full rain gear or they'd be soaked. Between the mud and the water, they'd be a mess," Jan observed.

Calvin nodded as he kept his eyes on the road ahead. A tree lay across the road ahead and he was trying to figure if there was enough room to make it around it. His decision was removed when Jack and Mac stopped, dismounted and quickly removed the obstacle. Jack walked to the Jeep and said with mischief in his eyes, "Sorry to disappoint you

Calvin. I know you usually drive over these things and that's half the fun, but I was thinking of Gel in there!"

"I understand. We'll do the fun course on the way back," Calvin replied. With that, Jan gave the back of his seat a thump. She answered before he could ask her what that was all about, "I'm just as much precious cargo as Gel is. Ask me before we do the 'fun' stuff."

"I know, I know. But where's the entertainment in that?" They chuckled as they prepared to move on.

They managed to travel another couple of miles with relatively clear roads when they rounded a sharp curve to find a significant landslide obstructing the roadway. The constant flow of water had undermined the soil covering the steep rocky slope above, sending it all cascading down the hillside and on the pavement below. They came to a sudden halt, barely avoiding hitting one another. The passengers in the Jeep jerked forward and slammed back into their seats.

"Whoa. That was close!" Jan exclaimed. "Gel, you okay?"

Evangeline winced as she straightened and said breathlessly, "Yeah, I think so."

"It looks as if they didn't hit one another or that heap of dirt. Everyone's getting off their vehicles, so they must be okay," Jan responded.

Calvin got out of the Jeep, followed by Jan and Paul. They surveyed the landslide trying to determine how stable the debris was.

Calvin and Jack walked closer to the mound of dirt looking up the hillside as they approached. A steep slope plunged below them and the guardrail that had separated the roadway from the drop-off had now disappeared. It was either flattened by the descending debris or had been dislodged and sent tumbling over the fifty foot drop below.

"We don't have a choice. There's only one route, that's for sure. We either go over it or turn back. The hill is too steep above and below," Jack observed.

"Well, now, that gives us a dilemma, doesn't it? What do you think?" Calvin asked as Mac joined them. "Is it stable? If we drive over it, is it going to trigger another slide?"

"Good question. First thing to do, I'd say, is to try tossing a few rocks on it from a distance and see if it starts moving again. If it holds, then we can try probing it with a log then try standing on it. If it holds, we might try the four-wheelers first to see if it will hold our weight one at a time," Jack offered.

"Yeah, I'd rather err on the side of caution with this one. I'm game if you are," Calvin responded.

"Okay, let's do it," Jack said before they had a chance to back out. "We'll start slow and easy. Let's gather a few rocks and there's a log that came down with the slide. It should work."

They tested the stability of the slide incrementally and it did not budge. The earth seemed sufficiently compacted to hold their weight. They soon decided to let Jack go across with the four-wheeler. He made it to other side of the debris field with no incident. Sonya then drove slowly over, followed by Mac then Sarah.

All eyes turned to Calvin as he restarted the engine. He surveyed the packed dirt where the others had travelled and steered into their tracks. Gingerly he crept up the mound of dirt; the ground did not shift beneath the wheels. He advanced a little more and still the ground under them held. They were halfway across now and it felt as if they going to make it to the other side when the wheels began to sink as the earth began to shift and buckle. The Jeep started to shake and slide sideways. Evangeline let out a shriek and grabbed the frame by her head. Calvin responded by urging the Jeep forward as fast as he dared.

Chapter 31

Lacey, Bert, Hildy and Sol gathered around the coffee table in the great-room of Lacey's house. However, drinking coffee was the last thing on their minds.

"It's serious. I know we've been Praying all along, but we have to gear things up now," Bert began. "It's no time for half measures. I would've been happier if we had the entire group here but with the roads as they are, I don't want to risk it. Beside, the phones are all down. We'll just have to Trust that the Lord has enlisted their efforts separately."

Murmurs of agreement were heard around the room. "The storm hasn't changed our original agenda. Our West Coast contacts haven't been wrong yet. We just have to expand our focus now with the ravages of the storm. We don't know how Jack's sister and aunt are doing in Wilmington, but we have to assume it's a bad situation. The limited information we have gleaned through our calls on the satellite phone combined with the original reports have shown devastation to that area. Igor continued to cut across a large area of the eastern seaboard then turned north," Bert continued with everyone's rapt attention.

Sol added, "The details of the damage and the deaths and injuries won't change the intent of our Prayers anyway. The Holy Spirit can help us fill in the details as we Pray."

Lacey added, "We still have to understand what our focus remains the same. We must realize that as bad as this disaster is, it's not the primary agenda here. It's just a prelude to a bigger and more ghastly plan. Our information is clear on this. Our people are pure gold and we can't be distracted from what we originally set out to do."

Bert nodded, "Lacey said it perfectly. We must remain solid and in unity on this task. Too many lives are at stake for us to let up now."

Hildy piped in, "But that doesn't mean we let up in our Intercession for Paul and Evangeline and their group."

Bert shook his head. "No, we can't stop saturating them in Prayer. It just means that we can't afford to divert our energies from our original call to Prayer. We just add to it. If any of us in this group or the other satellite groups lets down their guard, lives will be lost; more lives I'd say. There's no question that some will perish with this event, but we'll save many more through our efforts. And notice I said 'will' not 'may'. There must be united certainty in our results and the intent of the One providing the Protection; just as there is equal Understanding about the intent of the enemy on our soil."

"I couldn't agree more, Bert. We Prayed before Calvin and Jan left, but let's re-state our solidarity. Are all still Agreed on our original stance on this matter?"

One by one they renewed their pledge.

"Agreed."

"Agreed."

"Agreed"

"Agreed. Then it's settled. We can continue our meeting then. Bert, you have the floor."

The wheels of the Jeep spun then grabbed then spun again, as Calvin attempted to steer toward the hill side. The dirt continued to shift threatening to topple the Jeep on its side. In what seemed minutes instead of seconds, the tires grabbed the dirt again and moved the vehicle forward toward the solid pavement beyond. Once completely clear of the unstable earth, he put the Jeep in park.

Everyone sat silently, trying to gather their thoughts, their breathing slowly resuming. You could almost hear their hearts beating; their pulses were racing so wildly. Calvin finally drew a deep cleansing breathe, audible to the group.

"You can say that again," Jan said.

"I didn't say anything," Calvin muttered.

"Oh, yes you did. That breath said it all," Jan responded.

"That was close," Evangeline said in a whisper. She hugged the pillow in her lap a little tighter.

"Yes, but I never had a doubt that we would make it," Calvin assured them.

"You didn't?" Paul asked. "Because of your great driving skills?"

"Nope. I'm human and fallible. But we Prayed before we left and I had a sense of Peace that we would make it to town okay. We posted as many angels around these vehicles as it would take to get us to Moulton safely. I think we just put them through their paces though," he said flatly.

"I won't debate you about the angels at this point; whatever works. I'm just glad to know that we made it across," Paul grunted.

Paul, Calvin and Jan piled out of the Jeep for a closer look. "I'll be right back, okay, Gel?" Paul said as he went with the others. He didn't wait for an answer. Evangeline was left sitting alone in the vehicle again, turning as best she could to see behind her. *That was close! It's all getting crazy again, like yesterday. What a mess. What's next?*

The group of travelers crowded as closely to the edge of road as they dared. The landslide had been set off again, tossing more dirt and debris down the mound and off the cliff-like precipice beyond. Had they stayed in its path even seconds longer, they surely would have gone over the edge with the rocks and stones and tree branches they now could see beneath them. No one said a word, they just exchanged glances. That was sufficient communication for the moment. They knew what they had just escaped.

As they walked back to their vehicles, Jack said, "No more chances here guys. We'll take things a little slower even when the road seems clear. We rounded that corner almost too fast to stop in time. We don't know what we might encounter as we proceed. We'll likely find hazards in the open but hidden until you round a corner like this one. We have to remember what is below the surface of the pavement can be just as dangerous. We aren't going to lose anyone to injuries today. Is that clear?" Unanimous agreement followed this statement.

"It might take a little longer, but I'm all for making it there," Mac said as they climbed on their ATV's and the others headed back to the Jeep.

"Are we set?" Jack asked.

No answer came, but each of them started their engines and pulled down their visors. Jack was satisfied that his crew was ready and he put his machine in gear.

Audrey and Arthur Davidson, Jack's parents, sat before their television screen straining to see anything positive in the images that were before them. Scene after scene portrayed a dismal picture of the conditions in Wilmington, North Carolina. Both their daughter and Audrey's sister were there, presumably at the hospital, but they had no confirmation yet. The damage was thorough. Many houses were destroyed and those partly damaged, would require extensive repairs before they were again inhabitable. Flooding overwhelmed vast areas of the region and was taking a long time receding. It would take years to replace and repair the infrastructure of the city and surrounding district.

Already, there was finger pointing at all levels of government. Accusations of inadequate evacuation orders and planning abounded. The problems came on two fronts. First, there were insufficient resources compared to vast needs of the victims of this disaster. Second, the available assistance was going to be spread so thinly because of the widespread geographical range of the damage. This hurricane did not contain its path just to North Carolina. It continued not only north but also inland without a significant decline in strength. Manpower was overwhelmed as soon as it was deployed and the necessary supplies were depleted almost before they could load the trucks.

The most significant obstacle to administering aid was the impossibility of the task caused by impassable thoroughfares. They could not reach the worst-affected areas. It was an agonizingly slow and arduous endeavor to clear the roads and get the trucks to these regions. Airports were damaged and flights not only delayed but indefinitely canceled in many areas. The best that the officials could to do was airdrop personnel and supplies to the most desperate of regions.

FEMA was stretched to capacity. State and local officials were working through the priorities as best they could, however they could not get beyond the top of their lists. They understood that lives were at stake. However, the areas most directly affected looked as if they had been hit a nuclear bomb blast, so the work was tedious and often grisly.

Audrey left the room in tears. "I just can't look at it. It just makes me want to throw up. I'm so afraid for them now. It was bad enough before the television crews got there, but now it just makes me think that all my worst fears are going to come true. I never was this frightened when Laurie was still in the military. I always thought of her being behind the front lines, not exposed and vulnerable. In Wilmington, she was right in the line of fire. And Liz is so sick and . . ."

Arthur did not say a word. He flicked off the television and followed her into the kitchen. He put her hands in his and looked her in the eyes lovingly. No words could express his devotion to her and their shared pain at those images and descriptions of suffering. Under normal circumstances, it would have been too graphic for most people. In this case it tore at the very fiber of their souls. On what could they stand when their government was overwhelmed and rescue seemed impossible? That was the unspoken question hanging in that kitchen that afternoon.

The convoy moved slowly into the valley, mile by mile. The sun followed their track, glimmering through the trees overhead, signaling the complete end to the rain, a relief to each of the travelers. They managed to move on six miles before they stopped again. Jack motioned for caution as they neared another washout zone. This time the pavement was uprooted and washed down the embankment leaving exposed roadbed for about ten feet. It was complicated by the swiftly running waters over top of the remaining fill.

"I don't know how solid that dirt is there. With the water running over it, I can't see what's below. It looks like the water is at least a foot deep and running hard," Jack concluded.

"Well, it runs the width of the road. Even if we clear an area to the side to pass through, we don't know how solid the base is underneath," Sonya replied.

"The slope isn't that steep here. I'm just trying to figure a way around it. I don't think it would be as much problem for us but the Jeep could get into difficulties. I don't think there are a lot of choices. Either we go through it or turn back again. Problem is we have the landslide behind us now. We're kind of trapped, between a landslide and a washout. We might be out of options," Jack was brainstorming.

"Why don't we test it and if it seems solid enough, we can go through with the four-wheelers first. It doesn't look that bad. It's the water running through it that makes it seem worse," Sonya offered.

Mac and Sarah agreed that it did not look to be beyond their capabilities. Jack motioned for Calvin to inspect the trough. Calvin went to the edge of the ditch and stuck a branch into the water to gauge the depth. He poked the stick into the mud and said to them, "Well, it's soft on top but seems to have some rock under it. It might be tricky but I think we can manage it. You might get your feet wet though," he concluded with a grin.

Jack looked at Calvin, amazed at his brazen confidence. "You think getting our feet wet is our chief concern? All I want is for everyone to get out of here uninjured."

"I want the same thing, son. If you want, I'll go first this time. I can show you how to do it," Calvin declared.

"No, that's alright. We'll test it first. I don't want to risk our patient in there," Jack was starting to get frustrated with Calvin's attitude. He was not sure what irritated him the most, a challenge of his assessment or that he might be starting to doubt his abilities. Whatever it was, it was starting to put him on edge and he did not like it.

Calvin climbed back into his Rubicon and waited for the others to get ready. Jack started first and stopped just short of the drop-off. He wanted to be sure that there was no sink hole below him before entering into the water. Satisfied that the base was solid enough he proceeded through. The depth of the water was a little deeper than he first expected but he traversed the ditch with no difficulties.

Next Mac then Sarah crossed. Again they encountered no problems. Sonya followed their tracks and drove into the water-filled trough. As she reached the midpoint, her four-wheeler lurched and started to go sideways, throwing her off balance. She swayed precariously, but managed to hold the handlebars as the vehicle rose the other side. By the time she was up the embankment, she lost her grip and was thrown through the air and onto the ground in a sudden stop.

A collective gasp rose from the other three riders as they shut their engines and ran to see if she had been injured. Calvin threw open the door to the Jeep and ran to his side of the trough.

"Sonya! Are you okay?" Jack cried as he ran to her side.

Sonya sat up and brushed herself off. "Well, of all the dumb things to do!" she declared in disgust.

"What happened in there?" Jack asked.

"Darned if I know. I think the bottom is kind of sandy there. It might have shifted as I went through it.

Sarah asked, "Are you hurt? Can you continue to ride?"

"Oh, I might have a few bruises, but I think my pride is hurt more than my body. I'll probably feel that one tomorrow, but I can continue," Sonya replied as Jack helped her to her feet. "Oh, and Calvin, I did get my feet wet on that one."

Calvin held up his hands in surrender, "Sorry, I mentioned it. I'm just glad you're okay. Will you accept my apology?"

Sonya started to brush the mud off her rain suit, but soon decided that it was not worth the trouble and instead busied herself with adjusting her helmet. She nodded at Calvin and said, "Yes, sir, I will. Now, we'd better check things out before you try it. I hope it won't do it again with the Jeep."

They walked to the ditch and poked and prodded the bottom until they were satisfied that the Jeep could cross. Calvin got back in and put the Jeep in gear. He showed the rest of them his skill in negotiating the rough terrain. He crossed with no difficulties.

Sonya remarked, "I wish I knew what threw me there. It was as though the roadbed dissolved under me. Maybe the ATV was too small to pass like the Jeep. I don't know. I thought I had better control than that."

Jack leaned over and gave her a hug. "Your skill isn't in doubt. You can ride with the best of us. It was just a fluke. Let's just check out the vehicle and see that it wasn't damaged. Maybe we should trade. You try riding mine for a while and see if it works better for you."

"I should be okay. But maybe if you rode it, you could see if it's still handling okay. And thanks," Sonya replied.

"Thanks for what?" Jack asked as he released her from the embrace.

"Oh, for the vote of confidence and caring," Sonya said and smiled. Jack just looked at her and grinned.

"Okay, you two, we have to get a move on if we're to get to town before tomorrow," Mac called to them. Mac then turned to check Sarah as the other two busied themselves with their ATV's.

It was quickly becoming evident that the town of Moulton was a disaster area. Not only was there significant damage from the rain and the winds of the day and night before, but now the river running through it was becoming more turbulent as countless cubic feet of water descended from the upper elevations of the numerous mountains in the county. Seeley's Mountain might be the largest one in the region, but it was not the only one. Every inch of rain that started high on that range had to go somewhere and that somewhere was the East River. Unfortunately, Moulton was right in its path.

Historically, this spot along the East River had been a key location for the exchange of goods for furs when the first settlers came into the continent. It soon became a trading post and it was not long before the lure of a good source of fish and furs established a settlement in this location. That was long before anyone thought of building roads in this difficult countryside. The primary means of travel was up the East River, then known by the name the native population used for the waterway. The European settlers never did master the pronunciation of the river, so they called it after one of key leaders in the settlement instead.

Edward Eastman convinced a group of fellow colonists that there was money to be made in the mountains, despite the harshness of the environment. He had made alliances with the native tribes who had, in trade for goods, taught them survival in the wilderness country. It proved a lucrative allegiance for many years. Despite the turbulent years of the war for independence and other political upheavals, somehow the settlement thrived, through the combined efforts of Eastman himself and his son-in-law, Alexander Moulton. He linked with the vision of Eastman and together they forged a lucrative business. After Eastman's death, Alexander Moulton expanded the trading post and developed the settlement that grew into the town of Moulton that exists today.

Moulton now was a hub of activity for the region. Most roads from the surrounding mountain range funneled into this modest town on the East River. The topography encouraged the building of roads into this settlement and lately it had become a popular route down to the interstate highway. Bad planning and low budgets had seen the lack of construction of additional bridges in this section of the county. The powers that be would say it was because the mountains themselves did not lend themselves to the construction of additional roads across the river in that area. If the truth were told though, it would also reveal that there was a political struggle for control of government dollars in the region and Moulton had won. Unfortunately, now all evacuated residents were converging on one bridge that was significantly at risk.

As the waters of the East River grew angrier and more turbulent, houses that used to have spacious backyards overlooking the river, found their real estate shrinking by the minute. The rising river was beginning to overflow the banks and spill over usually dry ground. The vistas that had determined good property investment now seemed menacing.

The remnant of evil danced over the river. Igor as a storm was spent but its tentacles of torment fastened to the terrain and it brought the demon great delight. It was not finished with these mortals yet, not in the least.

The convoy of off-road vehicles meandered slowly down County Road 10 making their way closer to the town of Moulton. The East River could be heard far before it came into view, even over the rumble of vehicles. Jack perceived the sound in his chest before he actually heard it and brought his ATV to a stop. He signaled them to shut their engines.

"Do you hear that?" he asked Sonya.

They looked at one another, quizzical looks on their faces. They took off their helmets to get a better sense of what they were hearing.

Sonya looked at Jack and asked, "Is that what I think I'm hearing?"

"I am afraid so. That's the river. If we can hear it from here, I can hardly imagine what it looks like. It sounds like Niagara Falls. There must be an awesome sight ahead, that's all I can say," Jack responded solemnly.

"Oh, Jack," Sonya said shaking her head. She got off her four-wheeler and stood there, mouth agape and her eyes were imagining the scene that might await them in Moulton. "This isn't good."

"Yeah, we've had it rise in the spring, dangerously at times. But it's never sounded like this before," Jack stated and let out a long whistle. "We're in for it this time."

Mac and Sarah exchanged glances. They realized that it might be only the beginning of the hardest part of the trip. Their long and arduous trek to bring Evangeline to safety may be all for naught now. Anxiety began to rise in Sarah's chest. Questions danced around in her head about the futility of their quest. She moved closer to Mac searching his eyes for reassurance. She found only a vague hope in his eyes and that was quickly fading.

Mac whispered in her ear, "It'll be okay. Somehow it's going to be okay. Remember what Lacey said before we left. When it all seems lost, don't depend on yourself. Look to God for your Strength. That's probably all we've got now."

He squeezed her hand and she turned and hugged him. She needed to feel his muscular arms around her now. Somehow it was a reminder of the strength that seemed beyond her reach. "I needed to hear that. Thanks."

The four occupants in the Jeep sat and listened to the din in the distance. Evangeline shuddered at the prospect of more dangers. She just wanted to arrive at their destination without further adventures. She was tired and sore and about out of energy. An uncomfortable fear was rising within her again. She recognized it from the cavern. It was wrapped in a different package today, but it had the same sensation. *You're putting everyone at risk. It won't end well and it will be your fault again.*

She leaned her head back into the headrest and sighed. All the pain and despair she had been suppressing during the trip came crashing down on her. Paul responded by leaning forward between the seats resting his hand on her shoulder. He did not know what else he could offer at this point. They were stuck with an impossibly bad situation that was out of his control again.

Jan sat listening to the rushing waters and said nothing. She slowly bowed her head, closed her eyes and silently said a Prayer. Calvin just stared out the front windshield imagining the challenges that would be ahead.

"There's no sense putting this off any longer. We'd better get down there now and see what we have to deal with," Jack said as he started to put his helmet back on.

Sonya walked closer to his side and commented, "My rental house is by the river, you know, and it's definitely at risk. It's close enough to the shoreline that it won't escape this."

Jack responded, "I thought of that, but didn't want to say anything. There's not a lot you can do about it at this point though."

"Maybe not, but you know Tucker is likely to be still in his apartment behind my house, dead drunk," she answered.

"Nah, he's had lots of time to sober up since yesterday," Jack countered.

"Jack, you don't know Tuck as I do. He probably woke up yesterday and saw the storm and used it as an excuse to start drinking again. He's

. . . well, I don't think you know the problem he has with drinking," Sonya added uncomfortably.

"Sonya, sure he likes to party with the guys, but a drinking problem?" Jack questioned her.

"You don't know how many days he's not made it into work. Jack, I've caught him about to go on a shift and realized he was still drunk from his last bender. I've forced him to call in sick more times than I'd care to recall. He just wasn't fit to drive let alone show up for work. He'd be the one at the bottom of a ravine somewhere instead of the ones he was hired to rescue!" Sonya said in disgust.

Jack clawed back in his memory for situations where he had last seen Tucker. He had to admit that he had been with him mostly when the guys got together for a few beers to shoot pool or another off-duty event. Tucker liked to party with the best of them, but stay drunk afterward? *Why didn't I see the signs? What did I miss? Sometimes, when I met him in town he seemed a little crazy but I thought he was acting like that to impress the women. Was he just drunk and I didn't realize it? How could he get that past me?*

Sonya continued, "Jack, he's gone way beyond a social drinker. He's deep into alcoholism. I've tried to get him to get some help but he says he's just fine and just having a little fun; that he's got it all under control. But he's doesn't. Jack, he may be my cousin, but he's a drunk. That's all there is to it," Sonya said and started to look away as tears tumbled down her cheeks.

Jack got off his four-wheeler and took his helmet back off. He put his hand on her shoulder to turn her back toward him. "Look, I had no idea there was such a problem. If you'd said something, I could have talked to him about it."

Sonya sniffed and responded indignantly, "Jack, you were one of his drinking buddies. I didn't think you'd believe me if I did. I just didn't know what else to do."

Jack looked straight at her and continued, "Sonya, I'm sorry. If I had any idea, I would have talked to him about it; honest, I would have. Look, we'll stop by and check him. We'll make sure he's okay."

Sonya wiped away the tears on her cheek. She did not like Jack to see any weakness in her. She could always keep up with the guys on her crew and she did not know how he might respond to seeing her breakdown like this. "Thanks. It shouldn't take long any way. It's on the way," she added as she continued to wipe the tears away. Jack took her hand and brushed some dirt from her cheek. Sonya paused and looked into Jack's eyes, not sure what he meant by it.

Jack returned her glance and said gently, "We'll take care of things together. You don't have to manage Tuck alone any longer."

Sonya gave him a pained smile and whispered, "Thank you. I didn't mean for you to have to get involved in this but thank you, nonetheless."

"He's one of my friends too, you know. I should have been there for him. The least I can do is help him now. And I want to be there for you, too," Jack said awkwardly. He never was good with sentimental things and it was not easy for him.

"I appreciate it more than you know. Let's get moving then. The sooner we get there, the sooner we can get Evangeline where she needs to go," Sonya answered changing the subject. Jack nodded, holding her a moment longer and allowing Sonya to realize Jack was sincere in his pledge to be there for her. Sonya smiled and Jack slowly released his grip on her. Jack answered, "Yeah, we'd better get moving."

Sarah nudged Mac as she approached her ATV. "Looks like Jack and Sonya are an item."

Mac responded, "Could be."

"Well, I'm just glad something good is coming out of this mess," she commented. "It's good for them."

"Yeah, that's a good thing. A crisis can bring people together or tear them apart. I'm glad that it has brought them together."

"So am I," Sarah answered. "I'm also glad to have you here to help me. I hope you know that."

"Yeah, I know. We'll get through it all. You ready?"

"Sure. You lead."

Sam Fowler directed a crew to go house to house along a stretch of the East River just outside the Moulton town limits. They were carrying out an evacuation order imposed by the mayor and the sheriff's office. Resources were stretched to their limits and they were assisting the local authorities in getting as many people as they could to leave their homes before it was too late and the flood waters surrounded these buildings. Time was of the essence and he knew it. If only these people were not so stubborn to stay in their dwellings, he would be able to use his people where they supposed to be.

Sam was running on adrenaline now. He had continued to command the rescue operations as the storm had intensified through the evening and into the night. He had grabbed a few hours of sleep overnight when Jake Merkley came to spell him off, but his mind knew that every individual was needed and would not submit easily to sleep. His rest was minimal and now he was beginning to feel the effects of the exhaustion. He was nearing his forty-seventh birthday and his stamina was less than it was in his twenties. In those days, he would not have thought twice about the all-nighter, but now was a different story.

Sam called in to his radio, "What's the status now? Is the bridge still holding? Over."

"The bridge is intact. We're blocking all traffic across it though because the water is rising so rapidly, it could be submerged at any time. We aren't allowing anything but emergency vehicles through now. We can't take the chance of someone panicking partway across and blocking traffic. Over."

"Roger that. I hope we can clear these dwellings quickly and get back down there. I'll keep you informed as we go. Let me know if any reinforcements arrive and direct them over here. I want to release my crews to move downriver a little further. I think they'll be more useful closer to Central Avenue. Over."

"I'll let you know what we've got available. Over and out."

Sam shook his head in frustration. It was not the proper use of his personnel, but his hands were tied at the moment. These people had to be evacuated and now.

Bert walked to the large window in Lacey's great-room holding a book in his left hand. He glanced down at the pages before him and grunted. It was not easy waiting here knowing all the action was toward town. He shook his head and stared out the window again, studying the sky. It was now blue and clear, a sharp contrast to twenty-four hours ago. If not for a few missing branches, one would not suspect the ravages of the earlier storm.

He decided to go out on the veranda. As he closed the door behind him, Lacey rounded the side of the balcony and bumped into him. "Oh,

I didn't see you there, Bert," she said as she stopped abruptly. "I was just coming to get you to point out the lake to you. Look at the color of the water. All the runoff and debris has surely made a mess of the shoreline. The water is murky and looks like mud."

Bert walked with her down to the dock and inspected the water. "It's such a change in a short time. I wonder how long it will take for the water to clear."

"Well, I suppose it depends on how long it takes for the excess flow to come down the mountain. It looks like the water level is a lot higher than yesterday. The creeks are running like rivers still, so I expect that it'll take awhile," Lacey answered.

"If it's still running so freely here, I can only imagine how long it will take for the river to crest. It could keep rising for some time. That will make any spring runoff we've had lately look tame," Lacey mused.

As they stood contemplating the condition of the lake, they heard the sound of a vehicle by the house. They turned in unison to see Eli jump out of his truck and called to him. He spotted them and they waved him down to join them. He picked his way down the slippery hillside and was soon down by the dock.

"Whoa, look at the color of the water. Must be a lot debris coming from down the mountain!" Eli exclaimed.

"No doubt about it. What did you find over at Horace and Nan's?" Bert inquired.

"Well, Horace was being his usual handful. He got really confused last night with the storm so it was good Gertrude was there to help. There's a fair amount of damage all over the place: trees down on the road, houses, on the wires and the roads are a mess. A few people are out already doing make-shift repairs to the roads around their places. I'm not sure how effective that will be considering how much damage the road has sustained, but I guess if each resident does something it might help," Eli replied.

"It might make it easier if anyone needed to get out in an emergency though. Did you run into any neighbors?" Lacey asked.

"Only those were working on their patch of road. It looked like a lot of people might have high tailed it out of here before the storm escalated. Either that or they are too scared to come out of their houses," Eli commented.

"It looks like the general store might be closed for a few days. John was dumping pails of water from inside when I stopped by. A tree came real close to wrecking the place. He was fortunate to get away with only a little flooding with the roof he has on that place!" Eli chuckled.

"Yeah, he was putting off doing anything about it this summer. He said it was too hot to get up there. My guess is he might want to do it now though," Bert remarked. "Come on up to the house and we'll make some iced tea. You can tell us more about what you found. Then we can go down with you for another run and help with the repairs."

They carefully made their way up the slick slope. Lacey turned back to look at the vista. *Yes, the lake is looking murky and dark today. But this time you didn't get me or the ones I love. This time we're okay, you miserable demon.*

The ominous sound grew louder and louder as they approached the river. As the noise grew in intensity, so did their heartbeats quicken. The sense of impending disaster increased the closer they came.

Sarah did not know what to expect, but she was sure it was not going to be good. All hope of crossing the river and getting Evangeline to hospital easily was quickly evaporating. She realized that the challenges of getting down the mountain might be small compared to the situations that this river might cause. Disappointment was turning rapidly into dread.

Calvin and Jan did not speak as they rode along the final stretch nearing the river. They knew this section of road well, but it did not feel the same. It was as though the surroundings were willing them to stay back and away from the danger ahead. Paul could sense the mounting tension as he sat behind Calvin, but he did not want to convey his apprehension to Evangeline. However, she too could feel the mounting stress. It only fuelled her private fears. *You'll not survive this one even with all these people helping you this time. It's too big. I'm too big.* The same voice from the day before taunted her. The panic it instilled crept over her again. Bile rose in her throat. Silently, she sat awaiting the next decision that was out of her control.

Jack and Sonya rode ahead, side by side, as though to shield the view that awaited them as they rounded the last corner. Ahead and down a steep hill lay the East River, or at least what they once knew as that river. As they neared the intersection with Moulton Road, they had their first view of the waterway. One by one, they crossed the road and stopped their vehicles in the clearing above the river.

They watched in horror at the fury of the waters below them. Its wrath was enormous. It was now a monster, unleashed and intent on getting to an unknown destination down the mountain, down deep in the Earth. It wanted to get there yesterday, no longer content to meander and sightsee as in days past. This deluge had a mind of its own, a rage not seen for many a year here. The turbulence was astounding. Muddied water uplifted as it crashed against unseen obstacles below. Uprooted trees, splintered wood, sections of decks, even automobiles careened down its crazed path, pushing all in its way forward, downward away from the heavens above toward some hell below. This ogre was intent on destruction.

They stood silenced by the roar. No words were necessary. The scene below spoke volumes, like the waters themselves. The sound was deafening. They could feel the spray from the violent foaming waters even as they stood staring down on it from high above. They could taste and smell the destruction.

Jack leaned back on his four-wheeler sizing up this adversary. *Okay, it's big. It's a challenge alright. It'll show what you're made of Jack Davidson.* Jack clenched his teeth with a look of intensity Sonya had never seen. It frightened her as much as the churning waters below.

Sonya shifted on her vehicle. She felt an urgency to get Jack's attention away from the ugly scene below. He seemed drawn toward the force pushing those waters and it worried her. But even she had a difficult time looking away from the frothing waters.

Jack glanced at her as Sonya reached over and touched his arm. At first he stared at her as though she was not there, but finally broke free of the pull of the force in the waters below. He shook his head and took a deep breath. He was stunned. Each of them was staggered by what they witnessed. They had no means to defend against this threat.

"We should move on. Just take it easy and keep your eyes on the road," Jack finally said. He said this as much for himself as for the others. His eye was irresistibly drawn back toward that hideous river.

They rode carefully until they reached the first grouping of houses along the riverbank. It was an ugly scene, but they had to stop and watch. What they viewed made them gasp in revulsion.

The monster greedily ate at the shoreline across the river, licking at first, tasting then ravenously biting into the soil and roots. Like a voracious maniac, the waters devoured choice morsels first; then bit into the underpinnings of trees, decks, and now houses nestled along the once lazy river's edge.

Waves licked up, chewing the foundations of one house after another, leaving them precariously perched with no visible means of support. The weight of the buildings caused them to sag at first, signaling a sense of defeat in the wake of the monster's attack. It was soon followed by a low sigh, a gasp, then a crack from inside the structure. A wave of panic emitted from the house as timbers, one by one, in rapid succession, snapped like matchsticks when they no longer had any support beneath them. The groan of utter defeat was followed rapidly by the collapse of once fine construction into a heap of debris immediately swallowed by the raging torrent below, no evidence of habitation except parts of foundations.

Sarah drew a breath and held it at the sight before her. She seemed unable to find any air. Her horror at the sight of this devastation seemed to drain her resolve to continue. What could anyone do against this beast?

Mac leaned toward Sarah and slowly reached to hold her hand. Awestruck he said, "I've never witnessed such destruction from nature before. I thought the hurricane was bad, but this. Wow! I've seen images on the television before, but until you see it for yourself, you just can't imagine the forces involved. The sounds, the smells even! In person, well you just couldn't convey it through pictures alone."

They moved on a few hundred yards only to view a similar scene. Again the raging river devoured a home, cascading the debris into the turbulent waters, battering the pieces into unrecognizable pulp within minutes.

Jan and Calvin watched the river do its horrible work. They knew the source of this tirade. It was demonic and wicked. It was relentless in its working. This ogre would never be satiated with its current destruction. It had an unquenchable lust fuelled from the bowels of hell itself. Jan reached forward to touch Calvin's arm and he grasped her hand, realizing the true nature of the foe before them could never be battled by physical means alone. This force was not one God intended to be on His Earth. It was beauty transformed into the essence of evil itself. It was God's Love twisted into loathing and grotesqueness. Fingers of rage entwined themselves in these waters, turning life bringing liquid into tentacles of death.

Calvin squeezed Jan's hand. She looked over at him and nodded agreement. They knew what they were facing and what they needed in preparation. No physical training would suffice. The true character of the beast was not in nature alone, it was an adversary in the Spiritual realm that manipulated the physical. It was a clashing of forces in the unseen that resulted in what was evident to the eye.

Calvin solemnly said, "Lord, Prepare us with Your Word of Love and Truth and Power. You said that You would Supply all our needs according to Your Riches in Glory in Christ Jesus, so now is the time for that Supply. We need Your Presence and Your Hand upon us as we embark on this task at hand. We Thank You for Your ever present Love and Glory and Mercy. We place ourselves in the secret place of The Most High and abide in the shadow of the Almighty as we declare You as our Lord and Savior, Name above all names that may be named in Heaven and in Earth. In Jesus Name. Amen."

Evangeline repeated, "Amen." Paul mumbled the word, not sure what it all meant but knowing that this menace below them could not be tamed by human efforts alone. *We can use whatever help we can get. It couldn't hurt. It's been so crazy.*

Sonya turned to Jack said, "We'd better get going down to check Tucker. I don't have a good feeling about this."

Jack agreed and signaled the rest to move out. They continued along the road, carefully making their way across washouts and potholes. It felt painfully slow to Sonya who was feeling increasingly anxious about Tucker. *How stupid was I to leave him alone and not get someone to look in on him, especially with the hurricane in the forecast? I should have expected problems. I should have known I couldn't get back to do it myself. Instead, I was mad at him again for being too drunk to work. Now look at the situation!*

As they neared the stretch of river approaching Sonya's rental, they realized the river had risen higher than ever. The dock had disappeared and the force of the flowing water had eroded the shoreline so the house seemed to rise from the river itself. Gone was the sloping lawn with its patio and barbecue pit. Erased was the storage shed with the canoe. The car port had also vanished into the swirling waters that clawed at the ground below the dwelling's foundation. Wave after churning wave battered the quickly dissolving the ground beneath her home. Time was no longer on their side. Her home of three years was about to be swallowed by the advancing demon.

Chapter 32

Lacey poured five glasses of cooled tea and put out the lemon and sugar on the counter before her. As she set the empty jug back on the counter, Bert came back from the back porch. "There, I shut off the generator for now. We can put it back on in a while when we make the next meal. There's a balance between conserving fuel and keeping the perishable food cold in the fridge. Good thing you thought to stock up on the nonperishable items. We might be able to stop using the fridge soon if they can't restore power for a while."

Lacey agreed and took a sip from her glass and said pensively, "I know we've Prayed for Jack and Sonya and their trip to bring Gel to hospital, but I still don't have a good sense about it now. I just don't know what it's about by any means but it just doesn't sit right with me. I think we need to add something. We've missed some dimension to the Prayer somehow."

Hildy set her glass down on the counter and 'Listened' in her spirit to see if she could determine what Lacey sensed. She drew in her breath for a moment and reported, "You know, you're right. I don't know the details of what's going on, but I think it's an extra thing they're doing down there that we might have not covered before. We didn't add anything about . . . detours that they may encounter. I think that's it, yes, detours would be a good word."

Bert agreed, "You're right. I don't know how we could have been so negligent, but we didn't do that. Thank you, ladies. You've kept your antennae up and operational. We could have gone and gotten so busy doing stuff up here that we would have forgotten to keep Calvin and Jan and the group properly covered in Prayer. It's a moment by moment thing, isn't it? Considering the circumstances, we can't afford to let out guard down, for their sakes. It's good to do the physical things to help in the neighborhood, but if we forget to keep up the Prayer coverage over everything they may encounter, we've only done part of our job, have we?"

The group moved back into the library this time. Lacey pulled down two volumes from her bookshelves and laid them on the desk. "I think these might be helpful in formulating this Prayer," she added as she opened the first large book. One was a useful reference of Scriptures that covered crises. "I don't know that they specifically list this circumstance but we should be able to find something to reasonably match what we need for this occasion. Let me see. Storms, floods, yes, I think it'll do nicely." Lacey open her next book, a Message translation of the Bible. "This version will be appropriate for today's events, I think."

Sol and Eli found chairs near the desk, while Lacey and Hildy sat on the loveseat by the window. Bert perched himself on the edge of the desk poring over the Scriptures until he found a verse that hit a chord with his spirit.

"Heavenly Father, You told us that angels Hearken to the voice of Your Word, so we now give voice to Your Word in confidence that You will send Your heavenly army to battle on our behalf. As You Said in Psalm 91:

'You who sit down in the High God's Presence, spend the night in the Shaddai's shadow,
Say this: "God, You're my Refuge, I Trust in You and I'm safe!"
That's right–He Rescues you from hidden traps, Shields you from deadly hazards,
His huge outstretched arms Protect you–under them you're Perfectly Safe;
His Arms Fend off all harm.
Fear nothing–not wild wolves in the night, not flying arrows in the day,
Not disease that prowls through the darkness, not disaster that erupts at high noon,
Even though others succumb all around, drop like flies right and left, no harm will even graze you,

You'll watch the wicked turn into corpses.
Yes, because God's your Refuge, the High God your very own Home,
Evil can't even get close to you; harm can't get through the door.
He orders his angels to Guard you wherever you go.
If you stumble, they'll Catch you; their job is to keep you from falling.
You'll walk Unharmed among lions and snakes, and kick young lions and serpents from the path.
"If you'll hold on to Me for dear life," Says God, "I'll Get you out of any trouble.
I'll Give you the Best of Care if you'll only get to Know and Trust Me.
I'll Rescue you, then throw you a party,
I'll Give you a long life,
Give you a long drink of Salvation!"

Lord, we stand on Your Mighty Promises of Protection now. We stand in the gap for Calvin, Jan, Jack, Sonya, Evangeline, Paul, Mac and Sarah and whomever they are with. We Plead the Precious Blood of Jesus over them and whatever situation they may find themselves in now or may face in the future. Satan has no hold on them. Your Wonderful Blood Covers them now. We claim them for Jesus now. Those of this group who do not Know You now, we gather them under the Divine Covering of Your Blood to Shield them with our brother and sister in Christ, Calvin and Jan. We intercede on their behalf to keep them safe until they should themselves make the Decision to Follow You as their Lord and Savior. Until that time, we Claim Your Precious Blood as Protection for this group. We Love You and have full Confidence in The Mighty Word of Your Power and Stand united on that Word, in Jesus Name, we Pray."

Lacey continued, "Lord, You Said that if we Believe and do not doubt in our Hearts, that what we Pray Shall Come to Pass, we Shall Have what we Pray. Lord, we Believe that we Receive according to Your Word and Promises. We Know You are here in this gathering of two or more in Your Name. We stand firmly united in Your Word this day and forever. In Jesus' Name. Amen."

An echo of Amen's darted around the room. They continued to sit, quietly adding individual Prayer and Communion with their Heavenly Father. An air of settled Peace permeated the library. None doubted; although challenges may try to come against their friends, none would fail to rejoin them again.

The group of travelers pulled their vehicles to the edge of the road near Sonya's house. Sonya was the first to dismount her four-wheeler and run toward the house. Jack was close on her heels. He grabbed her before she could reach the front door, wrapping his muscular arms around her slender body. She fought him until he had her firmly restrained and she could go no further.

"Jack, don't! Let me go! I have to get in there. Tucker may be still in his apartment," Sonya protested and struggled against his arms.

"Sonya, slow down a minute. We can't just run in there like this. Hold on," Jack countered.

""We don't have time!" Sonya complained.

Jack held her and said calmly, "Sonya, listen to me. We have to go in with a plan; you know procedures as well as I do. We can't just run in like this," Jack spoke carefully and clearly in her ear.

Slowly she ceased her struggling as his words penetrated her panic. He eased his grip on her body. She turned to face him and said, "Then we'd better hurry and make a plan because we have to get in there now!"

Jack was about to respond to her when a loud groan issued from the building. The dwelling sensed its imminent demise and was moaning out in protest. The ground below the house was beginning to shift dangerously.

Jack called to Calvin, "Have you got any ropes in that Jeep?"

Calvin called back, "Done!" as he opened the back of the vehicle and grabbed the towropes and chains they used in their rallies. Jack called back to Calvin and the rest of the group, "Look, we need safety ropes. Anchor them. If this thing starts to go, we need you guys to pull us back. Let's hope we get out before it breaks apart!"

Sonya fumbled with her keys and finally found the right key to the apartment. Jack started to beat on the door as she inserted the key and released the lock. "Tuck! Tuck! Are you here?" Sonya screamed while Calvin sorted the ropes.

The house emitted another strange noise in protest of the eroding foundation below. "Calvin, tie Sonya off. I'll get in and see if I can find him," Jack yelled over the roar of the river below.

"No! Jack, you wait until we get a line on you too!" Sonya protested. But before she had time to finish he was inside the entryway.

Jack searched in the dim light for signs of Tucker. He soon found him asleep on the couch. Sonya was right in her prediction. He was snoring loudly as he slept in a drunken stupor. Jack ran to the sofa and yanked at him. Tucker cried in anger as Jack lifted him off the couch. Tucker staggered away from Jack and slurred, "Whadya think ya doing?"

Sonya ran behind Jack. She had a rope tied around her and two more to secure to Jack and Tucker. "Tuck, it's Sonya. You have to get out of here! Now! Let us help you."

Jack grabbed Tucker in a bear hug and dragged him toward the door as Sonya slung the rope around his waist and under his arms. Tucker squirmed wildly as they manhandled him toward the door. He yanked himself free from Jack's grasp and took a swing at Jack. Jack returned the favor and knocked Tucker flat on his back with a blow to the chin. Tucker collapsed to the floor in a drunken heap. Jack and Sonya wasted no time securing his line as they dragged him out the door.

"Pull him up the embankment!" Jack called to Mac, Paul and Calvin. They heaved on his limp body unison as Sonya and Jack guided him from below.

The building groaned and shuddered. The sound of splintering wood erupted, louder than the roaring river under them. The veranda tilted suddenly and began to explode under their feet. Sonya gasped and grappled with a nonexistent railing, arms and legs flying. Mac braced himself against the weight of Sonya's body as Calvin and Paul hauled Tucker the final few feet up the slope. Once Tucker was laying at their feet, they half-dragged Sonya up the muddy incline as she struggled to help them the rest of the way.

Below, Jack grasped, looking for a handhold by the side of the collapsing frame of the house. He managed to grab a branch of a tree overhanging the river as the remainder of the porch disintegrated below his feet. He fought for a tighter grip on the branch, a look of extreme determination on his face. His feet were dangling dangerously over the ten foot drop to the churning water below.

Sonya scrambled to the top of the embankment and turned to see Jack hanging, desperately trying to maintain his hold on the branch. "Jack! Hang on! We'll get you!" Sonya screamed.

Mac and Paul gathered the rope that had intended to be his tether and ran to the tree on which Jack clung. Mac threw the coil of rope, but missed the branch by a foot. He pulled it back quickly, wound up and tossed it again. This time it hit its mark and came within grabbling distance. The problem was that Jack needed both hands to maintain his precarious perch on the tree.

"Jack, can you get the rope? You've got to get the rope!" Sonya cried encouragement.

"I don't think I can let go long enough," he grunted, struggling to maintain his grip. "Just give me a second. I'll see if I can shift my arms."

Jack gingerly eased his hold and shimmied over closer to the rope. It was a painfully slow process as he knew he might lose his grasp momentarily. *Okay, Jack, now's the time to show them your stuff. Are you up to this task? Or am I going to take you out this time? I have you where I want you and you know it.* "No!" Jack yelled responding to the voice in his head. "No, you won't!"

Sonya was startled at his outburst and hollered down to him, "What?"

Jack ignored her question and continued to adjust his grip on the branch. The next move caused the branch to shake and sway. He was getting too far along the branch for it to balance his weight. Jack stopped his movement and studied the rope.

Thinking Jack was saying that he could not get at it, Mac called out, "Jack. Don't move! We'll try tossing it closer"

Jack was in no position to argue. The raging water splashed up on his boots below. The torrent seemed to intensify by the minute, the roar threatening to overcome all rational thoughts in his head.

Mac pulled the rope back, coiled it and swung again; this time coming closer to the base of the branch. Jack's face was a study in resolve. Sonya could see he knew he was running out of opportunities to reach safety. She held her breath as he shifted his weight on the tree limb. The branch dipped a little lower toward the water. Afraid to watch, she tilted her head back for a moment and looked into the sky. Under her breath, she whispered, "Come on, come on! I know you can do it, Jack. Come on. A little further and you can get it."

Jack eyed the rope and weighed his options. *What's it going to be this time? Are you able to get it? Or are you just another has been? This time I'm going to take you down! Are you man enough for this fight?* The voice was back and taunting him. Beads of perspiration formed on his brow, dripping into his eyes. A smell assailed Jack's senses from the foul water below. The odor was filled with death and Jack involuntarily gagged against the stench. *What's in that water? It smells like rotting corpses!*

Jack moved his arm further around the branch to establish a firmer grip to allow him to make a grab for the rope. His arm muscles strained, screaming at him as he readjusted his grasp. He could not afford to lose his hold on the tree; it was the only thing keeping him from a sudden drop into the churning menace below his feet. He gritted his teeth as he attempted to shift his weight to get the rope. It was useless.

"I don't think that I can let go long enough to get hold of it. I'll have a better chance if I can get my legs over the branch and maybe shimmy back," Jack called.

"Jack, I don't know if the branch can take it," Sonya replied.

"Well, I can't hang here all day. I have to try something," he yelled back, anger in his voice.

Paul moved closer to the tree, "Look, I can try climbing into the tree and maybe get you from behind or something. Just hang on a little longer. We'll figure it out!"

Sonya stopped him before he had a chance to do anything. "You don't have a safety rope on you either. We could lose both of you. Stop now!"

"Then get one on me, and I'll give it a shot," Paul declared defiantly.

"Paul, that tree looks like it couldn't take the extra weight with you on it. It looks like the roots are barely holding as it is. Let Jack figure it out. We don't need to risk both of you," Mac observed.

Paul looked up the tree, then down at the roots. It seemed hopeless. The erosion started by the rains from above now threatened to be completed by the swollen and violent river below. The tree was not stable and it was Jack's only lifeline at the moment. His predicament was beginning to look desperate and panic began to rise in Sarah's chest as she watched the scene from the edge of the road. Jack's feeble sanctuary was soon to be swept into the raging current.

Sonya looked more closely at the base of the tree in time to see the roots tearing from the ground. "Quick. Sling another rope around the trunk. We have to hold it up," she cried is desperation.

It was too late. As the trunk of the tree began to lean more and more, Jack dipped closer to the surface of the deluge. Water sprayed into his eyes obscuring his view. He blinked to clear his vision. He realized he was now sinking closer and closer to the deadly river below. Looking down, the gushing waters foamed and twisted, seeming to open to greet him, beckoning him in.

Chapter 33

Lacey sat bolt upright in her chair and said, "Oh, no!"

"What's the matter?" Bert asked, alerted by her tone.

"I don't know, but I don't think it's good," was Lacey's answer. "Bert, we're not finished here. I have no idea what's going on but I have never had such urgency to Pray in my life before."

Bert had learned long ago to take Lacey's Call to Pray seriously. It was no trivial matter. She dropped to her knees and began to implore the Lord for Mercy. "Lord I don't know, but I sense it's for Jack. You know his Heart, Lord. Only You Know whether he has yielded himself to You yet, nevertheless, have Mercy on him now. Save our friends. I know you would not have them perish. Oh, Lord! Give him more time to turn to You!"

The group continued in Prayer a few more moments when Lacey lifted her head and sat up. One by one, each person looked her way, puzzled looks on their faces.

Eli finally broke the silence and asked, "Lacey, what's up. Why did you stop Praying?"

Lacey sat quietly looking each in the eye one by one, formulating her thoughts. She finally broke the silence and said, "Because the Lord released me from the task. I don't know why. I don't know if the crisis is over, but I sensed that He said that I could stop. It was as though the outcome had already been determined. I just hope it was a good ending," Lacey murmured.

The mood of concern continued, though the Prayers had ended. The uncertainty about the crisis was perplexing.

"I've never been released from Prayer so suddenly before," Lacey commented. "I just don't understand it."

They rose from their positions, uncertain what had just occurred but each feeling a release from the burden to Pray. Slowly they filed out of the library and entered the great-room. The north side of the house was now in shadows, indicating that the sun was now beaming on the south side of the house. Time was advancing. Afternoon was well upon them. The day was starting to slip away.

Evangeline watched in horror from the Jeep as the drama was unfolding before her eyes. Unable to help, she was a mere spectator as these dreadful events played themselves out. She quietly kept repeating, "Oh, God. Oh, Lord. Oh, God. Help us God. Help us."

Sonya grabbed at the rope by Calvin's feet, desperate to get a line on the tree before it had a chance lean any further. Paul helped her fasten it around the broad trunk as it began to totter and sway before their eyes.

Sonya and Paul pulled back on the trunk trying desperately to support Jack's weight any way they could. They felt the tree strain against their arms, but it stopped its downward lean. Jack locked eyes with Sonya for a moment, but was immediately distracted as the remainder of the house groaned and screeched as the wood frames splintered and cracked like Popsicle sticks and plummeted into the raging river, sending sprays of water up several feet into the air.

Sonya gasped at the sight of her rental house slipping into the river. It was quickly engulfed into the tumbling waters before her, bouncing and rocking as it was carried away by the swiftly moving current. The house was gone!

Sonya looked up from the waters and into Jack's eyes; panic was quickly rising in her chest. She suddenly realized how futile their efforts were. She averted her gaze to the side as the embankment started to crumble, clump by clump.

Jack yelled to Paul and Sonya, "Get back or you'll slide with it. The tree is going. I'm going to try to jump if I can. Get out of the way."

Jack decided he was not going to hang complacently as the riverbank tumbled into the river, the tree and Jack with it. He was going to make one last desperate attempt at self-rescue. Short of that, he would at least try to direct his fall along the shoreline to give him the best chance of survival; although he did not like his odds. He tried to remind himself that he had managed to outsmart the best any river had thrown at him while white water rafting, so he could do this too. He knew however that he had always been wearing a life jacket and helmet during those adventures and never had any river been this turbulent.

He did not have more time to reflect on his predicament as the remainder of the embankment dropped in chunks and the last of the tree's roots dislodged, sending it crashing into the river. Jack attempted to swing himself close to shore as he tumbled. He grabbed at debris to try to slow his ride as he hit the water but the intense surge caught him immediately and it moved him with sudden intensity. He desperately tried to keep his head above water but was driven under repeatedly with the current.

Sonya screamed as she watched Jack fall. She ran along the shoreline, jumping obstacles as she came upon them, not bothering to register what they were. It was a race for Jack's life. She watched in horror as the river carried Jack along its crazed path downstream, never taking her eyes from his position for an instant. She stumbled a few times but gathered herself and ran, watching his form in the churning, angry waters. She lost sight of him repeatedly as the water forced him under, but each time he clawed back up to grab more air; until, finally, she lost sight of him altogether. She frantically scanned the tumbling waters to try to catch sight of his head or jacket or anything, but saw no sign of him. He had disappeared.

Jack struggled for control, frantically trying to find anything on which to grasp. The current was unbearably strong, ripping at his body; pulling and tugging at his clothes, his limbs, his very being.

"I've got you now, Jack Davidson. What are you going to do now?"

Jack was tossed violently into an eddy, twirling about, pulling him down, his body lurching to one side. He saw the changing colors and light about him. Water that seemed white and foamy turned dark and murky as he sucked below the surface.

Jack fought to break free from the twirling current, clawing at the merciless pull of the water. Downward it sucked his body, momentarily pinning him against a submerged log. His lungs were almost out of air and life. As he was about to black out from lack of oxygen, his lungs searing and depleted, the waters spit him upward into the daylight again.

Jack gasped and sucked in as much air as his lungs could contain as he broke the surface.

"Breathe, Jack. Yes, breathe, for it will be your last."

No sooner had Jack reached daylight and drawn in life-giving air, was he yanked under by forces beyond his control. Like tentacles entwining his body, the water encased his torso with unyielding might, distorting his body, moving him with such incredible velocity. He was catapulted back into the depths, engulfed again in darkness.

"What'ya gonna do, Jack? What'ya gonna do? I've got you now. I've really got you now."

Jack struggled to free his arms from the grip of the current. Willing himself to move, straining against the iron-like bands, he tried to swim toward the light. Holding his breath, resisting the urge to grab air from the water, he pushed upward. Straining, lungs searing with pain, he fought one surge after another.

"Let go, Jack. It's no use. Come to me now. You can't win against me!"

Without warning, the vice-like grip released. His body lurched to the surface. He could see light approaching his face, the life-giving air milliseconds away. Suddenly, he was hit with submerged debris. Face first; he felt a crack, pain exploding in his head and instant blackness.

"Gotcha!"

Chapter 34

Paul and Mac ran after Sonya but could not catch her until she slowed, in a desperate attempt to pick out any clue to Jack's whereabouts in the writhing waters. She continued to run for a hundred yards but could no longer see his form; no sign of clothing or the color of his hair met her eyes. Sonya stopped and sagged to her knees, gasped and heaved as she tried to catch her breath. "No-o-o-o!" she screamed from the depths of her Heart. It continued to echo in Mac's ears long after her breath was expended. She bent forward at the waist and beat the ground with her fists, pounding out her grief into the sodden earth. "No, no, no! This can't be happening. No!" she wailed.

Mac was the first to reach her. Sarah had run down the roadway and veered in when she saw where Sonya had collapsed. Paul looked on as Sarah scooped Sonya into her arms, each of them sobbing and rocking on the cold damp dirt. As Mac watched them comfort each other, it shook him right down to his soul. *I can't just give up like this. I have to keep looking. Maybe we can still find him.*

Calvin and Jan pulled up in the Jeep an instant later and watched the Heart-wrenching scene. Evangeline leaned out the window, wincing in pain as she strained to get a closer look, hoping beyond hope that Jack had been rescued only to realize it was not to be. *Your Prayers were useless. He's gone. I got him. He's mine!*

Mac and Paul exchanged glances wordlessly. What was there to say? No words could express their emotions. But still they wanted to do more, not content to accept defeat.

Mac was first to speak, "Calvin, we need to get the four-wheelers and follow the river and see if we can spot him. He might be able to stop somehow, grab something, anything. I just don't believe he'd give up. We've got to follow him down further!"

Paul and Mac stepped into open doors of the Jeep, grasping the door frames, not bothering to climb in as Calvin put it in gear and turned around, heading back to the four-wheelers. They jumped off the vehicle before Calvin could put it in park and ran to the ATV's. Paul called back to Calvin, "Take care of Gel for me." They were down the road before Calvin or Jan could say a word. Calvin slowly turned the vehicle around and parked it close to where they had left Tucker lying by the road.

Jan sat quietly for a moment before she spoke. "It's one of those times I have to have Faith when my eyes tell me there is no hope," she said softly, her voice breaking into a sob.

Calvin and Evangeline did not say a word. Calvin cut the engine. The silence was deafening in the vehicle. Evangeline began to weep softly at first, then with increasing intensity.

Evangeline drew the blanket up to her chin, like a child trying to hide. *This would not have happened if you didn't mess up this trip. He wouldn't have been here if you didn't need to get to the hospital. You caused Jack to fall in the river and now he's dead. It's always your fault when things happen. You are vile and wretched.*

"It's my fault," she said between sobs. "If I hadn't gotten myself hurt, none of this would have happened!" she wailed.

"That's utter nonsense!" Calvin replied. "We all make decisions every moment of the day. No one event causes a crisis. It was a series of decisions that brought us to this conclusion. You remember that. No one person caused this to happen, no more than you caused this hurricane to hit this area. Your accident was only one event in a series of unfortunate events. You did not cause this, Gel"

"But we wouldn't be here now if you didn't need to get me some help," Evangeline moaned.

Jan intervened, "Gel, it may seem like that to you, but Jack and Sonya would have come down here with or without you. That's what Jack and Sonya do in these situations. They're part of the Rescue Squad. Sonya works for them and Jack volunteers his time. They would have been here anyway."

"And our drunk friend over there participated in all of this too, you know, not just you," Calvin added as he pointed to Tucker who was now sitting by the side of the road, rubbing his swollen jaw.

Evangeline looked at Jan, then to Calvin, confused at first, then realizing what they had said rang True in her Heart. Their voices were so contrary to the one stabbing her inside her head. Why was she so susceptible to these attacks? Why was she so willing to take the blame?

Evangeline contemplated these things as she watched in a sad silence as Calvin got out and walked to where Tucker sat and knelt beside him. Mixed emotions boiled inside as she watched Calvin tend to the disheveled young man.

Sam Fowler was reviewing the list of residences that had been evacuated with Wally Truscott, the sheriff, when two four-wheelers rounded the corner. Mac was the first to spy Sam and pulled up beside him. He did not wait for the pleasantries of introductions. Mac immediately launched into a report of the incident.

"Sam! Am I ever glad to see you! It's Jack. There's been an accident," he said, nodding to the sheriff as he did.

Mac got Sam's immediate attention with this statement. "Whoa. Hold on. What's happened?" Sam asked.

"He's in the river. We followed him as far as we could, then we lost sight of him. He was headed down this way. We have to look for him," Mac explained.

Sam looked incredulously at Mac and repeated, "He's in the river?"

Wally Truscott stepped between the two men and said, "Hold on a minute, son. You'd better explain yourself better than that. What the heck is going on?"

Sam intervened at this point by saying, "It's okay, Wally. This is Mac Donnelly. He and his wife are here for one of Jack's training courses this weekend. And this is Paul Montgomery, another of his trainees. His wife was lost yesterday."

Sheriff Lancer nodded and "Okay, son, now I know who you are. What do mean Jack's in the river? What kind of foolish trick is he trying to pull now?"

Sam stepped in again. He was starting to get exasperated with Wally at this point. "It's not as if Jack would do anything foolish, Wally.

There has to be something serious going on. Okay, Mac. Explain what happened."

Mac took a moment to compose his nerves and described what had happened at Sonya's house, their rescue of Tucker and the disastrous result that landed Jack in the river.

"Well, disaster seems to follow you folks around, doesn't it?" Wally remarked sarcastically.

Sam looked away, trying to hold his frustration with this man. *Is there any wonder I want to deck this guy half the time?* Ignoring Wally for the moment, Sam asked, "How long ago was this, Mac?"

"We came when we lost sight of him. It's been just minutes. You've gotta help us look for him! It might be our only chance of finding him." Mac answered as he grabbed Sam's arm for emphasis. He was starting to get impatient.

Sam thought for an instant, pursed his lips and looked down the street. "Okay, I'll gather some guys. I'm strung tight now. Wally, I'm going to have to take my crew back. You'll have to do without us for the moment. We'll only have one chance at finding Jack. We have to do it now. With the speed of the current, he's probably passed us by already. Let's go."

Sam radioed to his crew to meet downstream at Lockney Bay. "If there's any chance of him getting to shore, it's there. The river shallows and under normal conditions slows a lot. Let's hope he survives that far." Sam left Wally standing there protesting that he needed Sam's personnel to save more lives than just one.

Sam turned away in disgust and motioned to Mac and Paul to follow him to his truck. "Can you believe that guy? I'm not taking many off that detail anyway. I'm not leaving one of my own guys hanging under any circumstance. No wonder I avoid him like I do. If I didn't . . . well, let's just say I might be in jail myself."

Paul said, "Kind of makes you wonder how he got elected."

Sam grunted and shook his head, "He's a politician more than a sheriff. He knows the right things to say to the right people. Let's get going. You guys follow me and we'll see what we can find. I hope Jack's as resourceful as I think he is. The other guys will meet us there."

They drove away with their thoughts badgering them along the way, each of them knowing that they may also be just a likely to be doing a body retrieval as not. The turbulent waters could easily have pulled Jack under then not allowed him to surface until he had a lung full of water.

The debris in the water would likely crush and kill him. The odds of survival were slim given the present conditions.

They arrived at Lockney Bay to find the usually placid cove was violently turbulent and rapidly piling up with debris. If anyone managed to survive the wild ride in the river without a life vest on, then they would hardly escape serious if not deadly injury by the wreckage that was continually accumulating here. Chunks of roofs and entire walls of houses were log jamming in the shallower waters. Even a car ricocheted off the amassed rubble into the deeper waters across the river. It was a grim scene to behold, given their reason to be there. None of them wanted to voice their true appraisal of the scene.

Sam's squad arrived a few minutes later and they divided into pairs searching in both directions, up and downstream trying to spot Jack's form in the water. They moved meticulously searching both the shoreline and in the current beyond. Paul was paired with Sam and Mac was with Larry Walters. They repeatedly radioed results as sections of shoreline and river were checked and eliminated.

"Okay, Parker, you move further downstream to see if he got by us. Larry, you continue to go back further and see if somehow he made it to shore closer to Moulton. I'm not willing to call this yet," Sam ordered. Sam was like a bulldog when he thought there might still be a chance of a rescue, even in these conditions. Sam knew Jack and if anyone could self-rescue it was him.

The search continued for over an hour. The same results were radioed back one by one. Not one party had found any sign of Jack or his clothes or jacket or any clue to his whereabouts. Sam was getting continual pressure to move his resources back into town where new events were erupting and getting out of control as rapidly as the river was claiming more property and the bridge was now severely compromised.

Sam finally radioed this message, his gut turning in knots, "Okay ladies and gentlemen, I have to call it. We need you back in town. We have a whack of incidents that need our manpower and can't wait any longer. Turn around and come back now."

Paul started to protest, but Sam waved him off saying, "Paul, I gave it all the time I can justify. I cannot afford the extra manpower. If Jack survived that ride down the river, he will show up and if he didn't, well . . ."

They walked back to the vehicle in silence. What was there to say? Sam's stomach was turning and boiling. Jack was the best friend he had in the world and he had to walk away from the search. *What would Jack do under the same circumstances?* That was the question that kept battering his mind. He was tormented as he climbed back in his truck.

"Paul, I want you and Mac back into town, too. I don't need you guys becoming another statistic today."

Paul looked away, staring over the churning waters before him one last time and conceded, "Yeah, I know. I need to get back for Gel."

Mac and Larry arrived back at that point, looking downcast and solemn. Larry shook hands with Mac and said, "Jack's a survivor. He can handle himself." Mac nodded in response, both of them knowing there was little chance they would ever see Jack alive again. Larry turned to join the rest of his squad in their vehicle.

Mac stood where he was for a moment pondering the outcome of the search, when Paul walked over and said, "There's nothing more we can do, Mac."

"Yeah, I know. It just doesn't seem enough though," he answered quietly.

"I know, but I need to get back and see what Calvin and Jan arranged for Gel. She needs me now too. I can do more for her than for Jack at the moment," Paul responded.

Mac looked down at the ground and rubbed the back of his neck, frustrated and said reluctantly, "I guess you're right. We'd better get back. I suppose taking off like that wasn't the best thing for her. Under the circumstances . . . I'm sure she'll understand."

"Yeah, under the circumstances," Paul answered.

Calvin and Jan had taken Evangeline to the triage station that was set up in a parking lot by the river park in Moulton on the north side of the river. The bridge access was blocked and even emergency personnel were being stopped from crossing. The authorities had serious concerns about its structural stability and the river level was about to surpass the bridge at any time.

They had spent an hour and a half waiting as Evangeline was assessed in the aid station by local medical personnel. When they finally let them in to see her they told them that the consensus was that she needed to be moved to hospital for further diagnostic testing. She was put on intravenous fluids because there was concern about internal bleeding due to her low blood pressure, but now they had to wait for an evacuation protocol to be put into place.

Calvin walked out of the tent in disgust. "I could have told them that they needed to take her to a hospital over an hour ago, for heaven's sake. It didn't take a brain surgeon to come to that conclusion!" he said in frustration.

"The good news is now it's in their hands to formulate an evacuation plan for her. And God's," Jan responded.

"Yeah, you're right. I just get mad at the bureaucratic nonsense and paperwork that needs to be done when there's an obvious emergency," Calvin responded.

"She must be stable or they would have been all over her like flies to an apple pie. That's a good thing," Jan said as she pulled him close to her. "But I'm glad to see you care so much. That's a good quality to have."

"You're a good woman, Jan Talbot. You balance my personality. You've kept me out of trouble all these years, woman," Calvin finished.

"Just don't you forget it, mister," was Jan's joking reply.

They turned as they heard Paul and Mac arrive on their four-wheelers. As they dismounted, Calvin and Jan walked over. "So? Any news?" Jan asked expectantly.

The solemn looks on Mac's and Paul's faces spoke for them as they shook their heads in unison. Jan drew in her breath and questioned, "You didn't find anything or is it bad . . . ?"

"No, we just didn't find any sign of him. There's a lot of river and a lot of debris. Maybe we were just looking in the wrong place . . ." Mac's voice trailed off.

Calvin looked away and replied, "You gave it your best shot. You can't expect anything more than that. Did you have any help?"

"Yeah, we found Sam Fowler and he put an entire crew on it with us, but …" Paul replied. "Where's Gel?"

"Oh, sorry, she's in here. Come with me," Jan responded.

Mac and Calvin stood outside the tent staring at the ground. No words were necessary. Mac finally broke the silence and asked, "Do you know where Sarah is?"

"Sorry, yes, I do. She's inside with Gel and Sonya. Sonya was distraught after you left. Actually, she was inconsolable. Sarah was worried about her and thought we should bring her with Gel."

They moved to enter the tent, when Calvin pulled him back. "Mac, be careful what you say in there with Sonya. She wanted to go with you but we wouldn't let her. She was so upset and in no condition to be of any help anyway. We finally convinced her that we needed her to help us with Gel and knowing how emotionally invested she was with Jack, she shouldn't go down there." Calvin paused and added, "Sonya overheard some nurse use the term 'body recovery' at one point and she went ballistic."

Mac nodded his understanding. He knew he wanted to see Sarah at the moment but facing Sonya would be especially hard. He had hoped to return with better news for her.

Calvin brought him near to where Sarah was sitting by Gel's gurney. The nurse on duty came over immediately and said, "I'm sorry but we can't have all of you in here like this. We need the room. Could some of you please move outside? We have to keep the way clear for new incoming casualties."

Sarah spotted Mac and hurried to where he was standing. He took her by the arm and steered her outside. She immediately gave him a long hug. She began to cry in his shoulder. Finally she lifted her head and said softly, "It's been awful here. Poor Sonya." She paused and choked back a sob. "You don't have any good news, do you?"

Mac shook his head and hugged her again. "No, we didn't find him." He stopped at this point then added, "There's lot of places on the river we didn't check. And we could only search on this side of the river so maybe . . ."

"Yeah . . . maybe . . ." Sarah agreed. Neither of them held out much hope in that 'maybe'.

"How's Gel doing? Did they figure out anything that might help her?" Mac asked.

"They examined her and determined that she might have ligament damage in her knee and a concussion, but there was no decision on the pain in her side. They're suspicious of cracked or broken ribs with possible internal bleeding; that much they conceded, but without x-rays and other diagnostics they couldn't be sure. They were about to move her to the hospital when they shut all passage over the bridge, even to emergency personnel. The only way to the other side is a ten-mile ride back to the east over roads similar to those we just came in on. They've been trying to plan a better evacuation method for the last twenty minutes," Sarah added with a tone of frustration in her voice.

Mac added, "So we're no further ahead than when we first arrived."

"Well, they've got her on an intravenous drip and they're working on the question of how to transport her to the hospital. That's a little progress," Sarah said.

Mac took Sarah by the hand and walked away from the triage tent. The sidewalk led to a park overlooking the river. On a normal day this would have been a serene place. Now it was a rude reminder of the wicked experiences they had endured over the last forty-eight hours. They sat on the first park bench along the path.

"How is Sonya doing? I understood she was upset earlier," Mac commented.

"So Calvin told you how upset she was, did he?" Sarah answered. Mac nodded and she continued, "She's starting to get hold of herself now. It's obvious she and Jack have a thing going on between them. She said to me that they'd not had a chance to get serious yet, but they had been doing a lot together lately, first with her work then when he came with the guys to Tucker's apartment."

Mac frowned when she mentioned Tucker's name. "Yeah, the parties. That guy needs some serious help."

"Yes, I think we realize that now, Mac, but Jack wasn't just there to party with the rest of the guys. Sonya thought he was there more to see her than to hang with Tucker's crowd. He came over helping with repairs, washing her car, and any excuse to be around."

Mac just stared ahead. His emotions were as stirred up as the white water below them. He did not know what to think about Tucker. His chest tightened as he thought back to the scene at Sonya's house. *How could things have gone so terribly wrong?*

"Sonya's in love with Jack, Mac. The irony is that they didn't really get a chance to solidify their relationship before this happened and now . . ." Sarah paused, "well, now they might not have that chance. It's so sad."

"Don't count him out completely. We don't know what happened to him. We just know we didn't find him," Mac said hopefully.

Sarah turned to face Mac on the bench and asked bluntly, "Mac, when you look at that river, the way it is now, what do you think of Jack's chances of survival?"

Mac stared at the crashing waters below and was silent for a few minutes as he pondered his answer. He could answer with his gut or he could say what the facts pointed toward. He was not sure which way he was swayed at the moment.

Finally, he looked up and answered, "We've been around some different people this weekend. I know how I would have answered that question a week ago. Now, I'm not so sure. My head says that there isn't a chance he made it out alive. But I know Lacey and Bert would be all over my case for even thinking that way. I know they've been Praying for us, even without knowing anything about this going on here. And Calvin and Jan have been for sure. I'm inclined to Believe that has some influence."

Sonya looked down at her hands as a tear trickled down her cheek. "I want their kind of Faith. It would make life a lot easier, don't you think?"

Mac nodded agreement. "Yeah, I just don't know where they get it from. It seems way beyond where I'm at."

Sarah explained some of her earlier conversations with Lacey and concluded, "She would say it's from spending time with God in His Word. I just haven't had that in our church, in our life. Maybe it's time we might consider changing what we do when it's over."

Mac took a breath and said nothing. He remembered the pace of life that they had left last week. It seemed a world away from Moulton. "I don't know how easy that would be, I'm afraid," he finally said.

"Lacey said she started her 'journey', as she called it, while working in the city in a demanding job. If she can do it, so could we," Sarah looked at him, hoping for his agreement.

Mac furrowed his brow and answered, "This means a lot to you, doesn't it?"

"Mac, you have to admit these events have been life changing. I mean, it's not often you go through this kind of . . ." she paused groping for a word to describe these last couple of days, ". . . trauma. We can just leave it and forget it. Or we can learn something from it and the people who marked us so deeply and helped us through it."

Mac did not respond. He just stared out at the river again.

"Mac, I want to take something positive away from this awful mess. Jan has been wonderful with Gel and Sonya and me. I want to be more like her and Lacey and the rest of them. That's all. I know that they're real people and they get mad and all that, but they've responded to all this devastation differently. They have Hope in the midst of it, when I wouldn't and maybe couldn't."

Mac hesitated before he responded, then finally said, "How involved are you thinking of getting in this?"

"Mac, from what I seem to understand, from what Jan and Lacey talked about, it isn't about being involved in some cult or anything. It's more about developing a Relationship with Jesus as a person, someone you can Rely on amid the junk of daily life. It is more about finding a good church with good Teaching about God and His Word. It's about understanding God and what He's like, then Trusting What He's said when those hard times come."

"You must have been having serious discussions with Jan and Lacey. It's a change in attitude," Mac concluded.

"Jan and I had some time to chat after things got settled down while you were gone. What she said made a lot of sense, with what Lacey and Bert and the rest talked about last night and this morning."

Mac was silent as he mulled over her words, then offered, "I suppose it might be worth investigating."

Sarah paused, considered how Mac might accept what she was about say to him. Finally, she added, "Mac, I know that I can't keep continuing on the way I was going. The worry and the stress isn't worth it. I need to be able to have an avenue of release. This sounds intriguing. Jan suggested a church we might visit when we get back home. She said they have a good pastoral staff with solid Teaching and classes and study groups. I'd like to go and investigate it at least."

Mac looked at her sincerely and answered, "Okay, we can try it and see what there is to it. I can't guarantee how much I can be there with work the way it has been, but, if it means that much to you, we can see what there is to all this."

Sarah smiled and gave him a hug. If Mac was agreeable, it was a place to start. That was a big step for him to concede that much and she would take what little he offered.

Sam Fowler was in a rotten mood since coming back from the search for Jack. He sat in his truck in the parking area near the triage tent and barked orders back and forth to his various crews through his radio. He was still in shock and could not believe what had happened.

The questions of how and why kept ringing through his head and he did his best to function, nonetheless. He looked up from his clipboard long enough to see Tucker Worley shambling across the parking lot coming toward him. As Sam got out of his truck he muttered under his breath, "Worley, you'd better back off. I don't know how I'll handle you now."

Tucker continued to walk his way and Sam could feel his hands closing into fists. Sam slammed his truck door and walked the other way away from Tucker. "I can't deal with this jerk," Sam continued to mutter, a little louder now. Sam walked to the triage tent, anywhere to be away from Tucker.

Tucker just kept following Sam until he reached his side. Sam pretended not to see him, but his gut was tying into a knot.

"Hey, Sam, have you heard anything about Jack yet?" Tucker asked him.

Sam swung around and stared at him, incredulous that he had the nerve to even come near him now. Not only had he not shown up for work during the worst storm in recent memory, he also had caused the almost certain death of his best friend. All that remained was finding Jack's body.

Tucker looked as if he had been dragged through the mud at a dirt track race. His hair spiked in all directions, his shirt was ripped and caked with dried mud. He had as much dirt on his face and arms as on his back. Sam could see that he was severely hung over.

Sam stood staring Tucker down, when Calvin walked out of the triage tent. He realized that a major confrontation was about to happen and stopped short.

Sam gritted his teeth and said, "Tucker, you need to get some help. I would have said 'before you kill someone' but it seems too late for that now."

Tucker leaned back and furrowed his brow trying to comprehend what Sam meant by this statement. "Whad'ya mean,' I need to get some help'? I was asking if you found out about Jack yet. Is he okay, man?"

Sam charged at Tucker and grabbed his shirt in his two balled up fists and pulled his face close to his. "Worley, what the #@+# do you care? If you hadn't been drinking like you were, none of this would have happened!"

Tucker's eyes popped big and round at Sam's response. "Whoa, man. What's this all about? What did I have to do with the house falling in the river?"

Sam held him there, bile rising in his throat, as he listened to Tucker's dissociation from the day's events. He wanted to blast this guy's head into the next county. He held him tighter and gritted his teeth. Calvin stepped forward ready to pull him off Tucker before he did any major damage.

Suddenly Sam shoved Tucker to the ground, spitting out these words, "You're just not worth the trouble it would cause." As Tucker lay on his back trying to regain his senses, Sam put his boot on Tucker's chest and said, "If you were smart, Worley, you'll stay away from me. You need some help, significant help. Don't show up anywhere near work unless you get it, you hear?"

With that, Sam walked back to his truck leaving Tucker in the dirt behind him.

Chapter 35

Sarah and Mac walked from the park at the sound of the commotion just in time to see the end of the altercation between Sam and Tucker. They slowed as they approached Calvin, who now stood near Tucker's sprawled body.

"Didn't know you had it in you, Calvin," Mac said, feigning shock.

Calvin whirled to see the two walking toward him and answered, "Well, as much as I would have liked to have been the one to set him on his butt, it wasn't me."

Mac chuckled and said, "We saw the end of it. I probably would have knocked him senseless. He got off easy this time."

Calvin reached out his hand and offered to help Tucker stand. Tucker waved him away, preferring to sit where he was. He realized he was in hostile territory. "Suit yourself, Tucker," Calvin responded. "I suggest you find somewhere to sober up then stay that way. We can help you find the right people to do that, if you're willing."

Tucker eyed Calvin with suspicion and started to get up. He was unsteady, staggering as he started to stand. Calvin grabbed him before he collapsed. "Let's get you inside the triage tent. They might at least get you hydrated with the right fluids this time," he said as he guided him toward the tent. "While you're in there, we can give you some help to find some resources about staying sober."

Mac helped Calvin steer Tucker into the tent and to a chair by the door. A nurse came to see what the concern was, but seemed a little disappointed when she found out that he was suffering the effects of a significant bender. Calvin drew her aside to explain the problem. He told her that he was Sonya's cousin and his part in the earlier events; she realized that he did indeed need some assistance after all.

"He's still kind of out of it. I wouldn't be surprised if he's dehydrated. He's been getting all his liquids from the wrong kind of bottle for the last couple of days. This lad needs some serious help, beyond just today. Can you be sure to arrange it?"

"This is a triage unit, not social services. We can hydrate him. But beyond that, once he's sober, we'll need the space for incoming casualties. The counseling will have to wait," she said officiously.

Sonya saw Tucker and walked to the chair where he was sitting. Mac and Sarah spied what was happening and joined her before anything nasty could erupt. Sonya looked at them then at Tucker, fire in her eyes. Sarah held up her hand to caution her, but Sonya went ahead and said, "Tucker Worley, I ought to kill you. Do you have any idea what you did today?" Mac grabbed her hand as she was about to strike his face. She fought his grip and tried to break free. Mac held firmly resisting her efforts. Suddenly she just stopped fighting him and said, "Never mind, there's no use talking to you when you're drunk anyway! Calvin's right, you need help. You're pathetic when you're like this. Let me out of here. I need some air; you're stinking up the place." With that, she rushed out of the tent.

Mac looked at Calvin and said, "I guess she might not be the one to make sure he goes to AA then!"

Calvin shook his head and agreed. "Yeah, you're probably right about that. He's got other family in town. That might be a better choice. It's best we get them involved instead."

Eli got out of his truck and Bert hopped out of the other side. Lacey, Hildy and Sol climbed down from the back seat.

"Well, I'd say that it's a good bit of work done. Look at us though; we're surely in need of a swim in the lake to wash up. Nothing like a little roadwork to get you dirty," Lacey commented.

"Do you mean that I might have missed my fashion shoot for Good Housekeeping?" Hildy laughed.

"Somehow I don't think I'd qualify at the best of times," Lacey responded.

"My dear woman, don't cut yourself short. You look mighty fine even in a pair of coveralls and rubber boots," Bert commented.

"Bert Lawson, you can come digging ditches with me any day!" Lacey laughed. "We'd better leave these boots out on the veranda. There's no sense tracking in any dirt."

"I'll leave these coveralls out here with my boots," Hildy added before she entered the house.

As they headed to the kitchen to get water to drink, Lacey said, "I'm glad we got out and worked on the roads. It's surprising what you can achieve when you mobilize the neighborhood. At least most of the gravel access road is passable now." She set glasses out on the counter and pulled out a large two-gallon water container. "It's good to see that the runoff is starting to slow. It bodes well for those living down the mountain and into town. Maybe the river will stop rising soon. I hate to think how bad it's been down there today."

"I wonder how Jack and Sonya made out today with the rest of the guys. It must've been quite a ride into Moulton, judging from the little we saw of the roads up here," Bert commented.

Lacey stopped pouring the water and said, "You know, I had a bad feeling about that trip this morning before we Prayed. I Hope they're okay." Lacey sighed and added, "I just have to Trust that God Provided for them. It's hard being up here and not knowing what's going on. I know we have the phone in the van, but I'm not sure who'd be available to call to get any information. Most of our friends would be helping with the evacuation."

Lacey continued to pour glasses of water for each of them and Bert suggested, "I have a couple of people I might call in Moulton. If there's any phone service down there, we could try to contact them and see what information we find. Let's get our swim to clean up then we can try making some calls."

Sol agreed, "That sounds like a plan. I hope we can get through to someone at least."

Lacey added, "It's strange though, I feel released from Prayer. It doesn't make sense because I'm sure there are other issues going on still."

Bert put his arm around Lacey's shoulders and asked her, "Did we Pray, Believing we Received when we Prayed?"

"Yes, we did, didn't we? I shouldn't question it, should I? It's Done. Either way, it's Done. I don't know how or why, but it is," Lacey answered.

"I have full confidence that God Heard our Prayers. Still I have the sense that something has gone terribly wrong. I just can't shake the feeling."

Bert knew enough to take Lacey's instincts seriously, but still was firm in his convictions about the Answer to the Prayer. "Lacey, we have no control over how or when the Answers come. Sometimes they are delayed and sometimes they don't look like Answers because we're looking for the wrong thing. Remember, just Stand in Faith."

"Thank you, Bert. Your gentle reminders are always helpful. I'll continue to stand on His Promises and not waver." She set her glass on the counter and added, "I think I'm ready for that swim now."

Sonya stormed out of the tent and into the parking lot. She stood there for a moment before she spied Sam in his truck. Sam looked up from his clipboard in time to see Sonya heading his way. He got out of the truck expecting her to be angry about how he had treated Tucker.

"Sonya, he had it coming. Honest, I could've done much more to him," he said with his hand up to stop her.

"Whatever you did to him, I would have done worse. Don't worry, I'm not peeved with you," she said, looking as if she were about to explode. "Sam, I just have to get back in the field. I can't sit around here any longer."

Sam raised his eyebrows at her and shook his head. "No, Sonya. I don't think you're in any shape to head back yet."

Sonya looked down at her clothes and realized for the first time that her clothes were smeared in dirt from her harrowing climb up the embankment earlier. She stared to brush off her pants. "Look, Sam, if my appearance is a problem I can go back and get changed at my house . . ." She stopped short at that statement, suddenly realizing she no longer had a house. Images of the events of earlier in the day flooded her memory and suddenly she blanched.

Sam put his hand on her arm to steady her. "Sonya, I wasn't referring to your appearance. I was referring to your emotional state. You've been through a lot today. I can't afford to have you in the field in your state."

"Sam, I can't sit around any longer, especially with Tuck in the tent. Please, please, let me get out and do something. I can't stand this waiting. Gel doesn't need me now. They're taking care of her just fine.

Paul and Sarah and Mac are all in there with her. I need to get out here and work now!"

Sam looked at her. She looked as though she might crack from the strain of the day. He knew he couldn't let her go out with one of the squads but he also recognized her need to get doing something other than waiting for news about Jack. "Alright, look, I can't let you go out in the field in your condition but I could use some help coordinating our efforts with the sheriff's office. You can help me with sorting this mess I've got here," Sam said as he pointed to the clipboard.

"I could hug you, but I won't! Thank you. Anything to get out of that tent," Sonya said exuberantly.

Sam leaned the clipboard on the back of his truck and explained the system he had been using to divide the teams. They were deep in discussion when Sam's radio signaled a call. Sam walked to the cab and reached in to retrieve the radio and answered, "Fowler here."

A voice at the other end called, "Sam, it's Parker Johnson. We have a report of an injured party down near Kelly Road. I'm close by and can head there now, if that's okay. Over."

Sam scanned the clipboard and answered, "Sure, it looks like you're the closest to that area anyway. Have you got enough supplies in the vehicle?"

"I've got as much as was available at the depot. They're running short on a lot of things, but we've got the basics to get by with for the moment. Over."

"Okay. Go ahead on down. Drive carefully because they said the roads down that way are bad. Don't take any unnecessary chances. Over."

"Roger that. I'll let you know what I find when we get there. Over.

"Okay, you do that. Over and out."

Sam lifted a few papers on the clipboard and jotted down some notes before he commented to Sonya, "Okay, so move Parker and Larry into the active column. They are unavailable until further notice."

Sonya and Sam climbed back in the truck as they got into a rhythm of working together. Sonya scribbled some notes on her chart as another call came in. This time it was from another crew down nearer to where Sonya's house used to stand. They were moved into the active column as well. They continued sorting through their deployments and receiving status calls, keeping them busy for the next half hour.

Calvin came out of the tent holding Jan's hand a few minutes later.

Sam watched as they walked to the park bench. *They've probably had enough of Tucker too by now.* Sam shook his head trying to break the negative thoughts that threatened to overwhelm him.

The radio chirped again. This time it was Parker reporting in. "Sam, Parker here. We've arrived . . . site . . . Over."

"Parker, you're breaking up. Adjust your radio. Repeat that last transmission. Over."

"I said . . . arrived. Going in . . . later."

"You're still breaking up. Let me know what you find. Over."

Sam stared at the radio in his hand, frustration mounting beyond his control. He slammed it down on the dash causing Sonya to jump involuntarily. She sat silently, biting her lip.

"These $&%* radios!" Sam muttered through clenched teeth.

Tears threatened to spill forth from Sonya again but she willed herself to contain them. The emotionally charged atmosphere sparked between them; their thoughts darting in the same direction but left unspoken.

Sonya ignored Sam's outburst of grief and frustration. The silence bore down on them until Sonya was tempted to bolt from the truck. Finally, Sam picked up his radio again, looking at it in disgust. "I thought we got these things fixed. How can I keep track of these guys with the radios working like this?"

Sonya looked down and shrugged, "I guess I've just gotten used to them working like that over the last few months."

Sam glanced over at Sonya with an expression of unspoken apology on his face and said, "I suppose you guys sometimes prefer it when they don't work. It gives you freedom to do your own planning when you want to, doesn't it?"

Sonya gave him a weak smile and answered, "Whatever you think. Just remember that I didn't say that."

With a lull in the radio calls, Sam got out of the truck to take a break. Sonya followed him out; thankful for an opportunity to redirect her emotions. Sam wandered to the triage tent and called back, "Do you want some coffee?"

"Yeah, do you mind getting it for me? I just don't want to face Tuck for the moment," she answered.

"Sure. Let me guess. Cream and sugar?" Sam asked.

Sonya smiled, "No, just cream, no sugar."

Sam ducked into the tent and Sonya watched Jan and Calvin as they walked through the park. They had made the circuit and were heading her way when Sam came back out with two cups in his hands with donuts balanced on top.

"Here, I brought you a snack too. They may be kind of stale though," Sam remarked.

Sonya accepted both the coffee and donut from Sam. Biting into the donut Sonya commented, "It might be stale but I didn't realize how hungry I was. It tastes good anyway."

"Yeah, it's something you get used to working this job. You grab what you can eat when you have the opportunity. Sometimes a stale donut tastes like filet mignon when you're hungry enough," Sam agreed.

Sam had popped the last bite into his mouth as his radio came to life with a call. "Fowler here."

"Parker . . . we found . . . coming in . . . roads bad . . ."

"Parker, repeat. You're breaking up again. Repeat. Over."

"Coming . . . I said we . . ." The rest of the transmission was just static.

"Parker, we lost what you said. Just drive carefully and get back soon. Fowler out."

Sam took a gulp of his coffee. "You think the county could spring for a better radio system than this!" Sam finally said in frustration.

Sonya agreed and took a sip of her coffee and grimaced, "Stuff isn't very good, is it?"

Evangeline had been lying on the gurney in the tent now for almost three hours and was starting to get restless. Thoughts were swirling through her head. The conflict within her was like the turbulence in the boiling river below.

Medical personnel attended to various casualties as they came in. Most had occurred when people stubbornly attempted to salvage as many possessions as they could before the river claimed their houses. Many had sustained fractures while carrying items out of disintegrating dwellings. Having waited far too long to vacate their premises, unstable stairs and porches that could not sustain their weight had given way as they tried to leave their houses carrying loads of valuables and memorabilia. Their possessions were forever swallowed by the churning waters and they lay broken and bleeding on gurneys, awaiting transport to higher care facilities.

These were the fortunate ones, because far more were not being brought into the triage center because they had not survived the river's tirade. As it pounded downstream, the river was now swallowing more victims than those who narrowly escaped with their lives intact but bodies battered and broken. Rescue and medical personnel were taken aback by the low number of live casualties.

Evangeline looked at the injuries the other patients and thought she was in good condition by comparison. She wanted to give up her bed for the more severely injured. Guilt washed over her for taking everyone's valuable time and space. She protested several times, requesting to be released to her husband's care while awaiting evacuation, but they would not permit this. She then began to wonder if they viewed her injuries as more severe than she had been led to believe.

Conflicting and confusing thoughts washed over as she lay on the gurney. *What if you have internal injuries that they don't know about? They're just leaving you here to slowly bleed to death. They don't care enough to do something to get you out of here. If your condition is so stable, why are you taking up valuable space in here? You've wasted everyone's time coming here.* Then the most nagging thought of all attacked her conscience. *If you weren't so careless and hadn't gotten hurt, Jack would still be alive.*

That was the essence of it. It was the pivotal conflict. Why had she caused Jack to fall to his death? Oh, those voices of worthlessness, how they badgered and harangued her. The Truths that Jan and Calvin had given her were rapidly being eroded like the shoreline beneath Sonya's precious home. Words of condemnation chewed at her mind causing the few strands of Truth she knew to crumble and crash. She lay their silently descending into a pit of depression and shame.

You haven't changed. Everything of value around you gets swallowed by your ego and vanity. You'd be better to go fend for yourself than take up space in here. Patients are coming who need care and if you stay someone may die because you took a bed from them. Leave this place before you kill someone else!

Her mind was awash with self-loathing, thoughts crashed like the waves in the nearby river. The smell of the dirt and blood on the patients nearby made her stomach churn and roll. The walls of the tent were beginning to press in around her, the air becoming suddenly oppressive and damp. Claustrophobia was moving over her now, sucking the breath from her lungs. She began to sob and gasp for air, as panic rolled through her body. All she wanted to do was get out of there, anywhere but in that tent.

Paul stirred a cup of coffee across the tent as he turned to look over at Evangeline. She was sitting up and trying to get off the bed. He ran to her as she was about to slide from the gurney.

"What're you trying to do? You can't go anywhere," he said as he grabbed her arm.

"I just have to get out of here! Look at those patients, they're hurt and they need the space. I need some air. Just let me get out of here," Evangeline responded in a panic.

"Gel, you need to lie down. It's okay; I'm here with you. What's the matter?" Paul asked.

Calvin and Jan came into the tent just as Paul was wrestling with Evangeline. "Whoa, don't you think it's a little early to have her up dancing?" Calvin exclaimed.

"It isn't my idea. She wants out of here now. I don't know what's gotten into her," Paul responded.

Jan walked to Evangeline's side and put her hand on her arm and said quietly, "Gel, it's okay, you can rest now." Jan stroked her arm and maintained eye contact with her and said soothingly, "We need you to lie back down. You can help us best by lying down."

Evangeline looked around wildly, still trying to maneuver herself off the cot. Jan continued to talk quietly and reassuringly to her. Gradually, Evangeline slowed her fighting. Her eyes became more focused and she realized Jan was talking to her. Jan caught her gaze and tilted Gel's chin to look directly at her. "Gel, it's okay now. You can lie down again. We're here to help you."

Evangeline turned her eyes down to the sheet in her lap and looked at the hand that had the intravenous line in it. She rubbed the tape holding the needle in place, pulling herself back into the reality of the tent. Her breathing slowed as she regained her composure. "I don't know what got into me . . . I just needed to get out of here. I couldn't breathe. The smell . . . it's awful . . ." was all she could manage to say.

Paul looked at Jan and she nodded to him, indicating that he needed to say something to reassure her. He hesitated a moment, then added, "Gel, honey, I'm here. It's okay now."

Finally, Evangeline relaxed as Paul eased her on the gurney. Her brow was still creased as her eyes seemed to search for an invisible assailant. Paul stroked her hair as Evangeline settled on the pillow. He whispered into her ear, "It's probably a reaction to the pain meds they gave you. Just rest now."

Evangeline shook her head and said, "I'm tired of just lying here. Why can't they get me out of here?"

Jan answered gently, "Gel, they're working on it. They have to make arrangements to move you to the hospital. The bridge is out and they don't want you to have to travel on those roads again. They're trying to find other transportation for you. It won't be long."

Evangeline went silent as she processed these words. Jan added, "Meanwhile, you're safe here and we'll stay with you to make sure you're okay. I know all the commotion around you must be frightening. But we're here for you."

Evangeline looked at Jan then to Paul. He nodded agreement. "I won't leave you alone again."

His words echoed in Evangeline's ears, yet, did not settle in her Heart. It was what she wanted desperately to hear, to believe. Doubt buzzed around her mind like an annoying bee. *Will you? Will you be there for me? Do you want to be here? Can I trust you?*

Jan spoke softly again, "Gel, we won't leave you alone in here. Paul is here. I'm here too. One of us will always be here. I'm sorry we left you. It must be disorienting in here with all the hustle going on around you. We're here now."

"Thanks. It's just all these crazy thoughts that keep jamming up inside me. It's been . . . hard. So much has gone on."

Jan frowned, realizing what was going on. "Those thoughts may feel like scrambled eggs now, but you listen to us instead. Don't worry about it; Calvin and I have you covered in Prayer. Things may feel confused and out of your control, but it isn't really. When I feel that way, I realize that the only One I can Trust is the One Who can make sense out of all this mess. I Pray and talk to God about the fear. I have a few favorite Scriptures to say when I feel all messed up inside. I know that the one bringing the fear isn't God and speaking God's Word at those times pushes the fear away. Fear doesn't stick around when you speak Truth."

Paul was about to protest, but Jan held up her hand, cautioning him to stop. Evangeline reached for Jan's hand and said, "I'd like to hear them. I need to quiet these thoughts. They seem like voices, pounding at me. Anything to stop them would be good. It's just been so confusing here, today, yesterday. It's just too much." She began to sob, tears rolling down her cheeks.

Paul settled down a moment, realizing he did not have anything better to offer her. He listened passively, hoping that Jan could quiet Evangeline's nerves, even if with her religious stuff.

Jan settled into a chair beside the cot and pulled out a small Bible from her sack. She began to read verses about protection and God's Hand of provision. Evangeline slowly relaxed her grip on Jan's hand and fell asleep. Jan quietly closed her Bible and gazed at Evangeline's peaceful face.

Paul sat there saying nothing. He was not ready to concede that Jan had achieved in such a short period what he knew he could not. *What is it about these people? Is it how she talked reassuringly to her or is there something else going on? I'm not ready to buy into this mumbo jumbo. If it works for Gel, that's one thing. But it's not for me. Maybe Gel needs that stuff, not me.*

Jan slowly rose from the chair. Paul looked up as she left. He shook his head, not being able to understand these people.

Chapter 36

Sam and Sonya went back to handling the radio calls. They had been unable to raise Parker or Larry on their radio for the last half hour, but blamed the malfunctioning units. They had been so busy taking other calls and dispatching units to the appropriate locations, that they had not given it much further thought.

Sonya looked up from her clipboard as she heard a Rescue Squad vehicle power into the parking area by the triage tent. Glancing at the papers before her, she realized that the SUV was the one driven by Parker. "Well, now we'll find out what we couldn't hear over the radio," she commented.

Both Sonya and Sam got out of the truck as Parker hurried to the rear of his vehicle and opened the back hatch. From their position across the parking area, Sonya watched as Larry and Parker maneuvered to remove a victim strapped to a backboard. The person was obviously in rough shape, covered in mud and missing a boot on one foot. Sonya and Sam started to walk across the lot and as they got closer; Sonya could make out the pattern on the person's shirt. She suddenly stopped short and gasped. It looked remarkably like the blue shirt Jack was wearing when he fell into the river. She suddenly broke into a run, trying to catch up to Larry and Parker as they carried the body into the triage unit.

Sam was close on Sonya's heels, overtaking her by the time he reached the tent. He too had realized what he was seeing and wanted to see if Jack was alive. As they charged through the door, Parker moved from the gurney, pulled Sonya back and said, "Let the doctors attend to him, Sonya. They need room to move."

Sonya protested and pulled away from him. "Parker, how bad is it. He's alive, isn't he?"

Sam held Sonya as Parker went to help Larry finish giving his report to the medical staff and hung an intravenous bag. "Sam, please let me go to him!"

"You know I can't. Let them work on him, Sonya. It won't help him having you in their way. Just give them time to do what they need to do."

The doctor was giving one order after another as they worked over Jack's lifeless body. It was obvious to even the untrained eye that he was in critical condition. Parker turned to grab a suction tube and caught Sonya's stare. He averted his glance toward Sam and shook his head, indicating that he should move her out of the tent. Sam immediately started to pull her toward the doorway. She resisted, but Mac moved in to help Sam guide her outside.

"Sam, I have to know how bad it is. Obviously, he's alive. Why didn't they let us know they found him; that it was Jack they were transporting?" she cried excitedly.

"The radios weren't working. They tried to tell us. I just couldn't make out their message. You heard it. The radio failed before they could tell us," Sam answered.

"Sam, I'm trained like the rest of you. I can help in there. Let me help!" Sonya said as she started to move back toward the tent. Sam grabbed her by the arm and pulled her back. She in turn pushed on the hand that was restraining her, trying to free herself from his grip.

Sam grabbed each arm as she continued to fight his grasp. He turned her to face him and spoke firmly, "Sonya, everything within me wants to be in there now. He's my friend too. He's probably the best friend I've ever had. I'd give anything to be in there helping. Just give them time to work on him. We're too close to this to be of assistance," Sam finished obviously in anguish himself.

Sonya looked at him, pain written all over her face. She searched his eyes for a sign he might back down, but found none. He shook his head as she finally understood his point. She pulled her hand to her forehead and started to cry. Sam put his hands on her shoulders and said plainly, "Sonya, I said it before and I will say it again, Jack's a survivor. He knows how to fight. He made it this far, he'll make it the rest of the way. If anyone can, he can." Sam said this as much for himself as for Sonya's sake.

Sarah burst out of the tent a minute later, a look of concern on her face. Mac drew her aside and asked, "It's really serious, isn't it?"

"Well, they are working on him pretty intensely. I'm no doctor, but . . ." Sarah responded. "Oh, Mac, he's got to make it . . . to find him then lose him again. I don't think Sonya could take that."

Mac gave Sarah a hug of reassurance. Somehow feeling his presence so close made her feel some hope. Sarah looked up and realized that Sonya was crying by Sam. Sarah whispered in Mac's ear, "I think I should go over and talk to Sonya. She might need some female company."

Mac released her and agreed. Sarah walked to Sonya and gently put her hand on her shoulder. Sonya looked up and realized who it was. Sarah whispered, "It'll be okay, you know. Jack's strong and in good shape; he's a fighter."

Sonya managed a weak smile but as Sarah drew her into an embrace, she began to weep. This time Sarah joined her as they were overwhelmed with all the emotion of the day's events. Finally, Sonya pulled away, embarrassed, and said, "I don't usually cry, especially in front of the guys, you know. Well, they'd think me weak or something. I just don't do this."

Sarah nodded, "I understand, but you have every right to do it now. This has been a nerve-wracking day, well, actually, weekend. I don't think anyone will hold it against you."

"It's just that . . . well, Jack and I . . ." Sonya fumbled with her words, not sure how to express her feelings.

"It's okay; it's clear to everyone how you feel about Jack. It's no secret," Sarah replied.

Sonya looked up quizzically, saying, "So it's that obvious to everybody?" She paused a moment and added, "You'd think I'd have realized it too before now. I mean Jack and I have hung out together and worked together, but . . ."

Sarah chuckled, "But you didn't see how much you've fallen for him?"

"It sounds silly, doesn't it? When you're so close to it you don't see it sometimes, I guess," Sonya replied shaking her head.

Sarah put her hand on Sonya's arm gently and responded, "Sometimes it takes something like this to solidify your feelings."

Sonya looked away as tears began to roll down her cheeks. "I hope

. . . that it's not too late." She took a long sigh and added, "We could've been together sooner if I hadn't been so dense."

"Sonya, Jack's strong. He's athletic and he's got that on his side. He'll make it. He's got to make it." Sarah said, trying to convince herself as much as for Sonya's sake. Then she added for emphasis, "After all, we didn't complete our course. He has to finish our training." Sarah sniffed back her tears as she spoke.

Sonya nodded but looked back toward the triage tent as she did. If wishing could achieve anything, she was putting her Heart into it now.

Chapter 37

Jan and Calvin sat with Paul by Evangeline's cot. The mood was somber as they listened to the medical personnel working over Jack's body on the other side of the tent. Calvin sat silently Praying. Jan fingered her Bible as she read Scriptures in a hushed tone.

Paul stared at his hands, his face set into a grim pose. His discomfort was palpable. Too many times, while covering stories, bodies had been pulled from all manner of disasters, only to have sheets pulled over their heads. It brought back unpleasant memories.

These were the thoughts Paul kept buried and to himself, rarely explaining the pain to Evangeline. Paul did not want these events to color their relationship. He had tried to be matter of fact about that side of his job. He wanted to remain removed, not emotionally drawn into other people's turmoil. As distant as he had tried to be, it still gnawed at him, especially on nights that he could not sleep on assignment away from home. Evangeline was not aware of it, at least he hoped not.

As he sat there listening to the doctors discuss their next procedure, Paul's mind drifted to past assignments. He thought about the distance he often maintained with Evangeline when returning home from covering a story. *Maybe I wasn't good at hiding my emotions from her. She probably sensed how I was feeling. She'd ask what was wrong and I'd withdraw from her for a while or go out with the guys for a drink. Maybe she knows more that I think. Maybe . . .*

A thought niggled at his consciousness, though he tried to ignore it. His mind wandered to past stories, then back to his life at home and to another assignment. Still there was a sense he was trying to avoid. He realized he had shut Gel out of that part of his life and she had reacted by being increasingly insecure about things, all manner of things. She seemed to have this need to prove to him that she was still attractive and outgoing and able to keep up to his need for challenges.

So what's the need for challenge all about anyway? Do I like it that much or is it about proving something to myself? I sometimes wonder why I do it. It puts it in a different perspective when you think about what's happened here. Gel's hurt, Jack hanging on by a thread; other people are dead or homeless. Why do we do the things we do? What motivates us? What motivates me? Why do I chase the next big story? Is it for the paycheck or the acclaim? Where does Gel fit into that anyway? Or does she?

Paul was pulled out of his introspection by Evangeline's soft voice. "Paul, what's going on?" she asked.

Startled, Paul looked up at Evangeline then to the other side of the tent. He was not sure what to say to her. *Do I hide it from her again or should I be honest with her. Can she take it? Maybe that's what's been bugging me all along. Maybe I haven't seen her as strong enough for the weight of the world. I've seen her as weak. But is this the time to test her strength?* Paul hesitated a moment longer until she asked again, "Paul, what's all the commotion over there."

Jan leaned over and said quietly, "They found Jack."

Evangeline squinted to get a better look across the room, realizing that there was a cluster of people around his gurney. "It must be bad. I mean, there are so many people working on him. Is he going to be alright?"

Calvin answered, "I Believe God Heals and that He has Heard our Prayers."

"But you don't know, do you?" Evangeline said in a hoarse voice.

"I wish I did. It would make every crisis in life easier. But I don't think God's finished with Jack Davidson just yet," was Calvin reply.

Paul looked at Calvin, curious about that answer. "You got some private information or is that a gut instinct?"

"More like gut instinct, I guess. Jack's got some good potential and we're Praying for him in Faith. That counts for something, I think," Calvin responded.

"Faith. You put a lot of weight in that, don't you?" Paul said flatly.

"It's the way we live, Paul. It's the way we Live, Pray, Worship, and face crises. Without Faith, we're lost in murkiness. Without Faith, it's all darkness and hopelessness. I don't know how we'd live through events like these. It keeps us Alive and trying." Calvin paused a moment, then continued, "I have Faith in a Good God. It may not always turn out the way I want it to, but I have Faith that God never intended it to end up that way either. He's Good and He'll Lead us to Good, if we'll Listen to Him and Follow Him."

Paul sat silently, staring over at the activity across the room contemplating what Calvin said. The silence was broken by Evangeline as she said quietly, "I want that kind of Faith too. I need it."

Paul looked at Evangeline, then at Calvin, then back to Jack. *Seems idealistic to me. If we'll Listen to Him. There's that phrase again. Lacey said that before, didn't she? I don't Hear Him. What did she say? I wasn't Listening. I wasn't Hearing Him in events or people. He's Talking and I'm not Listening.*

Evangeline asked, "What gives you Faith when you see things like this?"

Jan took Evangeline's hand and said, "I don't look at the circumstances. I look at what God Promised amid life's events. I've been Praying His Word for Protection and Healing and Guidance and Wisdom. These things pull us through. I Believe He Heals, so I say it. I Believe He'll Guide the doctor, so I say it. God said it, so I Believe and say it. It is as simple as that."

Paul grunted, "As simple as that? How do you Believe it?"

Jan answered, "Because I Believe that God is Honorable and will Honor His Word. He's Good and His Word is Good. He doesn't lie."

"You Believe everything He says?" Paul said incredulously.

"I don't debate His Word. If there's a question about anything, I look at what He says and that ends the debate. His Word is the Final Authority. It doesn't matter how bad it looks to my eyes, I choose to Believe His Word and speak that over what's happening," Jan responded.

"How does that change things?" Paul asked.

"Well, speaking about the bad circumstances won't change it. You already have that. I want to speak Change into my life, not more of what I already have. I Believe that there's enough Power and Faith contained in God's Words to Change situations," Jan stated.

"Words change situations? Then if I want a million bucks, I'll just say that too!" Paul responded mockingly.

"If God needed you to have it and you spoke His Words about it with Faith in your Heart, it would happen," Jan said definitely.

"Yeah, right; as if . . ." Paul spat the words out.

"If you had Faith in your Heart," Jan repeated.

"Faith. I guess I don't have much Faith," Paul said flatly.

"Oh, we each have a faith of sorts. It just matters what kind of faith. You had enough faith to drive your car here didn't you? You trusted the brakes to work, the gas pedal. Well, that's a type of faith, you know. There's also a type of faith that too many people have, although we don't to call it faith. Most would call it fear. But it's just messed up faith, turned around, tossed upside down; sort of faith in reverse. If you fear something enough, believing long enough that some negative thing might happen, speak it enough, then you'll get what you fear. I'm sure you've seen that happen in all your travels," Calvin answered for Jan.

Paul thought for a moment. He had to admit he'd seen people say that their father had died at fifty and they'd probably die then too, and sure enough, they dropped dead at fifty. He'd just put it down to genetics. *Wait a minute, they can't be right about this stuff!*

"I don't know. It sounds plausible but I've got to think about it. Your logic has to be flawed somehow," Paul answered.

"Suit yourself, but I'll still base my life on Faith. If I'm wrong, then it's helped me through some problems and often it's Changed their outcomes, too. If you're wrong, think about what opportunities you've missed to Change things, to handle crises, to avert them possibly," Calvin responded.

Paul said nothing in return. Ignoring Paul's comments, Evangeline leaned toward Jan and said, Help me Pray now, you know, with Faith. I think we could use it."

Jan smiled at Evangeline and quietly found a Scripture for Evangeline to lean on and lead her in Prayer. Paul shook his head and stood and walked to the other side of the tent, choosing to make himself another coffee instead.

Sonya stood outside the tent looking over the churning river. Her thoughts were boiling like the waters, dirty and cluttered with debris. She had a hard time putting two thoughts together; going on emotion and instinct. *How much more can I take? I can't stand anything else. Why*

doesn't someone come out here and tell us something? It must be bad. No, if he's dead, they would have given up already. He must be hanging in there. Oh, what's taking so long?

Back and forth her mind jumped around, presuming doom and death and hoping for a Miracle the next instant. Sam was right, she was useless the way she was. She was ready to break like an over-tightened guitar string.

Sonya was about to charge into the tent to see what was going on when Parker slowly emerged. He looked tired and worn out. Sonya began to fear the worst as he beckoned her over. She hesitated a moment, not sure she wanted to hear what he had to say. It was better to have no news than to hear the words she dreaded.

Sonya looked for any sign of hope in Parker's demeanor, but he would not give her any hint from his expression. Knowing she had to prepare herself for the worst, she paused and walked over. "What can you tell me?" she asked.

"He's stable now. He was beaten up on his trip down the river. He must have fractured some ribs and punctured his lung, because it had collapsed. We had a hard time getting a chest tube inserted, but he's breathing much better now. Once the lung inflates fully, we'll have a better picture of what's going on. The primary concern, as you know, is airway and breathing. Everything else comes after that"

Sonya stood staring at Parker, almost not believing her ears. *He's alive! He's really alive. Why did he look so serious then?* She let this information digest a minute before asking, "And his other injuries. What about them?"

"He's kind of banged up, as I said. He's not a pretty sight. He took a nasty contusion to his face; his left eye and cheek are swollen. No doubt he has a concussion, maybe facial fractures. I don't know the extent of the head injury; at least his pupils are equal and reactive. He's been kind of incoherent at times, you know mumbling stuff and thinking he's still fighting the current in the river. He seems a bit confused about how he got out of the river though. That's to be expected, given his head injury," Parker reported.

"But you got him stabilized, that's good. Any other fractures? What about internal injuries?" Sonya rattled off a list of possible problems she had imagined since they had rushed him into the tent.

"Well, he fractured his left ankle. I'm not sure how, but he might have escaped any other major fractures; although he's battered up and contused all over. It must have been one wild ride down the river. Considering all the debris in the river, it's amazing he wasn't crushed. He must have drunk half the river though. My concern is pneumonia from aspiration. There's a lot of junk floating in that water."

Sonya listened to Parker's assessment while eyeing the tent. Part of her wanted to know how he was, but the other half of her wanted to tear to his bedside. "So what about internal injuries?" she said hurriedly.

"We can't be certain until we get him to the hospital and do the diagnostics. His blood pressure is stable, so that's a good sign," Parker answered. "You can go in now, not that I think you want to," he added with a smirk.

Sonya said, "Thanks," and was inside the tent before the word hit Parker's ears.

The scramble of activity had subsided around Jack's gurney. Now only Paul, Jan and Calvin were standing quietly in front of his bed. They blocked her view of him, but when they heard her coming toward them, they stepped back so she could see.

Sonya caught her breath as she looked at his face; it was so bruised and swollen. He looked as if he had gone ten rounds on the losing end of a prizefight. Not only swollen, his face was scraped and raw on his forehead and cheek.

Jan whispered to Sonya, "He's alive and fighting. He gave the doctors a struggle when they put the chest tube in. He let out a few choice words! He's not ready to quit yet."

Sonya smiled at Jan as tears welled up in her eyes. Relief flooded her body as the pent up stress started to release. Jan put her arm around Sonya as she guided toward Jack's right side. "He can't open his left eye, so you'd best stand over here. He can't open the other one very well either, though," Jan commented.

Sonya scanned Jack's body, doing a quick assessment of his apparent injuries. Her mind was checking for and eliminating possible wounds. They had cut off his clothing and it lay in a heap at the head of his bed on the floor. He was partly covered by a sheet but his extremities were exposed. His skin was smeared in mud and blood, as they had not had a chance to clean him up, just stabilize him.

Sonya stood by his side and hesitantly touched his arm. He grunted and winced in pain, but opened his right eye as much as he was able. Bleary eyed, it took him a moment to focus and recognize that it was her.

She gave him a sad smile and said, "Jack Davidson, you'll do anything to get out of going on a date, won't you?"

Jack nodded slightly. "Nah," he murmured through swollen lips.

Sonya answered, "Not that I could take you anywhere looking like this, anyway."

Jack just grimaced in return. "Sorry, to 'dithapoint' you," he mumbled.

"I'm going to hold you to it though, you know that, don't you," Sonya said lightly stoking his arm. "I'll give you a few days to heal first," she added tears now streaming down her face. Her hand started to shake from the release of tension. She grabbed her right hand with the left one, trying to stop the trembling, but it was uncontrollable.

Mac and Sarah entered the tent and came by the gurney to see the Jack's pathetic figure on the bed. Calvin and Paul moved back over by Evangeline's cot to give them room. Sarah held tightly onto Mac's hand as they moved in closer to get a better look. Jack's face was so battered she hardly recognized him.

"Jack, it's Sarah, and Mac's here too. You gave us a scare," she said quietly. "We're so relieved that you're okay."

Jack tried to turn his head to focus on Sarah's voice, but the cervical collar they had put on him held his head in place. It was obvious he could not see where she was standing; his good eye was hardly focusing on his surroundings.

Mac added, "It's okay, buddy, you don't have to say anything. I just have to look at you to know you took a beating in that river. It must have taken a pint of blood out of your legs alone." Mac said eyeing the scrapes on his legs.

Sarah looked over at Sonya and realized how upset she was. She whispered, "He'll be okay. He's strong and healthy."

"Oh, I know all that. It's just . . . well, it was not knowing then assuming the worst and now seeing him like this. I know he'll be okay. I'm just so relieved . . ." Sonya's voice wandered as she sniffed and tried to wipe her tears. "I guess it's the stress release. I can't stop shaking. I'm not used to being like this. I take care of people like this every day."

Sarah smiled and put her arm around Sonya's shoulders. "You don't have as much emotional investment in those people."

"But I do. I often know them," Sonya countered.

"I mean invested with your heart, silly. You might not realize it but I think you and Jack are linked a lot closer than that," Sarah laughed.

Sonya paused a moment then realized what she meant. She looked a little embarrassed as she answered, "Okay, yeah, you're right. It might take me awhile to understand it all. I suppose I didn't realize what was happening between us."

"Then you were the last to know. We could all see it, girl!" Sarah gave Sonya a hug and added, "It's obvious. You love the guy and not as a brother, either."

Sonya began to sob again as she allowed her emotions to flow. New realizations crashed into one another in her mind and her heart. It was confusing, but at the same time, exciting.

"It's okay. It's been a hard couple of days. We're all a little bent out of shape," Sarah comforted her.

Sonya pulled away and grabbed for a tissue. "I don't know how I could have been so stupid. It took something like this to make me realize how much I care about him. It's so dumb," she said quietly. "And I almost lost him before I knew I wanted him. He was just always around, you know. We had fun, but more? I guess I didn't know what to expect from him, or me for that matter.

"Then when I saw him fall into that river, I thought my heart would smash apart. He was yanked away so violently, so senselessly. I watched him be swallowed by that awful river . . . ," Sonya's voice as small as it was trailed away to nothing. She could no longer speak.

Sonya gazed over at Jack bruised and bloodied body and reached for his hand. She stood for a moment, silent, tracing his fingers with hers. Jack attempted to open his one good eye and focus on her. Sonya managed a weak smile and said, "I'm glad you came back, Jack Davidson. You would have wrecked my day if you hadn't."

"Good to be back," he mumbled through his fattened lips. He squeezed her fingers and she took his hand in both of hers.

"This time maybe you could stay awhile," Sonya responded.

Sarah patted Sonya on the shoulder and motioned to Mac that they should leave. "I think these two need some privacy," Sarah said.

Sam stood outside the tent speaking with Parker and Larry when another transmission came through on the radio. He walked back to his truck to take the call as Mac came out of the tent with Paul. They turned as Mac asked them, "So how did you find Jack?"

"Oh, we didn't. Nathan Smiley was checking the waterfront by his place for washed up debris. I guess he was intent on scavenging whatever he could from the stuff that was washing ashore from upstream. He has a demolition business down the highway and you know, he'll do anything for a buck. He was sorting through all manner of junk in the bay and lifted a piece of siding that came from a house and there lay Jack. He said he looked as dead as any corpse you see on television," was Parker's reply.

Larry laughed, "Yeah, I would have given a thousand bucks to have seen the look on his face! Pretty near scared him into the next town when he poked at him with a stick and Jack groaned. I think it took ten years off his life. He figured him for a stiff for sure. I don't think he'll ever be the same."

Parker continued, "Anyway, he called it in and we headed out to see what was going on. We didn't expect to find Jack in that location. I'm still trying to figure how he landed up there, especially so far inside the debris field along the shore. I don't know how it happened, but there he was lying sprawled on the shore. His color was terrible. His breathing was compromised from the punctured lung and I think he took in a bunch of water into his lungs along the way. It seems incredible that he survived. You've seen the river; would you expect him to be alive?"

Paul shook his head and said, "Not from what you see down there, I wouldn't. I've covered a few stories about flash flooding and there have been times I've interviewed people who had freaky escapes. Some ended up in trees for days; others just grabbed debris and rode the waves till they hit the shore somewhere. None could explain how they survived. I put it down to dumb luck."

Larry agreed, "Jack must have had a lot of it then, because he was all the way out of the water. He must have crawled partway up the embankment afterward though, because Nathan said he didn't move him. He was high enough not to be pulled back into the water."

Parker added, "I still don't know how he made it that far into shore, though. He would have had to push his way through a whack of debris to get there. It doesn't make a lot of sense to me, but I'm glad someone found him when they did. I don't think he'd have survived much longer without medical intervention. You won't live if you can't breathe."

Sam came to where they were standing and announced, "Okay, we've negotiated with search-and-rescue air services to liberate a helicopter to airlift some patients out of here. I'm going in to talk with the doctors to determine who needs to go first. Parker, Larry, I need you to move them to the high school football field. It's the largest spot we've got free of power lines for them to land."

With that Sam went inside the tent, followed by Parker and Larry. Sam was wasting no time on the extrication. He wanted to be sure Jack was transported immediately. He knew Evangeline was also a priority because her blood pressure had been low all day and the likelihood of internal injuries was high.

Mac looked at Paul as they turned to enter the triage tent as well, "Do you think that means they'll take Gel with them now too?" Mac asked.

"I only hope so. She's been through a lot and I want her moved as soon as possible. We've been waiting too long already as it is. I know they were using the helicopters to rescue people who were stranded, but this is a priority too."

Mac countered, "Yeah, but at least her condition was stable. Some people wouldn't have survived had they not been plucked from their situations. They have to work through priority emergencies before being used for transport."

Paul frowned as he thought about other disasters he had covered in the past. He knew what Mac was saying was true, but it was different when it involved his wife. His patience was wearing thin and he wanted action now. He followed Sam into the tent, intent on getting his point across. Mac was close on Paul's heels knowing his friend could be like a mad bulldog when he was certain he was right. He knew Paul might not be inclined to be diplomatic about the matter under the circumstances and he did not want to alienate the medical staff.

Sam was already informing the chief-of-staff by the time they entered the tent. Before Paul could say a thing, he saw the doctor point to Jack and Evangeline. Paul watched as he directed nurses to prepare them for transport.

Sam caught Paul's eye and nodded to him as he walked over. "Gel, will be moved soon. We have a helicopter on its way now. We don't have a lot of time to lose. We have a window of opportunity to use the helicopter before it gets another call of higher priority. I'm sorry, Paul, there won't be room for you on board, but we'll have to arrange ground transportation down the river to the other bridge. It's holding at the moment. From there, you should be able to get to the hospital okay."

Paul moved to where Evangeline was being readied to move and tried to grab her hand. The nurse moved him out of the way as she pulled a sheet around Evangeline's shoulders. She then attached a portable intravenous pole to the gurney and quickly took her blood pressure and wrote the figure on her chart. Evangeline looked around the nurses to try to see where Paul was. He in turn was trying to get her attention from the other side of the nurses. Finally, as they moved her gurney, Paul walked beside her and said, "I can't come with you, but I'll get there when I can."

Evangeline reached out her hand to touch Paul as they wheeled her past. He walked apace with the stretcher and grabbed her hand. Evangeline whispered, "I love you."

Paul answered, "I love you too. Everything's going to be alright now. Hang in there, you hear me?"

Evangeline managed an apprehensive smile. Everything was happening so fast now. They had waited so long and now she was being ripped away from Paul so suddenly. They wheeled her outside to a waiting ambulance. They pushed her beside Jack's stretcher that had already been secured in place. Before Evangeline could say anything else, they closed the doors and pulled away. Paul was left standing in the parking lot watching the ambulance drive away.

They could now hear the helicopter as it maneuvered to the football field by the high school. The high-pitched ambulance siren wailed mingling with the beating of the helicopter blades as it passed overhead. Paul could do nothing but watch the helicopter's path as he crossed the parking area. Evangeline was out of his reach again, but this time he knew where she was. He might not be able to travel with her but he would not wait here wondering what was going on any longer.

Paul turned and saw Mac coming toward him as the helicopter cleared the trees. As he caught up to him, Mac informed him, "Calvin says he'll give us a ride down to the Lower Bridge Road. From there, we should be able to make to the hospital. It all depends if they keep her at the hospital here in Moulton or move her into the city. They didn't tell us what the plan was. Did they tell you?"

Paul shook his head, but turned immediately to find Sam. He was talking to Sonya by the triage tent. She seemed upset. As they approached, he overheard her saying, "Sam, I need to know where you've sent him so I can follow. Which hospital is he going to?"

Before Sam could respond, Paul added, "Exactly what I need, too."

Sam held up his hands in defense against the two, "I'll confirm it but

I think they're moving down to one of the hospitals in the city because they're already swamped in emerg here. They've got more than they can handle already. There's no sense dropping them here and them having to move them again. I'll confirm it and let you know."

While Sam went to his truck to get on the radio, Mac told Sonya of Calvin's offer to drive them to the hospital. Sonya looked at them then at Calvin's Jeep. "I don't know if we'll all fit. It might be kind of snug with five of us," she said doubtfully.

Mac eyed the vehicle and nodded, "You know, Sarah and I don't have to go with you now. It's most important for you and Paul to get down there. We can stay here for the meantime. We'll follow when we get hold of another vehicle. How are the roads down that way, anyway?"

Sonya answered, "I understand that they are in better condition than we encountered getting down here, but there are some bad washouts and flooded areas. The further south you go, the better it gets. Once you hit the interstate, it should be easy. Getting beyond these secondary roads will be the greatest challenge."

"Well, maybe by tomorrow the roads will be more passable for us. We'll probably have to rent a vehicle because I doubt ours will be accessible for a while. Those roads by the lake will take more than a day or two to repair," Mac said.

Sarah came out of the tent followed by Jan and Calvin. "We were picking through the remnants of Jack's clothing. We had to see if there were any personal effects he might want in his pockets. Somehow his wallet was intact and a set of keys. How would they survive that trip in the river and his boot didn't?" Calvin remarked.

Mac shook his head, "Hard to figure that one out. We were just discussing who should ride down with you to the hospital. There's only seating for four so I thought Sarah and I could stay here and catch a ride later. Maybe it would be better if we stay an extra day until the roads clear a bit. That way Jan can go down with you, Calvin, so you won't have to ride back alone."

Sonya looked down at the ground and offered, "You know, maybe I should stay here. Sam could probably use my help still and . . ."

Jan cocked her head, gave her an amused look and tilted her chin up so she had to look into her eyes. "Sonya, honey, I doubt you would be much good to him at this point. Admit it; your heart is with Jack. You might as well go and be with him.

Calvin looked at Jan and came over as she whispered in his ear. He spoke quietly back and she answered, "There's no need for me to go. Calvin won't come back tonight anyway with it getting this late and by tomorrow, driving should be a bit better. I should help finding you a place to stay for the night anyway. We have friends who would gladly help us out under the circumstances. They live right in town."

Before either Mac or Sarah could protest, Calvin added, "So it's settled then. Sonya, you and Paul grab your stuff and we'll head out. It looks like the river has crested. It hasn't risen in the last while so the other bridge should still be accessible." Sonya started to protest, but Calvin held up his hand. "Go ask Sam where they took them and we'll leave."

Sonya smiled, relieved that she could go after all. She trotted across the parking area to Sam's truck. Mac watched her go and added, "Jan, are you sure you don't want to go with Calvin? I'm sure Sam could find us somewhere to stay for the night."

Jan waved them off and said, "Oh, perhaps, but I think you'll like Jake and Beth's place better. They're nice folks and Beth's a great cook. If there's still no power, Jake can barbecue a mean hamburger in a pinch."

Sonya hurried back with the location of the hospital to which they expected to transport Jack and Evangeline. Calvin climbed into the Jeep before there could be more discussion. Paul joined Calvin in the front seat then Sonya took the back. Mac put his hand on Calvin's door and said, "Drive safely. We've had enough excitement for one day. We don't want to visit you guys in the hospital, too."

Calvin gave him a feigned expression of hurt and said, "You doubt my driving abilities after our trek down the mountain?"

"Just get there in one-piece," Mac added as he shook his head and closed the door.

Calvin fired the engine and backed out of the parking space. He turned the wheel and the Jeep roared out the parking lot, spitting up stones and mud as they left. Jan frowned and said, "Calvin Talbot. I know he did that for my benefit. He loves to try to bug me. He'll expect me to comment on that exit when he gets back."

Mac put his arm around Sarah's waist as they watched the Jeep travel down the road and out of sight. "So will you?" Sarah asked.

"Will I what?" Jan asked back.

"Will you comment on it when he gets back?" Sarah repeated the question.

Jan smiled and said, "You know, I don't think I'll give him the satisfaction. I'll just leave him guessing about what I thought about it. He knows what I think anyway. I've told enough times over the years. He ought to know by now."

Hildy and Sol carried the plates from dinner into the kitchen. Eli sat on the sofa across from Lacey and Bert in Lacey's greatroom. They had eaten informally around the coffee table. It had been a simple meal of sausages, salad and bread. They were weary but concerned that they had not yet connected with Jan and Calvin by phone. They had tried to call Jan's cell phone several times on the satellite phone in the van, but there had been no answer.

"Why don't we call Jake and Beth. If Jan and Calvin have had to stay overnight in town, they likely would stay with them. At least, they can give us a report on the conditions in town," Sol finally said.

Sol headed out the door before anyone could comment. He was already on the van phone by the time the others had made it out to the vehicle. "It's ringing. It sounds as if they have telephone service," Sol commented as everyone heard the sound over the speakerphone.

"Hello."

"Beth, it's Sol. We were wondering if you have heard anything from Jan or Calvin Talbot. They were headed into town this morning. We were hoping that you could tell us if they made it."

"Oh, yes. Jan's here with Mac and Sarah. I believe you met them at Lacey's," Beth answered.

"Oh, yes, we're well acquainted. We're glad they hooked up with you. Could we talk to them?" Sol asked.

Jan took the phone, while Mac and Sarah shared the extension so they could share in the conversation. Bert asked, "So you made it to town okay?"

Jan gave Mac and Sarah a look and answered, "Yes, we made it to town. It was an adventure. The roads were terrible. Some parts were treacherous. But we made it."

Lacey and Bert questioned, "Is Calvin with you?"

"No, he had to go with Paul and Sonya into the city to the hospital," Jan answered.

"They took care of Gel?" Hildy asked.

"Yes, finally, it took a long time to get them, uh, her transported because the bridge wasn't safe. We had to wait for a helicopter to airlift them out," Sarah answered.

"Them. You mean Gel and other patients?" Hildy questioned.

Mac answered this time, "Well, it's a long story. We had some trouble in Moulton before we arrived at the triage unit."

Bert frowned and asked, "Trouble. What kind of trouble?"

Mac paused for a minute. Jan and Sarah exchanged glances with Mac and Mac looked to them for some encouragement from them to tell them all the details of their day. Sarah nodded at him and he began, "The East River was a raging torrent when we arrived. It was . . . it wasn't like anything I'd seen before. Frankly, I'd be happier if I never saw anything like it again."

Bert looked at Lacey then to the others. It was plain that their Prayers were necessary after all. "So there's a lot of damage?"

Mac chose his words carefully, then started again, "The only way I can describe it would be to call the river 'Niagara Falls without the falls.' It was horrendous. The current cut into the shoreline and houses just fell into the water. You wouldn't believe it!"

Eli asked incredulously, "Houses. You mean many of them?"

Sarah answered this time, "Oh, yes. It was just awful! Then we came to Sonya's home. We had to get Tucker out of the building before it fell into the river, too."

Bert frowned and said, "Before it fell into the river? You mean Sonya's house was taken by the river too?"

Jan looked over at Mac and Sarah. She added, "Yes, unfortunately. But in getting Tucker out, we had an incident."

Bert took a breath and closed his eyes while saying, "Okay, Jan. You'd better tell us the rest of the story. An incident? It doesn't sound good. What happened?"

Jan hesitated a moment, but decided she may as well tell them all the details of their harrowing day. "In getting Tucker out, Jack was still on the veranda when it collapsed. Initially, he saved himself by grabbing a branch. Unfortunately, before we could rescue him, the tree was uprooted. Jack was sucked into the rapids and dragged downstream."

There a collective gasp on Bert's side of the phone. They were expecting the worst. "You're not trying to tell us what I think you are?" Bert replied, finally.

Mac answered, "No, it has to be some sort of Miracle. We looked for the longest time, but we couldn't find him. But some guy named Nathan Smiley came across him on the shoreline. He called the paramedics and they brought him in. Funny thing, though, no one can figure out how he got there on the shore. It seemed improbable given the conditions. I guess it doesn't matter, because they brought him into the triage unit and were able stabilize him then send him off to hospital for more care."

Lacey quickly asked, "Mac, what's his condition?"

"He probably fractured some ribs and punctured his lung. They had to put in a chest tube to re-inflate his lung. He looks as if he fought a bear and lost. He's all banged up and scraped and has a fracture or two. His face is battered and swollen. He's not a pretty sight, but he's alive to tell the story. Well, he'll be able to tell the story when the swelling in his mouth comes down."

Lacey hung her head. "That explains the Prayers, but that was a little too close. I wonder if that lad has any idea how much Praying we did today?"

Sarah answered, "Thank you guys for Praying. We sure needed it. That's obvious. I guess we didn't know what we were in for when we left this morning."

"We didn't know the details, but we sensed there was something wicked going on with you. We had a strong feeling to support you in Prayer, for a time at least . . ."

"For a time . . . ?" Sarah repeated.

"We felt we could stop; that the crisis was settled," Lacey finished her sentence.

"What time was that?" Mac asked.

"Well, it must have been about 2:15, I'd say," Lacey replied.

"That's odd. That was just after he fell in the river, long before anyone found him. You just stopped Praying?" Sarah questioned.

"I had a feeling of Peace. Like it was all taken care of," Lacey stated.

"You're sure about that? It seems odd you would stop Praying before we found him," Mac declared.

Jan sat there smiling and nodding. Mac and Sarah looked at her oddly, not understanding. Jan added, "God had already answered the Prayer, hadn't He? By that time, he was down the river and being scooped up the shoreline. It was just a matter of finding him, wasn't it?"

Lacey paused and added, "It sounds like it. We were released from the Prayer once the Answer was Sent. I'd wager he was Assisted by an angel or two."

Mac looked at Sarah and she returned the glance. She shrugged and said, "Whatever it was, he sure needed it. I'd like to Believe it was an angel. Do you think something like that actually happens?"

Jan piped in at this point, "I certainly Believe in angels. They've been sent to minister to us, as Believers. They respond to The Word spoken in Prayer. In fact, that's what dispatches them to our Assistance."

Mac shook his head incredulously. "Where'd you get an idea like that?"

"From the Bible Itself. God told us in His Word that angels respond to the voice of The Word. That's why it's important to speak the Word we Believe when we Pray. You may be reluctant to have Faith in this but it's something we deeply Believe," Jan answered definitely.

Mac raised his eyebrows while hearing her reply and asked, "Really?"

Jan said, "Really."

Lacey added, "Jan can show you later, I'm sure. But God did Promise it to us. He Promised us a lot more than that too. We Rely on It. It's the way we live or at least we try to. We sometimes fail, but we learn from those mistakes too. It's all about Faith."

Mac paused, so Jan continued. "Jack and Gel were airlifted out early this evening and Calvin drove Sonya and Paul to the hospital."

Hildy interjected, "Sonya went, too?"

"Sonya was broken up when we thought Jack wasn't going to make it back alive. And it didn't look good for a while, you know. She's smitten, that's for sure. It was obvious she needed to be with him at the hospital," Jan added.

Lacey chuckled and said, "I thought so. I knew something was going on between them. Jack mentioned her a few times, mostly in context with the Rescue Squad, but there was no mistaking the chemistry between them when they were together!"

Jan agreed, "There's no doubt about that and I think you'll find her hanging around in the future too. It's obvious where her heart is. The question is whether he realizes it yet. You know; guys and all . . ."

Mac shook his head at that jab. "I'm just glad they finally were transported to hospital. Between Gel and Jack, they have some recovering to do. That's some way to end a holiday."

Lacey answered, "Mac, I hope you excuse these events. This weather has been very unusual. We hope you'll come back to visit under better circumstances."

Mac replied, "We have to thank you for all you've done for us. We kind of intruded on your doorstep. It's been a hard way to get to know each other."

Lacey nodded and said, "Not an ideal situation, I'll give you that. But it sure plunges you into an instant relationship when you share something like this."

Sarah answered this time, "I couldn't have thought of better people to be put with considering what went on. I have to say you've given us a lot to think about. Thank you."

"You're most welcome. It's how we live, you know. It may be different lifestyle for you, but it is how we live. I'm sure we'll have lots of time in the future to discuss it further if you'd like," Bert added.

Sarah looked at Mac and he shrugged. He knew she was going to make a point of making Big Rock Lake more than a new getaway destination in the future. It would be nice to see it when the weather is good. Sarah replied, "Yes, I think we'd like that a lot."

Chapter 38

Six weeks later:

Lacey looked at Bert sitting across the dining table from her. Mac and Sarah were driving up with Paul and Evangeline this afternoon. Lacey had invited Bert to have lunch with her, so he could be there when they arrived. Now Lacey eyed his plate, realizing he had not eaten much of her goulash. She already knew why.

"I suppose it's time to make some decisions," Lacey stated quietly.

Bert nodded, "It would be better, I'm sure you'd agree."

Lacey looked at her hands before her, pondering her thoughts. The silence was deafening between them now.

The clock ticked on the mantle as she dipped deep into her heart for the words to speak. Finally, she looked up and smiled. "Yes," she said.

"Yes, what?" he responded.

The phone rang, startling both of them. Each looked at the phone then at one another. It rang again and Lacey's eyes questioned Bert's. He said nothing, but raised his eyebrows and nodded at the phone. The phone's insistent signal sounded again. This time Bert answered, "Go ahead. You need to answer it. It's probably them."

Lacey reluctantly picked up the receiver. "Hello."

A bright voice was at the other end, "Hi, Lacey. It's Sarah. We're about fifteen minutes out. I just wanted to give you warning that we're about to arrive. We've stopped at a gas station and should be there soon if you're ready for us."

"Oh, that's fine. Come right ahead. Bert's here already and we're looking forward to seeing you."

"Great! We'll be there in a few minutes. We can't wait to see you."

Lacey disconnected the phone and turned to Bert. "I suppose we'd better clean these dishes away before they arrive. Not that you ate much. I'll just put the dishes in the dishwasher while you clean the table."

Bert stood silently as she tossed him the dish rag. Lacey turned to the sink rinsed her plate. She slowly turned and smiled, "I meant what I said before. We should go to the West Coast like Andrea suggested. It would be good to see them all in person and discuss our thoughts about all of this."

Bert slowly looked up and asked, "And the other issue? What about that?"

Lacey smiled more broadly and walked back to him. She took his hand in hers and added, "Yes. I meant yes about that too."

Jack picked up the phone and punched the number for his sister, Laurie. This call would be a pleasure after the last six-week ordeal. It had been a confusing time during the days following Igor's attack on both of them. Laurie had no contact with her parents for a week following the storm as communications were significantly disrupted. Available phone service was being used for emergency personnel and personal calls could not be made from the hospital. Laurie put her name and Aunt Liz's on a list of survivors that had been posted on the Internet, but she had been initially unable to call them. The devastation that surrounded her could not be put into words and she was thankful that she did not have to speak with her parents while she was still in shock over all the destruction.

Jack could not make any calls either when he was first in hospital, although Sonya did notify his parents of his whereabouts on his behalf. The swelling in his face was extensive and it was soon determined that he had fractured his jaw and it was wired shut. Fortunately, they had just removed the wires and he could now talk and eat with freedom. He was cautioned to start with soft foods until his mouth and stomach adjusted to solid foods, but he was so looking forward to a nice juicy steak he could hardly stand it. He settled for his first normal conversation with his sister since the hurricane. Up to now, he had been only able to talk through clenched teeth and it had been frustrating.

"Hi! It's good to hear your voice. You sound a lot better." Laurie exclaimed.

"No more wires. I can open my mouth for the first time in six weeks. What a pain that was," Jack replied.

"I'm glad. It must've been rough not eating your favorite foods for that long," she teased. "Not that you usually do much talking. That probably doesn't make much difference."

"Oh, being able to eat is great. You have no idea. But Sonya makes me talk these days. Sorry I haven't called this week yet. I hated those wires so much; I wanted to wait till I got them out."

"It's okay. I'm glad to hear from you anyway. I'm preparing to fly back home now. It's been a rough six weeks here. It's kind of bittersweet though. We've been through so much together, with Aunt Liz's situation and with the aftermath of the storm, it is almost sad to leave."

"I'm sorry you had to handle things with Aunt Liz on your own. I'm amazed you stayed there this long though," Jack commented.

"Look Jack after Aunt Liz died so soon after the hurricane, well, there was so much around here that needed to be done. People were hurting so much over their losses. I suppose I was too. I missed Aunt Liz a lot. It just seemed logical to stay awhile to help the community out," Laurie answered.

"Laurie, you're a good person. Considering the stories you've told me so far, I'm sure they needed you. Your experience alone must have been appreciated. You have a good heart to help people," Jack said.

"Jack, you know, a situation like this hurricane is like no other I have been through so far. My expertise could only do so much. It changes you. I've seen things from a different side of things. Being here, you know, being a victim as much as anyone else, it's another perspective. I was used to being the professional who goes in after the fact, not a casualty," Laurie said quietly.

Jack paused, as he thought how true her words for him as well. "Yeah, I can relate to what you're saying. I had six weeks on the other side of things, too. It's kind of similar in some ways . . ." He went quiet.

"Jack, are you still there?" Laurie asked.

"Yeah, I'm here. I was just thinking about the craziness that went on around here. Funny, it was the same storm, but we both got butt kicked by it though we were so far apart," Jack answered.

"That was one mean hurricane. It was a freak like Hazel was. Twice in fifty years. Makes you wonder, doesn't it? Maybe it wasn't such a freak after all," Laurie pondered.

"Yeah, sometimes. So are you flying home today?" Jack asked.

"Well, I thought I'd take a detour to surprise Mum and Dad on the way home. I've been away so long now; what are a couple more days? I'm still on my leave of absence anyway. I've been on the Internet looking for cheap fares and I found one that will give me a few days out West before flying home," Laurie commented.

"You'll make Mum happy. I know she misses you. When she couldn't fly in after Aunt Liz died, I know she felt awful about it."

"Well, Jack, you know how things were here. No one could fly into the airport anyway, with the condition it was left in. It'll be better to have a memorial service in the spring. It's a good excuse for everyone to get together in Wilmington when the weather is nice. We'll all probably need a vacation by that time anyway," Laurie countered.

"You're right; if we don't wait so long that it runs into my busy season. I'll have courses starting again once the roads are passable after the spring thaw," Jack responded.

Laurie countered, "Don't worry. I know about your schedule."

"It is my livelihood, you know," Jack reminded her.

"You're not giving it up after all that happened?" Laurie teased.

"No way! It was just a fluke. Now that I have the wires out and that cast taken off my ankle, I can get back to work and it will be business as usual. Hey, even my ribs aren't hurting anymore, so nothing should hold me down." Jack sounded offended.

"Just kidding, brother. I know you won't stop teaching your courses. It's what makes you, you. I might as well cut out your heart as stop you doing that. Speaking of hearts, how are things going with Sonya these days?" Laurie asked.

Jack smiled at the mention of her name. If anything had changed in his life, that would have to be it. "Great, just great. You'll have to meet her soon. I think you'd like her a lot. You're alike in many ways. She has spunk like you."

"Oh, so she won't take any of your guff, huh?" Laurie laughed.

Jack chuckled, thinking back on his recovery days. She had said he was not a good patient. "Nah, she made me behave. But I managed a few things she didn't know about anyway. Did you know that you can drink beer through a straw?"

"How'd I know you figure out a way to do that? You should go easy on that, you know. Otherwise, you'll be looking like Uncle Stan and even acting like him. Ugh," Laurie quipped.

"I know how to take care of myself. Don't worry," Jack said defending himself.

"Yeah, like when you fell in the river?" Laurie asked.

"That's not fair. You said you wouldn't bring that up against me." Jack said.

"Okay, so sue me, I'm your sister. I'm concerned about you. You need to take care of yourself."

"I'll let you get away with that one last time. It's probably the nurse in you. But promise me you won't bring it up again."

"Agreed," was Laurie's reply.

"Call me when you get to Mum and Dad's," Jack added.

"I will. You take care of yourself. I mean really take care this time. I love you and don't want to lose you," Laurie said as she ended the conversation.

Jack added, "I do too. Talk to ya later."

Paul was behind the wheel as they turned the corner and came into view of Lacey's house. Evangeline was seated beside him with Mac and Sarah in the rear seat of Paul's SUV.

Lacey and Bert came out to greet them as Paul parked the vehicle. Bert was first there, shaking hands with Paul as he opened the door. "I see you have a new vehicle," Bert commented as he eyed the shiny blue paint.

"Well, after our last experience up here, I thought we should come prepared," Paul answered with a laugh.

Bert shared the chuckle, but added, "I hope you found the roads better than on your trip home. They've done a lot of reconstruction in a short time. I hope that doesn't mean they blew the road maintenance budget for the winter already. We all might have to get snowmobiles in that case!"

Mac and Sarah opened their doors and piled out, as Paul came around to help Evangeline from the SUV. He was careful to help her step down from the vehicle and handed her a cane as she balanced herself on her good leg. She reached back into the vehicle to grab her purse then straightened to walk to where the others were standing. Lacey gave her a big hug, followed by Bert.

"I'm so glad you could come. Since we visited that time when you first got out of the hospital, you've made considerable progress. You're getting around so much better," Lacey commented.

"Well, I'm just glad that I could have the surgery to repair the ligaments right away. Waiting for further diagnostics would have prolonged my recovery. I can get around well now. I still use the cane for rough ground. I just don't want to take a chance of twisting it. It's come so far so soon, I don't want to mess it up," Evangeline replied, smiling at Lacey's comments.

Bert helped Mac and Paul with their bags as Lacey and Sarah guided Evangeline up the stairs to the veranda. As they went through the door, Evangeline giggled, "You know, you guys don't need to hover so closely. I can manage by myself now."

Sarah put her arm around Evangeline and answered, "I know that, but coming back here just makes me want to protect you a little. It's where all this started and I guess I feel guilty that you got hurt up here."

Evangeline eased herself on the leather sofa and replied, "For heaven's sake, you have nothing to feel guilty about. You didn't cause my injuries,"

The men walked in with the luggage, laughing as Mac said, "These cases are so heavy, maybe the girls are planning a weeklong trip this time!" Mac laughed.

Sarah frowned as she overheard the comment and protested, "The weather is getting cooler now and I didn't know exactly what clothes to bring I wasn't sure how warm or cold it might get, especially in the evenings in the mountains."

Mac responded, "I think you must have half your closet in here," as he lifted her suitcase. "You shouldn't have any trouble finding the right clothes to wear judging by this case."

Sarah feigned disgust at his remark, realizing he was trying to tease her. "I like to be prepared. Don't you, Gelly?"

Evangeline came to her defense, "Oh, absolutely. We need the right apparel for the weather."

Lacey intervened at this point, saying, "You boys stop it now. You've given these women too much grief already. Just appreciate how they like to dress for you. I think they're looking beautiful, don't you, Bert?"

Bert raised his eyebrows and set the case on the floor he was carrying to get a closer look at the two women. "Yes, I'd have to agree with you. No doubt about it."

Sarah remarked, "Mmmm. Well, you're a diplomat. I think we probably look a little better than the last time you saw us up here, at least. Anything is an improvement over that."

"I'll be honest with you. My appearance was the last thing that was on my mind that weekend. To begin with I was scared of wild animals and by the end of the weekend, well, I just wanted to get out of here alive," Evangeline answered honestly.

Lacey sat beside Evangeline and gave her a hug. "I hope this weekend turns out far better this time. You can relax and have fun. We're just glad you were up to making it here so soon."

"I wouldn't have missed it for the world. I'm glad we came before it gets too cold. The colors are wonderful already. Back home, the trees are hardly turning yet," Evangeline answered.

"Well, yes, the elevation does make a significant difference here. I even notice that the trees haven't turned much yet down by Moulton. They're at least a week behind us," Lacey responded.

Bert added, "If you look further up the mountain, you'll see that some leaves are already dropping so even that extra elevation makes a difference. You picked the right weekend for the foliage, that's for sure."

Mac asked, "How's Jack doing? Is he around?"

Lacey responded, "Well, he'll be over shortly I believe. I'll call to let him know you've arrived. Sonya will be coming when she gets off work," Lacey said as she arose from the couch to get the phone. Bert handed it to her as she reached the telephone table. She took the phone and punched in Jack's number.

Bert added, "He's progressed well, all things considered. He was in rough shape at the start though. You know about that. At least they had the two of you in the same hospital. Did you get to see him very much, Gel?"

"Well, I was a little tied up initially. They had me stuck with tubes and wires for the first few days. That surgery knocked the stuffing out of me. But who needs a spleen anyway? People do without them all the time!" Evangeline said lightly with a sheepish grin.

Sarah nodded acknowledging Evangeline's attempt at humor. It was not lost on her how much Evangeline had been through in the past few weeks. She favored her sprained shoulder and the cane was another reminder that she was not yet ready to do any extensive physical activity.

Lacey disconnected the phone and reported, "Jack said he would be over when Sonya arrives. She gets off work at 2:30 then has to drive here. That should give us some time to visit," Lacey commented. "Sonya's been living here with me since her house was destroyed. I thought she might want to be closer to town and her job, but opted to stay up here. She said she wanted to be here to keep an eye on Jack once he got out of the hospital, but I think she just wanted to be with him. The two have been inseparable lately," Lacey chuckled.

Lacey and Bert offered them refreshments and they made themselves comfortable in the great-room. Bert had started a fire to take the chill off the room and they soon were catching up on each other's lives. Mac and Paul talked about work and the travels they had been doing. Paul had taken assignments closer to home for the first month, but had resumed travelling over the last two weeks, although for shorter durations. Mac, on the other hand, had been to Seattle, San Diego, Vancouver, BC and London, England since they were last together.

"Do you ever get tired of the travelling?" Lacey asked.

Mac answered, "Well, I could do without all the waiting in airports. That part I don't enjoy, I'll admit. I love the work that I do, although it can be stressful at times. It's great travelling to all those cities, but I don't see much of them while I'm there. I wish sometimes I could just do the *Star Trek* thing and say, 'beam me up, Scotty'. It would be a lot easier. The jet lag can be brutal at times, especially when I have to go into meetings the moment I arrive at my destination."

Sarah added proudly, "Mac's good at what he does. He's been getting contracts lately because those firms have recognized the quality of his work. It's hard on him though that he has to travel so much. We've been talking about our alternatives, but such is the nature of the work."

"Paul, I read your articles about the widespread effects the hurricane has had on the local economies. They were insightful, I thought. You mentioned features that many people wouldn't have considered. I suppose your experience up here had no bearing on your writing?" Bert commented.

Paul chuckled, "Nothing like a little inside information to change your perspective on a story. There's a big difference covering a story from the outside in, than from the inside out. I want to thank you for your permission to quote you. It added to the believability of the pieces."

"Always glad to oblige. I'm glad that someone finally told our side of the story about living in a rural area. Too often it's the big cities that get all the publicity and, consequently, the majority of the dollars for repairs after a situation like this. It's nice to finally have a voice," Bert replied.

Evangeline added, "I wouldn't be surprised if he were up for another award for that series. He sparked a lot of controversy and people are still talking about those articles. There've been many letters to the editor commenting on his viewpoint. Maybe there'll be some legislative changes to prepare for the next disaster."

"Well, there's no doubt that they're still in a mess over this one. The systems are still inadequate to evacuate people and administer aid amid the crisis. As we've watched over the last six weeks, they're still swamped in red tape for financial assistance. Temporary housing around Wilmington is inadequate. Although in some aspects it differs from what they encountered with Katrina, in other ways it seems they haven't learned a heck of a lot. It's the bureaucracy. It bogs down the system of implementation. Too many people are still without housing and even medical care in some regions," Paul reported.

Lacey remarked, "I heard that, as with Katrina, many effective strategies came from Christian ministries. They came in from all directions and administered direct aid to people, from the very first day. They often made the authorities at most levels look silly. While they were fighting about whose authority took precedence, churches from many states and larger ministries were supplying water, food and temporary shelters. As the storm caused such widespread destruction over so many states, so did the mobilization of ministries. I think I heard some surprising statistics about the number of churches involved in local and national aid."

"You're right. Sadly, it seems when government gets involved, bureaucracy abounds. What I witnessed in the worst hit areas was people helping people. It was awesome to see. You're right though, the most effective efforts often came from church based groups," Paul added. "It might take years for some of those areas to recover at the rate the government machine is working."

Bert shook his head and said, "It's unfortunate that it takes a crisis of this proportion to see the goodness in people. Don't get me wrong, secular groups did wonderful work, too, but the ones that seemed already prepared came from ministries. I'm glad that they had the apparatus in place before the events happened because they mobilized so quickly."

Paul responded, "Jack's sister, Laurie, was helpful when I got down to Wilmington to hook me up with sources for my articles. What you've said is consistent with what I found when I arrived. Even a month after the fact, it was still true. Civilian organizations were providing shelter and relocation services."

"I just wish people could do that for one another regularly and not wait for a disaster to mobilize. It's just unfortunate that you don't see that more often," Lacey commented, followed by nods of agreement.

Mac smiled and added, "Perhaps you could start something like that, Lacey. After all, you people already seem to have a good network established up here."

"Thanks for noticing, but it will take a humungous effort to mobilize the larger areas into operating like this. Villages and towns may be talked into it, but cities would require an effort of different proportions. Often people in cities depend on government agencies to provide for their needs, either that or they don't trust anyone. Paul, could you start a call for that in your articles. You probably know people who could mobilize the urban centers."

Paul paused and looked at Lacey for a moment. You could see the wheels turning in his head. "You've got me thinking about another idea for an article. You guys have a way of stimulating ideas. I don't know where it'll take me, but you never know. I hope you don't get me in trouble over this."

Bert cocked his head and asked, "So did your other comments get you in hot water?"

Paul answered, "Not hot water as such, but I did get warnings not to overstep my bounds from a couple of civic administrators. They reminded me that I could cause more trouble than help if I phrased things improperly. They didn't want any civil unrest in areas that had their infrastructure already compromised. Inciting mob mentality where policing was difficult would be detrimental and foolish."

Bert nodded, "Yes, I can see their point, but it isn't something you have to do immediately. You can spark the conversation over time. Keep it in people's memories long enough that it doesn't get forgotten until the next disaster. That's all I'm suggesting."

Paul countered, "I can only do that if my editor will allow me. He answers to the publisher who has connections up to the mayor's office and into the state building. If he catches any grief from those levels, you can be sure he'll stop any articles that are too controversial. These guys aren't comfortable with pressure that doesn't agree with their politics. I have to tread a fine line at times."

Bert frowned, "I have noticed a slant in articles in the newspapers at times. The old principle of balanced reporting, presenting both sides, doesn't always hold. It is a sad reflection on society."

Paul added, "Well, I know who's writing my paychecks. Don't quote me on this but I've seen what can happen to writers on staff who won't toe the line. They try to make it seem like it was the reporter's decision to look for a job elsewhere, but really, what would you do if you no longer got prime pieces to write? You'd get tired of writing obituaries after a while too."

Bert continued to frown as he said, "That's unfortunate because the words you write influence how people think. You have a role in determining the pulse beat of society. You can shape the perceptions of people, how they look at events and situations. Over time, that can change how people react to the circumstances in which they find themselves. I've seen newspaper, magazine and television reporting that can whip people into an emotional frenzy or calm them according to the words that were spoken. Unfortunately, it's been my experience that they either jack up emotions that require a cool head or calm them over issues that should cause a commotion. It isn't always responsible reporting that gets to print or to air."

Paul nodded, but said nothing. He paused to consider his words, when Lacey added, "I understand the predicament you're in Paul. You must feel like you're in a difficult position sometimes. Have you ever considered writing books instead of working for the newspaper?"

"Yes, then I'd only have one source of income. I've put some ideas together for a book already but I don't think that the paper would approve of everything I've written. I figure it's something I could get published when writing at the paper has run its course. Now that my column has been picked up for syndication and I have a broader readership, I might have a shot at it. I'll just have to pick my time, that's all."

"Well, your words are important, there's no doubt about it. You have respect in the industry, from what I have gathered. Choose your words carefully, because they can shape the future," Lacey stated.

Paul looked her way and responded, "You give me credit for more power than I have. How much power that has in the overall picture, well, I kind of doubt it rocks much ground here."

"You'd be surprised, Paul. Even my books have motivated some immovable people of this world. You may not have been exposed to my genre of writing, but I have stimulated some controversy among the Christian community, even from this backwoods mountain. At least, it has sparked discussions that have started a movement of change. Don't cut yourself short. Words move people," Lacey finished.

Paul nodded and added, "I read that novel you gave me. Your characters weren't conventional, I'll admit and you presented some interesting concepts. I just don't know how practical they are for living these days. There's so much going on with the changes in technology and the intensity of living. I'm not sure that the Bible is that relevant to current society when you come down to it."

Bert nodded at Lacey. She smiled and answered, "Paul, I've often heard that comment from those who haven't had much exposure to God's Word. On the contrary, I would have to say that the Bible is even more applicable to living today than ever. The more I delve into it, the more it has explained to me why things are happening in the world as they are. I feel more assured of God's Presence every time I open the Bible. There's nothing in this world today that is taking God by surprise. He Predicted it all and Told us about it. Did you read the suggested passages in the book?"

Paul nodded but said nothing. He looked away for a moment then added, "You might have a point about a few items. The erratic weather patterns have increased as well as earthquakes and armed conflicts, but we've always had wars and hurricanes."

"Yes, it isn't so much about them occurring; it is more about their frequency and intensity. Because I know that Jesus Knew beforehand that they would occur, it gives me Confidence that the other things He Spoke about are sure too. He gave me a pattern after which to live my life so I can have Confidence that if I Do those things about which He Spoke and He Himself Did, I can have the same Results. I've Done them, at least in my recent life, and it has been life altering."

Paul looked challenged and defensive. He asked, "How so?"

Lacey was enjoying the conversation now. She explained, "I take words seriously, very seriously; the words I listen to and see and the words I speak and write. They have power to influence my thinking and the thinking of others. I just try to keep them consistent with God's

Word and His Will for my life. He Spoke words of Wisdom and Power and if I line up with and speak those Words, I can have the Results contained in those Words. He said so Himself and He Did just that. He said that He only Spoke the Words He Heard His Father Speak. He Said we are to Do what He Did, so my goal is to speak Words like His. He also Said that we can Do What He Did and more. It's an exciting principle to live out."

Paul reflected on her words before answering, "But is it possible? You must get angry like the rest of us, say things you regret."

Lacey laughed, "Oh, yeah, too often, but less than before. When we Believe in Jesus as Lord and Savior, He provided us an out. He Said that if we mess up, we can come to Him, Confess, Repent, be willing to Change and He Gives us Forgiveness and Cleansing to start over. Then it's up to us to remember His Words the next time and let them Guide us into speaking and doing it Right."

Lacey continued, "I've fallen many times over the years, believe me. I've done a lot of Repenting then accepting His Forgiveness. The trick is not carrying the baggage from the mistakes into the future. He's forgotten it so I should not stay chained to it. The only thing those memories need to do is remind me what words I want to stay away from in the future. I also need to remember His Words about me instead of the condemnation the world would want to put on me."

"Yeah, but people don't easily forgive and they like to remind you that one false move will cause you to lose your job or reputation. That's the reality of life. You make it sound so easy. It isn't that realistic, is it?" Paul argued.

Lacey looked down at the coffee table for a moment, carefully choosing her words. "That's why I start my day with the Words of God in my Heart. I remind myself of His Words before I go out into the fray. I put those Words on like a garment that protects me from the insults of this world. I coat those Words inside my heart so they buffer the words of people who don't always understand the circumstances. I know that God Understands and He Knows where I'm at. When I Ask Him, He gives me the Words I need for that day and I put them on like a suit before I go into the world. It's how I've learned to live and it works."

"It sounds like a lot of work to me. Who has time to do all that? You just have to take life as it comes," Mac jumped into the conversation.

Bert decided to add his comments, "It doesn't have to take much time, just consistency. You do it daily. Start by rising ten minutes earlier to read God's Words and after a while you'll look forward to the Insights that come during that study, realizing how it has helped you the previous day. Before you know it, you give it a half hour and feel naked if you go out without it. It becomes a way of life. I've saved myself time by the Information I have gleaned through my conversations with God. He has a way of giving back time that you give to Him."

Paul looked skeptical but Evangeline nodded her head. Agreeing she said, "I've started to do just that. Sarah and I have met with that church group you suggested we contact. They've taught us some thought-provoking things I had no idea about before. While recuperating, I've had time to think about it. With the resources they've given me, I've learned so much! I've begun to look at things differently. It's so practical. I know I'm just a baby in all this, but I've tried it on small stuff and it works. It kept me positive when life seemed overwhelming and I felt so helpless after the surgeries; especially, when Paul started to travel again and I was alone to do things for myself."

Paul looked over at Evangeline and raised his eyebrows, "So that's why you let me go? I thought it was a little odd you didn't object to my leaving."

Evangeline smiled and nodded, "I guess I've Changed a little. I haven't been so intimidated by things lately. I know that I've just begun in this, and yes, I've had my ups and downs. But considering how challenging life has been lately, I've survived better than I first thought I might."

Sarah leaned over the coffee table to pat Evangeline on the leg, "Gelly, you have Changed and it's great to see the Transformation. I know it's been good for me, too, especially with Mac being away so much on business. I feel more secure and at peace. I don't feel so alone, I guess."

Paul leaned back and held up his hands, "Okay, I give up. I'm outnumbered. So it works for you and that's great. I've still got to think about it. Give me time."

Sarah and Evangeline looked at each other and giggled. Sarah added, "Sure, just try to keep up, will you?"

"No guarantees. I've got a lot going on. I'll get to it when I can," Paul grunted.

Chapter 39

Jack heard Sonya pull into the parking area and he looked out the window. He watched as she opened the vehicle's door, gathering her backpack with her as she got out. He smiled, inwardly happy that she had arrived. As she stepped down from her tan SUV, she glanced at Paul's vehicle and hesitated. She looked as though she was considering whether to go directly to Lacey's to say hello to the guests or to drop into Jack's place first. In no more than a moment she turned down Jack's path and he walked to the front door to greet her.

Jack opened the door before she had a chance to climb the steps. "Jack, you startled me. I didn't realize that you saw me coming," Sonya exclaimed.

The day's growth of beard on Jack's face was broken by his rugged smile, disarming Sonya to the core. Jack responded, "Sorry, I was just waiting till you got here to go to Lacey's. I'm glad you stopped in here first though. We can go over there together."

"Well, I'll go in with you but I need to get changed and showered before I can be sociable. I am such a mess with all this mud," Sonya responded.

Jack smiled and responded, "Didn't even notice it on you, Countryman."

"What are you trying to say, that I'm always this dirty coming to see you or you'll take me as I come?" Sonya asked feigning offense.

"No, just looking at you. I'm used to the mess," Jack teased.

Sonya mocked a hurt look at him, "You try staying clean in the mud on Harrow's Road. We went to a rollover near Chaney's and it was one job to extricate the passengers. You'd think people would slow their driving given the road conditions. They've done a lot to improve the roads but they sure aren't that good yet."

Jack reached over and rubbed a streak of dirt from Sonya's chin and said, "I suppose it keeps you in a job though. People will be people. They do dumb stuff."

"Judging from what I encountered this week, I should never be out of a job. With the lost hunters on Wednesday and this accident, there's been no shortage of stupidity. It just makes me look forward to coming to see you at the end of the day," Sonya answered and gave him a kiss. "Oh, I better be careful or I'll get you dirty too."

Jack looked at her then held her a little longer and returned the kiss. As he released her, Sonya smiled at him and said, "Well, that was nice. Miss me?"

"Yeah, you could say so," Jack replied.

Sonya smiled back and added, "I'm glad. You know we should probably go to Lacey's now. After all, you promised to visit with everyone, didn't you?"

Jack cocked his head and said, "Yes, but you might have to help the invalid over there."

Sonya looked around and answered, "I don't see any invalid around here. He must have left. I just see you. No more wires, no more cast. The ribs are mostly healed. I'd say the sympathy ploy won't work much longer!"

Jack pretended to stoop and hobble as he shut the door behind them and they started down the steps to go to Lacey's place. Sonya playfully gave him a light shove in disapproval. She shouted, "Enough, already!"

They were still laughing when they arrived at Lacey's house and Sonya opened the door. Everyone turned to see what all the joviality was about as they almost tumbled through the door.

Lacey started toward the entryway at the commotion, saying, "Well, that was quite an entrance! Welcome, I think."

Sonya and Jack straightened themselves and looked sheepishly at the gathering in the great-room as they quickly started to remove their boots. Paul and Mac headed to the foyer to shake hands with Jack and Sonya while Sarah waited with Evangeline on the couch.

Lacey went into the kitchen as the greetings were taking place and returned with a pot of coffee and mugs. Bert helped her make room on the coffee table as she returned to the kitchen to get plates and a coffee cake that had been cooling on the counter.

Sarah's eyes brightened as she saw the cake. "So that's the aroma I smelled when we came in! I thought we would have to wait till dinner to have some."

Sonya remarked, "I hope you don't mind but I want to shower and change before I come to join you. Save me some cake though, will you?"

Jack quipped, "Not a chance Countryman. You know how it is with us hungry men. First come, first served."

Sonya called down the hall as she headed for the guest room, "Don't even try it, Jack Davidson!"

Everyone laughed and Lacey gave Jack's hand a playful slap as he reached for the cake. Sarah gave Lacey an approving look as she saw how comfortable Jack and Sonya had become with each other. Lacey nodded back. They knew what the other was thinking.

By the time Sonya emerged from her bedroom, there was a hum of conversation about the changed appearance in the area with the fall colors.

"The lake looks so different with the reflection of orange, red and yellow," Lacey described. She looked over at Sonya as she entered the room, having transformed from her grimy uniform into casual snug fitting jeans and blue sweater. Her hair swung freely around her shoulders, a sharp contrast to the tightly bound ponytail she wore to work. Lacey commented, "Speaking of changes, don't you look nice."

Sonya smiled in reply and glanced at Jack to see if he approved. He smiled and reached for her hand as she approached. The chemistry between them was obvious and Evangeline could not wait to comment, "Looks like you guys are a couple now!"

Sonya grinned broadly and Jack smirked in response. Sonya answered for the two, "It's amazing what a disaster will do for a relationship."

Sarah laughed and said, "I suppose you saw Jack at his worst recently. Was he a good patient?"

Sonya threw her head back and said broadly, "Whoa, no way. He was just awful. Do you know what it's like to be around a man who can't eat solid food? I have never seen anyone use sign language to complain so much! Considering how active he usually is, nursing a broken ankle and ribs on top of a broken jaw was the test to any new relationship. I must either be nuts to be still here or maybe there's something to love about the guy. Maybe I just felt sorry for him. What do you think?" she added as she looked at Jack.

"Must be the sympathy I needed. She stuck by me no matter what I threw at her. Nah, she just must be crazy. Well, maybe crazy about me," Jack joked.

"Oh! Such arrogance! Maybe I should just leave now that you're on your feet, Davidson!" Sonya laughed. She moved away from him as if to leave, but he pulled her back and she landed in his lap. He pretended to wince in pain as she tried to straighten.

"Ooh, I am still injured. You can't go yet," Jack moaned.

Everyone laughed at the scene, but obviously love had blossomed on the shores of Big Rock Lake.

Mac took a sip of coffee and asked, "So Jack, all joking aside. Are you going to be able to resume your courses soon or will you wait till spring now?"

"Oh, I already have my first group coming next weekend. I'll start with something easy though, just to see how it goes. You know, something like a navigation course," Jack added as he rolled his eyes.

Mac responded, "Oh, yeah, like your last one was so easy!" And everyone laughed.

Sonya leaned to him and added, "Why didn't you tell me you had one booked already? What if you're not ready yet?"

Jack shook his head, "I've had way too much fun sitting on my butt for the last six weeks. It's time to make some money and stop sponging off Lacey's generosity. She's been nice not to charge me rent since I've been injured, but now's the time to get back to work. It'll be a piece of cake."

Sonya gave him a look that could kill but realized she had no way to stop him either. "Well, I could help you if you need me."

"It might be a good idea. I was thinking of taking on a partner some time anyway. I'll have to think about it . . ." Jack responded.

Evangeline laughed and asked, "Partnership, what kind of partnership?" She was trying to get more information about the seriousness of their relationship.

Paul nudged her and whispered, "Don't be nosy."

Jack smiled and added, "No telling what might come of this. We'll have to see how she handles the customers!" Jack was leaving everyone guessing, including Sonya. Sonya gave him a quizzical look, but he did not elaborate any further.

Lacey leaned into Bert's ear and whispered a question and he nodded back at her. Lacey cleared her throat and started to say, "Well, speaking of partnerships, Bert and I have an announcement to make."

Everyone looked over at the pair. Lacey smiled warmly as she took Bert's hand. "Bert has asked me to marry him. I am sorry to say that . . ."

Eyes widened as it sounded as though she had turned him down. An involuntary gasp came from Evangeline as she anticipated what she might hear.

". . . I made him wait a few days while I asked the Lord for His full Blessing. I told him 'yes' today."

Evangeline and Sarah whooped in delight as everyone gathered to give both Lacey and Bert hugs and handshakes.

"I knew it. You two seemed right for each other while we were here!" Sarah said. "When will it be?"

"Oh, well, we haven't made any plans yet, but I guess it could be soon. I don't want anything big or fancy, just close friends; people who mean something to us, like you folks," Lacey answered as she looked at Bert for his consent.

Bert nodded his agreement. "We have to call our pastor to officiate as I can't do our ceremony. I may be a pastor but I'd rather just be the groom on that day!"

Lacey put up her hands. "Okay, folks, enough frivolity. Who's going to help me in the kitchen with dinner?"

The afternoon drew into evening and soon the dinner was over, leaving groaning bodies on the couch.

"Lacey, if you keep feeding us like that, we may never leave here," Mac commented as he loosened his belt a notch. "Bert, you'd better look out. You'll need to buy a treadmill to stay in shape eating such good cooking."

"Oh, don't worry about me. Lacey is so active; she'll have me walking the mountain trails, skiing in winter and travelling the countryside with her book tours. I won't have time to sit still for long. We're planning to travel to the West Coast to visit friends. I'm going online this evening to check flights."

Sarah asked, "An early honeymoon perhaps?"

"Well, not unless I can arrange the wedding this weekend!" Bert answered.

"I would almost go for that and have a party later to celebrate," Lacey commented. "The planning for weddings can get so out of hand."

Sarah nodded and looked at Mac while she said, "Tell me about it. My mother went nuts over our wedding plans. I love her dearly but the wedding almost ruined our relationship. She was so manipulated by our relatives that we almost came to blows over it. I wanted a small, simple wedding and she started to push us to arrange something suitable for some celebrity. I had a complete meltdown before she listened to reason."

Lacey asked, "How big did it get?"

Sarah answered, "Oh, I pared it to a hundred people from the four hundred relatives and business associates she wanted to invite. I insisted on having the wedding where Mac and I were living at the time, not back home, so it effectively excluded all the casual acquaintances from the guest list. Fortunately we're still speaking after that fiasco." At that, Mac grimaced as he recalled the events.

Lacey nodded at Bert and added, "See that was one of my reservations. You proved my point exactly. I love you Bert Lawson but a large unmanageable affair is out of the question. I just want close friends to celebrate with us."

Bert held up his hands and said, "Enough. I've heard enough. I'm sure we can arrange that, no problem. I'll just let you handle all the calls from the neighbors for the next five years, if they still want to speak to us!"

Lacey sighed and realized she was in a no-win situation about this. She was thinking it would be easier to elope.

Chapter 40

Saturday dawned with promise of blue skies. Although warm for October, a morning dampness from an overnight fog still hovered in the atmosphere and draped itself over the landscape. The group had retired early because Mac and Sarah, Paul and Evangeline were tired from their trip up to the lake. Lacey was up early and stood in the kitchen looking over the misty, still waters below the house. She sipped her coffee as she pondered the muted reflection of the multicolored trees in the waters beyond the dock, their brilliant hues softened by the lingering haze.

Lacey turned as she heard tentative footsteps coming down the hallway, Evangeline was attempting a soft tiptoe gait with her cane. She spotted Lacey when she neared the kitchen.

"Oh, I thought that I might the first up. Well, I should've known from the smell of the coffee that I wasn't," Evangeline whispered.

"Don't worry, I am usually up early anyway," Lacey replied. "Come look at the view. It's marvelous."

Evangeline came up beside her and looked out the kitchen window. "Now that's something you don't see in the city! You're so fortunate to live here."

"You'd like to live in the country? I thought that you didn't like all the animals here," Lacey observed.

"Oh, the view I like. The animals I'd have to get used to. I supposed they wouldn't be bad if I knew how they might behave. It's more the fear of the unknown that spooks me," Evangeline replied.

Lacey paused a moment and said, "Yes, fear can do that." She then turned from the window to look at her, asking, "Have you got your jacket handy? We could go out on the veranda to sit for a while. I enjoy this part of the day so much. Each day opens with such promise. Everything is new and reenergized in the morning. It's a fresh start no matter what has gone on the day before."

Evangeline quickly fixed herself a cup of coffee and put on her blue tweed blazer. She walked carefully out the door and followed Lacey around the wrap-around veranda to the back of the house. The air was damp, but still comfortably warm for an autumn day. Evangeline breathed the clean air and sighed, "Everything seems so unspoiled here. It's such a sharp contrast with the city. Even in a park, there's always background noise. The only things you hear by the lake are birds and squirrels. It must be so easy to unwind here."

"Yes it is conducive to relaxation most times. It's a good environment in which to write I'll admit. But, as you saw a few weeks ago, it has times of stress like anywhere," Lacey replied.

"Yes, but when it is calm, it's really calm, isn't it. The city always maintains a tempo. It never idles," Evangeline observed.

"Do you regret living there?" Lacey asked.

"I never gave it much thought. It's just where Paul and I settled; mostly because we work there so it's a natural place to be. I don't like the traffic and the smog. It's just where we live now. If our lives were different, we could move; maybe in a few years."

"You haven't always been there though. Sarah said something about a time when you were living on the West Coast," Lacey probed a little more.

Evangeline's face clouded as the memories flooded in from that period of her life. She looked away as she said, "Yes. I spent time in Los Angeles."

Lacey asked softly, "It wasn't a good time in your life?"

Evangeline paused and did not say anything. She felt exposed in front of Lacey. She feared what Lacey would think of her if she knew the details of that part of her life. Tears welled in her eyes, threatening to escape.

Lacey turned to her and said, "You know, we've all made mistakes in our lives. We can learn from them and let them go. If we have Repented to The Lord, He Forgives them all, completely."

Evangeline looked down at the stained cedar boards and said, "You have no idea the things I did. It isn't that easy to erase." She turned away from Lacey, visibly uncomfortable with the path this conversation was taking.

Lacey moved closer to her and turned Evangeline to face her. "When I said that He would Forgive everything, I meant anything. His Forgiveness isn't like mankind's forgiveness, like His Love isn't like ours. There's nothing He cannot Forgive if you honestly hand it to Him."

Evangeline looked away, avoiding Lacey's penetrating gaze. She pulled herself away from Lacey, then took a few steps and stopped. She looked over the crisp colors of the autumn leaves but only saw the murky grays of darkened memories, bringing with them unbearable emotions. She looked out of unseeing eyes, consumed by images grotesque in their recollection and began to sob openly. "You have no idea what I did. If you only knew what happened, you wouldn't say that. I . . . I was such an evil person back then. I allowed myself to . . ."

Lacey followed Evangeline and pulled her into a hug. Evangeline stood there, arms stiffly by her sides, unable to receive the affection, but wept in deep heart wrenching gasps. Tears streamed down her cheeks. Lacey allowed her to empty her deep inner anguish, patiently waiting for the pain to subside. As Evangeline allowed the emotions to tumble forth, she slowly nodded her head into Lacey's shoulder and accepted her embrace.

"I don't know why I'm doing this to you," Evangeline said between sobs. "Every time I am around you I seem to lose it somehow."

Lacey patted Evangeline on the back and stroked her hair. "It's okay. Maybe you just need to let it out. You have to tell someone eventually; if not me, at least to God. He will Forgive you. I promise you that. Nothing is a surprise to Him and nothing will shock Him. He knows already, because He watched you do it."

Evangeline pulled away in anger, saying, "Then why didn't He stop me? Why did He let me ruin my life? I did things that . . ."

Lacey looked down at the grass below the deck and answered, "Because He gave you the right to choose, Gel. It was the risk He took with each of us. But He gave each of us the right to choose how we'll live our lives. We don't always make the decisions He planned for us. I'm an example of that."

"What do you mean? Look at your life here. You live in this idyllic setting, are about to marry a great guy. You write successful books.

What do mean you're a model of a messed up life?" Evangeline asked incredulously.

"I could ask you the same thing. Your life looks wonderful. You teach school to an amazing bunch of kids. You're married to a successful writer, who's very good looking. You yourself are a treat to look at; you could be a model. What could be wrong with your life?" Lacey countered.

Evangeline looked away from Lacey and took a few steps toward the stairs, tempted to run rather than pursue this conversation. Lacey waited for her to stop, knowing that she would. She sensed Evangeline desperately wanted to be open with her. Lacey spoke gently, "I did things in my younger days that were probably worse than you could imagine. I think I know where your pain is because I've lived it."

Evangeline turned to her, angry now. "Did you let yourself get used by people only to find they didn't care about you? Did you degrade yourself? Do you look at yourself in the mirror and wonder how you could ever have been such a fool?"

Lacey was crying now too. She paused and nodded. Evangeline looked at her unable to understand what she meant.

Evangeline finally said, "Nothing you have done could match my stupidity. I scratched an all time low when I was on the West Coast. I just don't know how I could have been so naïve."

Lacey answered so softly, Evangeline could hardly hear her say, "Not as low as I went, not that low. I spent five ugly years in California. I might just as well have prostituted myself. The end effect was no different."

Evangeline stood staring at Lacey, mouth agape. She couldn't believe her ears. "But you're in ministry now. You seem so far from that. What could you have done that was so bad and still be here living like this today?"

Lacey sat on the railing and hung her head. "I went to Los Angeles on the promise of great opportunities to work for a marketing firm." She paused, choosing her words as the memories barraged her brain. Evangeline stood staring at her, unconvinced.

"I was good at what I did. I had a lot of innovative ideas. I moved up the ranks quickly. My employers liked my work and I pulled in lucrative clients for them. Everything was going so well, for a time at least. Then they hired more talent, especially this one new guy, Jackson. He was a threat to me, a go-getter. He was determined to out-produce me for the firm. He liked the perks I had. You know: the car, the vacations, the big condo, and the opulent parties. The pressure to produce was enormous. The competition was outrageous . . ."

Evangeline nodded as she listened to Lacey speak words mirroring her life story. The details may be different but the essence was identical.

Lacey continued, lost in her mental images, "I worked unbelievable hours. I was exhausted all the time. I started drinking excessively at parties. I was desperate to lure new clients to the firm, to maintain my status as top producer. I had to devise new ideas, things that hadn't been done before. I drank too much then I needed energy so I popped pills to keep me awake into the night when there were deadlines. The more I produced, the more Jackson crept closer on my heels. He generated better layouts and more ideas. My bosses were disappointed with my results. I was desperate, willing to do anything to maintain the prestige of my position. And believe me; I did anything . . . everything . . ."

Evangeline stared at her, still not believing what she was hearing. She shook her head, not understanding that Lacey was not describing her experience.

Lacey finished quietly, "I slept with any guy who I thought could advance my position, erase my sorrows, or get me a fix. I wallowed in the trash of my own making, and all for what? I pretty much prostituted myself for money, prestige and notoriety. So how much worse could your situation have been than that?"

Evangeline stood still, hardly able to breathe. Gradually, sobs overtook her and tears streamed down her face to her tweed jacket. For a few minutes, neither woman moved, each choked with overwhelming, dark memories. Finally, spent of emotion, Evangeline limped to Lacey and hugged her. This time, Lacey stood arms limp at her sides. She was drained, laid open and exposed before Evangeline.

Evangeline finally caught her breath enough to say, "I can't believe that what you just told me was not my story. I went . . . to work for the publicity division of a publishing company and freelanced writing television scripts on the side, but I ended the same way you did. I . . . I couldn't tell anyone, not even Paul . . . the details of what happened there . . . I let myself be taken advantage of . . . in every way. I destroyed my self-worth . . . and for what?"

Lacey looked up now and turned toward the serene scene below them. The memories that flooded her brain were crashing into words that contradicted their essence. *I have Forgiven every one of those acts,*

Lacey. I already Forgave you. Do not torment yourself again with these memories. I tossed them in the sea of forgetfulness. Do not let the accuser bring them up again. I Love you now as I Loved you then; no more, no less. I Love you still. Don't turn from me. I Love you.

Conflicting emotions barraged Lacey's soul. Her heart was speaking Love, her mind was crashing into emotion. She fought to focus. Love was speaking His Words into her Heart again. Forgiveness. Cleansing. Purification. Redemption. She was reawakening to the Truth. Her head tilted slightly higher. She let those words warm her like the sunshine that was peeking through the trees now. Bathed in His Light now, she smiled through her tears and turned to face Evangeline.

"I asked myself those very questions. You have no idea how I asked them. It seemed so senseless and left me empty, barren, and useless, to myself and others. I was at the point of suicide. I was scared, so full of fear I hardly wanted to get out of my condo to go to work. Once at work, I dreaded going home. I didn't know what I would do next to hurt myself. I wanted to die, but wanted to live at the same time. I was so confused.

"Then one day I met a man. Well, actually, I ran head long into him. He almost scared the life right out of me. I was running for the elevator in my building when I careened into him as he was coming out. I fainted in his arms. I think I must have scared him as much as he terrified me. Anyway, when I came to, there was this big hulking man leaning over me. I was too frightened to run, but he was just standing there with this worried look on his face. Somehow I knew he wouldn't hurt me. I wouldn't let him call the paramedics so he helped me to my apartment. It could have been a foolish thing to do, but it turned out to be the best thing that ever happened to me."

Evangeline sat on the railing beside Lacey, listening intently. Lacey paused, gathering her thoughts; memories intertwined. She took a deep breath and faced Evangeline.

"That man changed my life. He was genuinely concerned for me. He literally picked me up and set me back on my feet. He stuck by me. He Loved me like no one had for a long, long time and didn't seem to care what I had done. He had Jesus in his life and just lived like it. I didn't know what to make of him; I didn't know how to trust anyone at that point in my life. But he Loved me; that much was soon clear. He was there for me.

"I didn't change immediately. You must realize I fell deeper and ran a little further, thinking I could make it on my own. But I ran smack into a brick wall of my own making. I had nothing left by then, no job, no money, no self-respect, nothing. I was empty and hit bottom. Only then was I was ready for an alternative. Anything was better than where I found myself. So I turned back to that man who supported me that night."

Evangeline looked into Lacey's eyes and asked, "Who was he? Who was that man?"

Lacey smiled and a Peace spread over her face that almost made her glow. "His name was Warren McCrae."

"Warren? The man who was your husband?" Evangeline asked incredulously.

"One and the same. He took me, as shamed and dirty as I thought I was; he took me as I was and accepted me as another stranger on the road to Jesus."

"He knew what you had done yet married you anyway?" Evangeline repeated the question.

The words stung Lacey to her core. They were the very words she had spoken to herself many, many times. Words. *They're just words, you know. Sticks and stones will break my bones but words will never hurt me. Hah! Yes, oh, yes they hurt. They sting and stick and maim and erode the soul. Yes, words count.* Lacey drew in her breath deeply and paused a little longer.

Lacey finally turned toward Evangeline, "I was lost, alone, so desperate, fear-filled and ashamed. I felt dented, bent, and unrecognizable, so far from what I was supposed to be . . . whatever that ever was . . . until I received a letter; a Love letter it was. I can recite to you ."

Evangeline sat still, stunned by Lacey's words. She waited as Lacey continued, "It said,

"Dear Lacey,

I Love you so much.

All I have ever done has been to find you and bring you to me.
I Love you so much, with all that I am.

My Love is so intense I would die for you. It hurts me to see you so sad, so ashamed, so filled with fear, so desperate. I Love you with all that I am. I would give you everything I have if you would turn to me and Love me back.

I would give you Love for self-hate, Purity for your shame. I would take your fear and share my Faith. I would Love you if you would let me. Will you . . . let me? Will you let me Love you, pour my Love on you and in you?

I want to be your hero, your life partner, your confidant, the one you smile at in the morning and say good night to at night. I want to be your 'all in all'. I Love you that much. I will; will you let me?

Will you?

I Love you, Lacey. I Love you with all that I am. Love me and I will Love you and give you all I have. I will hold nothing back and I will never, ever leave you. I Love you, Lacey. Can you Love me?"

"I will never forget those words," Lacey's voice trailed off into silence. She stood still, eyes open but focused inside with her memories.

Evangeline sat stared at Lacey, mouth agape. The silence hung heavily between them. Finally Evangeline spoke the thoughts swimming in her brain, "How beautiful." She hesitated before she spoke again, "But he died and he did leave you, Lacey, didn't he?"

Lacey responded softly, "Yes, he died but he never left me."

Evangeline furrowed her brow and asked, "I . . . I don't understand. He didn't leave you? He died, how could he not leave you? He's still in your memories?"

Lacey smiled softly, "Well, Gel, He didn't leave because Warren didn't write those words. Jesus did. God wrote that Love letter to me, using Warren's pen. He was just the messenger. He spoke God's Words of Love into my Heart. I now Know it was God Speaking through him into my spirit and soul."

Lacey paused then added, "He came and spoke those words into my life at the very moment I was at the end of myself, desperate and hurting beyond human endurance."

Evangeline just stared at Lacey, eyes disbelieving. Lacey added, "And yes, Jesus did die, but only so I could be Free. He was Raised from the dead and still Lives today. He Lives with me always. He's still with me every day."

Evangeline sighed deeply, confused, "I don't understand. That letter was from . . . Jesus . . . God?"

Lacey anticipated her question, "Yes, those are God's Words to me and He speaks those Love Letters to me daily, knowing how often the accuser wants to remind me of my past. It's my daily dose of Love and Forgiveness."

Evangeline cocked her head and frowned, "The accuser. You mean a person?"

"Well, Satan, he's a spirit being who hates God and everything that He stands for," Lacey answered. Evangeline looked at her narrowing her eyes as she tried to take in her words.

Lacey continued, "You know, that inner voice; the one that reminds you of your past? That nagging voice; that one that beats you up every time you try to do something and don't quite make the mark? That voice that brings those niggling fears, those second thoughts when you felt everything was finally going right? The one that reminds you that you're damaged, dented and beyond repair?"

Evangeline stood and stared at Lacey, her heart beginning to pound in her chest. *How does she know about that voice, those thoughts?* Her eyes darted around her, wondering who was feeding her this information. Finally, Evangeline turned away, looking for a place to bolt should she need to escape. Softly she answered, "How do you know?"

Lacey rose but stood still, tempted to take a step closer to Evangeline, but realizing how fragile and exposed she must feel, she merely said, "Because it's the same voice that abused me for years, that punished me and accused me, that would not let me go."

"You?" was Evangeline's response.

"Yes, me. I'm no different from anyone else. I was susceptible through circumstance, through bad choices. Because I thought I knew what I was doing, that I could do it so well . . . on my own. And I failed miserably. And when I tried to come back to where I started, I didn't know who I was anymore. I didn't recognize myself. I didn't even know where I'd started from any longer. I was so far from what God Created me to be, I figured there was no hope. And that nagging voice remained."

"That voice . . . keeps coming back. Why?" Evangeline whispered.

"Because I let him do it. I let that demonic voice continue on and on and on in my head, attacking my Heart and soul. I didn't know that I didn't have to take it. That there was a way out. I just didn't know."

"A way out? A way to stop it?" Evangeline asked incredulously.

"Yes, if you put your Trust in the right place, away from self and on the One Who Loves beyond all known love. His Desire is not like those we know here in this world. His Desire is only for Good. He died to Prove that to us. He made a Way available to us, if we will just come to Him like a child, Innocent and Trusting, He just asks us to come to Him willing to admit that what we have done so far just hasn't worked. That anytime we seem to experience joy, it has been so fleeting and transient, disappearing into an intangible mist and gone. When we realize that we can't do it by ourselves and want more than we can do for ourselves, then we're ready to meet Him, to Accept Him and What He offers."

Lacey stopped talking. Evangeline stood overlooking the placid lake, her mind racing, her heart beating in her ears. A blue jay cried in the pines above their heads, but she did not hear it. Lacey words tumbled through her head like the waters over the rocky stream by Jack's house. Memories flooded her eyes. Shame spilled over her, like a dark veil, threatening to engulf her.

Lacey whispered, "I listened to His Voice, His Words, not the accuser's. I Love you. I will never leave you, nor forsake you. I will Forgive every time you miss the mark, however foolish or shameful the decision. I am willing to Love you and Forgive you. Will you let me? Will you let Me have those memories? Will you Trust Me?"

Evangeline froze, all thoughts stopped. She recognized the Voice. Where had she heard it before? *That voice, so soft. Trust Me . . . Trust Me. In the cave. He said it, didn't He? Trust Me. And I did. But . . . can I again?* "I want to," was the only thing she managed to whisper in response.

Lacey whispered gently, "Then you can. Just tell Him so, that you know you've messed up and want a Better Way, His Way. That you want Him as Lord and Savior of your life and want to follow His Ways as He Teaches you. It's as simple as that. But it's your Choice and your Choice only. No one can do it for you. You decide in your own Heart."

Evangeline was stunned. She searched for words but could find none. She stood there shaking all over. She suddenly realized that she was facing a defining moment in her life. Here she was in the wilderness that had tried to take her life and she was facing the possibility of a New Life.

Her mind raced with memories and shame and desolation while

desperately wanting to grab the Hope that Lacey had offered her. Could she? Should she? It would take Ultimate Trust. Trust, that was big. *Why Trust her more than anyone else who's offered you freedom. Remember, you thought the drugs and alcohol would give you peace. What did it do for you? Nothing. Why should this either? Marriage didn't bring you freedom; it only gave you unrealistic expectations. Why this?*

Chapter 41

Paul awoke to find Evangeline gone from the room. He dressed quietly and wandered out into the kitchen, drawn by the aroma of the coffee. He was pouring himself a cup when he spotted Evangeline on the veranda with Lacey. He could see both had been crying. He watched with curiosity, but hesitated to go out and interrupt their conversation.

He had been concerned for Evangeline since she had been released from the hospital. Although she had handled things better than he had expected, she did have times when she withdrew from the world, becoming moody and despondent. He had put it down to the trauma of their first trip here, but wondered if there was more to it when she would not discuss it with him. He felt inadequate to handle it himself.

Paul hoped some 'woman talk' would ease Evangeline's stress but wondered what caused it and how Lacey might be trying to help. He remembered his discussions with Lacey and felt a little uncomfortable. She had a way of making him squirm in his insecurities. He still was trying to figure what made this woman tick and how she seemed to know what he was thinking.

He shook his head and took another gulp of coffee. He was about to turn away from the window when he saw Evangeline give Lacey a heartfelt hug. She was crying but seemed happy, nonetheless. *Maybe she's dealt with whatever was bugging her.* He moved into the great-room and set his coffee on the side table. *Could be I'll have the old Gel back now.*

A cool draft rushed from the top of Seeley's Mountain. A movement of unrest rustled the trees then shifted toward the ground, creeping down its slopes. The remnant of a storm unfinished was stirring toward the lake. It would not allow this opportunity to incite fear to slip by. The shame and guilt it carried would penetrate and take its stand against its foe again. It determined that it would release no prisoners on this mountain.

"Okay . . . I have to admit I can't do it by myself. I want Jesus to Help me . . . there's no question of that. I just . . . well, I don't see how He can just make all these memories stop . . . badgering me. I've accepted Him as Lord, so why doesn't it just go away?" Evangeline asked weakly.

Lacey paused, choosing her words carefully. A slight breeze feathered across her face. Evangeline shivered as the morning dampness penetrated her thin jacket. She looked toward the door to the house and said, "I'm getting cool, maybe we should go back in."

Lacey looked at her carefully and smiled. "Bear with me a moment. Give me your jacket."

Evangeline looked at Lacey as though she was crazy. "I'm getting cold out here. I don't think so."

Lacey continued to smile. "Trust me. You'll soon understand. Just give me your jacket. You're cold. It isn't taking care of you like you need it to anyway."

Evangeline looked at her blankly but slowly began to undo the buttons one by one. She shook her head as she started to remove the thin coat. Finally, she handed it to Lacey who had removed her long, oversized wool coat.

Lacey handed the long, red coat to Evangeline and said, "Here put this on. It should take care of you."

Evangeline accepted the coat and started to put it on, as she saw Lacey try her small jacket on for size. Evangeline was engulfed in the fabric of Lacey's garment. It had a furry lining that immediately brought warmth and comfort to her body. Lacey, on the other hand, looked ridiculous in Evangeline's puny garment.

Evangeline laughed when she looked at Lacey. *She's lost it now.* "What do you think you're doing? That'll never fit you. No offense, but it must be two sizes too small!"

Lacey continued to smile at Evangeline and answered, "Are you warm, comfortable now? Has it taken care of your problem?"

Don't listen to her. She could not deny how she felt. "Yes, but, Lacey, you can't possibly wear that jacket!"

"No, it doesn't take care of me any more than it did you, does it?" Lacey replied.

Don't listen to her. She's not all there. There's nothing that can change what you are. You are what you made yourself. Live with it. "Of course not," was Evangeline's slow reply.

"Well, think of your efforts to make things better like your jacket. They're inadequate, small and ineffective. You try to stop the thoughts and words from battering you with guilt and shame. You try to think other thoughts, but they keep coming back and back and back, don't they."

Evangeline furrowed her brow as she tried to follow Lacey's analogy. *Stop this nonsense. She's just trying to confuse you. Nothing can change what you've done.* She nodded her head. Despite the mounting confusion in her head, she recognized that Lacey was speaking from experience now. "Yes, they're always there, not far from the surface."

Lacey nodded slightly in encouragement. "So how did you feel when you wrapped my huge, long coat around you?"

Evangeline said nothing for a moment, contemplating her response. "Well, Warm. Not only was your coat big and cozy, but your body heat was still in the coat, like it was alive, still part of you as you gave it to me."

Now Lacey knew Evangeline was starting to follow her line of thinking. Encouraged, she continued, "Exactly. So this jacket of yours never was effective for you, as it won't be for me, right?"

Evangeline chuckled as she looked at Lacey in her jacket. It strained at the seams to contain Lacey's muscular torso. It only covered such a small portion of her body, it looked ludicrous. *She doesn't understand where you come from. You have your reasons for wearing it.* "Well, fashion isn't always practical. It's the way we dress in the city, in my world."

"In your world and 'the' world. It flows with what others think is best for you; ideas, fashions, fads of thinking and thus dressing. It's all about ways of thinking, isn't it?" Lacey asked.

What does she know about you, what you think? Evangeline fought to focus on what Lacey was saying. The voice in her head was getting annoying. Evangeline answered slowly, "Ye-e-s. I guess you could say that."

"Okay, stay with me for a moment. So the coat made you warm?"

Don't answer her, she trying o confuse you. Lacey watched as Evangeline struggled with her thoughts. Finally, she answered, "Yes, it made me feel . . . comforted, taken care of," Evangeline added.

"Well, think of this jacket of yours as all your efforts, by yourself . . . small, inadequate, even dirty, soiled."

Evangeline's smile evaporated suddenly when she realized what Lacey was getting at. She stared at her as Lacey continued, "I took that for you and gave you what I had that was far, far better to do the job."

Evangeline nodded agreement, still staring at Lacey but saying nothing. Lacey continued, "Let's say my coat is Jesus' Sacrifice, His Blood. Wearing this coat is like being washed in Jesus' Blood, wearing His Royal Robe. When people look at you, they see the Robe, not you, but Royalty. God sees Jesus when He sees you washed in The Blood. He sees you Forgiven, Pure, White and Cleansed. He doesn't see your messes and stains. He sees the Royal Robe and assumes you are as Clean as Jesus; Spotless, without blemish."

Evangeline nodded slowly, her thinking was catching up to Lacey's line of Reasoning. Images were flowing with Lacey's words now.

"I took your inadequate jacket, your efforts and put it on me, because I Love you and want the Best for you, so you can be completely cared for. I did it for Love and no other reason, because it does me no benefit other than Love."

Evangeline stood staring at Lacey; silently, as she focused on the ideas that came from Lacey's words.

Lacey spoke softly now, "You said that you felt the warmth of my body heat, like it was alive, part of me. Well, put on Jesus' Sacrifice, His Robe, His Words and you Have Part of Him around you and in you. He *is* Alive in you, keeping you warm, keeping you Safe, Protected, Cared for. He's in you, not just around you. He is part of you.

"The more you get to know Him through talking to Him in His Word, the more you can Trust Him to Do everything He Promised to Do for you. He said He would Forgive you and Cleanse you when you confessed those times you messed up. He Will. He Gave you His Robe to wear and took yours from you. He took your inadequate efforts to care for yourself. He took your sins and sicknesses and lack and whatever makes your life a mess and put it on Himself and took them all away. They're now gone. They're erased and neutralized by His Blood. He doesn't see them on you anymore, so don't take them back."

Nothing will make your sins, your stains go away. You did them. Jesus didn't do them. You did. "But I still did them. It doesn't change the facts. It did those things. I chose to do them!" Evangeline countered.

Lacey looked down by the lake and pointed to the mist rising above the water. "See the mist over the lake?"

Evangeline followed Lacey's outstretched hand and saw that the sun glinting off the mist now. Lacey continued, "What is the sun doing to it?"

"The warmth of the sun is evaporating the mist. It's disappearing," Evangeline answered.

Lacey nodded and added, "Like your sins, my dear. When you truly Confess your sins and your fears to God, His Love takes them and burns through those sins and fears. His Love makes them Disappear, as if they never, ever, happened: like that mist is now gone. You can go on Forgiven and Cleansed. He tossed them in the sea of forgetfulness. He doesn't remember them any longer. If you remember anything, remember His Words that Tell you about His Forgiveness, not the memory of what you did. It's been Taken Care of, like wearing this coat has taken care of you. It is Done, Finished in God's mind."

Evangeline stood there staring down at Lacey's long, flowing red coat wordlessly. It was all beginning to make so much sense.

The breeze rippled across the lake now, noticeably stronger now. At the same moment, the sun erupted from behind the mountain, displaying brilliant autumn colors that had been hidden by the misty twilight. The waters below now moved in rhythm with the wind, but they still reflected the dazzling hues through every wave.

As the rays of sunshine broke through the trees and warmed the earth, the mist disappeared. Gone was the uncertainty in which the fog draped the mountain. Every crevice soaked up the early morning warmth, renewing itself for another day. All traces of darkness disappeared.

It was a day renewed.

Evangeline leaned on the railing as they overlooked the lake. The sun seemed brighter now, her Heart lighter. Lacey removed Evangeline's jacket as she said, "Oh, that sun feels marvelous. It's so warm for this time of the year. I love it!"

Evangeline agreed and looked down at Lacey's coat. The words about what this coat represented warmed her even further. She knew that they would stay with her for a long, long time. She wanted to remember this feeling in the future, when those voices tried to return. Now she was content to revel in the newfound Glow that surrounded her.

The two women stood wordlessly taking in the warm morning sunshine as the leaves danced about in the breeze. It promised to be a grand new day.

Chapter 42

Mac joined Paul in the great-room. They were talking sports, debating whose favorite teams would do better as the baseball season moved toward the World Series. Paul and Mac turned as Sarah came down the hall looking bright and cheery. She had showered and was dressed in jeans and blue sweater, complimenting her brown hair.

"You look refreshed this morning," was Mac's comment as she entered the great-room where they were now having coffee.

The outside door closed with a thud behind them as Lacey and Evangeline came into the house followed by Bert, who had just arrived. Sonya came out of her room after hearing all the commotion. She was still wearing her pajamas and was looking sleepy.

"Well, it looks like everyone is up already," Bert said as he took off his jacket. "Are you ready for some good news?"

Lacey looked over in his direction from the kitchen, where she had started to make another pot of coffee. "Good news this early in the morning? You've been up with birds I gather."

Bert smiled back at her and replied, "Well, I did some of it last night before going to bed and some this morning. I booked us plane tickets to Seattle for Tuesday morning, then we can drive to see our friends from there. They're a good price so I grabbed the seats while they were still available."

"That's good. No grass grows under your feet Mr. Lawson, that's obvious. I'd guess then you won't be the procrastinator of our new family," Lacey observed.

"I emailed Marty to see if he could officiate at our wedding. Before I finished on the computer, he had emailed me back. He must have been up early this morning too. And . . ." Bert paused for emphasis, "He said he'd be pleased to do it and . . ." Again Bert stopped until he had everyone's attention, "he'll be available on short notice if we want to elope as you said, Lacey!"

Lacey smiled and shook her head. "You actually asked him that?"

"Of course, if it pleases you to escape a big wedding and have a party later, then so be it," Bert replied.

Lacey smirked at him, astounded that he had worked on it so quickly. "I'm impressed. So, who's invited to the wedding, other than you and me?"

Bert stood, saying nothing for a minute before he answered, "Well, maybe you'd like to plan that part with me. I only sent out an e-mail, after all. I didn't think about the details yet." Everyone laughed at his response. Evidently, he was eager to have Lacey as his bride.

Lacey walked to where he was standing at the threshold of the great-room and gave him a kiss on the cheek. "I appreciate your efforts. It just surprised me that you were so prompt. We can plan the details while we're away on our trip. It's a long flight so we should have lots of time to talk about it."

He put his arm around her waist and kissed her back and replied, "Sounds good to me."

Lacey turned to the assembled group and asked, "So who'd like bacon and eggs for breakfast?"

Evangeline excused herself to shower and change once breakfast was over and the dishes were done. Paul watched her walk down the hall. She had been quiet during the meal preparations and while eating. He was wondering what had transpired with Lacey earlier, so he followed her into their guest room.

"You have a nice conversation with Lacey this morning?" he asked as she gathered her toiletries for her shower.

Evangeline paused what she was doing and thought about her words before answering. "Yes, it was good. It was nice to have another view of some of my questions and thoughts about what happened the last time we were here. Lacey has a good ear to listen."

"You both seemed upset. Was there a problem?" Paul asked. He sounded like the reporter now.

Evangeline realized that she was not ready to share the details of her conversation with Paul yet. She hardly had time to digest it herself much less tell Paul what it was about. "No, no problem, we just touched on some emotional stuff. You know how we girls can get. Lacey helped me see things from another perspective. She also told me a little about her first husband, Warren. She seemed to love him a lot. I know she loves Bert, but there was also something special she had with Warren, I think. It's sad that he died."

Paul nodded and seemed satisfied with her response. "I just didn't want you upset by this trip up here. I'm sorry if it has been hard on you."

Evangeline stopped what she was doing and slowly turned toward Paul. It was not like him to be so considerate of her feelings. It felt odd to hear. "Thank you. What sparked that? It's unlike you to say something like that."

Paul was standing by the bed looking at the floor, but glanced up at her briefly, then away again. He said awkwardly, "Well, you obviously were upset when you were talking to Lacey, so I figured something had to have happened. Maybe it wasn't such a good idea to come up here so soon. It was pretty traumatic for you."

Evangeline walked to where Paul was standing and sat on the bed. "No, I think it was a good thing we came. I needed to work through a few of my emotions. Being back here, talking to Lacey, has been a good thing. She helped me. Crying can be good; it's not always bad. Sometimes you have to let it go and crying helps."

Paul wandered to the other side of the room and turned to look out the window. He added, "That's good. I'm glad for you . . . Look, I'm sorry if I haven't been as supportive as you needed me to be during your recovery. With work and all, I guess, I could have been there for you more . . . or . . ." Paul was groping to understand what might have sparked her earlier emotional episode.

Evangeline set her toiletries on the bed, rose and walked to the window with him. "If I'm honest, I probably was a little distant with you too. I had a lot of pain and pent up feelings to deal with. I admit it was difficult, but I guess I might not have been the easiest one to be around sometimes. It's good to get back up here. It's like picking up and staring over where we left off, before all this nonsense happened. Only maybe it can be better than before." Evangeline took Paul's hand in hers and added, "Being up here on this mountain seemed to have given me a clearer perspective on what happened. Lacey has a way with words."

"You used to say that about me," Paul replied.

"Yes, but she's a woman. Thankfully, you're not. I love you for who you are, but sometimes a woman can speak to another woman so she hears differently; in ways a man can't," Evangeline added. "I love your way with words, too. You are gifted in what you do."

Paul looked over at her and smiled. It had been a while since she had said that to him and it felt good. "Thanks. Maybe I'll write something just for you. You used to like that, didn't you?"

Evangeline drew her breath, realizing how long it had been since he had done so. She bit her lip and answered, "Yes, I did. I liked it a lot. I guess life has moved so fast lately, we've kind of forgotten those little things. I used to write you things too, as I recall."

Paul smiled and tilted her chin toward him. He lightly kissed her lips. "I can do that for you again."

Evangeline tilted her head to lean on his chest and embraced him. "I guess seeing Bert so excited about marrying Lacey, it makes you think, doesn't it? I'd like that spark back in our lives too."

Paul was quiet but returned the hug. He finally added, "Yes, I would like that too."

Shortly after breakfast Sonya left with Jack to go into town. As they returned, they were in an especially jovial mood, laughing and teasing each other as they entered Lacey's house. Sarah and Evangeline exchanged glances as they watched the two interact so well together. They were romantics at heart and wanted to see them with an announcement of their own soon.

Jack and Sonya smiled at the two women as they realized they were being watched. Sonya wandered into the kitchen to grab a cup of coffee and started chatting quietly to the women, while Jack moved into the great-room where the television was on the sports network.

The men were soon discussing football, touting their favorite teams and players. The women finally had enough of the conversation and told them they wanted to get outside and get some fresh air.

"With this nice weather, we can't be stuck in front of the television watching sports. Let's move outdoors. At least, let's go outside on the veranda!" Sarah exclaimed.

It was soon decided that Sonya and Jack wanted to hike up the mountain. Sonya spoke with a professional tone, "Jack, if you think you can run a course next weekend, then you had better test your ankle while you have me around to watch you. If it swells like a pumpkin, you might have to change your mind."

"No problem that a little ice pack won't fix," was Jack's retort.

Lacey and Bert walked out of the library in time to hear his disclaimer and Lacey gave Jack one of her 'looks', which stopped his bravado quickly. "Just stay out of the river this time! Okay?" was her response.

Jack gave Lacey a pained expression and shook his head in disgust. He then turned to Sonya and gave her the grin that melted her resolve every time. He could get away with anything when he did that with her. "Okay, so you try hiking today and we'll see what happens," she finally conceded.

Before long, Mac and Sarah decided to accompany them. Paul reluctantly left Evangeline behind with Lacey and Bert, as she realized the trek up the mountain would be out of the question for her. She encouraged him to go as she knew he wanted to get out and get some exercise.

They left with a parting command from Evangeline, "Now don't fall in any holes on that mountain, you hear?" They laughed as they set out down the road.

Bert retreated into Lacey's library to use her computer to check his emails, leaving Lacey and Evangeline to themselves. They wandered down to the dock to enjoy the sunshine.

Evangeline was eager to ask Lacey more questions, "You said earlier that you learned that you didn't have to listen to those awful voices. How did that all come about for you?"

Lacey responded with a smile, "Warren was a special man, gifted in teaching the Love Letters of God, as I call the Bible, The Word of God. He helped me see that God had given me Authority to Listen to and Obey His Word, His Voice; that I could Speak His Words, like He spoke them with Faith. In doing so, if I truly Believe God's Words when I Speak them, that accusing demon will flee from me. His Love is His Word because that is Who He is; He is Love, and that Love Banishes those demon voices.

"It took time, diligence in studying His Word enough that it became Real to me in my heart. And one day, I realized that when I spoke that Word, those thoughts became less frequent and finally stopped. I'm not saying they never came back; after all, Satan tries repeatedly to take you where he had you before. But each time it happened, I spoke God's Words back to him. I didn't debate the guilt and the shame. I just spoke God's Word from my heart and that little demon fled each time."

"Those thoughts, do you still think them?" Evangeline asked.

Lacey paused and looked down at her hands, "I wish I could tell you that those thoughts never come back. And I will indeed admit that it's been a while since they've come. They stirred up again during the week-end of the storm. It was probably a ploy to batter down my resolve to Pray; to make me feel unworthy to Speak God's Word. Then, today, when you spoke about your situation, well, there they were again. Funny how you think you have it all licked then it comes along and broadsides you."

"Oh, I'm so sorry I brought it up for you," Evangeline apologized.

"Nonsense, it only proves to me the Power of the Spoken Word of God. No matter the situation, it works every time if you Believe it when you Speak It. His Love banishes Satan from the premises every time . . . however that demon brings it up. Just remember learning to walk in it is a process over time. With good teachers and other mature Christians to hold you accountable, you'll improve in it. Just stick with it. You took the first step today when you brought your past into the Light; don't stop, ever."

Evangeline laughed lightly, "And here I thought I might have a quick fix to my problems. How many years has it been for you?"

Lacey stopped and thought for a moment and said, "It must be twenty-five years now and I still work at it daily. I'm in The Word and talk to my Father consistently about things I need to stay current in. He Leads me, Guides me and is completely Faithful to His Words, His Promises."

Evangeline hesitated before she asked the next question, "Even when Warren died?"

Lacey drew in her breath a moment and Evangeline almost regretted asking, but Lacey continued, "Yes, even when Warren died. Jesus never let me down for one moment."

"But Warren died. It was an accident, wasn't it?" Evangeline pressed.

"Well, an accident, of sorts. You know, in some ways, there are no accidents. To some degree there's often poor decision making involved. I learned that from experience. Most times, if you know all the details, you find that someone in the situation wasn't listening to Instructions, Warnings. Often, there are several people involved who've dropped the ball," Lacey answered.

"How so?" Evangeline furrowed her brow as she asked.

"Warren went out on a fishing trip with friends. He had planned it for some time and looked forward to it. He was getting together with some old school chums, a reunion of sorts."

"Sounds like something my uncle used to do," Evangeline commented.

"Yes, it wasn't that unusual for him either. It was just a fishing trip. He left on Friday to go to Marlow Lake. He met the guys there. They had a good afternoon of fishing that day and he called me the next morning before they headed out again. The forecast was for intermittent storms, you know the kind that happen with humidity. I warned him to be careful, that I didn't want him out on the water in bad weather. He assured me that they knew what they were doing, that they had been fishing since they were all kids."

"Well, the weather started beautifully; you know, sunshine and hot, although a little humid. As the day wore on I had an uneasy feeling about things, foreboding. I called the fishing camp, but the caretaker said that the men had already had lunch and were back out on the lake. He had warned them about the uncertain weather but they had chosen to go out anyway, promising to head to shore at the first sign of a storm."

Lacey stopped for a moment, gathering her thoughts. Evangeline prompted her, "Did they get caught in a storm?"

"Well, the weather started to get iffy, so they headed back to the fishing camp. They did what seemed prudent. Because they wanted to be back home for Sunday morning church, they packed and left early trying to beat the bad weather back into town. He called me and told me that they were headed home and I was relieved."

"You had sensed something was going to happen?"

"Yes, but my 'radar' wasn't accurate, I guess. Because, I thought it was all about them being out on the lake during a storm, and I was so wrong. Once they started home I just let my guard down, you know, figuring it was all okay. But it wasn't over. Coming home seemed like the smart thing to do. So I didn't continue to Pray and Listen to God."

"So what did happen?" Evangeline leaned in to listen, curious.

"Warren was travelling alone in his car and was maybe ten miles from home. He came to an intersection with a traffic light. He had the green and advanced through. I guess he didn't see the other car coming from the east until it was too late. The guy ran the red and broadsided Warren's car on the driver's side. He probably never knew what hit him. They said he was probably killed instantly. I only hope so . . ." Lacey's voice trailed off and she paused to collect her emotions. "The other driver was drunk and walked away with hardly a scratch and Warren was dead."

Evangeline looked into the water below the dock, hesitant to ask, but finally responded, "So God tried to Warn you but your Hearing wasn't accurate."

"Well, God tried to Warn us, well me, I guess, but I made some inaccurate assumptions about it all. I thought I knew what was going on and I was wrong. I've learned more about Prayer since then, and about our adversary. God was trying to Warn me to continue to Pray but I just shut Him off once I thought Warren was doing what I would have done. My smarts, my reasoning . . ." Lacey paused, gathering her thoughts.

"Warren just did what he thought was logical to do. He probably wasn't Praying either, having just finished a getaway with the guys. He did the sensible thing according to the weather. Sometimes we just go ahead and do our thing despite His Warnings. We have a will and the ability to decide. God always provides sufficient Resources to make a good Decision. All we have to do is ask Him then Listen. But do we Listen, really Listen, especially when the answer is contrary to our reasoning? Do we Do what He suggests? All too often, we don't. It's been a sad lesson that I've learned. Even the most seasoned Believer misses it sometimes, with tragic consequences."

"I'm so sorry, Lacey. It must have been difficult for you," Evangeline replied.

Lacey gave a rueful laugh and answered, "You have no idea. I learned a lot about Listening to God and Obedience in that experience, although it took me awhile to see it clearly. Time has a way of teaching us things, helping us see things more clearly. I will never take His Leadings lightly ever again. And I won't stop Praying until I am Released from the task."

Evangeline stared into the water lapping up against the dock, pensively. Finally, she spoke softly and asked, "You and Warren were strong

Believers at that point, weren't you? Why didn't God protect Warren? Why would He have let him be killed?"

Lacey sighed and answered, "Well, God doesn't usually just mess with our affairs here. He doesn't force us to do anything. He gave us the ability to make Decisions for ourselves. He doesn't leave us alone in it all. He's available to us, if we ask for His Help. I didn't invite Him to interfere and He did try to Warn us. We just didn't Hear His Leading all that well. I stopped Listening and Warren did his own thing. He decided to go home, at that time, on that particular route. A few moments earlier or later could have made all the difference. I can't be responsible for his actions, his not Hearing God for Direction. Warren made choices. I know that God would have been talking to Warren, too, not just me."

Lacey turned to look at her and continued, "It's all about choices. Do we Listen, do we Obey what He's telling us or do we assume we have it all taken care of and do it our way? It isn't about a single choice that we, ourselves, make; it's also about the choices of people around us. That man decided to drink then climb into his car, drive to that intersection and go through the red light. It takes a series of bad decisions to turn an event into a tragedy. God probably warned a whole whack of people in that whole incident; each doing what they wanted and not Hearing, not heeding the Directions."

"I haven't thought of it that way before. God does Speak to us more than we think, doesn't He?" Evangeline murmured.

Lacey nodded and added, "Ah, yes. He talks a lot more than we Listen and Obey. So much misery could be avoided if we Listened instead of just talked at God. He has a lifetime of Wisdom to share if we only learned to tune our Listening to the right frequency." Lacey sighed and smiled, "But fortunately, God is Merciful, granting us second chances and thirds and fourths and more if necessary. He brought me Bert. I have truly been Blessed."

Evangeline turned and hugged Lacey long and hard. She whispered in her ear, "Thank you for confiding in me. I think you have changed how I think about things forever. I don't think I can look at simple events as coincidences anymore." She released Lacey and added, "I think I was supposed to meet you."

Lacey sighed and replied, "Well, the circumstances surely weren't ideal, but yes, He did plan for us to meet." Lacey looked over the lake, up toward Seeley's Mountain and continued, "Out of all the places you could have been that weekend, this setting was probably the most unlikely for you to be; a survival course was not your prime choice of activities. But you came anyway. The timing was not God's Best Plan for you, but because you decided to be here when you did, He did get me to Prepare for your arrival. I did sense that much."

"Yes, and I did sense that I didn't want to go that weekend. I'll admit that I preferred to go to a concert in the city instead. I gave my tickets to a friend so I could come. Paul was set on planning it for that weekend because of his schedule at work, and Mac was free too. I didn't have much of a choice," Evangeline added.

"Well, sometimes we are schedule-driven instead of Spirit-Led. You can't blame Mac and Paul, especially because they aren't tuned into the Spirit. My point is that God didn't Plan the hurricane; He just Planned for the two of us to meet. God Knew you needed to talk to someone who had gone through similar circumstances as you had. He had to link us somehow. The gift of the orienteering course was the hook to get you here, but the timing was your own choosing, or at least Paul's. The chances of all the other factors falling into place to cause the crisis and your injuries, well, I don't believe that came from God. That was from an evil source that was building for some time, waiting to strike. It was unfortunate that it came together when you arrived to meet me."

"Almost makes you think something was trying to stop us from meeting, doesn't it?" Evangeline commented. "Your life, your decisions and experiences were so similar to mine. I know I wouldn't have talked to anyone else about it. I couldn't for so many years, not even with Paul. I was . . . so . . . well, ashamed, I guess. I . . . felt . . . that no one would look at me the same way if they knew the details of my life . . . my bad choices. It just seems that our meeting was meant to be. But it also does look like Satan wanted to stop it."

Lacey nodded and said, "Yes, it does, doesn't it? But that storm was bigger and was about more than just the two of us. It was a product of a lot of fear and unbelief in a lot of people, building over a long period. The overall effect of that awful storm was to produce even more fear, which that demonic force wanted to use to stop any Faith from being seeded in anyone. I'm just glad our little group knew to Pray before, amid and after that storm. I'm sure the outcome wasn't Satan's original plan for us."

"Despite all the damage and the injuries and deaths?" Evangeline asked.

"Yes. Up here, we affected a small corner of the region though. Remember, our group is little. I'm certain there were others Praying, but you know as well as I do, there aren't that many people these days who take this seriously, much less know they can even do it. A small group of us against such a large storm, well, I don't like those odds. By the time it got here, it had a mighty head of evil steam behind it; like a locomotive with no brakes. A storm like that has considerable fear fuelling its movements. It had effectively produced what it planned to do over a long and fear-filled path."

"Yes, it sure produced devastation in the area; well, along its entire course," Evangeline agreed.

"But you know, it did divert its path at one point early on and it was owing to a concerted effort of Prayer," Lacey added.

"It did? How so? Where?" Evangeline asked incredulously.

"Well, I don't know whether you knew that it was headed straight for Jamaica at the beginning of its trek through the Caribbean. It stalled for several hours off the coast of Jamaica, looking initially like it would take a direct hit. Then it suddenly moved northward. I have it on good authority that there were hundreds of people Praying and Declaring their Faith in God over their island. It stopped the storm in its tracks for a period and when it couldn't find the fear it wanted it just moved on elsewhere. There have been amazing testimonies that have been coming back to us over the last few weeks. God gave us the Authority to speak to storms in Faith. They did it and they were spared the full onslaught of that demon entity. It is so exciting to see Faith Manifested."

"That's surprising and all because of Prayer?" Evangeline said shaking her head.

"Yes, Prayer and standing in Faith on God's Faith-filled Word," Lacey responded.

"That opens possibilities in life doesn't it? It sounds so exciting," Evangeline said as she looked at Lacey with exhilaration in her eyes.

"Yes, it takes diligence in getting into the Word to build up your Faith in what God told us is ours. It doesn't happen overnight. But we can change the results of many things if we join in Faith, declaring God's Word over our situations," Lacey stated matter-of-factly.

Evangeline nodded, "Prayer works."

Lacey smiled and put her hand on Evangeline's shoulder, "Yes, Prayer works even when we don't understand the why or the how and just follow His Lead. Prayer does work."

Chapter 43

By the time the hikers had returned, Lacey and Evangeline had fresh baked biscuits cooling on the counter and the aroma of garlic and herbs wafted through the house from the roast beef in the oven.

Bert greeted the group as they entered the front door. "We were about to send a search party. That must have been some hike."

Mac smirked and replied, "We sort of took the long way back down the mountain."

Lacey wiped her hands on a dish towel as she came out of the kitchen. "My guess is that you guys didn't just hike the usual trail. Where'd you go?"

Sonya looked up from unlacing her boots and said, "Hah. Usual trail, not exactly! Jack wanted to go exploring, against my better judgment."

Lacey cocked her head and furrowed her brow, begging a response from Jack. He looked at her and put up his hands in defense. "Look, it was a nice day for a hike. It wasn't that far."

Sonya rolled her eyes and commented, "It wasn't the distance that was the problem; it was the terrain. You must have been planning that trek since you were in hospital. You and your curiosity! Good thing we were with you when you decided to explore this one."

Bert walked out from the great-room and said, "Okay, spill the whole story. Where did you go?"

Sarah pulled off her jacket and hung it on the coat stand by the door. "We started looking for your infamous hole, Gelly. I still don't know how you fell into such a minute space, backpack and all! It just amazes me when I looked at it again."

Evangeline looked down and murmured, "I suppose anything's possible when you're taken by surprise as I was. It wasn't something I planned. I'm not that big, you know."

Sarah laughed, "No, you're not, but sometime you'll have to look at it when you're more able. I still marvel at how you fit through the opening. But we didn't stay there long. The men started talking about the caves up there and decided to do some investigating. That's where this little adventure got interesting."

Everyone got quiet as they eyed one another, deciding who would continue the story. Lacey gave Jack a long, disapproving look. He started to avert her stare, but decided to be the one to speak. "Well, I was talking to a few guys over the last few weeks and heard some stories about the caves; you know, the old tales."

Sonya broke into his narration, "You didn't do a whole lot of talking in the last few weeks, honey. You did more listening with your mouth wired shut!"

Jack gave her a grimace of disgust as he hung his vest on the coat tree. With his boots off, he was visibly limping as he made his way into the great-room. Lacey moved into the kitchen to grab an icepack as he made himself comfortable on the couch. "I heard about a long-abandoned entrance to the caves, to the west of where we found Gel that day. I just wanted to investigate a little. It wasn't that far."

Sarah chuckled as she plopped herself on the couch opposite Jack. "Yeah, it wasn't that far, but the configuration of the cave gave us some problems!"

Mac agreed as he sat beside her, "It wasn't the easiest thing to negotiate."

Lacey walked to Jack and heaved his foot on the coffee table, while placing a cushion under it. Next she placed the icepack carefully over his obviously swollen ankle. He started to protest, but the look she gave him stopped him short. Raising her eyebrows, she asked flatly, "Okay, Jack. Should I ask you about what you found or will I get a more honest answer from Sonya?"

Jack shrugged and looked at Sonya as she sat beside him. He remained quiet as he realized that he was out-numbered. Sonya smiled and nodded back. "I'd better tell about it because he's still defending this little expedition. Well, it made for an exciting afternoon at least. Gel, didn't you say that you heard noises down in that cave; like you weren't alone down there?"

Evangeline's eyes widened as she sat beside Sarah. "Are you telling me, I wasn't hearing things? What did you find?"

Sonya answered, "Well . . . we're pretty sure it is the same cave you were in, but just the other end of it. This adventure wasn't my plan, believe me." She gave Jack another look, then continued, "Considering the time of year, I didn't think it was wise to do much cave exploring. Jack said it was too early to worry about animals bedding down for the winter yet, but I had my doubts."

Bert set his drink on the coffee table and commented, "It depends on the year and the weather. They'd be preparing for the winter, but I doubt they would be heading in for their final hibernation this early."

Sonya shook her head, "Well, you guys are the hunters. I didn't like that there was only one escape route. I'm not saying that I'm claustrophobic, but I do like safety. Against my better judgment, we ventured in some distance. It was so dark in there and awkward to move about. We only had one flashlight, so it didn't help much." Sonya paused in her story for dramatic effect and continued, "We continued in until . . . I spied it."

Bert, Lacey and Evangeline stared at Sonya as she paused in the story. Mac and Sarah nodded in unison. Evangeline finally could not contain herself anymore and blurted, "Spied what?"

"Evidence that a bear had been using the cave for shelter some time; you know, scat. That was when we realized that we probably shouldn't be in there in case it decided to come back. We didn't want to be caught invading a bear's den, if you know what I mean!"

Lacey laughed and said, "Right! Face to face with a bear with one exit. Sounds smart! Not something I'd like to do."

Sarah made a face and answered, "Oh, yeah. We got out a lot faster than we went in, I'll tell you. We realized that those noises you heard that day could've been a bear at the other end of the cave. It must have been looking for shelter from the storm that day. It looks like you were fortunate that the rocks narrowed so much that the animal couldn't get through."

"I knew I wasn't crazy. I thought so! It echoed so much in there that I couldn't tell what I was hearing. I was so scared . . . the water was running so hard . . . noises all melded together. Oh, my. If I'd known for sure what that noise was . . ."

Paul stood behind Evangeline and put his hand on her shoulder. "What would you have done?"

Evangeline paused and blanched a little. She searched for an answer and finally said, "It's good I didn't know. I probably would have panicked even more than I did. Then I wouldn't have been able to do anything to save myself."

Lacey added, "Looking back on the events of that day, I still believe that you had some . . . well, Divine Intervention."

"Oh, there's no doubt in my mind about that! I've had some time to contemplate that happened and given my injuries, I know that I couldn't have done what I did without some Help. I was desperate and adrenaline counts for something, but with my leg and my wrist and shoulder like it was, it shouldn't have been possible to climb at all. Maybe God Sent an angel my way."

Paul frowned a little at this information. Sarah smiled and agreed, "Seeing what the cave looked like, well, I know I would have needed an angel to Help me out of there."

Sonya added, "It has had me a little puzzled, given what I saw when I went in the cave to rescue you and the extent of your injuries, how you managed to do what you did. It seemed odd to me, although, I'll admit that I've seen some strange rescues over the last few years."

Paul was glad to change the subject and added, "Sonya, I'd like to interview you some time about your experiences. Well, you and Jack would make a good story. You've seen just about everything that can happen up here, I'm sure."

Jack shrugged and said, "Actually, you probably would want to talk to Sonya and Sam Fowler. That's their area. I'm trained, but don't do rescues every day. They encounter the worst of it. Believe me, I don't make a habit of using the Rescue Squad with my courses either."

Paul laughed and responded, "No, I didn't think so. I just thought you might add color to the story; maybe add 'the rest of the story' kind of information, if you know what I mean. You'd understand more of how situations get out of control. You know, how people might get lost in the bush."

Jack nodded and added, "Yeah, and now I know how people slip into unknown holes, too. I never thought I'd have that experience."

Mac piped in at that point, "Well, I think your story of survival in the river might make good copy too. How did you get out of the river? You never told us that part."

Jack was silent but serious. He shook his head and said nothing for a long time. He contemplated an answer that he did not have. Finally he answered slowly, "I have no idea. I can't explain it. One minute I was under the water, fighting to come up for air and as I was about to break the surface I was hit full on with a log or something, I guess. I don't remember much. The next thing I knew, I was on the shore. I have no idea how I got there. No idea at all."

The room was quiet for a while; the only sound was the ticking of the mantle clock. Thoughts rolled around in each of their heads. The explanations were as varied as the people in the room. Lacey, Bert, Sarah, Evangeline and even Mac could conceive of the possibility of the presence of angels Sent through Word Inspired Prayers. Paul, Jack and Sonya were completely perplexed by the impossibility of the rescue under natural circumstances. It made no human sense how Jack was spared from death in the angry river.

Jack muttered under his breath, "Beats me how I got out of the river. For all I know, someone dragged me out. I have no memory of it."

Paul quickly interrupted his musings, "Still it would make an interesting piece, if you're up to talking about it. You have insights into the whole wilderness thing that the typical survivor wouldn't have. If you'd allow me to, I would love to explore doing an article or even a series of pieces. It could be quite good."

Jack nodded slightly and said, "If you think so, I could help you out. But make sure you talk to Sam and Sonya too. I can't tell you much about my experience, except that it was stupid to get into that situation. I should've known better."

Sonya rubbed Jack's shoulder and said, "You were a hero. Without you, Tucker would be dead now. Don't beat yourself up."

Mac piped in, "So where's Tucker these days?"

"Oh, he went into detox then a rehab center. He'll be released soon. My aunt made sure he was cared for. She was shocked about what happened. I think it made Tucker think about a few things too. Thanks to Calvin's friends in town, it sounds as if he may be connected to some good people when he gets out. At least, I hope he is. Most of it depends on Tuck himself. He has some decisions to make," Sonya explained.

Mac nodded, "If those events don't get your attention, not much will. He'll need good friends and a support system in place or he'll just go back to his old way of living for sure."

Bert added, "We've been in touch with him and he seems to have a genuine desire to change. He's still young. I think what happened had a significant impact on him, once he sobered up. He was pretty shook up; knowing that Jack was almost killed. Once he knew the details, he felt responsible. Jack is his friend after all."

Paul said skeptically, "Well, booze changes a person and has a habit of drawing people back into its lifestyle if you aren't careful."

Bert commented, "Sounds like a person who knows that from experience?"

Paul responded, "My father was an alcoholic. He was never committed to getting sober. Heck, he never made a commitment about anything in his life."

Bert responded, "I'm sorry to hear that. If he'll give it a chance, Tucker has a bunch of people who care for him, who'll help him make it work. We'll see how it goes."

Paul still did not look convinced. "I hope so. I've seen it work for some people. I've done an article or two about success stories. But I've also done stories about the victims and the losers. It could go either way."

"Yeah, it's based on decisions. We're Praying that Tucker will make good ones. And we're willing to be there for him too, to hold him accountable, if he'll allow us to. Not to condemn him, just to support him toward good decision making. We know some good people who've been there, who know the path he's been on. They've come a long way themselves. They've already connected with him. So time will tell," Lacey stated.

"That's good. I'm glad to hear something good might come out of that situation. It looked bleak," Paul replied.

Sonya answered, "Yeah, I was ready to kill him. It's taken me some time to reflect on it all and, well, he's my cousin and we were close at one time. I'm willing to give him another chance. Lacey has helped me see it from another perspective. Otherwise, I am sure I would've just written him off completely."

Lacey smiled at Sonya and realized that their long heart to heart chats had not been for naught. *Yes, maybe more good than bad has come out of these last few weeks up here.*

Lacey rose from the sofa intending to check the roast. Her attention was soon diverted by the arrival of a vehicle in the parking area. She quickly recognized it as Calvin and Jan's jeep. As she headed for the door to welcome them, another two vehicles crested the hill and pulled in as well. Sol and Hildy greeted Eli as he got out of his truck and they started down the path to the house.

Lacey looked at the vehicles, then she glanced back at Jack and Sonya who were grinning. Suddenly she realized that they had been up to something while in town earlier in the day. Lacey opened the door and stepped outside as Jan met her at the door with a casserole dish in hand and Calvin carried a brightly packaged gift. Lacey soon understood that Jack and Sonya had arranged a gathering for their engagement.

Lacey was about to protest when Sonya interrupted, "Well, can you think of a better time to have it? With everyone visiting, it was a good time for a reunion and celebration. Hey, anytime's good for a party!"

Before Lacey and Bert could comment any further, more vehicles arrived filled with well-wishers. Hildy had coordinated the food brought by the guests and soon a sumptuous table of dishes was put out for all to consume. Guests dropped by the remainder of the afternoon, bringing more food, cards, small gifts and best wishes to the soon-to-be married couple.

Jan and Calvin laughed at Lacey, saying, "It's probably the worst kept secret in the county. We were just waiting for the two of you to come to your senses and make it official. You were made for each other, admit it."

Bert intervened, "It might be so, but Lacey had to be ready for this step."

Lacey responded, "To be fair to Bert, there's no doubt, I love him. I had to be sure though, that I was following God's Lead, not mere emotion. It's a big decision, one affecting the rest of our lives. I want to make his life better than it would be without me. I think I'm ready now."

Bert smiled at Lacey and put his arm around her. "I only hope that I can bring half of what you bring into this marriage. I can promise to bring to you the best I know how to be. With the Lord Leading us, I'm sure that we'll bring out even Better traits in each other."

"Well said!" Calvin agreed. "Congratulations!" It was followed by applause from the crowd.

The afternoon slid into evening before anyone knew it. People came and went. Before long Calvin, Jan, Sol, Hildy and Eli were the only extra guests who lingered as the night wore on. They had finished cleaning all the dishes and had settled into the great-room before a comfortable blaze in the fireplace.

"So we have the diehard few remaining from our unfortunate weekend in August." Sol commented. "It's a reunion, as well as a celebration."

"You could say that. I hope most of us are in better condition than the last time we left the place," Sarah commented.

"I think we're all on the mend, so to speak. And the roads are vastly better, that's for sure. It might take a little longer to finish cleaning the property damage though. Aside from the houses that are still being fixed, there were so many trees and branches down that it may take until next year to get through it all, especially if the snow comes early this year," Jan responded.

"I imagine the insurance claims around here must have been horrendous. With all the trees around here, the damage to houses, power and telephone lines must have been staggering," Paul commented.

Bert nodded his head, "Yeah. It was insane. We were almost two weeks without power up this way and, even now, the more remote hunting camps haven't been reached. That won't make the hunters particularly happy. It'll bring new meaning to 'roughing it' for some of those lads."

"I suppose it's one of the hazards to living up here, but what are the chances of a hurricane causing damage in this area? It's been far more likely in the past to expect an ice or snowstorm in the winter or spring flooding, not a hurricane," Eli answered.

"Considering how unpredictable the weather's been lately, I'd almost expect anything. Better be prepared than be taken by surprised, I guess," Calvin replied as he put his cup down on the coffee table. "At least this year there should be no shortage of firewood for burning. Speaking of that, it looks like it's time to throw another log on this fire."

Calvin stoked the fire and soon the blaze sprung to life again. They sat entranced, as they watched the flames dance and spark in the stone fireplace. Evangeline snuggled against Paul's shoulder staring into the flames, enjoying the warmth it provided. Jack and Sonya sat against cushions on the floor in front of the coffee table, while Sarah and Mac curled together on the oversized recliner. The rest of the group was perched on the sofas and scattered chairs brought in from the dining room.

"Are you drifting off?" Paul asked Evangeline.

Sleepily she responded, "I think I might have dozed a little. The fire is so peaceful and I was up so early this morning. Maybe it's time for sleep."

Paul yawned as she said this, "Sorry guys. No offense meant to the company. I think it must be the good clean air up here and all that great food. I'm more tired than usual too. Do you mind if we sneak away and go to bed?"

Lacey and Bert gave them their blessings and they wandered down the hall to the guest room. Soon Mac and Sarah were following them to their room. Jack and Sonya wandered to the front door and out on the porch to talk for a few minutes alone. About twenty minutes later Sonya came back in alone and excused herself to her room. The houseguests were all now in their private quarters and the house fell silent.

Bert and Lacey remained by the fire with Sol, Hildy, Calvin, Jan and Eli. No words were spoken as they studied the flames before them. The warmth of the glow before them was comforting, but it was apparent each was in deep thought.

Finally, Bert spoke quietly. "It's good we're together tonight. I don't know about you folks but Lacey and I have had a sense of urgency about the situation on the West Coast. I'm not sure what the specifics are, but the rumblings have already started. I spoke to Matt Knox and they are moving people around. Their group has organized a daily Prayer effort already. The sooner that Lacey and I get there, the better. They'll need support for their efforts. Thus far, their warnings have not been heeded, so they need our help."

Murmurs of agreement could be heard from the group. A solemn silence engulfed the space. The reflection of flames leaped from face to face in the dimly lighted room. Their expressions were hard to read, however, their Hearts were unified with concern.

"Well, I'd say that we've done all that's possible in this physical realm. It's now out of our hands, except our Prayer efforts. That's something we can always do and we might as well put this time together to good use before we leave," Bert stated firmly.

Lacey replied, "I agree. Are you sure that they have positioned people appropriately?"

"Oh, as well as they can, considering they don't have any idea of the timing of events. They're as ready as they can be under the circumstances. Safety has always been a primary concern. None of our efforts will be any good if our people get hurt. You know that as much as I do. Our experiences here have taught us that if nothing else," was Bert's answer.

"I suggest that we move into the library for more privacy. It would be better to keep interruptions to a minimum," Calvin added.

"What if we are all wrong about this? Couldn't this be a way off in the future?" Eli questioned.

"You know, it could be, but I doubt it. And I also hope we're wrong because many lives will be saved. But you know as well as I do that all the signs point to our being right about it. We've had too many people getting the same sense of urgency on the matter to ignore it. And, listening to the news reports lately, it proves that it's already begun, at least the preliminaries anyway," Bert replied ruefully.

Lacey looked each of them in the eye one by one and said, "It really doesn't matter. If we're wrong, we've spent some time in Prayer. That's never a loss. If we're right, well, then we can stand before God and say we did our part to minimize the aftereffects of all of this."

With that they entered the library one at a time, silently closing the door behind them.

Jack went to his computer and checked his emails. He scanned down the list and found one from Laurie. He opened it and found a cheery message about her flight to Seattle and trip to their parent's home. She was having a great reunion with Mum and Dad and wished he could be there too. He winced when he thought about the attention he would get from his mother if he were to go too, considering how soon it was after his near mishap in the river. He could do without all the mother-smother. *It's better that you have your visit there this time without me.*

He typed a short response, telling her that everything was going well where he was. He was glad to go back to work and start some cash flow again. Although he was sorry he could not be there with her, he'd make a point of visiting her once she got back home when his slow season started. He asked her to say hi to Mum and Dad then signed off.

He continued to check his other emails and finally turned away from his computer. He was feeling content with life and eager to resume work next week. *It's funny how a little time off work can give you a better attitude. Only a few weeks ago I was getting frustrated with the clients. Now the next training session can't come soon enough.*

The Prayer meeting ended and each person went a separate way home, off to a night's rest. They were satisfied that they had done all they could at the moment but also had an uneasy feeling that their lives might change radically in the next hours, days or weeks. Most thought that time was not on their sides on this issue.

Lacey's household was up early, with breakfast done and cleaned up by 8:00 a.m. Bert arrived shortly after the last dish was put away in the cupboard. Evangeline and Sarah had just retreated into their rooms to put the final touches to their packing.

Bert was eager to get their Sunday morning activities under way. They attended a small church in Lofton where their friend, Marty Cortland, was the pastor but Bert often filled in for him when Marty had to be away. It might be a small church by city standards, but it had a dynamic congregation and was by no means dead in a Spiritual sense. Both Lacey and Bert loved that God's Presence was perceptible the moment one drove into the parking lot.

"So is anyone planning to join us at church this morning?" Bert asked Lacey as he watched as Paul and Mac brought the first bags out to the SUV parked in the yard.

"Actually, yes, it looks like Sarah and Evangeline are quite eager. Mac is interested and Paul sounds if he'll come because the rest are going. He's not convinced it is a good use of his valuable time away from work. We'll have to see what the Holy Spirit does in that man's life. It isn't our job. But I'll not give up Praying for him," Lacey replied quietly.

"I didn't think you would," was Bert's reply. "Is Sonya up yet?"

"Yes, but she has to be available for on-call work this weekend. I think she isn't ready to make the leap into regular church attendance just yet either," Lacey answered softly.

"I'm not giving up on her or Jack at this point. God has a plan for those two as well," Bert replied as Lacey nodded.

Mac and Paul opened the door and looked in, hoping to see some activity from the women. When he saw nothing happening, Paul kicked off his shoes and started down the hall to the room that he and Evangeline has shared for the weekend. Sarah poked her head out the guest room door and said, "Good, you're here. Evangeline will need help for sure, but I'll also need Mac's assistance with my bags upstairs. I think they got heavier since we arrived somehow."

Paul glanced back at Mac and commented, "I didn't think those girls had a chance to go shopping while they were here. How could the bags get heavier?"

Sarah smirked and answered before Mac had a chance to make any smart remarks, "Well, knowing we wouldn't get a chance to explore the area, Lacey did give us a few souvenirs of our trip to the lake. She also gave us copies of some of her books, autographed and everything! That might be what is making the bags so heavy."

Paul veered into the guest room, while Mac brought up the rear and headed upstairs to their bedroom. He quipped, "There's never been a time that you didn't come back with more than you arrived with. How heavy is it this time? Do I need a fork lift?"

Sarah rolled her eyes and pointed to her suitcase on the bed, "You might want me to put the books in a separate bag; they're kind of heavy."

Mac groaned as he lifted the suitcase, moved it down the stairs and started down the hall. As he went by the kitchen where Bert and Lacey were listening to all the grumbling, he said, "Thank you Lacey for the books. We appreciate receiving them, but you might have suggested she pack them separately. I might have to send you the bill for my hernia operation at this rate."

Lacey chuckled at the complaining and moved toward the door as the women arrived with their hand luggage. They planned to leave straight from church to return to the city. Lacey asked, "All set then?"

"I think we have everything. If we're missing anything, it will be an excuse to get together again, won't it?" Sarah answered.

"I don't want to wait for any excuse. I want to keep in touch and get together for more talks. I really enjoyed our time together," Evangeline exclaimed as she gave Lacey a big hug. "You don't know how much I appreciate your candor yesterday," she whispered in Lacey's ear.

Lacey smiled and pulled her back so she could look her in the eyes, "I meant everything I said yesterday. Don't you ever forget it," she said quietly. Then louder for Sarah's ears as well, she added, "You both have my e-mail address, so you can get me wherever I might be. You also have my cell-phone number. So you have no excuse not to be in touch. We could conceivably get together when we fly back into the city from out trip. You could meet us somewhere near the airport for dinner."

Evangeline was especially eager, "Oh, that would be great! We'll have to make it a date then."

Mac came back into the house pretending to be injured from his efforts to pack the vehicle, "After all of that exertion I might not be able to help with the driving on the way back home."

Sarah came to Mac's side and added, "Oh, I think the time in the church service should give you time to Heal. I'm expecting awesome things to happen there anyway."

Lacey grabbed her Bible from the counter as she ushered them out the door and replied, "You never know what'll happen. The Holy Spirit is full of surprises in our services. It always promises to be a wonderful meeting with The Lord every Sunday." Lacey closed and locked the door behind her and they were ready to leave.

Evangeline nodded toward the car as they walked down the path, "I wonder if Paul is ready for this?"

Bert replied quietly, "That's okay. The Holy Spirit Knows where he's at and He's ready for him. That's all that matters."

Chapter 44

Paul was first out the door of the church following the service, followed a few minutes later by Mac. Sarah and Evangeline lingered behind, talking to some women with Lacey.

Paul stood uncomfortably on the outside steps, peering in the open door of the church occasionally, wondering if Evangeline was ready to leave. She had her back to him so he could not catch her attention. Mac realized Paul was eager to get back to the city. "The girls like to talk. They're excited about the service. It might be good to let them wind down a little before they get in the car though."

Paul shrugged and replied, "Yeah, you might be right. We might as well let them sit in back together so they can gab away all they want."

Small groups of people lingered outside the church, but slowly the crowd thinned as they made their way to their vehicles. One by one, vehicles pulled away from the church. A truck and a car traveling toward the church caught Calvin's eye as he came out the sanctuary door. He smiled and waved as he realized that Jack and Sonya were arriving.

Paul followed Calvin's gaze and saw Jack and Sonya as they got out of their vehicles. They sauntered up the hillside toward them and Jack greeted them, "I thought we might catch you before you guys left. Sonya was called to go down to work this afternoon, so we thought we'd head in for lunch before she goes. Do you want to join us?"

Bert had arrived in time to hear Jack's question and asked, "Where were you thinking of heading?"

"Oh, probably we'll go into Moulton because I have to work right afterward. What do you think? The Carleton Diner sound good?" Sonya replied.

Bert looked into the church, searching to see if Lacey was ready to join them. "I'm not sure if we want to go all the way into town today. We have some packing and preparations to do for our trip on Tuesday. I'll see if I can extricate the women from the sanctuary so we can ask them."

Bert wandered in the doorway as Lacey turned to join them with Evangeline and Sarah. He repeated the invitation as they joined Jack and Sonya. By this time, Jan reached the group as well.

Sarah and Evangeline were enthusiastic about the idea of having lunch before they started their journey. "I would love to eat before we leave. It's Mac's turn to do the driving and once he sets the GPS for home, it's hard to make him stop for washroom breaks, much less meals!" Sarah exclaimed.

Mac looked pained and Paul slightly annoyed as it was obvious he wanted to get back to town. Evangeline piped up, "Oh, yes, please save us from the forced famine! I'm already hungry. There's no telling when we'll eat otherwise."

Paul was about to protest when Jack answered with a grin, "Well, we need to keep the ladies happy, don't we? There's nothing like a cranky woman to travel with." Sonya gave Jack a shot to the arm and a warning look.

"Watch yourself, Jack Davidson. You still have to deal with me until I go to work," Sonya replied with a laugh.

Mac looked at Sarah who was nodding agreement and he realized that the women were ganging up on the men on this. He turned to Paul and said, "I think we'd be further ahead eating before we go at this rate. 'Happy wife, happy life', as they say."

Paul shrugged and said, "Sure, you're the driver on this end of the trip. Anyway, we have to eat and the company will be good. We'll have to trust you that the food will be too."

Jack answered, "So it's settled." He turned to Bert and Lacey and asked, "What about you folks?"

Lacey looked over at Bert, squinting her eyes, "I don't think we can fit that in today. Since Bert purchased our tickets for our trip so quickly, it doesn't leave much time to prepare. I still have laundry and packing to do. There must a dozen other loose ends to take care of before we leave on Tuesday. Any other time and I'd love to join you."

Sarah nodded her head, "I understand. It's hard to get ready when you entertain guests right before you leave. I know I need a lot more notice before I travel."

"Oh, I've learned to be flexible, especially on some of my book tours. If my agent arranges last minute interviews, I have to change my plans at the drop of a hat. This is one trip I would like to think about before I leave. I'm not sure how long we'll be away yet, so I want to make sure that things are taken care of to give us the flexibility to stay as long as needed."

Evangeline commented admiringly, "It must be nice to be able to just go when you want to like that."

Bert smiled, "Well, I am retired from full-time work. It helps that I work only when I'm needed and available. Maybe if Paul eventually moves into freelance writing you could do that too, if you weren't still teaching by then. But you have a lot of living to do before that stage."

Lacey added. "And who knows, even a couple of kids in tow too in the future?"

Paul rolled his eyes and added, "Oh, you women have it all planned, don't you? Let's slow down a little!"

Jack sensed Paul needed to be rescued from this conversation so he interjected, "So anyone else want to join us for lunch?"

Paul grinned at Jack's tactic. Calvin and Jan begged off as well. By that time, Sol, Hildy and Eli had joined them. Jack also invited them but they too had plans for their day.

"I'm glad you guys made it to church with us. It sort of gives you a better picture of our little community of Faith here. These are good people and we have good Teaching with Marty as pastor. I hope you can join us again some time," Sol commented.

Evangeline nodded, "I was impressed with his message on asking the Lord for Wisdom. Goodness knows, we need that these days."

Lacey nodded, "Just ask and He'll Answer you, as Marty said. Stay in His Word and He'll give you the Wisdom before you even Ask. He Knows what you need before you do."

"I'm looking forward to getting into His Word more now. You've been such a source of inspiration to me. I want to thank you so much for our conversations. I hope you don't mind if I keep emailing you my questions. I'm sure I'll have so many," Evangeline almost bubbled as she gave Lacey a big hug.

Lacey held her in the embrace a little longer a whispered in her ear,

"Just remember that you are Forgiven and He doesn't hold anything against you. You're totally Forgiven in His eyes no matter what those voices want to say. You have the Word with which to counter them. Say the Word and remind Satan that you are a child of the King."

Evangeline hugged Lacey even harder and whispered back, "I will. If I forget, I know you'll remind me, right?"

Lacey answered, "Absolutely, no doubt about it."

Evangeline released Lacey as a little tear trickled down her cheek. "I'll miss you. We'll have to get together once you're back from your trip."

Paul looked at his watch and said, "We'd better get going or we won't have time to have lunch before we leave." Paul turned to Lacey and added, "Lacey, I want to thank you for such a great visit. It was far more relaxing this trip than the last one."

"Well, I'm glad you enjoyed it. It would be hard to top your last stay for excitement though. At least we had a good reason for a party this time. I want to thank you for such a wonderful celebration last evening," Lacey responded.

"That was Jack and Sonya's little surprise for us all. And everyone pitched in together to make light work. Good people make a good party. You guys must be well loved to attract so many well-wishers on short notice," Sarah answered as she gave Lacey, then Bert a hug. "You have a good trip and please, stay in touch with us."

Bert nodded as he turned to shake hands with Mac, adding, "You people might have more trouble with remembering us. After all, you're busy people."

Sarah put her hand on Bert's arm, "There's no way I'll be too busy for you. You've made a mark on my heart that I'll never forget."

Lacey glanced at Jan and smiled. "Well, hurricane Igor sure got all our attention. I hope the way we responded was positive for everyone concerned. It's just the way we do things."

Sarah gave Hildy a hug and added, "Well, keep doing it like that. I think I'll take a little piece of this community home with me in my heart. While in our traffic jams and stress, I'll dream of being back here again."

Paul shook hands with each of the men in turn. As he approached Calvin he paused and added, "I don't know whether I had a chance to adequately thank you for all your help getting Evangeline to hospital. Without your driving expertise, it would have been a far different result."

"It was nothing. I'm just glad I was available to give you a hand. God has a way of putting the right people in your path when people are Praying for you," Calvin responded.

Paul looked down at the ground for a moment, then finally answered, "I'm not sure I understand it all, but it did work out that day. So thanks again for all your help."

The church bell rang out above them signaling that it was now 12:00 noon. Mac checked his watch and declared that they needed to start their journey. They exchanged final hugs and handshakes then piled into their individual vehicles, leaving for their various destinations and activities.

Evangeline looked out the window of the SUV as she waved a final farewell to Lacey, Bert and their friends. The sun shone brightly as she watched the small church retreat from her view. She realized that she wanted more than she could explain to be connected to the God she had met in this community in the wilderness.

An hour later the four travelers piled into the SUV and said their final farewells to Jack and Sonya. The foursome extended invitations to have them stay with them in the city for a weekend urban adventure. They had exchanged emails and phone numbers and made promises to stay in touch. Jack and Sonya watched as they drove across the bridge that crossed the now sedate East River. Ten more miles and they would catch the interstate down to the city.

Jack gave Sonya a kiss and they headed back to their vehicles. Sonya had to leave for work and Jack planned to head back up the mountain, stopping by at John's Market Square for some local gossip on the way. It was back to the usual routine of daily living again.

Mac deftly maneuvered the SUV around the many winding curves of the access highway while maintaining his part in the various conversations that flowed as they settled into their journey home. By the time they reached the interstate, Paul was already mentally outlining his next article and planning what he would have to do to obtain the background information he needed to make it stand out from the others he had written.

Mac eased into the rhythm of interstate highway driving and his mind wandered to his next business expedition to Chicago at the end of the week. This trip promised to be especially challenging. He mentally calculated the ways to make this trip more profitable and less taxing this time. He enjoyed the strategizing before a job began and he was already transitioning into his work groove.

As they descended into the valley that wound down to the city, Sarah and Evangeline chatted happily for the first hour but had moved into a pleasant silence, quietly contemplating their weekend away.

Sarah's mind meandered from the serenity of the lake to the sights passing their vehicle. The pace of life had already picked up while traveling the four lane highway, but she attempted to maintain the peace she had attained up on the mountain. She had purposely planned an easy day at school the next day, knowing her energy levels might be low after the trip. She knew she could incorporate the sights and sounds of their journey into her teaching. The children were a challenge at times but she loved their energy and enthusiasm. It always motivated her to come back with equal passion for what she did.

Evangeline gazed beyond the glass of the SUV, at first watching the passing scenery and vehicles. She had been quiet for about an hour now, contemplating the events of the last few days. Images of the purple wild flowers and rock cuts along the roadside blurred as her mind reviewed the conversations she had with her new friends. The words that struck her most dramatically had been the ones she had shared with Lacey. Her remarkable candor and compassion deeply touched her heart.

Evangeline slipped quietly into the recesses of her thoughts and realized that she wanted so much to attain Lacey's strength of Faith and Love toward God and others. If Lacey could climb out of such a pit of pain and shame with God's help, surely she could as well. It seemed daunting to start, but Lacey had assured her that it was indeed possible. Seeing where Lacey was today gave her a Hope for the future as never before. She smiled as she realized it was the first time she had not felt afraid of what the next day would bring. Faith, Hope and Love; what wonderful gifts she had received on this trip.

Lacey and Bert watched out the jet's window as the view below blossomed from indistinct fields and rivers into a well-defined landscape of houses and streets and even individual vehicles. They held hands and

Prayed for a safe and uneventful landing, as well as a productive visit with their West Coast brothers and sisters in The Lord.

Bert grinned at Lacey and she realized that she was about to embark on her first adventure with her fiancé. Lacey liked the sound of that word, but looked forward even more to the time when they would be joined in marriage. She warmed to the notion that they would soon become a true team as husband and wife; working together on whatever exploits the Lord had Planned for them. They were embarking on a new phase of their lives and that was exciting enough in itself. However, they sensed that what was ahead would challenge them more than anything they had ever faced. This time they would handle it together, strong in their Faith in God and His Promises. This threefold cord would not be easily broken.

They watched as they made their final approach on the runway. Bert squeezed Lacey's hand and they whispered to each other in quiet agreement, "We are truly here for such a time as this."

The end

CPSIA information can be obtained at www.ICGtesting.com
Printed in the USA
LVOW130350291112

309234LV00002B/10/P

9 781449 767556